DISCARD

REDEYE

A NOVEL BY

RICHARD AELLEN

RED

EYE

DONALD I. FINE, INC.
NEW YORK

Library of Congress Cataloging-in-Publication Data

Aellen, Richard.
Redeye.

I. Title. II. Title: Redeye.
PS3551.E45R44   1988   813'.54   87-86266
ISBN 1-55611-082-0

Manufactured in the United States of America
10 9 8 7 6 5 4 3 2 1

For M.N. at R.H.M.

CHAPTER

1

THE WOMAN HE DREAMED OF KILLING WAS NOT HIS wife. Her name was Lisle Beaumier and she was a stranger. He knew the details of her apartment even before she ushered him inside. He knew that in the kitchen there was a row of copper pots hanging diagonally above the stove and that the bedroom contained a twin bed covered in Chinese brocade and in the bathroom there was a claw-footed tub with a shower head attached by a hose that lay like a pink snake curled in the bottom of the tub. All these things Paul Stafford knew as he kissed Lisle Beaumier and planned to kill her. He was prepared.

Paul has no reason to dream of death. The night was quiet and warm with only a faint breeze to disturb the curtains shrouding his open bedroom window. From the back yard came the chirp of crickets and soft rustle of leaves against a rusty drainpipe. It was April. Above the distant rooftops the peak of the Washington Monument was visible, its white spire pointing like a finger to a three-quarter moon that bathed the city in moonlight. Lying in bed, Paul groaned and turned restlessly, fighting the images that forced themselves into

1

his mind, making him an unwilling participant, a perilous seducer, a cold-blooded killer.

The girl in the dream was provocative and alluring and knew it. She had honey-blonde hair, jade-green eyes and lips that surged naturally forward in a seductive pout. As soon as the door clicked shut behind them, she pressed against him, reckless and more than a little drunk. He kissed her and let his hands slide down her back. When he pulled her hips against his, she murmured in anticipation. Her tongue came dancing into his mouth.

Curiously, Paul was aware of the dream even as it aroused and repelled him. He was caught, just as he had been in other dreams, unable to wake up before the final terrible moment. He could feel her breasts beneath the sheer fabric, could smell the perfume that enveloped them, could hear the little animal sounds she made as her hands slid down his body. Imperative fingers unzipped his pants and pulled him free.

"El Rancho Grande," she laughed, echoing the refrain of the floor show they had seen earlier.

He wanted to tear the dress away and shove himself against her but it couldn't be done that way. The death had to appear accidental. Instead, he forced himself to step back while he slid out of his clothes. Shirt, tie, pants, underwear—he dropped them all in a pile, careful that nothing should fall from a pocket.

Eager to please, Lisle Beaumier followed. She pulled the dress over her head and tossed it aside, then stepped out of her slip, revealing full breasts with tiny flat nipples, rosy with passion. The black bikini panties with lace trim slid quickly to the floor and she stood before him, confident in her nudity. He picked her up and carried her to the bathroom. She gasped with surprise when he placed her in the tub.

"I want to see you wet," he said, turning on the water.

"I am wet. See?"

She ran a finger between her legs and offered it to him. The water curled across their feet, a little too hot. He adjusted the temperature, then asked if she had any bubble bath, knowing from an earlier, surreptitious visit that she did. He poured the powder into the bath and sat facing her as bubbles rose around them. He let his fingers enter her, enter the taught, silken folds of flesh as her fingers pinched and stroked and fondled, bringing him closer and closer to the climax they could never share.

With legs wrapped around one another they pressed close, twisting and thrusting. Lisle's forehead glistened with sweat. She held his waist and rocked back and forth on his fingers, panting with dry lips and a glazed expression until she could stand no more. She pulled away and got to her knees.

"Come, come to bed."

But he couldn't let that happen. Much as he ached to bury himself in her, there must be no indication that Lisle Beaumier was anything but alone tonight. And so, reluctantly, he stood up and stepped out of the tub onto the rug. It was time to finish.

"Wait," he said when she started to follow him. "I must kiss you dry."

"You better hurry."

She stood with suds sliding down her stomach while his lips followed a towel across her body. He began at the neck then moved to each breast and down to her navel across her glistening abdomen to the delicate pink lips nestled behind warm pubic hair. He moved his feet slightly each time so that when the time came to act, his feet would be dry. Lisle watched with a benevolent smile until he was crouched in front of her. The tang of her arousal was still on his tongue when he gathered his feet and lunged upward.

She started to say something as the heel of his hand slammed into her chin, snapping her teeth shut and breaking her neck with a muffled crack. She fell backward against the wall and collapsed beneath the bubbles. When he lifted the body her head rolled back, revealed a tongue nearly severed—

Paul sat up quickly. His heart was pounding, his breathing deep and ragged; the pajamas tangled around his body damp with sweat. Because he was alone, it took him a moment to realize that he was still home and not on assignment tracking a story in some foreign land. Then he remembered the argument with his wife. Joanna had gone downstairs to watch television, nursing her grievance with a late-night movie and a drink. She hadn't come back.

Paul untangled his legs from the sheets, got up and went into the bathroom. He splashed cold water on his face, tilted his head back and breathed deeply. Tiny rivulets ran down his neck and slid down his chest until absorbed by the cotton fabric. The image of the woman swam before him, the woman he'd killed. He could still hear the quick intake of breath as his hand caught her chin, still smell the faint aroma of her perfume. The nightmares had come before but it had never been a woman he killed. Always before it had been a man.

Paul went downstairs. Joanna was asleep on the couch, bathed in the sullen light of the television. She'd pulled an afghan comforter over her as a blanket, leaving her bare feet sticking out from beneath its tasseled hem. One hand lay sandwiched between her cheek and a maroon throw cushion. Her thin lips were parted slightly, giving her mouth a fullness normally absent except in anger or lovemaking. Asleep, she looked even younger than her twenty-eight years. A bottle of Remy Martin had overturned beside the couch, leaving a small stain on the rug.

Paul picked up the bottle and placed it on the coffee table. He considered carrying Joanna up to bed but decided against it. Waking her might rekindle the argument they'd had earlier. Paul had been reviewing copies of Rockland-Birdwell inspection reports on a laser component for the Star Wars program when Joanna had come in. She had picked a report at random and inspected it. Her hands were narrow, with long, delicate fingers marred only by her habit of biting her nails.

"What story is this?"

"SDI. Rockland-Birdwell is faking progress reports. Changing test criteria so the components pass and they stay on schedule." Paul leaned back in his chair. "The question is, did they do it to fool the Department of Defense or did the DOD do it to make SDI look more formidable to the Russians?"

He was referring to the upcoming Mutual Defense Treaty, which involved a trade of "defense technologies"—the American laser-based Star Wars program and the Russian's secret RF wave transmitter, popularly called the Nevsky Project. The subject didn't interest Joanna. She slid her hand across Paul's shoulders and toyed with the hair on his neck.

"Are you coming to bed?"

She wore a pale blue silk chemise that matched her eyes and she stood close enough for her hip to touch his shoulder.

"I want to see what I've got here first."

Joanna dropped her hand.

"Paul . . . I want another child."

He kept working. After a moment she said, "Aren't you going to answer me?"

"Did you ask a question?"

"I said I want another child."

"We already had a child."

And he died, Paul thought.

"The house feels empty. I feel empty. I want another child—"

"No."

"Paul—"

"I don't want to go through it again."

"*You* go through it?"

"I don't want us to go through it."

She moved in front of him and stood holding her elbow, keeping her voice calm with an effort.

"Paul, what happened was an accident. You know that, don't you?"

"It's the way I feel."

He turned his attention to the reports.

"You were the one who wanted a family," Joanna said. "I wasn't even thinking about it when we met."

"Then nothing's changed."

"Everything's changed. We started a family. You said you wanted four children."

"Not anymore."

"When did this—when did you decide this?"

A strand of long dark hair had gotten into the side of her mouth. She flipped it aside.

"I've been thinking about it for a while."

"For how long?"

Since Jason died, he wanted to say. Since the morning after the funeral when I woke up and saw you sleeping, as peacefully and innocently as if nothing had happened.

But it had happened. Sixteen months ago Joanna had taken Jason and driven down to visit her parents in Charlottesville. They lived in a large, rambling country house on a hill overlooking the town. Jo had gone shopping, leaving Jason with her parents—her mother, who was preparing food for a Christmas luncheon, and her father, who was in the basement refinishing the floor. When Jo left, Jason was in the basement, helping his grandfather. At some point he went upstairs, and from that point on each of the adults thought he was with the other. Nobody noticed when he went outside. Nobody heard him fall through the thin coating of ice that covered the swimming pool. By the time they found him, it was too late.

Joanna knew what Paul was thinking.

"It's not fair," she said softly. "I didn't kill him."

"But you couldn't protect him and neither could I. Neither one of us could."

"You think it's my fault, don't you?"

No, he thought, as the same recurring rationalizations came twisting and turning through his mind. Nobody's fault. Forgive and forget. Forget that you took him to Charlottesville, forget that your parents were so damned oblivious that they let him die not fifty feet from the house, forget that I wasn't there that weekend, forget that we had a son at all.

He suppressed his anger and said, "No."

"Is it mom and dad? Is that who you blame?"

"I don't blame anybody."

"Yes you do."

He turned on her then, staring at her while he spoke in a hard voice.

"He's not here, okay? He's not here, not a part of the world any more. Nothing he might have done will happen now; nobody will know him—friends he would have had, a wife, children . . ."

Joanna's eyes filled with tears; she put her hands over her ears and left the room without waiting for him to finish.

Paul felt a momentary urge to follow her but it faded quickly at the memory of his last glimpse of Jason . . . He had carried his bag of toys to the car and watched as he and Jo drove away, Jason with his Macy's Snoopy from the Thanksgiving Day parade pushed against the window, waving its paw goodbye. The look of trust in the boy's eyes wouldn't leave him. There were no excuses in raising children. None at all . . .

Now, as he watched Joanna sleeping, Paul tried to rekindle the feeling they'd once shared. He imagined making love to her while she slept. Her beauty still attracted him, her physical presence still aroused him, but he wanted her now without commitment. He imagined her body responding instinctively while she remained asleep, the white skin flushed with pink, her hips moving to his rhythm, her legs straining beneath him.

Paul knelt to kiss her. His knee touched a cold spot, the spilled brandy, and images from the nightmare returned, thoughts of death and mutilation. Joanna became a stranger to him, a pale woman with cameo features floating in a sea of black hair spreading across the pillow like ink on water. Images of death, decay crowded his brain.

From past experience he knew he wouldn't be free until he purged the nightmare from his memory.

He went upstairs to his office, took out a yellow tablet and began to write. The nightmares were rare, but when they came he used them as the basis for mystery stories that he sent to Black Cat Mystery Magazine. The money wasn't much but Paul enjoyed seeing his name listed as an author of creative fiction. Somehow it seemed more impressive than a reporter's byline.

He wrote quickly, using both sides of the paper, and threw the finished sheets into an open drawer. Two hours later, when the world outside had turned gray and three-dimensional, a voice behind him said, "Have you been working all night?"

He turned with a start. Joanna stood in the doorway, the afghan comforter wrapped around her like a cloak. She looked tired. Paul got up and went to her. She leaned into his embrace and he buried his face in her hair. They stood silently for a moment.

"Have you?" she asked again, her voice muffled by the afghan.

"I had a nightmare."

She paused. "The kind where you kill someone?"

"I almost woke you up."

"I'm glad you didn't," she said. She had never had a nightmare in her life.

"It was a woman this time."

"Me" she asked, showing a spark of interest.

"No, nothing like you. Besides, her name was Lisle Beaumier."

"You know her name?"

"I always know their names."

"How did you kill her?"

"Broke her neck." He didn't mention the seduction that preceded the killing.

"Broke her neck," Joanna repeated glumly, almost as if that was to be expected. She wasn't a morning person. As she left the room she said, "I'm going to make coffee. I feel like hell."

At breakfast they treated each other with the diffidence of exhausted boxers. Paul checked the Washington *Post* and compared the coverage to that of his own paper, the Washington *Herald*. The *Post* was a better paper but Paul felt no envy. The *Herald*, which was still trying to build its credibility and prestige, went out of its way to accommodate him. He was a star at the *Herald*. At the *Post* he'd be just another award-winning journalist

Joanna gave a satisfied grunt. She had the Arts & Leisure section spread out on the kitchen table.

"Thank God it got in. See? They ran the story on Luis."

The article concerned Luis de Cuevo, the Brazilian artist whose show was opening tonight at the Gallerie L'Enfant. Joanna was assistant curator at the gallery and had been working with Cuevo, setting up the show. Paul glanced at the story and noted that the accompanying photograph wasn't contrasty enough and that Cuevo's work didn't show up well. It was all planes and angles and geometric forms. Cuevo himself stared haughtily at the camera like some sort of imitation conquistador. It wasn't a world that interested Paul and he doubted that Joanna's interest would last. Since he'd met her, she'd been involved in famine relief, architectural preservation, sailing, the theater, and now art.

"Will you come to the opening?" Joanna asked.

"What time is it?"

"Five-thirty until eight. We'll have free champagne. Maybe I can seduce you."

If it was a veiled reference to their sporadic sex life, Paul couldn't tell. Recently whenever they made love he sensed a kind of desperation that had never been there before. Joanna's need forced him outside himself and made it difficult to feel close to her.

She was still in her bathrobe when she accompanied him into the attached garage. The door opened at the touch of a button, grinding and clattering as it worked its way into the ceiling. The damp, musty air stirred slightly and light poured in revealing the two cars: Paul's Audi and Joanna's Alfa Romeo.

She stood on her tiptoes and kissed him hard and then bit his lower lip. He jerked back. There was a faint taste of blood, like a tin spoon, along the inside of his mouth. She stared at him.

"It's easy to hurt each other," she said. "Not hurting each other is hard."

She went back to the kitchen before he could answer. The slight quaver in her voice defused his irritation and he felt a sudden tenderness. She was still unpredictable, aggressive and tender in a way that made her the most attractive woman he had ever known.

Half a block away a man sat in a darkened room watching a video monitor. The monitor showed the front of Paul's house. Beside it another monitor was trained on the back of the house. As the Audi turned onto the street the man noted the time on a page filled with previous departures and arrivals. He picked up a walkie-talkie and spoke tonelessly.

"Decker Six, Decker One."

The responding voice was equally dry, flat.

"Decker Six, go."

"Alpha departure."

"Copy alpha departure."

"You got it."

"Lucky us."

The man replaced the walkie-talkie, stood up, stretched, then sat down again and opened a paperback novel.

Half a world away an overweight police inspector stepped off an antiquated elevator and made his way to an apartment where a group of spectators stood craning their necks for a peek inside, like pigeons searching for breadcrumbs.

"*Allez, allez,*" the inspector said as he waved them aside.

Inside the apartment he was met by a uniformed officer who led him to the bathroom where the body of a young woman lay curled in the bathtub, one arm draped awkwardly over the edge. The victim was naked, her skin wet and slightly furrowed, as if she'd been too long in the shower. A photographer with a fancy camera was taking pictures.

"The water was on when they found her," the officer was saying. "That's how the concierge knew something was wrong. No hot water this morning."

"An accident, I suppose?"

"Broke her neck when she fell. See the bruise on the chin?" He shook his head sadly. "Such a waste of a pretty girl."

"Do we have a name?"

"Lisle Beaumier. Nobody special."

The electronic flash went off, momentarily blinding the two policemen before the white-coated attendants arrived and took the body away.

CHAPTER

2

PAUL STAFFORD DIDN'T HAVE MUCH OF AN OFFICE AT the *Herald*, but then, he didn't spend much time there. The office was more of a status symbol, separating him from the ranks of reporters who sat at desks in the city room beyond the glass wall. Paul rated an office because of his title: investigations editor. Twice a week he met with the paper's three investigative reporters and offered counsel and advice. Once a week he met with Managing Editor Bernie Stern and defended his counsel and advice. The rest of the time he devoted to his own stories.

On the day that the CIA men showed up, Paul was in his office talking with a young photographer named Dicky Lazarus. Because Paul shot his own photographs he was sometimes sought out by those who wanted to straddle the worlds of words and pictures. Dicky had been trying to get pictures of Angelo Vespucci, a notorious mobster who was testifying before a Senate subcommittee. Twice he'd been roughed up by Vespucci's bodyguards, and Paul had offered to show him the "Stafford Switch." They were about to leave, first for lunch, then Vespucci, when the girl at the reception desk called to say that two men from the Central Intelligence Agency were here to see him.

Paul glanced at Dicky, who seemed impressed.

"We'll have to wait on lunch," Paul said.

"Is this an ongoing?"

Dicky was new enough to Washington to be excited by a visit from the CIA but smart enough not to show it.

"An in-depth report on homosexuality in the CIA," Paul told him.

"Really?"

"These two guys share a houseboat on the Potomac."

Dicky whistled. "Explosive."

Within minutes the entire building was alive with rumors: Paul was doing an exposé of the CIA, Paul was being arrested as a spy, Paul was actually a CIA agent, Paul had taken unauthorized photos of a secret military base. In the city room outside the window, heads began peering over the maze of cubicles as news of the CIA men spread.

Paul picked up two motor-drive Nikon cameras from the desk, handed them to Dicky.

"You keep this stuff," he said. "I'll call you when we're done."

"You're sure you don't want a witness?"

Paul shook his head. "You look too tempting. They might make a pass at you."

The look on Dicky's face showed how little he liked that idea. He was an east-coast kid given to hip jargon and a faintly punk look: pleated gray pants, checkered suspenders, a blue tee-shirt and over-size lavender sportcoat with sleeves rolled to the elbows. It was no wonder Vespucci's men tossed him before he got within a hundred yards of the guy.

Outside the window the CIA men were visible coming toward them. One looked heavier than the other but they were both clean-shaven and neat in a way that made their conservative suits look like military uniforms. Like soldiers in civilian clothes, thought Paul. Or Secret Service men without sunglasses. He wondered if this was something to do with the Rockland-Birdwell SDI story.

Dicky slid out the door as the CIA men approached. Paul reached into his pocket and touched the shutter release of his Ricoh FF-90. The FF-90 was a small, fully automated camera that Paul used for grab shots. There was a faint click followed by a tiny whine as the electronic flash began charging. Outside the door Dicky paused to give the CIA men a look of distasteful appraisal as they entered the office.

"Mr. Stafford?" said the older man. "My name is Hugh Roark, senior investigator, Central Intelligence Agency. This is my assistant, Maurice Singer."

Singer closed the door to the office before acknowledging the introduction with a nod. He was thin and pale with an expression as blank as a store-window mannequin. Roark, on the other hand, had an easy going manner and disarming smile that was at odds with his calculating, restless eyes. Both men flipped open identification cards and tucked them away just as quickly.

"Have a seat," Paul said.

Hugh Roark immediately took the single upholstered chair while Maurice pulled over one of the two molded plastic chairs along the wall.

"What can I do for you?"

"We have a problem that only—"

Paul lifted the Ricoh from his pocket and casually took a picture. The flash stopped Hugh in mid-sentence and caused Maurice to bounce up from his chair as if spring-loaded.

"Very clever. Now give me the camera."

"I beg your pardon?"

"The camera or the film, I don't care which."

Hugh said, "Easy, Maurice."

"He's got our picture."

Paul said, "I won't publish it without your permission."

"You won't publish it at all. That film leaves here in my pocket."

"Sit down, Maurice," Hugh Roark said quietly. The younger man turned toward his boss. "What happens if we end up on his hit list?"

Paul said, "Side view's good." And then snapped another picture.

Hugh saw it coming and managed to get a hand in front of his face but Maurice was taken by surprise. He turned to Paul with a murderous glare, but Hugh stood up and put a cautionary hand on his partner's arm.

"Easy," he said, then turned to Paul. "Mr. Stafford, whether you know it or not, there are times when taking photographs of field agents can be construed as a threat to national security. We could go to court and force you to turn over your film."

"If it was wartime you could," Paul said, "and if you were both engaged in covert operations. But this isn't wartime and the Washington *Herald* isn't a battlefield and I don't think that talking to a photojournalist constitutes any sort of covert operation.''

"Then let me put it this way. We came here to talk in good faith. If you continue this kind of harassment we can come back with a subpoena and a U.S. marshal. It's up to you.''

"Okay, no more pictures.''

Paul slid the Ricoh back into his pocket, laid his hands flat on the desk and waited. He'd had his fun, now he just wanted to know what the two men wanted. What was it Maurice had said? Something about a hit list?

The two CIA men sat down and Hugh pulled out a metal rectangle slightly larger than the size of a domino.

"You don't mind if we tape-record the conversation, do you?''

"What for?''

"It saves time taking notes.''

He placed the device on the edge of the desk.

"That's a tape recorder?''

"One of our own design. Ninety-six minutes on a permanent micro-filament. You don't mind, do you?''

It was a rhetorical question, Paul knew. If they wanted to tape the conversation, they could do it with or without his knowledge or permission.

"Suit yourself.''

"First of all,'' Hugh said, "let's make sure we're talking to the right man. You're the author of five stories in the Black Cat Mystery Magazine, is that right?''

Paul grinned. "What is this? What are you guys pulling?''

"It's a simple question.''

"I've got two Pulitzer Prizes—photo and journalism, both—and Langley sent you out to talk about a few pulp stories in Black Cat?''

"Are you that author?''

They were actually serious, Paul realized.

"I wrote the stories. What about it?''

Hugh pulled out a notebook and glanced at it. "Your first story was 'Ace High, All Die,' in which a man named Dan Kelso was murdered by drowning, is that correct?''

"I just told you I wrote the stories.''

"Bear with us, please, Mr. Stafford. I want to lay a factual groundwork before addressing the substantive issues of the case.''

"Case? What case?''

Hugh gave him the benevolent-uncle smile. "Please, if we can finish reviewing the stories I'll explain in a moment. Now your second story was, let's see . . ."

" 'Death Sport,' " Maurice said impatiently. "Jurgen Manheim."

Maurice kept his eyes on Paul so there could be no mistake: he had the facts memorized. Hugh's smile faded slightly but he took the interruption in stride.

"Yes, that's correct. As the author, I assume you remember what death you devised for Jurgen Manheim?"

"A fake suicide. Shot in the head."

"Exactly. Then a year and a half later came 'Twist of Fate,' in which a man named Maxwell Durning fell while mountain climbing and broke his neck. Nine months later, in 'Odd Corpse Out' you have a victim named Jim Wilson executed gangland style and his body placed in the trunk of his car. Two years after that, a man named Frank Schrader is poisoned in 'The Grief Merchants.' " Hugh raised his eyes from the notebook. "Is that an accurate summary of the stories published to date?"

"You didn't summarize the stories, you summarized the murders." The nightmares, he wanted to say. You summarized the nightmares that prompted the stories.

"It's the murders that interest us, Mr. Stafford." Hugh's eyes scanned Paul's face for any change of expression. "I think you know why."

"I have no idea why."

"Those were real people, Mr. Stafford. And you either killed them or you know who did."

Paul laughed. "What is this? Did Buddy put you up to this?"

"I wouldn't laugh if I were you," Maurice said.

"What should I do—confess? Colonel Mustard with a candlestick in the dining room? Come on, guys, deliver the punchline. Whose idea is it? Where're the balloons? Where's the funny card?"

"It's not a joke, Mr. Stafford. Two of those who died were our people—agency employees—and the other three were assets. Provided us with confidential information about Soviet and Warsaw Pact activities."

"Oh, sure, sure."

"I'm trying to be honest with you, Mr. Stafford. We could do this differently, you know."

"Like *terminate* me?"

Maurice snorted. "This is getting us nowhere."

"Are you going to help us, Mr. Stafford? Or should we let it be known that you're a security risk and under investigation for murder? As you know, Washington is a small town. People might not be so free about talking if they didn't trust you."

What the hell were they telling him? That he killed people by dreaming about them? Ridiculous. And then he had another thought. He was doing an investigative piece, an exposé of defense contract misappropriations. There had already been offers to buy him off and at least one indirect threat. It wasn't the first time he'd been pressured and it struck him that maybe this was part of the deal. A way to make him think he was implicated in murder so he'd lay off the investigation. But to make him believe that characters in his stories were real? And he was somehow responsible for their deaths? It seemed a farfetched way to pressure him.

Paul stood up. "If you want to charge me with killing fictional characters, go ahead. My guess is you end up in the funny farm before I end up in court. Meanwhile, I've got work to do . . ."

Hugh took a small piece of paper from the notebook and handed it to Paul. It was an obituary notice from a French newspaper. Paul was fluent in a number of languages but even without French, the name was like a slap in the face:

> BEAUMIER, Lisle Jeanette, age 27 years,
> beloved daughter of Helen and Jacob
> Beaumier, 14 Rue Tilsitt . . .

Paul sat down quickly. A week earlier he'd typed the Lisle Beaumier story and sent it to Black Cat. He hadn't even gotten a response, but these men had obviously read it. Read it and then what? Recognized Beaumier's name from an obituary? He checked the date, knowing what he'd find. The girl had died on the night of the dream. Weird, indeed.

When Paul looked up, Hugh was watching him. "I'm glad to see we finally have your full attention."

"Lisle Beaumier . . . is real?"

"Was real. She was having an affair with Terenti Vlasik, the Russian ambassador to France. She was also reporting to our Paris station. Lisle Beaumier was working for us."

"A spy?"

Hugh shrugged. "You weren't aware of the obituary?"

Paul glanced at the clipping again. It made no sense. None of this did. He shook his head slowly.

"Then how did you know?" Hugh asked.

"And why did you publish your knowledge?" Maurice added. He was leaning forward, elbows resting on the chair, the fingers of his right hand toying nervously with a rubber band.

Paul felt as he had after the accident, when he first heard the news about Jason . . . the sick sensation in his stomach, the feeling of disorientation, of life being out of control, of everything being a mistake.

"All of them?" he said slowly. "You're saying they were all real, all those people?"

"The names are real, you know that. You *must* know that."

"No."

"Let's not play games," Maurice said "The names and the circumstances of death are recorded exactly as they occurred. All but one was made to look like an accident—something only the murderer could know. Which means that either you're the murderer or you know who is."

"I didn't murder anybody—"

"Then how do you know their names? How do you know the way they were killed?"

"All I know is what you've told me. How do I know this thing is real?"

Paul flicked the clipping toward Maurice, who grabbed it as it fluttered through the air.

"How do I know your I.D.s are real? How do I know anything you've told me is real? I don't know anything about any murders and I don't know anything about you. For all I know, you're making this all up. How do I know? I never saw you before in my life."

Hugh took out a business card. "Call this number."

"What's that going to show me? Some anonymous voice on the other end says, 'Yeah, sure, this is the CIA. Sure, they're our guys. Sure, you can believe anything they say, including some cock-and-bull story about agents dying from mystery stories.' I can get an unlisted phone number and say the same thing." Paul picked up the phone and imitated a secretary. " 'Good Morning, Central Intelligence Agency.' " He slammed the phone down. "You can be anything over the phone. I do it all the time working on stories."

He stopped, aware that he was talking too much and too vehemently. His visitors regarded him silently. Paul stood up, moved over to the door and opened it.

"Try Bob Woodward at the *Post*. See if he believes you."

Before he left, Hugh placed his card on the desk. "My number's on the back in case you change your mind."

When they were gone, Paul sat staring at the door until Dicky popped his head in.

"Are they?"

"What?"

"You know—sword swallowers?"

Dicky opened his mouth and poked a finger at his throat.

Ignoring him, Paul picked up the phone and called Stuart Meeker, the editor of Black Cat Mystery Magazine. Whoever the men were and whatever they were after, Stuart had let them see his story and Paul wanted to know why.

"Hey," Dicky said. "Are we going, or what?"

"Wait a minute."

"I'll be in layout," he whispered loudly.

Black Cat was published in Boston. After an initial bit of confusion about whether Stu had left for lunch or not, the editor came to the phone and apologized for not having called as soon as he read Paul's story.

"Like it a lot," he said. "We'll run it sometime in the fall."

"By that time half the world will already have read it."

"What's this? You're saying somebody else is publishing it?"

"I'm saying somebody else is reading it. I just had a visit from two men who saw the story and you've got the only copy outside of my desk."

"*Two* men?"

"What's going on, Stuart?"

"I guess one of them was Mr. Johnson, huh?"

"Who's Mr. Johnson?"

"He's a collector. He loves your stuff. Bought all our past issues with Paul Stafford stories and he wanted a first peek at anything new. A very wealthy fellow, Paul. A little eccentric, maybe, but willing to pay in real live dollar bills. I thought I'd humor him and maybe he'd get interested in some of our other authors. Does he want your autograph?"

"How much did he pay to see the story?"

"Oh, I don't know . . . twenty, not more than a hundred. Something like that."

"Meaning what? A hundred?"

"You've got to realize, Paul, that with the postal rate and printer's costs going up, we've really been squeezed. I didn't see any harm—"

"A hundred bucks for a peek?"

"Actually, for the original manuscript. We made a Xerox for the office. Like I say, he's a collector. He's got the original of *Treasure of the Sierra Madre*, so you're in good company."

Treasure of the Sierra Madre, my ass, Paul thought. But he admired the detail. Details made deceptions convincing. He knew. He'd used plenty of phony ploys backed with convincing details in pursuit of a good story.

"What's his full name?"

"Bob. Bob Johnson. He's a real fan."

Dicky Lazarus was standing in the doorway, pointing to his watch. Paul said goodbye and hung up.

"We got to get going," Dicky said, "if we're going to catch Vespucci."

Paul wrote Lisle Beaumier's name on a piece of paper and told Dicky to take it to Kathy Craven in research.

"Tell her to look for an obit in *Le Matin*. This date." He wrote it all down.

"Paul, it's almost one o'clock. '*Uno heura*,' as they say at the Miami *Herald*. Vespucci's going to be gone by the time we get there."

"We'll make it. Get the car. I'll meet you downstairs. Go, go."

Dicky left quickly and Paul made another call, this time to Ron Farquar, a case officer at the FBI. They'd first met when Paul funneled some information Ron's way during the Tongsun Park investigation. Since then they'd traded favors. I.O.U. city, Paul thought as he waited to be patched through.

"Farquar."

"Paul Stafford, Ron. I need a favor."

"If I can."

"Two names: Hugh Roark and Maurice Singer. My understanding is they're CIA. I need confirmation."

"You digging something on the CIA, Paul?" The idea intrigued him.

"You'll be the first to know. How about the names?"

"Not so easy. We've got a reciprocal—they keep off our grass, we keep off theirs."

"Confirmation of employment, that's all. I want to know if I'm dealing with real spooks or someone playing a game with fake I.D.s. Can you do me?''

''Twenty-four hours.''

''I'll check back. How're the kids?''

''Teeth, Cub Scouts, ballet lessons and He-Man. How's the wife?''

''Art patrons and champagne. They're opening a new exhibit tonight. She's okay.''

''That's 'Roark'—R-O-A-R-K—and 'Singer' like it sounds?''

''Yeah. Roark about sixty, Singer maybe half that, hard to tell, a bloodless type.''

''Invisible ink in his veins.''

''Maybe. I'd like to know ASAP.''

''Doesn't everybody.''

By the time he hung up, Paul had half-convinced himself that Hugh Roark and Maurice Singer were fakes.

CHAPTER

3

IT WAS THE FIRST TIME THAT JOANNA HAD GONE TO
bed with a man she didn't love. Luis de Cuevo was talented and
handsome and made no secret of his desire for her, but Joanna didn't
love him and he didn't love her and she told herself, if Paul hadn't
broken his promise it never would have happened.

He was supposed to meet her at the gallery for the opening of
Luis' show. The event had been well attended, although not a packed
house. They'd had a brief moment of panic when the caterer called
saying that the delivery truck had broken down, but they found a
replacement and the hors d'oeuvres arrived in time. A violinist in a
Victorian evening gown had been Joanna's idea and was a great success. Everything had gone well and she'd had just enough champagne
to begin looking forward to seeing Paul and getting over the tension
of the morning when the phone call came.

"Something came up," Paul told her. "I can't make it tonight."

"Where are you?"

"Still at the office. Checking obituaries for you'll never guess
who."

20

"Can't it wait until tomorrow?" she asked, not liking the undertone of irritation and supplication in her voice.

"*It* can, but I can't. Besides, smiling at pretentious art patrons give me lip cramps."

"We'll be here until eight-thirty."

"Look, it's important, okay?"

As if that explained everything. Important. Everything that Paul did was important.

She knew that work was good for him, that it kept him from dwelling too much on what happened to Jason, but she also knew that it had become a thing between them. Paul was traveling more and working more evenings at the *Herald*, leaving her alone, and lonely, with only a snifter of brandy to ease the pain of her own memories. Most of the time she kept the pain to herself, tried to show a warm, happy facade, hoping and needing to lure him back to the intimacy they'd enjoyed before. But it wasn't working. Witness this very morning. Part of him was missing now. There were times when she felt he stared at her as if she was a stranger, and when he watched her undress it was without warmth. Their lovemaking had become sporadic, perfunctory.

From the phone came an angry chirping sound. Joanna was still holding the receiver. She replaced it and glanced around to find Luis watching her. He stood at a punch bowl, surrounded by admirers. When he caught her glance he excused himself and picked his way through the crowd, deflecting the attentions of those who would intercept him until he stood beside her.

"Your husband?"

"He's not coming, it seems."

Luis nodded, as if this was to be expected. When he spoke again it was in a lower, more intimate tone.

"A few of us are going out for drinks afterward. I would like you to join us."

And that's how it started. Or continued. They had already spent ten days working together, hanging the show, and Joanna was well aware that Luis found her attractive. He was self-centered and egotistical, but the simple fact that he *wanted* her was . . . a comfort, a reassurance. After Paul's call, all the loneliness, regret and guilt of the past months seemed to rise up inside her. And so she'd left with him, ostensibly for a quick drink with his friends.

The friends turned out to be a chubby art historian and her husband, both from George Washington University, and an expatriate Brazilian poet with an Israeli girlfriend. After a half hour of touching, then rubbing his leg along hers, Luis separated her from the others and took her to his hotel room. They exchanged their first embrace in the taxi, and by the time they arrived at his hotel, the hair around her neck was damp from his kisses.

Once inside, Luis lifted the mirror above the dresser and brought it to a chair next to the bed. He put his arm around her waist and struck a haughty pose.

"You see? We fit well together."

He's trying to be clever, she thought. Luis, with his narrow face, prominent cheekbones, high forehead and thin hair swept backward as if blown by the wind was so different from Paul. He wore a black tuxedo that looked elegant next to her mauve silk dress with its paint-splashed pattern of turquoise blue, yellow, green and black.

Watching the mirror, Luis slipped his coat off and tossed it to the dresser. He pulled off the bow tie and said, with a smile, "You do the rest."

He kept his eyes on the mirror as she removed each stud from the shirt. He was sure of himself now, no need to rush. It probably happened all the time, she thought. He probably took a lover every time he opened a show. For him, it was routine. For her . . . ? Hardly routine. She hadn't planned the evening to turn out this way. She hadn't planned for *anything* to turn out as it had.

She finished removing his studs, hesitated. Luis pulled off his shirt and tossed it to the floor. He wore no tee-shirt, his chest was flat and brown with a thin ridge of curly dark hair. He slid his arms around her and pressed her face against his chest. The smell of his body, cologne mixed with perspiration, was so *foreign* . . .

I must be going crazy, she thought.

Luis lifted her face, brushed his lips against her cheeks, then kissed her hard. Before undressing her, he removed her earrings. He did it gently, twisting the loops as if he'd designed them and knew every curve. He let his hands glide over her body, moving from her shoulders, down her stomach to her thighs. He lifted her dress, gathering it as he did so that all she had to do was raise her arms for it to slide free. As he knelt to remove her pantyhose he let his hand slide between her legs, brushing his fingers against her.

She shivered and closed her eyes. As he undressed her, he whispered how beautiful she was, how rich her hair, how smooth her skin, how perfect her breasts, how much he *wanted* her. Naked now, she allowed the sensations to spread like fire whenever he touched her. It had been so long since she'd felt wanted this way . . . It was like an affirmation of her womanhood, of her passion and grief and her *right* to the terrible, needing coalescence of body and spirit that had been missing for so long.

It was after midnight when Paul got home. The house was empty but that didn't surprise him. Joanna often stayed out late after an opening, sometimes until dawn. She liked to sit in smoke-filled bars with clutches of artists and intellectuals and discuss esoterica like the death symbols in Eric Fischl's work or the merits of Neo-Futurism. Paul had little patience with such talk and rarely went with her. He frankly looked forward to the day when Joanna lost interest in the whole phony art scene and moved on to something less pretentious and self-indulgent.

He went to his desk, flicked on the light and picked up the phone. He'd had a busy day. After leaving the *Herald* he and Dicky Lazarus had gone to the Sumac Club and set up the Vespucci ambush. When the mobster came out, Dicky went in low, pushing between the barrel-chested bodyguards, who promptly shoved him aside, creating an opening for Paul. By the time the guards grabbed him, Paul had gotten three shots and switched cameras. The film that the guards tore from his Nikon was blank. The second camera lay nestled under his arm beneath his coat. It was kid games, really, but it gave him a sense of satisfaction all the same.

When he got back to his office some time after six he found two messages on his desk, one from Kathy Craven and one from Ron Farquar. Kathy had left two copies of Lisle Beaumier's obituary, one from *Le Matin* and one from *France Soir*. Ron's message was equally succinct: both subject identifications confirmed.

The messages stunned him. Until that moment he hadn't realized how much he'd convinced himself that the CIA men were imposters and their story a fake. Now he knew: the story was real, the deaths were real, the people were real—and so were his dreams. But how?

Paul went to the research department on the second floor. Half of the room was divided by 4x8 sheets of plywood, a temporary condition necessitated by the new computer installations. All the files and records were bunched together in rows on the one side of the room, leaving little space for tables. Luckily, only three people were working the room. He recognized Pam Markowitz but the other two were strangers. A lot of new people had joined the staff recently, mostly college graduates—'C and E's,' the veterans called them. Cheap and eager.

Pam briefed him on the temporary layout and gave him a computer terminal. Paul started with the obituaries, checking the time periods that coincided with when he remembered dreaming the stories. It was a long process. He knew the publication dates but his memory of the dream dates was hazy. The other problem was that he had no idea of which city in which country the victims might have died. Roark had said that two of the victims were CIA agents. He discounted Jurgen Manheim and concentrated on the other four: Dan Kelso, Max Durning, Jim Wilson and Frank Schrader. He began checking U.S. obituaries, giving himself a five-week envelope around the estimated time he had the dreams.

After an hour the only thing he had to show for his trouble was a building headache. Here he was, looking for fictional people in a real world. Kelso, Durning, Wilson, Schrader—they were creatures of his imagination, the stuff of dreams and nightmares. He had no idea who they were. In the stories they died early and quickly. Usually they were bad guys with lots of enemies, to make the job of determining the killer more difficult.

At one point he thought he had Jim Wilson. The name cropped up in the L.A. *Times* at about the time Paul would have dreamed it. A Hollywood talent scout named Jim Wilson died in Beverly Hills when he backed his Mercedes into a swimming pool and drowned. The date was about right but the details were wrong. In Paul's dream, Wilson's throat had been slashed and his body stuffed into the trunk of his car. Aside from the name, the only other similarity was the car. Each man owned a Mercedes.

At which point Paul went to the lounge, got a ham sandwich from the machine and called Joanna to tell her he wasn't coming. Ten minutes later he was back at work. This time he checked the German press for the name Jurgen Manheim and scored a bull's-eye. An obit in *Berliner Zeitung* reported that Manheim, a fifty-nine-year-old resident of West Berlin, died of a self-inflicted gunshot wound. It was eerie to see the man's name in print, as well as the details of the dream: the same gunshot to the right temple. In the story he wrote afterward he made Manheim left-handed to provide a clue for his police inspector. He doubted that the real Manheim was left-handed.

He doubted that anyone knew it was a murder. If it was a murder.

Paul felt his mind turn into a hall of mirrors. Every time he looked at a set of facts from one angle, another set of facts became an impossibility. A fifty-nine-year-old German had died and he'd dreamed it, just as it happened. Or had his dream made it happen? He remembered these old bull-session arguments in college about the nature of reality. Was the world a subjective perception or an objective phenomenon? If you weren't there to perceive it did the world exist? Or did it exist only because you perceived it?

He became aware of the conversation at the other end of the room. A girl in jeans and a khaki shirt was complaining to Pam about the fluorescent lights. A study had shown that fluorescents produced a flicker that caused headaches.

"See those things," the girl pointed at the ceiling. "It's like being bombarded with radiation. They should have flicker filters over them."

A tight feeling of claustrophobia came over Paul as he listened to the girl argue her inane ideas. He got up and went outside. The night was warm and the sidewalks were busy. He walked quickly and then began jogging. Without destination, he sought motion. He ran faster and faster, dodging pedestrians and dashing between cars. He narrowly missed a couple stepping out of a restaurant and the man shouted after him. Paul swerved from the sidewalk and ran full bore along the side of the road, feet pounding, breathing in loud gasps, until he collapsed in Franklin Park and lay on the lawn staring at the stars, the smell of fresh grass all around.

During the Vietnam War Paul had served for two years as a helicopter pilot. He remembered his flight training and how, the first time he had been given all three flight controls, the machine seemed to take on a life of its own, turning and bouncing and sliding all over the sky. It was as if the controls reversed their function at his touch so that every attempt to correct a condition caused the machine to gyrate even more wildly out of control. He felt the same way now. The more he learned about his dreams, the less sense the world made.

Paul watched the stars for a while, and then as the dampness from the grass began to make itself felt he got up and went back to the *Herald* Building. Pam was at her desk reading a book. Everyone else had gone.

"You left the terminal on," she reminded him.

"I'm not done."

Pam grew bored with her book and offered to help. Paul gave her a list of the names before remembering she was one of the few who read his stories in *Black Cat*. She looked puzzled when she read the names.

"These names are familiar," she said. "Who are these guys?"

"Confidential."

"Kelso . . . Manheim . . ." Suddenly it hit her. "Wait a minute, these are names from those mystery stories The ones you write for that magazine."

"You've got a good memory."

She frowned and Paul held up his hand. "Don't ask."

"This isn't an assigned piece, is it?"

"I'm logging the terminal time 'personal.' "

"These *are* names from your story, aren't they? Or are they real people?"

Paul told her that he'd received libel threats from the relatives of people whose names were the same as the ones he used. He was checking the other names to see if there was a potential of other suits. Satisfied, she set to work and fifteen minutes later came up with a new Jim Wilson, this time in a story by Newsweek titled "Americans at Risk Overseas." The article detailed the increasing number of kidnappings and killings of Americans by terrorist groups. Pam pointed to a paragraph that read:

> In Karamursel, American James S Wilson was found dead in the trunk of his Mercedes-Benz. His throat had been cut and the body left with a message calling for the expulsion of all U.S. military bases in Turkey. Wilson was an employee of the USAFSS.

"What's the USAFSS?" Pam asked.

"U.S. Air Force Security Service. They run a signals intercept sta tion at Karamursel."

Pam was impressed. She gave a low whistle and said, "Our *Her ald* reporters know *everything*."

The truth was that Paul had covered the Turkish invasion of Cyprus in '75. The resulting American arms embargo made the Turks mad enough to shut down the Karamursel intercept station for some thing over a year. It had been big news for a day or two and made a lot of intelligence officers mad who didn't give a damn about Cyprus as long as their eavesdropping stations were secure.

"They can't sue you for this one," Pam was saying. "Jim Wilson's a common name and this one died in Turkey while all your stories are in the States, right?"

Paul agreed that there was probably no threat of libel action. He wondered if Wilson was one of the agents that Hugh Roark mentioned—or was he merely an "asset"? He went back to the computer, but by this time his eyes ached and he had a roaring headache. Flicker-filters, he thought, remembering what the girl had said.

Now, sitting at his desk at home, he still had the headache. It wasn't the kind of headache aspirin could cure; he needed answers. He took Hugh Roark's card from his pocket, placed it beside the phone and dialed the number. One ring and a woman's toneless voice answered.

"Six seven five one," she said.

"This is Paul Stafford. I want to talk to Hugh Roark."

"Paul Stafford," she repeated. "One moment, Mr. Stafford."

There was a faint click on the line. Paul imagined the tape rolling in a listening room the size of a sound studio.

"Is it an emergency, Mr. Stafford?" Her voice sounded as if it was pieced together from computer tones.

"Call and ask him."

"We're patching through now. In case of a disconnect, what number are you calling from?"

Paul gave her the number and she put him on hold. Prerecorded classical music flooded the line; Prokofiev's *Peter and the Wolf*. Paul wondered what they'd do if he hung up. Probably send the marines over. He smiled, thinking that Joanna would call this another example of his knee-jerk rejection of authority. The music stopped abruptly and Hugh Roark's voice came on the line.

"Mr. Stafford?"

"You said to call if I wanted to talk. Okay, I want to talk."

"Are you in any danger?"

"Why should I be?"

"It's after midnight, Mr. Stafford. I'm just doing a situation assessment. Are you in danger?"

"Not that I know of." Situation assessment . . . the officialese always offended him.

"And you're willing to cooperate with us?"

"I'm willing to trade some answers. I'll tell you what I know and you tell me what you know and maybe we can both figure out what's going on."

"I can't promise any deals. Not over the phone like this. We have to talk first."

"The sooner, the better."

They made arrangements to meet the next day at a restaurant near DuPont Circle. After they hung up Paul took a shower and went to bed. By the time Joanna got home, he was asleep. He felt her climb beneath the sheets but it wasn't until the bed began to shudder that he realized she was crying.

"Jo?"

No answer. He reached over and turned on the light. Joanna lay on her back staring at the ceiling, her dark hair tangled and wet with tears.

"What happened?"

He touched her cheek but she turned away. There was a crescent discoloration on her neck, the mark of a lover.

The world glided to a stop. Staring at the mark of another man's passion, Paul felt a deep emptiness, not unfamiliar, that had been with him a long time now.

"Who was it?" he asked, surprised that his voice sounded so calm. Joanna turned and hugged him, hard.

"Hold me, Paul," she whispered. "Hold me, please hold me."

He put his arms around her, aware of the smell of cologne in her hair, on her skin.

"I love you," she said in a low voice. She repeated it like a chant or incantation. "I love you I love you I love you."

Paul remained silent. He could feel conflicting emotions leap and whirl as his perceptions of Joanna shifted. She was lover and betrayer, wife and enemy, giver of joy, bringer of pain, a stranger, a woman's body surging and trembling against him.

He became aroused. When Joanna realized it she pulled up her nightgown and guided him to her. She was still wet. He entered without preliminaries, quick and angry. Joanna locked her legs around his waist, grabbed his buttocks and pulled him close, her fingernails digging deep into his flesh. The pain spurred him on. They watched each other's eyes as they made love, staring like enemies, teeth clenched, bodies slamming until they bruised. Slowly, Joanna's expression changed. Her eyes dilated, her mouth parted and she whimpered each time they met, faster and faster until she exploded with a cry and held him close.

Her climax was a cue for his release, but this time Paul felt the opposite sensation, a dying away of passion, a moving away from intimacy. He became still. Joanna sensed what was wrong. Keeping him inside, she changed positions, sitting astride him, her hands braced against his shoulders. She began moving, seeking his rhythm, willing his climax. Paul closed his eyes and matched her movements, searching for the lost tempo. They met again and again, the rhythm increasing and decreasing and increasing until they were both flushed and glistening with sweat and the sheets lay tangled on the floor. Finally Joanna pushed free and moved to take him in her mouth.

"Don't," he said.

"You didn't come."

"It doesn't matter."

She stared up, her chin on his stomach. She moved down again but he held her tight.

"You'll taste *him*."

She froze and then rolled away to the side of the bed, sat there with her back to him, shoulders rising and falling as she regained her breath. When she spoke her voice was empty, tinged with bitterness.

"You're a withholder, Paul. You hold everything back. Even this."

He said nothing. Anything more might end it for them, end the marriage right there. And no matter what he felt, or didn't feel, he knew he didn't want that.

CHAPTER

4

KARL ALEXANDER SAT JAPANESE-STYLE BESIDE THREE other instructors from the Eichwalde Combat School. They wore the traditional white karate *gi*, each with a black belt, as did their opponents. The men were participants in the annual Armed Forces Karate Tournament, held at a military base near Potsdam, twenty miles outside Berlin. It was an event that Karl had won five times previously and was favored to win again. Only one person doubted his ability to win and that was Karl himself.

Mizu no kokoro, he thought, recalling the karate maxim "A mind like water." *Mizu no kokoro*. He repeated the phrase mentally in an effort to rid himself of the dark thoughts and terrible memories that drifted through his mind ever since the latest mission. He had killed a woman, and it was a woman whose memory had returned to haunt him. Not Lisle Beaumier, but another woman, someone whose very name he had repressed, whom he hadn't thought about in thirty years, never wanted to think about again. He swept the name and the bitter memories aside. Now was the tournament. Now he needed clarity of thought and concentration of will. *Mizu no kokoro*

The contestants on either side of Karl were from various branches of East Germany's Armed Forces. They sat outside an eight-meter-square area that had been marked with yellow tape on the polished wood floor of the gymnasium. This was the contest area. Beyond it was an official's table with a time keeper and recorder, while the four judges were stationed at each corner. The bleachers were sparsely filled with other armed forces personnel. From windows high up near the ceiling came narrow bands of sunlight that struck the dark floor and turned it a glowing amber.

The first part of the tournament were *katas*, formal exercises composed of a number of karate movements and executed by a single individual in fixed sequence. An air force man was performing now, hands and feet flashing, bare feet squeaking against the hardwood floor as he battled imaginary attackers. Karl could tell that the man was attempting a complicated pattern beyond his abilities. He would not score well. Karl, on the other hand, had chosen the Heian Number 4, a comparatively simple *kata* but one he knew intimately and could perform perfectly even when distracted, as he was now.

What was on his mind was that he'd lost control on his last mission. Not during the killing of Lisle Beaumier, but afterward, with the Algerian girl. He had lost control and that was dangerous. As a member of the Staatsicherheidienst—the Stasis—East Germany's equivalent of the KGB, he couldn't afford to make mistakes. He had been activated as an assassin in 1981 after the Bulgarians bungled the assassination attempt on the Polish Pope. Having demonstrated their ineptitude and very nearly implicated the KGB, the Bulgarian Durzhavna Sigurnost was replaced by East Germany's Stasis as Moscow Center's preferred agency for "wet" work. Karl had killed six times since then, but Lisle Beaumier had been the first woman. And her death unlocked long-buried memories of his childhood and of the woman who had dominated his early years, the woman whose name still made his stomach tighten with fear. Tante Inge.

He saw her again, rising like a specter in his memory, dressed in her scavenged clothing, layered like a gypsy queen, the bitter mocking lips turned inward, her hair an unnatural henna red, her eyes mirroring the unpredictable moods that seized and shook her like a tree before an autumn wind. It was her eyes that terrified him, trying to read their expression, hoping she wasn't angry, afraid that if she was happy it was only a prelude to some new cruelty. Her eyes mirrored her passions, alternately glazed with tears of self-pity or sparkling with alcoholic euphoria or smoldering with perverted sexuality that made his childhood a nightmare.

"Meeow kitty," she would call him to her bed. "Put me to sleep. Put me to sleep like a kitty cat."

Karl knew what she meant. He would have to crawl beneath the covers and lick her most secret places. Sometimes she would rub chocolate on herself as an added inducement.

"I have a chocolate mouse tonight," she would tell him. "Be a little kitty and eat my chocolate mouse."

Childhood memories . . . The tawdry apartment was his prison and Tante Inge was his jailor. He had been been kept indoors, fed and pampered and coddled and shampooed like a show dog. He remembered how she brought home candy and bathed him and touched a drop of cologne to his forehead as a prelude to turning him over to the furtive, heavy-lidded men who came to the apartment and used him like a woman, pushing his face against the rough sheets or forcing him onto their laps, thrusting into him as they fondled his genitals. And afterward, when all he wanted was to crawl beneath a blanket and hide, Tante Inge insisted on cleaning him with endless scrubbings and enemas of scalding water.

The only time he felt safe was at the mass graveyard in Treptow, where he imagined his mother lay buried. He had never known his mother. She had died in the streets, blown apart by an American bomb, and Karl would have died as well if Tante Inge hadn't rescued him. She'd told him the story many times, emphasizing her own courage and his subsequent ingratitude. And so he endured her until the day he'd run away and joined a gang of wild children living in the rubble of Berlin . . .

The sound of applause brought him back to the present. The air force man had finished his *kata*. Now it was Karl's turn. Quickly he emptied his mind of disruptive thoughts and imagined a white, luminescent screen, pure and clean and free of memories.

The loudspeaker announced him: "Oberstleutnant Karl Alexander, the Heian Number 4."

As Karl stood up, Heinrich Lammers, a new instructor at Eichwalde, wished him good luck. Karl's two other teammates, who knew him better, said nothing. Walking to the contest area, Karl was aware of the stiffness in his legs. He wished he had paid more attention to flexing his muscles while he was sitting.

He made the ritual bow to the officials, took his position. The

Heian Number 4 involved twenty-seven movements; Karl would execute them in forty-three seconds. The movements would take him forward from his starting position, then diagonally to the right and left,
reversing direction to a position behind the starting point and through
a series of movements that concluded back at the original position.
When done skillfully enough, the shadow opponents could be imagined as clearly as if they'd materialized out of thin air.

Karl took a deep breath and began. He stepped to his left, blocked
an incoming blow with his left hand and countered with a knife-hand
right and a front kick. He moved smoothly, never stopping except for
that fraction of a second that marked the culmination of a strike or
block. At those moments all physical and mental energy became
focused at a single point, like the rawhide tip of a whip when it
explodes in a loud crack.

The room, the spectators, the white-garbed contestants—all faded
from Karl's consciousness as he moved into the *kata*. His mind fused
with his body, his muscles became an extension of his will. He
moved with the grace and energy of a young man although the lines
around his eyes and the salt-and-pepper hair suggested a man in his
forties. Rigorous physical training kept him lean and hard; when the
mistake came, it was not his body that betrayed him but his mind. He
lost his concentration.

Karl felt it as soon as it happened. He had just completed the thir-
teenth movement, a *riken-uchi*, or backfist strike. The next movement
involved a 225-degree turn to the left, but even as he felt the sweep
of air over his arm he knew that his center of gravity wasn't low
enough. He overstepped the fourteenth position by six inches. To the
casual observer the mistake was imperceptible, but Karl felt it and the
judges would note it. A mistake on a simple *kata*, the Heian Number
4. Even if he performed the rest of the exercise correctly, he would
finish six inches from his original position. The only alternative was
to correct during one of the other movements, weakening its execution.

His momentum carried him through a left-and-right punch to the
mid-section, and then he stopped. The silence grew loud as spectators
sensed that something was wrong. Karl straightened, turned to the
judging table and bowed.

"I apologize," he told the officials. "I cannot participate in the
tournament."

Ignoring the buzz of surprise that rippled through the audience and the whispered exclamations of his own teammates, he turned and left the gymnasium. In the locker room he took off his *gi* and changed into civilian clothes. From outside he could hear the announcement: Oberstleutnant Karl Alexander, representing the Eichwalde Combat School, had withdrawn from the tournament. The sound became momentarily louder as the door opened and Heinrich Lammers entered. He came quickly down the long row of blue lockers and stood before Karl with a worried look. Heinrich had blond hair and strong features that were too broad for his round face.

"Are you ill?"

"It's poor form to leave the contest area," Karl said cooly.

"But . . . are you all right?"

"As you can see."

Karl lay the heavy twill jacket on a bench, placed the pants on top, then rolled the *gi* into a bundle. He ignored Heinrich, who was too young, too eager and too much a part of the new generation for Karl to feel comfortable with him.

"It is a family matter?" Heinrich persisted. "Your wife, your children, they are in good health, *ja*?"

Karl looked at him. "If they weren't, what would you do?"

"Anything I could do to help, Herr Oberstleutnant."

Heinrich came to attention as he spoke. Karl knew what the young man wanted. He'd heard the rumors about Karl—that his occasional absences, ostensibly to advise combat schools in other Warsaw Pact countries, were actually wet assignments for the KGB. Heinrich was eager to do this type of work himself. He had already confided his ambition to Karl, who professed ignorance and was unresponsive.

Now Karl told him, "You can help most by winning your match today."

"I will, sir. I'll win for both of us."

Karl could feel Heinrich's eager eyes on him as he walked away and an unkind thought crossed his mind, that the boy's opponent would foul and land an *oi-zuki* to Heinrich's wide, pumpkin face.

He did not return to the training ground at Eichwalde but drove instead toward the city. The road rose and fell as it followed the Spree River past the rolling farmlands and pine forest that bordered Berlin. This was Karl's favorite route, one he normally drove at high speed, enjoying the feel and movement of his Mercedes 280 E. Today he drove slowly, unwilling to acknowledge that the appetites he'd begun to satisfy in Berlin's hedonistic Western Sector were no longer a game. It was no longer the pretense of violence he craved but the real thing. The experience with the Algerian girl had proved it.

Fassi, that was her name. She had come to his room at the Hotel Angleterre, the same room, according to the maid, in which the American writer, Ernest Hemingway, had once stayed. The Angleterre was known for its modest elegance and well-insulated rooms, which made it ideal for Karl's purpose. When he was on assignment he always stayed at expensive hotels, where privacy and the dollar were equally respected. His money was real and his documents were false and this was his protection.

Fassi arrived with an assortment of leather gear and a willingness to participate in bondage—for an extra fee, of course. Karl had specified a small woman, young and thin and limber, a *chicky girl*. Fassi was taller than he would have liked, but otherwise she fit his description exactly. She was angular and lithe, with small budlike breasts and narrow hips. Her full brown lips curved inward and became glistening pink where they framed strong white teeth. Her eyes were wide and expressive, but the impression of innocence was mitigated by the assurance with which she set down her purse and bag and surveyed the room. Her hardened expression didn't fit the adolescent body, but Karl was confident that he could reduce her to a frightened child quickly enough.

He gave her a moment to admire the room, which was decorated in pastels of lime and peach and gold and contained a double bed whose bedspread matched the floral design of the wallpaper, a coffee table flanked by two upholstered chairs, and a large dresser. After a few moments chatting she told him that her safety-word was "enough"—all other protests he could ignore. Karl pretended to agree and told her to go into the bathroom and remove her makeup. He wanted her looking fresh and young, just as he had been with Tante Inge. While she washed her face Karl inspected the devices in a shopping bag. He noticed with a professional's eye that the shopping bag was from Cartier. The little whore's employer paid attention to details.

Karl spread the leather goods on the bed, feeling as he always did the mixture of anxiety, fear and anticipation. He noticed, too, the faint buzzing sound he associated with these episodes. Barely discernible now, he knew the sound would increase in volume, reaching a crescendo at the moment of climax. The analytical part of his brain categorized these and other symptoms of what he considered an abnormality even as he accepted and indulged it. Karl did not delude himself. His safety lay in the recognition and control of his sickness.

Fassi had brought the items he asked for: an assortment of leather thongs, a ball gag, a combination headband-chinstrap studded with metal rings, handcuffs, and an enema bag. Karl tied two of the thongs to the metal rings on the headband. While he did this Fassi undressed. She hung her dress in the closet, placed her undergarments on a chair and approached him, thin and dark, ribs faintly visible under glistening walnut skin, the diminutive breasts topped by prominent dark nipples. She had shaved her pubic hair.

"You want me on the bed?"

"Put this on, first."

Karl handed her a white tee-shirt. She slid into it without comment. The tee-shirt was large but Karl had cut away the lower half, revealing her body from the navel down.

"Now this."

He tossed her the headband. She inspected the two thongs dangling from it and half-smiled in recognition.

"We are going to Auteuil this afternoon, *mon bête?*" she said, referring to the famous Paris racetrack.

"Put it on."

Fassi buckled the strap around her forehead and chin. The two thongs dangled like pigtails past her shoulders to her waist. He handed her the enema bag.

"Fill this with hot water and hang it up."

While she was in the bathroom Karl put out a "Do Not Disturb" sign and locked the door. He drew the drapes, turned on the lights, then cleared off the dresser and pulled it away from the wall. He took a roll of pink ribbon he'd bought at a gift shop and cut four long strips. These he placed on top of the dresser. By the time Fassi returned he was undressed and waiting. Lying across the top of the dresser, Karl instructed her to tie his hands and feet with the ribbon to each of the four legs. Humming softly, Fassi went about her work.

"Tighter," Karl told her. "Come on."

"These little things? They will never hold a big man like you."

"They're not meant to."

"Ah, you will be a brute today, *n'est-ce pas?*"

"Don't talk unless I tell you what to say."

She shrugged and continued about her business. When she was done, Karl lay across the dresser as if embracing it. The surface was hard against his chest and face, the edge cut into his thighs, awakening fierce memories and forgotten fears.

"Now bring the enema bag."

Silently she went to the bathroom and returned, the bag in one hand, the white nozzle attached to its orange hose in the other.

"Come at me with it," he instructed. "Tell me I've been a dirty boy and you're going to clean me."

She came toward him, the bottom of the white tee-shirt sliding back and forth across her stomach.

"You're a very dirty boy," she said in a sultry voice.

"Not seductively. You mean to hurt me. You're *going* to hurt me. You know it and you want me to know."

The girl assumed a severe expression and began again.

"You've been a very dirty boy," she said. This time her voice was hard, her attitude more what he remembered. A shudder ran through his body as the old hatred brought the taste of bile in the back of his mouth. The buzzing inside his head increased. He was growing hard.

"Keep repeating it. Tell me I'm dirty and you're going to get me clean. Come up slowly and try to do it."

She did as he asked. Karl strained against the bonds and pushed his cheek hard against the dresser. Eyes closed, he remembered the terror of childhood, the garish basement apartment with its heavily perfumed bedroom and Tante Inge coming toward him, just as the girl was coming toward him now.

His body tensed. "*Bitte, bitte*, Tante Inge. Please, no."

"A very dirty boy and you have to be punished."

He felt her coming closer and he strained against the bonds, remembering all the times he'd wanted to escape and been forced to endure. The dresser was sharp against his thighs and pressed uncomfortably against his erection. The smell of the bedroom rose in his memory, the smell of Tante Inge's perfume and of his own fear.

"Dirty boy has to be cleaned for his own good."

"I'll be good," he whispered, but the words were drowned by the angry buzzing that filled his ears. "Please, please, Tante Inge."

"Has to be cleaned right now—"

The nozzle touched him and all of the submerged fear and rage exploded as he ripped free of his bonds, rolled from the dresser and landed on his feet in a crouch. Fassi, taken by surprise, could only stare, her mouth a gaping pink O.

Karl grabbed her ankle and tumbled her to the floor. Before she could react he was on top of her. He shoved her arms beneath his knees, grabbed the enema bag and held the nozzle to her lips.

"*You* take it. Here, here!" Karl insisted.

She pulled her arms free, tried to push him away. There was fear and panic in her eyes, and angry desperation as she began to fight back. She scratched at his eyes, forcing him to drop the bag and grab her hands. He leaned forward, bent his arm and directed an elbow into her solar plexus, then lunged to the bed and got the ball gag. Fassi rolled to her side, legs drawn up, gasping for breath. Karl shoved her onto her stomach and sat on her narrow haunches as he shoved the ball into her mouth from behind. He moved quickly, never stopping, compelled to act, compelled to use the girl as he would an enemy, an object . . . as he would have used Tante Inge.

Pulling her arm back, he handcuffed her before flipping her over. Fassi was breathing in deep gasps now. Her eyes were fearful but wary, like a trapped animal. Karl wanted her emotions bared as completely as her body. Pushing beneath the flimsy tee-shirt, he sank his teeth into her skin. Fassi pulled away frantically, the force and suddenness of her movement making him lose his grip. She slid out from under him, kicking, trying to push free. Karl grabbed at her but her heel caught him in the temple. The blow brought tears to his eyes. Fassi scrambled to her feet. For a moment she stood over him, hands pinned behind her back, headband tight across her forehead, mouth distended by the ball gag. She looked from the door to the window, then ran for the door.

Karl rolled to his feet and went after her. This time she was ready for him. As she got to the door she kicked it once and then surprised him by turning and aiming a kick at his groin. His defense was instinctive; he caught her ankle in a cross-arm block, yanked upward and with a muffled cry she fell backward to the floor.

Her attack infuriated him. He had been through enough pain—more than enough. It was her time to endure and his time to punish. Instead she had tried to turn the tables, tried to hurt him.

Holding her ankles, he dragged her across the room. The rug scrunched the tee-shirt up around her armpits. Grabbing it, he lifted her and pushed her face down onto the dresser and took her, using her the same way he had been used as a boy, a sacrificial victim to the pain of his childhood, as if everything that he had endured could be transferred to her.

He felt no sympathy for the girl. She was an adult who chose to sell her body for sexual sport. If the trauma he inflicted was more than she bargained for, it was little enough compared to the hell of his childhood and no worse than what many a pimp had done before him.

Swept up in his contorted passions, Karl failed to notice when Fassi's eyes rolled back and she lost consciousness. Only after he climaxed and was lying with his cheek resting on her back did he become aware that she lay limp and had stopped breathing. In pulling her head back he had compressed her windpipe, cutting off her air. It took ten minutes of mouth-to-mouth resuscitation before she was breathing properly again, and during those minutes Karl realized the extent of his danger.

The episodes with prostitutes had started innocently enough as a reward for his first assassination. At first he limited these diversions to those times when he was far from home. Then he began going to West Berlin, seeking out the parlors that specialized in the types of sexual activity that attracted him. He kept this aspect of his life secret, telling himself that safety lay in controlling the impulses, not suppressing them.

But the accident with Fassi proved what he had suspected for some time—that the episodes were becoming increasingly violent and that instead of his controlling the dark needs inside him, they were coming to dominate him, overcoming his common sense, testing his strength of will and finding it lacking . . .

Karl left the road and drove through the neighborhood of Treptow. He stopped briefly to buy a red rose from a flower vendor, then continued to the Cemetery for Unknown Victims of Fascism. The cemetery wasn't large or well known. It consisted of a small field of well-tended grass surrounded by a two-foot-high stone wall. As a boy, Karl had helped build the wall, using the rubble from buildings shattered by the war. For this he had received a bowl of potato soup and half a slice of bread each day—a great deal at a time when many were starving.

But it wasn't for these memories that he'd come; it was for the memory of his mother, the stranger who had given him life and who linked him with unknown past generations, with aunts and uncles and grandparents and myriad ancestors lost to him but nonetheless real.

Karl walked slowly across the grass to the center of the field, where a statue stood, the only object to disturb the broad expanse of green grass. The statue, cast in bronze, was of a woman on her knees, head bowed, hands covering her face, hiding her features, leaving her identity unknown. As a boy he had come to the irrational conclusion that his mother had posed for the statue, and over the years, whenever he thought of his mother, it was this figure that came to mind.

He sat down with his back against the pedestal, tilted his head back and stared up at the hidden face framed by tufted white clouds that inched their way across the sky. The sound of children playing kick-ball on a nearby street came to him and their delighted laughter reminded Karl of what he had lost. He was a father with three children of his own, but his children were strangers to him. Too much was hidden—from them, from his wife, from the world at large.

"It can't go on," he said softly, twirling the rose idly between his fingers.

He sat for some minutes, breathing deeply, lost in thought. His fingers slowed and the rose became still. He saw clearly that the danger was inside him. Danger to his job, danger to his family, danger to his own personality. A choice had to be made. Either he resigned from the Stasis or he gave up the poisonous interludes with prostitutes. There was no middle way.

He closed his eyes and let his mind drift. He knew what the answer would be—what it had to be. Finally he got to his feet and stood in front of the statue, staring at the bronze hands that were as familiar as his own. A cloud passed over the sun, momentarily painting the grass a darker shade.

"Never again," he said quietly. "It stops now."

The resolution made him feel better. He drove home and found Magda baking May Day cookies while listening to the television. The two girls were still at school but Willy, their youngest, was in the back yard playing with a neighborhood boy.

Magda greeted him with a kiss, her upturned nose cool against his cheek, her hands held wide so as not to get dough on his clothes. There was a time, early in their marriage, when they delighted in each other's bodies. After the birth of their first child, however, Magda drew back from sexual experimentation and settled comfortably into a motherhood that Karl found excluded and comforted him at the same time. They were dutiful toward each other, nothing more.

"You're home early," Magda said. "Is Uncle Alex coming with us?"

Karl was suddenly alert. Alex Ikhnovsky was his mentor, a Russian KGB colonel who had been responsible for Karl's education and then his career in the Stasis.

"Coming with us where?"

"To Zinnowitz. Didn't he call you at the school?"

"No. Did you talk to him?"

"He called here just after you left. He said you invited him to come to Zinnowitz with us, which I don't mind but I wish you'd ask me first."

"I meant to," Karl said automatically.

The truth was that he hadn't talked to Uncle Alex in months and hadn't invited him along on their May Day holiday. The old Russian hated the beach. For him to invite himself along meant that something was wrong, something that he couldn't talk about on the phone but needed to discuss in person.

Karl was sorry he hadn't returned to the office, although when he thought about it he realized that Uncle Alex wouldn't call him there. Phone calls at Eichwalde were screened. Knowing the Russian as he did, Karl was certain that Ikhnovsky wanted to keep their meeting as casual and private as possible.

His thoughts were interrupted by Magda banging on the kitchen window. Outside in the back yard the two boys were fighting over a tree branch. They paused to look up.

"No sticks, Willy," Magda called out. "Put it down." The boys pretended not to hear and went back to their struggle. Magda banged on the window again, then turned to Karl.

"Make them stop that."

He opened the back door and yelled at the children. Both boys dropped the stick and turned to face him.

"Leave it alone," Karl ordered, trying not to sound severe but not succeeding too well. It annoyed him, these children who had everything and still weren't satisfied but had to make trouble.

He closed the door and stood for a moment watching Magda roll balls of dough and shove them onto a pie tin. He had come home early thinking to make love to her before the girls returned from school, but not now. He was worried about Uncle Alex, and he felt like a stranger in his own home.

He went to the garage, got out his tools and changed the oil in the Mercedes. He would not waste the afternoon.

CHAPTER

5

ONE HUNDRED MILES NORTH OF BERLIN, THE RESORT
town of Zinnowitz sits on a low-lying peninsula thrust into the Baltic
Sea. The town is bordered by hotels and guest houses facing an endless expanse of windswept dunes. One of them, the Apart-Hotel
Nordsee, is a modern facility that offers, in addition to rooms and
apartments, a tennis court, saltwater pool, sauna and sunbathing
lawn. It was here that Alexander Ikhnovsky, former non-voting member of the Politburo and retired chairman of the KGB, came to meet
Karl Alexander, the man he considered a son, the man who had taken
the Russian's name as his own, the only man he could trust with his
life.

"And God so loved the world He gave His only begotten
son . . ."

The words came unbidden to his mind and caused him to smile. In
his old age, bits and pieces of religious ceremony came washing up
on the shores of his consciousness like nautical debris after a ship-
wreck. Ikhnovsky hadn't been to church in over sixty years, yet
recently the sound of the wind in the birches took on the harmony of

voices raised in liturgy, the smell of exotic pipe tobacco would startle him with the remembered aroma of incense, and the task before him called to mind God's sacrifice of His only son to save the world. Only Karl needn't be sacrificed. Not if everything went according to plan.

Ikhnovsky shifted uncomfortably. The rental car, an East German Trablant, was small and cramped, particularly for a man of his bulk. In his younger days he'd had enormous strength and energy. When he was seventeen he'd lifted a dead horse to free a fallen comrade. Another time, drunk and daring, he'd dangled one hundred feet in the air, holding onto a rope by his teeth. During the Krondstat Rebellion he'd taken nine rebel bullets and had still been among the first wave to breach the ramparts of the fortress. "Iron Man Ikhnovsky," they had called him. But no longer. The years had thinned the once-massive limbs and caused the flesh around his neck to sag. Only his trunk retained its characteristic girth, as if all the flesh had shifted position, withdrawing to this one location.

Keeping one hand on the wheel, Ikhnovsky reached back and massaged his neck, which had become stiff. He thought longingly of Mischa, his driver during the many years the state had provided a limousine to whisk him back and forth to work. Now that he was retired he was no longer *nash*, one of the privileged few who had the General Secretary's ear. Not this General Secretary, anyway. Not the man who was willing to sign a Mutual Defense Treaty with the Americans and trade Russia's Nevsky Project for the so-called Star Wars technology. Trading a cannon for a bow and arrow—that was how General Gulst termed it.

Thinking of his fellow conspirators reminded him of their last meeting a few days ago in his dacha outside Moscow. He remembered their faces as they gathered, ostensibly to celebrate his birthday, actually to solidify their opposition to the Defense Treaty. There was Gulst, thick and stalwart, Likhacev with his disdainful smile, Pilayan with the self-righteous tilt to his chin.

Strange how different they were, each drawn to opposition for his own private reason: Gulst to protect the Nevsky Project, Likhacev to move himself closer to a position in the Politburo, Pilayan because of his fear of the Americans. None of it mattered to Ikhnovsky, who saw the threat of the Mutual Defense Treaty as cultural rather than physical.

The rich cultural heritage of the Soviet Union and the exhilarating frontiers of Marxism were being diluted by the West. Ikhnovsky knew how easily his country could become a pale imitation of America, like Canada or Western Europe. Another culture sapped by materialistic cravings, its people driven by superficial goals, eyes and ears assailed by garish advertising slogans and minds engulfed by television trivia.

Ikhnovsky recalled the day when his father had marched off to the Tsar's war and his mother had taken the family to church, where they sang and prayed for his father's safe return. *Gospodi pomuli*—even now the empty ritual phrases echoed in his mind. *Gospodi pomuli.* The prayers had availed nothing. It was not prayer that changed the course of history, but concerted action. The sort of action that was necessary now to save his country

In his room at the Apart-Hotel Nordsee, Ikhnovsky changed his clothes, then went downstairs and asked to see the manager. Herr Oster, a portly man impeccably dressed with razor-edged sideburns and a rather flat face, hurried out to meet him. There was an air of officious subservience about Herr Oster that Ikhnovsky associated with the worst extravagances of the German character. Adopting an appropriate arrogance, Ikhnovsky presented Herr Oster with his briefcase, which he demanded be locked in the hotel safe.

"I shall place it there myself, Herr Ikhnovsky," the manager promised.

Watching the man strut away, his trousers tugging at his buttocks with each step, Ikhnovsky wondered what Herr Oster would say if he knew that inside the briefcase there was a map of a United States Military Ocean Terminal, a modified Sony radio housing a CIKOP-34F receiver with voice decryption capability, and fifty thousand American dollars?

Ikhnovsky left the building and went down to the beach, where he found Karl and his family. They were dressed in swimsuits in spite of the cool temperature and brisk wind. Sand peppered his ankles as he made his way toward them. Although he had little affinity for the sea, Ikhnovsky had changed into what he considered beach attire: a navy-blue sweater with white shorts belted high on the stomach. His legs were surprisingly thin for a man of his bulk, like those of a seagull marching across the beach. He wore leather shoes without socks, and already the sand was abrading his heel.

Karl greeted him warmly and Magda only slightly less so. The three children were dutifully polite. Bridget and Katrina actually curtsied, a gesture that struck Ikhnovsky as incongruous given the red spandex swimsuits they wore. Little Willy, the youngest, shook his hand solemnly and then raced back to his excavation in the sand. A handsome family, Ikhnovsky thought. The type of family he might have had if the years hadn't passed so quickly and the demands of trying to forge a new society hadn't been so all-consuming.

Without being told, Magda went to get another beach chair. It was early in the season and the beach was only moderately crowded. A number of people had rented rattan windbreaks, self-contained benches with backs that extended some six feet high. Others lay on towels and blankets scattered across the sand. A young couple walked arm-and-arm in the surf, a boy and his dog played tug-of-war with a towel, and from a distant radio came the melody of a popular tune.

"Sit down, uncle," Karl said, pointing to one of the two beach chairs. Once Magda was out of earshot, he gave the Russian a questioning look.

"So?"

"A crisis, Karl. We will speak of it later."

"But you—you are all right?"

Ikhnovsky shrugged. "A young man trapped in an old man's body. I am all right."

Magda returned and the two men shifted their conversation with ease that came from long practice. They spoke of the weather, of the children's progress in school, of Magda's volunteer work at the War Widows Home, of Ikhnovsky's health and of Berlin's recently relaxed border restrictions.

Ikhnovsky noted Karl's casual manner and approved. They hadn't spoken since the phone call a few days earlier, during which the Russian had been able to reveal nothing of the real purpose of his visit. He knew that Karl was curious, yet few would guess that beneath his casual pose, eyes half-closed, arms and legs draped carelessly over the chair, Karl was alert as a cat.

Magda was relating a humorous incident about a motorist who became lost in fog and drove into the sea the night before. Ikhnovsky put on a polite expression and listened without hearing. Magda had a milkmaid's freckled cheeks, blonde hair and blue eyes and a full figure that had once been voluptuous but now overflowed the edges of her two-piece bathing suit. Her interests were a traditional German hausfrau's: kitchen, church and children. She laughed easily and Ikhnovsky felt she was oblivious to Karl—to the complex personality beneath the simple facade.

Which was Karl's greatest asset, Ikhnovsky thought—that ability to function with such credibility in two different worlds. Most killers were lost and lonely men who lived without families and had few friends. They were social misfits whose secret passions knew no allegiance and this made them suspect. But Karl was different. He had grown up in the devastation of post-war Berlin, surrounded by death and dying, and despite the fact that he never spoke of the time before they met, Ikhnovsky suspected that Karl knew no difference between life and death. At some deeper level, the two states were the same to him. This was what enabled him to be a husband, a father and a killer, each with equal success.

On the beach the two daughters had joined their brother at their sand construction. They whispered among themselves and every so often turned to look toward Ikhnovsky. Finally Katrina got up and came to him, urged on by gestures from her sister. She stood awkwardly, rubbing a strand of wet hair against her cheek.

"Excuse me," she said. "Excuse me."

Magda reached over and put a hand on her daughter's shoulder while she finished describing the new addition to their house, then said, "What is it?"

"I have a question," Katrina said. She turned to Ikhnovsky. "Uncle Alex, Willy said something stupid. He says that in Russia you eat bears. Is that true?"

"Kati!" Magda said, but Ikhnovsky waved her objection away.

"No, no, no, she's right. We used to eat bears."

The little girl's eyes widened. "You did?"

"We ate field mice, too."

"Field mice!"

"Anything we could find. This was before the Revolution, when the Tsar took all the food for the soldiers and left the people to starve. So we had to eat whatever we could find. Shooting a bear would be lucky because a bear could feed a whole village."

"Oh." Katrina wrinkled her nose with distaste, then ran back to tell her brother and sister the terrible news.

"You shouldn't encourage her with such stories," Magda told him.

"All true, all true. We ate mice and pigeons during the Revolution."

Magda shuddered. "I think I would starve before I ate such things."

Karl said, "That's because you don't know what it's like to be hungry, Magda. Believe me, you would eat anything."

"A pigeon, perhaps, if I—"

"Anything."

For a moment, Karl fixed her with hard eyes empty of emotion. Then, as if someone had flicked a switch, the warmth came back. He smiled reassuringly. "I ate squirrels in the Tiergarden. Uncle Alex knows."

Magda looked uncomfortable. "You mean . . . after the war?"

"When else?" Karl stood up. "I'm going in."

He walked briskly down to where the surf tumbled and melted into the sand. The children ran after him, dancing in his footsteps and shrieking with excitement as he dove without hesitation into the sea. He swam with smooth, powerful strokes, shoulders glistening in the sun, his body lifting and falling on the incoming waves. How different he was, Ikhnovsky thought, from the dirty, half-starved little boy that he had first seen so many years ago.

"He never talks about those years," Magda said lightly.

She gave him an oblique look, inviting his confidence, but Ikhnovsky had no wish to confide in her.

"Terrible years," he said.

He closed his eyes and pretended to doze. The sun was warm where his face was sheltered from the breeze. Memories came unbidden . . . he saw again the old building on Liebnechstrasse in which the KGB offices had been located for many years after the war. The multi-story Italianate building was one of only a handful to escape the Russian shells and American bombs. It was surrounded by a wrought-iron fence, guarded twenty-four hours a day, with access strictly controlled. As *rezident* of the Berlin Section, Ikhnovsky had chosen the building precisely because it lent itself to tight security measures, and so it came as a particularly unpleasant surprise to discover an intruder.

Ikhnovsky had been on his way out when he heard the shots. He hurried downstairs and discovered a commotion in the yard. A janitor had discovered a boy in the basement. The boy had broken free, run out the back door and scaled the fence. By the time the soldiers arrived, the boy was on the other side, running across the snow-covered earth. The guards fired but the boy disappeared in the ruins of a neighboring building. The sergeant was certain the boy had been hit.

Ikhnovsky went with them and discovered a trail of blood in the snow. Following it through the debris and rubble of the bombed-out building, they found the boy sitting on the ground, his back against the wall, face contorted with pain. Although it was January, he wore only ragged pants and a frayed coat two sizes too large. His feet were wrapped in rags and were bleeding. His leg had been shattered by the bullet. The sergeant raised his rifle but Ikhnovsky placed a hand on the barrel, then picked his way through the debris. At his approach the boy pushed himself against the wall with the desperation of a wild animal. Ikhnovsky stopped in front of him.

"Does it hurt?"

In answer, a defiant stare. The Russian knelt and reached forward. Instantly the boy lashed out with a crude knife. Ikhnovsky parried the blow with a gloved hand but felt the blade cut his palm. He stood and kicked the boy's leg. Hard. The boy fainted. Ikhnovsky picked up the knife as the sergeant and guards came running forward.

"Should we call the police, sir, or shall I take care of the little Nazi privately?"

"Take him to the hospital."

"The hospital?"

"Have them fix his leg."

"Sir, he broke into a secured building and—"

The back of Ikhnovsky's hand connected with the sergeant's face.

"I will not give the same order twice," he said, then walked away without a backward glance.

An investigation of the basement revealed a crawl space behind the boiler where the boy had been living. The floor of the space was covered in newspapers and old rags, like a nest, and a window curtain blackened with soot had been hung to conceal the opening. It appeared that the intruder had been there for some time.

Ikhnovsky visited him in the hospital. The boy lay in a metal frame bed, his leg in traction. They had cleaned his face and brushed his hair but his eyes were still those of a wild animal's.

"They tell me your leg is going to mend."

The boy watched him warily, without speaking.

"How did you get inside the building?" Another pause. "Come on, nobody's going to hurt you now. How did you get in?"

"The coal chute."

"The door to the coal chute has a padlock."

"The frame is rusted loose. I got the whole thing free."

"You pulled the frame with the door attached?" The boy nodded.

Ikhnovsky smiled to himself. The frame would be repaired immediately.

"You were living in the building. Why?"

"I was cold."

"You're from the rubble gang?"

Ikhnovsky didn't expect an answer and got none. Years after the war huge portions of the city still lay in ruins, inhabited by groups of homeless children known as rubble gangs. They became beggars, petty thieves, pickpockets and con artists. Their only loyalty was to other members of the gang and their only credo was survival at any cost.

"What's your name?"

The boy stared at him, his gray eyes blank. His thin cheeks and taut skin reminded Ikhnovsky of photographs he'd seen of victims of Nazi death camps.

"Come on, I want to talk to you. My name is Alexander Ikhnovsky. What are you called?"

"Karl."

"Karl what?"

"Karl Drei."

"Drei—three." Karl Three, the third in his gang by that name.

"How long were you living in the building, Karl?"

The boy shrugged.

"Days?"

He nodded.

"Weeks?"

The boy nodded again. In the building for weeks. A stowaway inside KGB headquarters in Berlin. A boy of what? Seven or eight? A boy had slipped through their security system and remained undetected for weeks? He knew what they would say at Moscow Center if they ever found out. And they would find out. Like anyone else in a position of power, Ikhnovsky had rivals who would be only too glad to see his reputation damaged.

"Can I sit here, Karl?"

The boy moved to the far side as the Russian sat down. Ikhnovsky took the boy's knife from his pocket. The blade had evidently been made from a piece of scrap metal. The shaft extended between two pieces of wood wrapped in electrical wire. "Where did you get this?"

"I made it."

"It's very sharp." Ikhnovsky held up his palm. "See what it did?" The boy tensed. "Yes, it's a good knife." Ikhnovsky held out the knife, handle first, to Karl. "Go ahead. You may need it when you get outside."

Karl took the knife and slipped it under his sheet.

"You're a clever boy, Karl. I could use a boy like you. How would you like a job?"

Taken by surprise, the boy's features softened, and for the first time Ikhnovsky could see behind the fear and desperation to the child hidden within.

"You would have enough to eat, your own room, warm clothes. In return you would be my eyes and ears on the street. A rubble boy is invisible. You can go places, see and hear things others would never be exposed to. How would you like that?"

"I would have food?"

"All you can eat."

"And shoes?"

"Shoes and wool socks to go with them."

"And I could sleep in the basement?"

"No, not there. But in my apartment, there's a cleaning closet behind the stairway. I'll have the landlady clear it out and it will be your bedroom."

Karl stared at him.

"When will I start?"

"You've already started. One of your jobs will be to test the security of all Soviet buildings—just like you did this time."

Ikhnovsky's subsequent report contained a stinging indictment of Major Bobkov, the security chief. After all, hadn't Ikhnovsky hired a rubble boy to penetrate the KGB building? And hadn't it taken the security force three weeks to discover this? What if the boy had been an enemy agent rather than one of his own people? Ikhnovsky recommended that a new security chief be sent, this time one who couldn't be fooled by a mere boy.

And so it began, a relationship based on expediency that became, in time, that of a father and son. Karl filled a void that Ikhnovsky hadn't known existed. At first this embarrassed him. He had, after all, hardened himself against emotionalism and sacrificed his personal life to building a new society. But after Karl began living beneath the stairway, the Russian found himself making excuses to avoid the drinking bouts of his peers in favor of a dinner at home with the boy, a quiet conversation and perhaps a game of chess.

For his part, Karl idolized and adored his mentor, so much so that there was never any doubt in his mind about what he would do when he grew up: he would join the KGB. The greatest disappointment of his young life was when he revealed this ambition to Ikhnovsky, who was forced to explain that only native-born Russians were allowed into the organization. But the East German intelligence agency would surely take him, Ikhnovsky would see to that.

Karl's life began on the day Alexander Ikhnovsky came to see him in the hospital. Of the time before they met, he never spoke. When Ikhnovsky sent him to grade school, he chose his mentor's first name as his own. He had been Karl Alexander ever since . . .

Now these memories warmed the old Russian as much as the sun and lulled him to a sleep where he dreamed of onion-spired churches and cheering crowds and clumsy wood toys carved by a man with bushy eyebrows and a thick brown beard. The man was his father but it was long ago, and the man seemed so young, so very young, so very long ago . . .

CHAPTER

6

KARL ALEXANDER TOOK THE LOOSE COINS FROM HIS pockets and arranged them in a neat stack upon the dresser. The currency was East German, the color and weight of aluminum, larger and lighter than its West German counterpart. Karl arranged them according to size, from largest to smallest, until they formed a graduated cone. It was a habit left over from his childhood, when a single *Pfennig* meant the difference between a crust of bread and starvation. The feel of the coins reassured him. Money was security. Money meant that he would never be enslaved by circumstance the way he had been as a child; the way he had been by Tante Inge.

Karl turned from the dresser and selected a coat from the closet. He had rented the largest and most expensive apartment at the Nordsee, one with two bedrooms and a living room with kitchenette. From the open doorway he could see Magda and the children sitting in front of the television. Willy was asleep on his mother's lap but the two girls lay on the floor, heads propped on their hands. His family gave Karl the same sense of security as did the stack of coins on the dresser.

53

Karl was not wealthy but he was privileged; there were many ways that a senior member of the Stasis could augment an otherwise modest salary. The anti-fascist barrier, known in the West as the Berlin Wall, was invisible to Karl. Merely by flashing his I.D. he could pass freely from one sector of the city to another. He was immune to his country's currency restrictions, and his car was never searched. A man with Karl's extensive underground connections in the West and a privileged position in the East would have to be a fool not to make money.

Magda said something and the two girls laughed. Karl cocked his head to one side, listening, like a wolf alert to approaching game. At times it bothered him that the world of children was inexplicable to him. He knew nothing of their carefree manner and easy laughter, and on those occasions that he tried to join them, his attempts were forced and unnatural. Having had no childhood, he had no concept of a child's world. His only world had been Tante Inge.

Karl checked his appearance in the mirror, then said goodnight to Magda and the children and received a dutiful response from each. As he got into the elevator and pushed the button to the third floor, it occurred to him that he felt closer to Uncle Alex than he did to his own family.

He had been dismayed to see how old the Russian had become. Over the phone Ikhnovsky's voice had sounded strong and gruff—still the same voice that he remembered as a boy, the voice of a man who'd first appeared to him as a giant wearing a khaki greatcoat and a fur hat bearing the emblem of implacable military might, the red star. But this afternoon, when Uncle Alex played with the children, he was not so steady on his feet, and when he fell asleep in his chair his chin disappeared in the slack skin of his neck.

The elevator doors opened. As Karl stepped out a middle-aged man with a giggling young woman entered. The woman had dyed red hair and wore a tight-fitting black dress. She bumped into Karl, said, "Excuse me," and gave him a casual appraisal that made no secret of her approval. Karl paid no attention, but as he walked down the hall he found himself mentally replacing the lascivious look in the girl's eyes with one of pain and fear, just as he had done with the Algerian whore, Fassi. With an effort he pushed the image aside and concentrated on the immediate surroundings—the determinedly cheerful yellow walls, the fire extinguisher at the end of the hall, the muffled sound of a television.

He found Ikhnovsky's door and knocked. When the Russian appeared it was evident that he'd just taken a bath; his hair was damp and he wore crisp slacks with a pale silk shirt. Meeting now, they embraced again, this time with a warmth that underscored the limited significance of their earlier public greeting.

"Ah, Dreitsky, Dreitsky," the Russian said, using the nickname he'd given Karl as a boy. He held the younger man at arm's length, and Karl was surprised to see a sadness behind the joy in his eyes.

"Are you in trouble, Uncle Alex?"

"Soon enough, soon enough. Have you got the time, yes?" Ikhnovsky took Karl's wrist and turned it so that he could see the watch. It was a modern, digital design, but Karl knew he wasn't looking for the time. The watch was a Stasis design; if the digits flashed, it indicated the presence of a transmitter. Did Uncle Alex really think his room at the Nordsee might be bugged? He felt his senses sharpen. The Russian was not a man to harbor groundless fears.

Ikhnovsky grunted, reassured. He turned away, motioning impatiently to the television.

"Find us a good program, something to take our mind off our troubles."

Karl performed the ritual precaution, turning the volume up on a documentary about sailboat racing.

"Yes, good," Ikhnovsky called to him.

He was unscrewing the mouthpiece of the phone. Only after he removed the microphone and placed it on the table did he motion Karl to sit down.

"Come, come," he said, speaking in Russian. "Now we can talk."

They sat at a round formica table near a picture window that looked out over the sea. Below them the beach was bright with floodlights, but beyond it the water merged into darkness and only the white foam was visible, advancing on unseen waves like pale snakes sliding sideways through the night.

"Karl," Ikhnovsky began somberly, "what I have to say will jeopardize your career, the safety of your family, perhaps your life. If there was any other way . . . if I was young enough, if I could turn back the clock inside this old man's body and become like you, a man in his prime . . ."

He sighed. Karl watched and waited. He knew the old man's

moods well enough not to try and hurry him. Ikhnovsky placed his hands on the table and shook his head.

"What the mind wills," he said, "this body can no longer achieve; what the eye sees, these hands cannot grasp."

Karl slid his hands across the table. "Use these, Uncle."

Ikhnovsky smiled. "I know you have little interest in ideological concerns, Karl, but are you not aware that the socialist world has reached a dangerous crossroad? Our ideals are no longer closely held, our commitment has faded, and the great dream of the Revolution is dying. You are young, but I remember our vision of a new world, a vision that made us strong, so strong we could prevail even when we made mistakes. But this heritage is slipping away, and with it, the whole promise of the future."

Karl listened but the words had little effect. He knew the benefits of Marxism and the weakness of capitalism and the evils of imperialism, but he knew these things as dogma, as subjects that he learned in school. Karl was not an intellectual. Political concepts and abstract discussions mattered little until they led to action. He had only one allegiance—to Alexander Ikhnovsky, and only through him to the state he served.

"It's not nuclear weapons that will destroy us, Karl, it's cultural sabotage. Can you see that? No, no, I bore you. Very well, then. Let me show you something that may make an impression, even on your pragmatic soul."

Ikhnovsky crossed the room and lifted a briefcase to the bed. He unlocked it and pulled out a video-cassette.

"You've heard about the Nevsky Project, I assume?"

"The Soviet version of the American Star Wars program."

The Russian shook his head, waving the cassette in the air as he carried it to the videotape recorder.

"Wrong, wrong, wrong. That is what everyone thinks—that the two systems are compatible. And no wonder, since our illustrious General Secretary intends to trade the fruits of Soviet science for the so-called Star Wars program."

Karl knew what he meant. The General Secretary was flying to Washington at the end of the month to sign the Mutual Defense Treaty. The agreement provided for an exchange of defense technologies between the Soviet Union and United States, with scientists from each country working on both systems. The first system to be operational would be deployed for the benefit of both nations. The treaty had many critics, American as well as Russian.

Uncle Alex continued talking as he inserted the video-cassette.

"But I let you judge for yourself. See what the Nevsky Project is capable of. The Americans talk about their Star Wars and laser systems, still years in the future, seen only in Disneylands and Hollywood movies, while we—we *have* a system capable of erecting an electronic shield around every major city and military installation in the country."

The television screen flickered and the scene of sailboats was replaced by momentary hash that cleared as a title appeared: "Department of Research, Strategic Rocket Forces, Project N-181: Contents Classified *Top Secret*."

"You still have your sources, Uncle," Karl said with admiration.

"I am not alone, Karl. There are others."

The first scene showed what looked like a huge satellite dish over fifty feet in diameter with a long spiked pole extending from the center. The dish was housed inside a laboratory. Other scenes showed huge dynamos and multi-paneled control rooms. Men in white lab coats worked on machinery and occasionally one of them would catch sight of the camera and smile self-consciously.

"Very short frequency radio waves," Ikhnovsky explained in a voice that sounded as if he'd memorized certain facts. "Sixty gigahertz. A chip gun is what the scientists call it. It can destroy the microchip circuitry of a missile's guidance system. Watch. Watch this now."

Massive doors on one side of the building opened onto a broad field. The field overlooked a distant lake. Instinctively Karl noted the geography and tried to place it. He couldn't be sure, but it might be the Aral Sea.

The scene shifted to a launchpad where a missile sat pointed at the sky. In the corner of the screen white video numbers began a countdown from thirty seconds.

"The countdown is for activating the Nevsky signal," Ikhnovsky said. "The missile is launched first."

Karl nodded, said nothing. The tape reminded him of early German rocket tests he'd seen of the V-1 and V-2, except that here the quality was better. At five seconds the missile vaulted into the air. A slow-motion camera tracked it out over the lake. Moments later the countdown reached zero and the Nevsky transmitter was activated. Immediately the missile went out of control, began to tumble and then exploded. The camera followed a plume of smoking debris into the lake.

"And *that* is what the General Secretary wants to give the Americans," Ikhnovsky said with disgust. "The Nevsky Project, in exchange for what? Blueprints."

"A radio wave did that?"

"You see the possibilities? An electronic umbrella over every major city and military installation in the Soviet Union. Impervious to the advanced electronics of modern delivery systems."

Karl was impressed. The Nevsky Project had been kept secret and reports of its capabilities varied wildly. This was the first time he'd seen anything concrete.

"It's already operational?"

"As you see."

The tests continued, each with the same result.

"Then I don't understand," said Karl. "Why trade with the Americans if you have the Nevsky transmitters?"

The old man gave him a fierce look.

"If *we* have the Nevsky transmitter. Why speak as if it were separate from you? From the GDR? From the rest of the Warsaw Pact? This is *our* technology."

Karl nodded, thinking that Uncle Alex's patriotism seemed to become more extreme with age.

"We, then. Why don't we just deploy the Nevsky transmitters and forget the treaty?"

"The cost. Look there." Ikhnovsky indicated the last test, in which the missile escaped unharmed. "The power requirements for Nevsky wave-transmission are tremendous. As you see, the range in the tests is still limited. What we need are superconductors—technology that the Americans can provide."

"Forgive me, Uncle," Karl said, "But that sounds like a reason to sign this Mutual Defense Treaty. With a Nevsky transmitter using superconductors, both countries could deploy defensive screens without being vulnerable to the other."

"Without being vulnerable to missiles," Ikhnovsky corrected.

"You mean the danger is from manned aircraft?"

"I mean the danger from another Nevsky transmitter. Watch this now."

The screen had gone black but a new title announced the next set of tests. This time it was a Soviet T-54 tank that sat in the middle of the field. As Karl watched, two men brought a dog and lifted it into the tank, where it was harnessed in front of a video camera. The men left, closing the hatch after them. The scene shifted back to the tank's interior and the countdown numbers appeared. The dog waited, glancing up toward where the men had disappeared and occasionally pulling against its harness. When the countdown reached zero it let out a silent yelp, twisted violently and wrenched its head back, gnashing blindly at its shoulders. Then it collapsed and after a few quick convulsions lay still. The scene shifted and the technicians were shown pulling the dog's body from the tank. They held it up, smiling, like big-game hunters with a trophy.

Ikhnovsky stopped the tape.

"Sterile destruction," he said quietly. "That's what they call it. With more power a tank battalion could be stopped in its tracks. With enough power, the population of Tokyo or New York could be wiped out—and all without disturbing a single brick."

Karl, not usually impressed by new technologies, found himself talking in hushed tones.

"The effect is the same on humans?"

"All forms of animal life," the Russian said. "The electro-chemical impulses of the brain are just as susceptible to it as microchips."

Ikhnovsky removed the video-cassette, and the television returned to its normal program, a comedy about a man trying to learn to ski. "You see why the Nevsky project can't be allowed to fall into American hands?"

"Has the General Secretary seen these experiments?"

"Of course, he has. That's what makes his decision all the more criminal. To hand over to the Americans the weapon for our own destruction . . ." Ikhnovsky shook his head. "Can you imagine a transmitter orbiting the earth? Powered by the sun, making use of superconductors?"

"I thought you said it was cultural sabotage that worried you, Uncle."

"Cultural sabotage and physical destruction go hand in hand. The first prepares us for the second. I worry about both of them. That's why I've come to you. I want you to help save my country, Karl. Our country. The General Secretary has lost sight of what his mission is, what all his dealings with the United States are supposed to serve. He has become seduced by the wine of peace, corrupted by compromise, ready to sacrifice our heritage to economic expendiency. He must be stopped.''

"I'm not another Lenin, Uncle."

"Ignaty Grinevitsky," Uncle Alex said slowly.

Karl's smile died as he realized the full import of Ikhnovsky's words. Ignaty Grinevitsky was the man who assassinated the Russian Tsar, Alexander II. Every schoolboy knew that.

"But," added Ikhnovsky, "I don't ask you to sacrifice yourself, as happened to poor Grinevitsky."

"What do you ask, Uncle?"

The Russian pushed himself out of the chair and went to his briefcase, which was lying on the bed. He pulled out a manila envelope, drew from it a folded piece of paper and handed it to Karl, who spread it on the table without comment. It was a map of a shipping terminal. The legend and the building designations were in English, which Karl read without difficulty. He was trained to be fluent in both English and French, the languages of the Western occupation forces in Germany.

"Military Ocean Terminal Bayonne?"

Ikhnovsky nodded. "Bayonne, New Jersey, in New York harbor. I draw your attention to Warehouse E."

Karl ran a finger down the index until he found what he was looking for. Ikhnovsky, standing behind him, placed a hand on his shoulder.

"Before I tell you what is inside it, you must know two things, Karl. First, that this is not an official assignment. If you undertake it you will be given a two-weeks' leave of absence, ostensibly as an adviser to our KGB training facility in Yaroslavl. This will be a lie. You will disappear for thirteen days. When you return, you will be a hero, but you must never speak of it and no one can ever know."

"And the second thing?"

"If you fail, it will mean my death."

"Then you will live a long time, Uncle Alex," Karl said quietly. "What is in the warehouse?"

Ikhnovsky did not smile but Karl could see the satisfaction reflected in the old man's eyes.

"What *will* be in the warehouse three weeks from now is a shipment designated *QL 4416 H5*. The shipment is composed of Redeye shoulder-launched missiles on their way to the contra rebels in Nicaragua. One of the Redeyes will not reach its destination. Instead, you must steal it and shoot down a Soviet Ilyushin 62." He paused, then added, "I think you know who will be on the aircraft."

"The General Secretary?" Karl said.

Ikhnovsky nodded. Karl searched the old man's face; his intent was reflected in his eyes.

"Explain it to me."

"The Redeye shipment arrives by rail on the twenty-third. The ship, the *Coralis*, is a civilian vessel under long-term contract to Military Sealift Command, which will take the Redeyes to the rebels. It will arrive on the twenty-fifth. Between the arrival of the Redeye shipment and the *Coralis*, you must steal one of the Redeyes in such a manner that the theft cannot be detected."

"Steal an American missile? Why not use one of our own?"

"Because the attack must appear the work of an American patriot. A fanatic dedicated to destroying the Soviet Union."

"And who is this patriot?"

"I leave that up to you, Karl." Ikhnovsky patted his shoulder. "I leave too much up to you, I know."

"You challenge me."

"Because I have faith. I put my life in your hands." It was the most important argument for the mission he could put to Karl. More effective, Ikhnovsky knew, than talk of the glory of the Soviet Union.

Karl remembered something he had heard about the Redeye missile. "I thought the Americans replaced the Redeye with the Stinger."

"They did. That's why they're giving these to the Nicaraguan contras. That's why this shipment is unusual. The Bayonne terminal is not normally used for missile shipments and the security will not be as tight."

Karl began to consider the attack itself and its political ramifications. "The General Secretary . . . Are you sure?"

"Listen to me, listen carefully," Ikhnovsky came around the table and sat opposite him. "I do not come here alone. There are forces in Moscow just as determined as I to rid us of the current leadership. They want to do this before the Mutual Defense Treaty is signed. They will fail in this attempt unless the General Secretary is destroyed and his so-called reformists discredited. We will do both, you and I, in one stroke. When the General Secretary's aircraft is shot down, the world will see the fallacy of even attempting détente with the Americans, and the reformists will be leaderless."

"But to shoot down his aircraft . . . there must be defensive systems. Countermeasures, electronic jamming, air-to-air missiles . . ."

Ikhnovsky waved his hand. "Yes, yes, of course. The Ilyushin is fully protected with sophisticated countermeasures. Nothing as primitive as a Redeye could succeed as long as the plane's infra-red defenses are engaged. But they will not be engaged. Only the display panel, which will indicate to the crew that the system is armed and operating properly."

"You can do that?"

"I told you, Dreitsky, I am not alone in this."

He returned to his briefcase and brought out two more items. His movements were quick and energetic now, like those of a young man. He was happier than Karl had seen him in years.

"I have everything you need." He handed Karl an expensive-looking Sony radio about the size of a walkie-talkie.

"Made by Sony, modified by our electronics expert. This will pick up all aviation frequencies as well as Alpha voice-encrypted Soviet air-to-air communications. I will show you how it works. You will also need this."

Ikhnovsky handed him a manila envelope and Karl pulled out a photocopy of a U.S. Army training manual. In large type across the front he read: *Operator Manual*: REDEYE Air Defense Guided Missile System XM41E2.

"You'd better memorize it," the Russian said. "The Americans would give you a rude welcome if they discovered this in your luggage."

Karl nodded absently, his mind on the political consequences of the Redeye plot. It was one thing to wage war against the enemies of the state, but this was not another assassination of a spy or a traitor. This was the head of the Soviet state. He suppressed an urge to ask the names of the other conspirators. He had never questioned Uncle Ikhnovsky before. Besides, the information that the Russian brought was in itself enough proof that the conspiracy represented a significant portion of the Soviet hierarchy. Sensing his unease, Ikhnovsky said, "Something is wrong?"

Karl shook his head, smiled. "Just taking a deep breath, Uncle."

A distant look came to Ikhnovsky's eyes. "We are going to save the Socialist heritage, Karl. You and I, and a lovesick girl named Marina."

CHAPTER

7

"I WISH HE'D OF CALLED ME AT MIDNIGHT," MAURICE
Singer told his partner. "I would have called him back two hours
later just to change the rendezvous."

"And let him have control?" Hugh asked with a smile.

Both of them knew that Company doctrine specified the primary
responsibility of a case officer was to maintain control of his asset.
Maurice grunted. He had his own opinion of Company doctrine and
of how to control men like Paul Stafford.

The two men were waiting at the Trio, a popular restaurant near
Dupont Circle. They sat at an outdoor table next to a wrought-iron
railing that separated the dining area from the sidewalk. After three
months of intensive surveillance—expensive surveillance—finally there
was some action on the Stafford case.

"You think he got instructions from our local *rezident*?" Maurice
asked, referring to the KGB chief of the Soviet embassy.

"He's just as likely to get a bullet from them as instructions."

"Because he's blown?"

"Because he's blown the assassinations."

"He did it on purpose."

"Maybe."

"Why else?"

Hugh nursed his coffee and said nothing. Theoretically, he was training the younger man, but he half-suspected that Maurice was there to keep an eye on him. Hugh knew his own reputation well enough. Ever since the Iran debacle he was considered second-string material. Nobody had ever told him so, but nobody needed to. His subsequent assignments had proved it to him. It was only because he and Jock Lewis, the new deputy director of intelligence, were old friends that he'd been put on the Stafford case.

Hugh Roark had been dealt an odd hand. He'd joined the Company after World War II and served as a case officer first in post-war Vienna and later the Middle East. His instincts were good. He had a knack for recruiting and running agents, and in each station he quickly built a reliable, high-quality network. At one point it was widely assumed that he would someday inherit the position of deputy director of intelligence. But when Hugh returned to the States he discovered he had no patience for political maneuvering. His career reached a plateau, and for a number of years he remained a perennial candidate for great things. Then he had the misfortune to be named chief of station in Tehran two months before the Shah of Iran was deposed. When the CIA came under intense criticism for failing to predict that event, Hugh became a convenient scapegoat. Since then he'd been marking time, waiting for retirement. The Paul Stafford case was an intriguing exception to the routine jobs he'd been stuck with. What made it more intriguing was that his educated instincts told him that Paul Stafford was telling the truth. In this he was at odds with Maurice, who, as a poor judge of character, automatically suspected guilty motives in everyone.

"So what do we know?" Maurice asked rhetorically. "We know that before we caught Stafford's stories the deaths were all classified as acci dents—all except the Wilson case. And with Wilson the death was designed to look local, not Soviet. To make a murder look like measles takes high-level talent, so the question is, why would Moscow waste it by having Stafford publish the truth in a mystery magazine?"

Maurice gave Hugh a sidelong glance, inviting him to respond When the older man said nothing, Maurice delivered the answer him self.

"Unless they were testing us to find out how thorough our security office is. How about that?''

"Maybe," Hugh said. His eyes ranged over Maurice's shoulder, scanning the street, watching for Paul.

"But you don't think so?"

Hugh sighed. "If they were going to test, they'd use something less damaging than assassinations. Remember how close the trail got to Moscow when the Bulgarians blew the job on the Pope? If we make murders out of these accidents and connect them to Moscow, the smell will make the Chernobyl meltdown look like a picnic. I can't see any way that Moscow wants those stories published."

"Then where's he getting the information if he's not getting it from them?"

"Maybe we'll find out."

Hugh nodded toward the street, where Paul Stafford was coming toward them. He wore what Hugh considered a typical journalist's outfit—jeans and an Oxford shirt with a herringbone jacket. When he caught sight of them, Paul changed direction and came directly to their table, stepping over the iron railing. Hugh thought he looked haggard. Probably up all night, trying to decide what to do, how much to tell.

"Different color every day?" Paul said, gesturing to the rubber band Maurice was twisting between his fingers. It took a moment, but when Maurice realized what he meant, shrugged and said, "Whatever the morning paper is wrapped in."

"The *Herald*?"

"The *Post*."

"Yeah, they got the best rubber bands."

As an exercise in one-upmanship the exchange was a minor one, but for Hugh it added another detail to the emerging portrait of Paul Stafford, who had evidently noticed Maurice's habit the day before. An observant man, Stafford.

A smiling waitress appeared with coffee and menus. Paul ordered a slice of pie; Hugh and Maurice, on an expense account, ordered full lunches. When the waitress left, Hugh began the conversation by telling Paul he was surprised but pleased that he'd decided to cooperate.

"It's a two-way street," Paul told him. "I'll tell you what I know, you tell me what you know."

"I'd like to do that," Hugh said, "but I can't agree to conditions until I know the nature of the information you intend to provide, plus how deeply implicated you are."

"That's easy," said Paul. "But you won't like the answer."

"Try me." Hugh was smiling but his normally restless eyes were still now, alert and watching Paul closely.

Paul took a deep breath. When he spoke, his voice was flat. "I have nightmares. I dream about killing people and when it happens, I write stories about it. I don't expect you to believe it, but there it is. All of it."

The rubber band popped off Maurice's fingers and landed in the sidewalk. "Dreamed it? You mean like, made it up? Like it didn't happen?"

"I know it happened. Now I do. What I don't know is *why* I dreamed it."

"What does that mean?" Maurice demanded. "You came here to ask us the same question we're asking you?"

"You wanted to know what I have to do with the killings. I told you. What I want to know is the circumstances—particularly on Kelso, Durning and Schrader."

"Why them particularly?"

"Because I already know something about Manheim and Wilson. I know when and where they died, but I don't know if they were— what? Agents or assets? Aren't those your two categories?"

"Or enemies," said Maurice.

"Were they enemies?"

Hugh said, "They were both assets."

"In case you didn't know," Maurice added.

"I didn't. I got my information from the morgue. Files and research."

The waitress brought an apple pie. There was a slice of cheese draped over the top that Paul lifted with a fork and placed in an ashtray. After the waitress had gone Paul explained how the dreams came sporadically but in vivid detail, including names. Maurice expressed his disbelief while Hugh watched silently, occasionally raising a question or making a comment to soften Maurice's abrasiveness. After repeating himself half a dozen times Paul asked about the other deaths, the ones he hadn't tracked down. Maurice became quiet and glanced at Hugh, who was absently stirring a bowl of vegetable soup long since grown cold.

"You make me feel like a man with one foot in the boat and one foot on the shore," Hugh said slowly. "On the one hand we know you weren't physically present when the killings took place—you weren't even in any of the same countries. On the other hand this story about dreaming up the details is something I just can't accept. If you'd give us something more to work with—''

Paul stood up. "I don't have anything more to work with. I've told you all I know and one way or the other I'm going to find out the rest. When I do, you guys will be the last to know.''

He left without a backward glance. The two men stared after him and Maurice said, "Did he really think we were going to believe that?''

Hugh gave him a sharp look, then got up quickly. "Take care of the bill,'' he said.

Paul was already in his car when Hugh caught up to him. He leaned down and peered in the open window on the passenger's side.

"Wait a minute, Mr. Stafford. I have a proposition for you. Would you be willing to take a polygraph?''

"A lie detector?''

"If you can prove you're telling the truth I'll go along with you. Maybe we can help each other. But I've got to have something besides sweet dreams and fairytales before I put my ass on the line.''

Paul stared at him a moment. "If I take the test, you tell me what you know?''

"If you *pass* the test.''

Paul thought about it a moment, then nodded. "When and where?''

"I'll call you.''

As the car pulled away, Hugh wondered what they were going to do if his instinct was right. What if Paul Stafford really was telling the truth?

The note was waiting for Paul when he got home that night. The house had been cleaned, the rug vacuumed, dirty clothes washed, the dishes put away. The note was on the dining room table beneath a saltshaker.

> Dear Paul—
> We are not this kind of people. I have to get away—I need time to think things out. I would say I'm sorry but you would say that's an excuse. If you need shirts, the laundry ticket is in the top drawer of my dresser. I'll call you in a few days. Believe it or not, I still love you.
>
> —Jo

Paul felt a rush to anger. She had stayed in bed that morning when he left for work and he had never had a chance to tell her about the CIA men. Now, when he needed her as an alibi and as a witness, she was gone.

He crumpled the note and threw it across the room. It had taken him ten years to build a career and during that time his philosophy had been *run fast, run lean and run alone.* Not until he was near the top as a journalist did he figure he was ready for marriage and its commitment, and not until Joanna was he willing. Very willing. She was twenty-six, he was thirty-eight, and each ignited the other. They were smart and quick and bright and they lived with a sense of special dispensation, as though immune from the mundane considerations that burdened the rest of the world. They woke up gladly to each new day and mined it for all the exhilaration and laughter it could bring and then fell asleep in one another's arms, rocked by ebbing waves of passion, exhausted, full, content.

When Jason came they incorporated him into the vision they had of their lives. They planned to travel with him, expose him to foreign countries, to other races and religions; they would teach him foreign languages, make him part of a new, enlightened generation, a citizen of the world. He became an extension of their dreams, and with his death their world came tumbling down . . .

Paul poured himself a drink and wandered through the house, trying to guess Joanna's intentions by what she'd taken. He looked in her closet, her dresser, the bathroom. Some clothes were gone, some shoes, makeup and toiletries. And birth control pills. A glance inside the medicine cabinet showed him that. He felt a stab of jealousy at the thought of her with Cuevo. And then he thought of last night; of the marks on her body, the desperation of their lovemaking, the recriminations followed by the empty silence as they lay back-to-back, not touching. He saw her now as if through the wrong end of a telescope, distant, almost like a stranger. A stranger running away . . .

The next day Paul followed instructions from Hugh and arrived at a nondescript building on Sixteenth Street. He took an elevator to the seventh floor, to an office labeled "Barrington Associates." The receptionist, a middle-aged woman in a cashmere dress, sat behind an L-shaped desk reading a newspaper. She announced Paul on an intercom and a moment later Hugh Roark appeared. Paul noticed that he wore a coded blue identification badge. After exchanging a brief greeting Hugh ushered him to an interior room with off-white walls, a salmon rug and simple upholstered furniture of white ash. Maurice was waiting with two other people, all wearing blue badges. Hugh made the introductions.

"This is Bob Gonzales, our technician, and Doctor Annie Helms, with our office of medical services."

Paul shook hands with Gonzales, a middle-aged man with a droopy Arab-looking moustache and a glistening, peppermint smile. Then he turned to Annie Helms, a tall, willowy woman in a beige suit. Her pale greenish eyes regarded him from behind black-rimmed glasses and she greeted him with a no-nonsense handshake. Except for her teased blonde hair, she was all business.

"What kind of medical services do you provide?" Paul asked.

"My branch is in charge of things like candidate profiles, personality testing, character analysis—personnel services."

"Psychiatric testing?"

Behind the glasses Paul caught the quick blink of surprise, followed by a slight smile.

"I hope you have no objections."

"No, no, some of my best friends are blonde psychiatrists."

Her smile broadened slightly.

"I asked Dr. Helms to be here," said Hugh, "because I've got to consider the possibility that you're telling the truth. And if you are, well, we're going to have to look in . . . in unusual directions for the answers."

"Meaning inside my head?"

Hugh spread his hands. "That's where you say you find the murders."

"Or they find me."

"Shall we find out?"

The test itself took an hour. After Paul signed a consent agreement Hugh reviewed the form and nature of the questions, which were to be answered either "yes" or "no." Bob Gonzales had him take off his coat and roll up his sleeves so he could attach the machine. Gonzales explained what he was doing as he went along, all very friendly and reassuring, except that it did nothing to reduce Paul's feeling of being readied for the electric chair.

"This strap is called a pneumograph," Gonzales said. "It measures changes in your breathing. This device is just a standard cardiograph—have you ever had a cardiograph taken, Mr. Stafford?

Nothing to it, really. And these are galvanic sensors that measure the skin's resistance to electric current.''

"One-ten or two-twenty?"

"Heh, heh. No, nothing like that. We use one point five volts of direct current. You won't even feel it.''

Once Paul was hooked up, Hugh asked the questions while Gonzales sat off to one side, monitoring the machine. Annie Helms and Maurice sat on a couch along one wall. Maurice was on good behavior today. He said nothing to Paul, but sat quietly, whispering occasional comments to Annie. Once the questions started she put up a hand to silence him and focused on Paul.

Hugh began with simple, obvious questions: "Are we in Washington, D.C.? Do you live in Arlington, Virginia? Is your name Paul Henry Stafford?" Then came more relevant questions: "Did you dream of the death of a man called Dan Kelso? Did you know that Dan Kelso was the name of an employee of the Central Intelligence Agency? Had you received any information about Dan Kelso prior to dreaming about him? Did you receive any information about the manner of Dan Kelso's death from any source other than your dream?''

Hugh asked each question in a calm, unemotional tone and paused before asking the next one. Interspersed with the relevant questions were more of the innocuous ones designed, Paul assumed, to provide a contrast in readings in case he was lying. They did each death in turn—Kelso, Manheim, Durning, Wilson, Schrader, Beaumier. Even though he was telling the truth, there was a tightness in his stomach that Paul associated with childhood visits to the dentist.

They ran through the questions once, took a ten-minute break, then ran through them again, asking the same questions in a different order and having Paul offer double responses. The double responses took twice as long because each question was asked twice with Paul answering first "yes" and then "no." Hugh assured him that this was standard procedure in sensitive cases because it gave them a direct comparison of high and low stress responses.

When it was over Bob Gonzales disconnected the polygraph and took his graphs and charts into another room to analyze them. Hugh and Maurice followed but Annie stayed behind. She handed Paul a medical form and asked him to fill it out.

"You mind if I get a drink first?" Paul said.

"There's a fountain down the hall. I'll show you."

"I can find it."

"You don't have a blue tag," she said. "Security."

"You have a lot of secrets in this building?"

"Well, some. Or so we like to think."

There was a soft, Southern lilt to her voice that Paul found appealing. Following her down the hall he found something else appealing: a fullness in her buttocks that was unexpected considering her narrow body. When they returned Annie sat quietly on the couch while he filled out the form. The first part detailed the state of his physical health; then came questions about mental illness. Had he ever undergone psychiatric treatment? Had he ever been institutionalized? Had he ever been diagnosed as having this or that condition? Had any of the following drugs ever been prescribed? Had he ever suffered from dizziness, hallucinations, hot flashes, cold flashes, blackouts, premonitions, visitations . . . ?

He had almost finished when Maurice came into the room. "Dr. Helms, we've got a readout."

He held open the door for her. After she left, Maurice stood with his arms crossed, eyeing Paul.

"You look unhappy," Paul said. "What's the matter, I passed the test?"

"There's a tiny percentage of the population that doesn't have guilt feelings, no matter what they've done."

"And you think I'm one of them."

"It's a more logical explanation than dreaming."

But when Hugh returned with Annie he said, "Bob gives you a clean bill of health, so instead of solving a mystery we've got a bigger one. Let's see if we can pool our resources and come up with something."

Hugh was carrying a briefcase, thin as a cigarette pack with a combination lock. He lifted it to the table, opened it and brought out a manila envelope. Now that he'd made the decision to trust Paul, he gave him the details in a brisk, businesslike manner.

"First case, Dan Kelso. He was one of ours, working out of the Hague. Officially he drowned when he fell from a ferry crossing the English Channel. Death listed as an accident. In your story, 'Ace High, All Die,' the killer strikes him in the stomach before throwing him overboard. A nice touch. The first breath he took would have filled his lungs with water. Second case, Jurgen Manheim, one of our assets, but unreliable. He was a black-marketeer who ran goods back and forth between East and West Berlin. We never completely accepted the suicide but never questioned it either. Manheim was an opportunist, expendable. Third case, Max Durning, another asset. Durning was one of Bertil Lindstrom's assistants. You're familiar with Lindstrom?''

"Swedish scientist. I think nominated for a couple of Nobel prizes, never got one.''

"He's a physicist. Durning was one of his assistants. The Russians got a lever on him and had him delivering data from Lindstrom's research. We caught him, turned him and gave him something different to pass on to the Soviets. You remember a few years back, when the Russians lost some key scientists in an accidental explosion?''

"The Karpov Institute accident.''

"It seems the formula had a flaw. Anyway, Durning's death was in retribution for the stuff we had him pass the Soviets. Durning died in the mountains on a hiking trip. Looked as if he fell down a ravine and broke his neck. Nobody questioned it, but in your story you've got a killer who snaps his neck with a blow to the jaw. The same way, in fact, Lisle Beaumier died.''

Paul nodded. In his mind he saw the face of each victim, no longer imaginary, but a real person, killed before his eyes.

"Fourth case, Jim Wilson. You already know the details here. Wilson was a cryptographer who pretended to go over to the other side. I can't give you details on this one but you know about as much as we do about the killing. Except it wasn't right-wing Turks who did it. Fifth case, just last year: Frank Schrader, one of ours, died on vacation in Jamaica. An autopsy showed a heart attack. In your story, Schrader was popped with a spray gun of hydrogen cyanide.'' Hugh shook his head. "We should have caught that one. Hydrogen cyanide's an old KGB trick—leaves no trace and reads like cardiac arrest. Anyway, that's what we know. Now what about you? Can you tell us anything else? Anything more about the dreams, when or why they come?''

Paul shook his head. "I put all the details in the stories. As far as the dreams go there's no rhyme or reason. I've made time charts, tried to remember what I ate the night before—there's nothing.''

"What about the killer? Do you ever get a name on him?''

"The killer? I'm the killer. In the dreams, it's always me.''

"But you don't get a name, like you do on the victims?''

"Get a name? From where? It's not like turning on the television and watching J. R. Ewing kill his wife.'' Paul let out a deep breath.

"It's as if I experience it, not watch it. While I'm dreaming I am the killer."

"Wait a minute," Maurice said. "Assuming he's telling the truth—"

"I thought we just proved that," Paul said.

"Okay, okay." Maurice had been standing against the wall, watching skeptically. Now he moved forward. "I was just thinking, what he said about the television. I read somewhere about a man living close to a radio transmitter and he actually heard the programs in his head. The frequencies resonated in—it was either a tooth or one of those little bones in his ear. Anyway, isn't it possible his house is in the path of some kind of transmitter from a surveillance setup? That he's picking up the murders like this man picked up radio signals?"

Paul shook his head. "I didn't even have my house when I dreamed of Dan Kelso. And when Durning died I was in El Salvador."

"Not only that," Hugh added. "There would have to be more than a transmitter. Somebody would have to be filming and broadcasting the murders. Not very likely."

"*Nothing's* likely," Maurice said. "But it's a lot more likely than dreaming things up out of thin air. We all know those stories weren't just coincidences. Even *he* knows that."

Maurice pointed to Paul, who said, "I'm not deaf and blind, Singer."

"Well, you don't think they're coincidences, do you?"

"No, I don't think they're coincidences."

"Okay then, that's my point."

There was a long silence, broken by Annie Helms' quiet voice. She had been sitting on the couch, studying Paul's medical report.

"You mentioned here that you sometimes have premonitions, Mr. Stafford."

"It's more like an instinct. Usually when I'm out on a story and things don't feel right."

"Can you give me an example?"

"Yes, but I don't see . . . Well, okay, there was the time in Afghanistan when I was with a rebel unit that was going out and I was set to go with them. We started in the morning and were crossing a stream at the edge of town when I got a very uneasy feeling. I decided to go back and do an interview with a convoy leader I'd been trying to get to and who had just showed up. That night the men didn't come back. It turned out they'd been ambushed, all killed. That kind of thing. You spend enough time in combat zones—starting back in Nam—and you begin to develop a sort of sixth sense. Sometimes it's strong, sometimes less so. And sometimes you act on it, sometimes you don't.''

"But these premonitions are only feelings? Not like the images you have when dreaming?''

"Not the same thing at all. I don't know how to describe it exactly, but the whole experience is different. The premonitions are part of me that feels uncomfortable but the dreams—while I'm asleep it feels like I'm being . . . invaded. Almost as if someone's taking over my body . . .''

Maurice was trying to light a cigarette. Now he looked up. "What does that mean? You're a victim of some sort of demonic possession?''

"Please,'' Annie said, then returned her attention to Paul. "Mr. Stafford, you consider these dreams to be unpleasant, unwelcome occurrences, don't you?''

"They're sure not pleasant.''

"And you prefer to forget them as soon as possible?''

"That's why I write them down. As soon as they're part of a story I can forget about them.''

"I wonder if you'd mind doing the opposite. I wonder if you'd mind thinking back, going through each dream, detail by detail, so that we could see if there was something you perhaps overlooked.''

She was leaning forward, legs crossed with both hands resting on the upraised knee. There was an eagerness in her eyes, an anticipation.

"I'm sorry,'' he said. "Once I write it down I put it out of my mind. When I read the stories now, there are things that seem brandnew—that's how much I've forgotten.''

"Only consciously, Mr. Stafford. Subconsciously the mind is a repository for everything you've ever seen, heard, smelled, tasted or touched. Everything of significance, that is. Those things that make the strongest emotional impact are the easiest to retrieve. Your dreams certainly belong in that category.''

"Are you talking about my mind or a computer?''

Maurice cleared his throat and gave Hugh an uneasy look. Hugh said, "What are you suggesting, Doctor?''

"If Mr. Stafford will agree, I'd like to hypnotize him. By doing that we can return to each dream, relive it, and perhaps access details that are missing from the stories.''

''You really think you can do that?'' Maurice asked. It was evident by his tone what he thought the answer was.

''We can try, if Mr. Stafford is willing.''

They all turned to look at Paul, but he kept his eyes on Annie Helms. ''You'd be the one to do it?''

''Yes.''

''Alone?''

''We'll establish whatever conditions make you most comfortable.'' She took off her glasses as if to emphasize her sincerity. ''If you'd like it to be just the two of us, then that's how it will be.''

She had a long, oval face, Paul noticed, and her greenish eyes reflected the room, bowed and distorted, with him in the center of it.

''Okay, doctor. You've got a deal.''

CHAPTER

8

THEY MET THE NEXT DAY AT THE ELITE DINER, A CAFE that had been redone in the style of the 1950s. Having lunch was Annie's idea, a way of getting acquainted and building trust before she tried to hypnotize him.

"Hypnosis is a two-way street," she told him. "If you don't want to be hypnotized, I can't make it happen. You've got to want it."

A middle-aged waitress whose uniform included bobby socks and a pillbox hat took their order. The pink and gold flaked formica table was framed in chrome and the thick padded seats were upholstered in turquoise vinyl. A huge Wurlitzer jukebox glowed in one corner and the menus were in the shape of a 1959 Cadillac.

While they ate, Annie explained that hypnosis was too often misunderstood by the public. It wasn't a method of controlling another person against his will. No one could be hypnotized against his will or made to do things while hypnotized that weren't in keeping with his basic character.

"It's only the conscious mind that's hypnotized," Annie said, "not the subconscious mind. And the subject has to be a willing participant.''

"Is that a reassurance or a warning?" Paul asked.

"Both. From reading your file and watching you with Mr. Roark and Mr. Singer, I'd say you're a man who likes to be in control. But part of undergoing hypnosis involves relinquishing control. If you're unable or unwilling to do that . . .''

Mention of a file got Paul's attention.

"What file did you read?"

Annie was crumbling crackers and dropping them into her soup. At the note of hostility in his voice, she glanced up and said, "The agency file. You've been under investigation for three months, you know.''

"No, I didn't know." He hadn't considered the possibility of a long-term investigation, but it made sense. They would put him under surveillance, hoping to discover a link to the murders, and only when that failed would they confront him directly. Paul's mind flashed back over the events of the previous three months, seeing them now from a new perspective, a third party's, a Peeping Tom's. Had they tapped the phone? Bugged the house? Had they been listening to every intimate conversation and argument?

"Maybe I shouldn't have mentioned it."

"I don't like to be spied on."

"Normally you wouldn't have been. But innocent men were murdered and the evidence indicated that you knew how and why. Given that, an investigation doesn't seem inappropriate.''

"They weren't innocent men. He's an innocent man." Paul pointed at one customer, then at others. "That one, those two—they're innocent men. But your people were agents and assets, playing spook games. They weren't just garden-variety innocent men.''

She nodded. "And your sympathies are with the innocent public rather than with those who protect them.''

"The 'innocent public' doesn't need *protection*, it needs the truth— after that it can usually protect itself.''

Annie changed the subject to Paul's family. She already knew some facts: that his father had been a German soldier who died before he was born; that his mother, Greta, had met and married a young American army officer, Ralph Stafford, who was stationed in Berlin after the war; that Ralph had brought his new wife and her son back to America, where the couple subsequently had three daughters; that Ralph had divorced Greta five years ago to marry a younger woman.

"A bimbo and a boat," said Paul. "That's what dad wanted after he retired from the army."

"It sounds as if you don't like your father."

"I don't respect him, that's all."

"Because he left your mother?"

"Because he ran a cowboy operation in Vietnam. He went over there to get a promotion, knew it all before he arrived. Of course, he'd tell a different story. He'd say if more commanders had been as aggressive as he was, we could have won the war. I guess we have what you might call 'basic philosophical differences.' "

Annie probed gently into his past, listening carefully as Paul told her about his experiences in Vietnam. For three years he flew Huey troop carriers in and out of jungle clearings no bigger than a back yard. He went to Vietnam naive and optimistic and came back angered by the false hopes raised by politicians and army generals every time they wanted more troops to throw into the morass. The only accurate information about the war seemed to come from journalists who went to the battlefield and reported what they saw. Paul had planned to make the military his career, but after his experience in Vietnam he decided to resign his commission and become a journalist.

"My first story was about fragging—soldiers killing incompetent officers. It caused a big scandal at the time. Dad never forgave me. He said I'd betrayed the army—which meant him. I told him I was sorry but I felt he and his buddies had betrayed their commands. That pretty well summed up our differences. I doubt if we've spoken a dozen words since."

"And your mother?" Annie asked.

"She was caught in between. Dad's whole life was the army but I was her son. She was German and remembered how Germany rationalized its way to war—not that she equated the U.S. with Nazi Germany. Anyway, she got an ulcer trying to keep the peace between us."

Paul picked up the sugar dispenser and held it over his glass of iced tea but nothing came out. The spout was clogged.

"Where is your mother now?"

"Isn't that in the file?"

"I'd like to hear it from you."

Paul cleared the spout with one prong of his fork, then added sugar to his ice tea.

"She lives in Fort Lauderdale," he said brusquely. "She keeps books for a country club and teaches German once a week at Broward Community College. Now ask me something that's not in the file."

"Are you close to her?"

"Sure. I'm the oldest, the only son, it's natural. What about you? Are you on good terms with your mother?"

If he thought the question would put her off, he was wrong. Annie was as forthcoming about her own history as she was curious about his. She had grown up in South Carolina, had a doctorate from Duke University, was divorced, had one child, a girl named Shelly. Paul's expression must have shown his surprise because she held up a finger and said, "I know, I don't look old enough to be a mother."

It wasn't that she didn't look old enough, it was that her flat stomach and full breasts seemed like strangers to the rigors of motherhood. Paul doubted if Annie Helms would appreciate this kind of appraisal, so he said nothing.

Annie called the waitress and ordered a vanilla milkshake for dessert. When it came, she removed the cherry and tipped the tall glass forward to bring the straw to her lips.

"Let me ask you something, Dr. Helms—"

"Annie."

"Annie, then. You said you graduated from Duke University, right?" She nodded, her cheeks hollow as she drew the liquid through the straw. "Isn't that where they give degrees in things like extrasensory perception?"

"The official designation is Paranormal Psychology."

"Is that the degree you have?"

"That's one of them. I'm also a board-certified psychiatrist, if that's a more reassuring credential."

"Then in your dual capacity as both a board-certified psychiatrist and paranormal psychologist let me ask you this: what do you think's causing these damn dreams?"

"I'd rather wait until we have a little more data before venturing an opinion."

He smiled. "Be brave and venture a wild guess."

Annie's head was bent low over her glass but her eyes remained on him.

"Don't worry," Paul said. "You won't scare me off."

From the bottom of the glass came a hollow slurping sound. Annie wiped her mouth with a napkin, pushed the glass aside and leaned forward to speak in a low, intense voice.

"I'll give you my best guess, which is also my best hope." She took off her glasses and looked directly at him. "I think you may be a receiver of some form of mental energy. I think that every so often, for whatever reason, your mind becomes sensitive to someone else's sensations, which you experience in your sleep as dreams."

She watched him, eyes showing her excitement.

Paul laughed uncomfortably. "You think I'm some kind of ESP freak?"

"In the broadest definition of extrasensory perception, yes."

"Oh, come on."

"What do *you* think?"

The question took him by surprise. Ever since he had discovered that the murders were real, Paul had been looking for a rational, a logical explanation. Whatever deep-seated suspicion he had along the lines Annie now suggested, he suppressed. He was a journalist, after all, a man of hard facts, not a member of some California mantra-of-the-month club. In his experience there was always a rational explanation for even the most bizarre occurrence if you looked long enough and dug deeply enough. Instincts he could believe in. Instincts and premonitions like the one that saved his life in Afghanistan. But the death dreams were different. There was no explanation for them except the one Annie suggested—the one he had rejected until this moment. His smile faded. "You think that's possible?"

"I know it's possible, Paul. I know it's happened before, but only under extraordinary circumstances. The most common incidents of telepathic communication are associated with death—usually the death of a loved one. The largest body of documented evidence comes from World War II. In one case a sailor's ship was torpedoed and his wife woke up dreaming of flames at the exact moment her husband died. In another, a soldier was killed and his mother woke up with a burning pain in the same place her son was shot. The cases go on and on, all involving death and the simultaneous dream by a loved one. So you see, your pattern fits the others except that *your* dreams are recurring."

"And I don't dream of just dying, I dream of killing."

"And you're not a loved one, in close harmony with someone else's emotional state."

She sat watching him with her glasses dangling from one finger, swinging them back and forth in a way that Paul found oddly appealing.

"So where does that leave us?" Paul asked.

Annie shrugged. "Let's go find out."

They returned to the CIA's Sixteenth Street building, to a small room with walls covered in a soundproof material that looked to Paul like a tightly woven rug. There were no windows. The furnishings were a small desk, three chairs and, of course, a couch. Annie had him remove his shoes and lie down. From a closet she took two pillows, which she gave him with instructions to make himself comfortable. Then she brought out a metal stand with a glass ball, about two inches in diameter, suspended from a chain.

"You're kidding," Paul said. "A crystal ball?"

"Would you rather concentrate on some other object?"

He made a wry face and shook his head. Annie positioned the ball above him, then took a tape recorder and placed it on the desk where she could reach it from her chair. She turned a switch that changed the lights from direct overhead to indirect baseboard lighting.

"It's easier on the eyes. You ready?"

"I guess."

Annie turned on the tape recorder and settled herself in a chair beside and slightly behind him. The room was quiet except for the hushed sound of air-conditioning. When Annie spoke, her voice had a husky, melodic lilt, gentle yet insistent.

"I want you to concentrate on the glass ball," she began. "Concentrate on the ball and listen to my voice. Let your mind empty of thoughts, let it become as clear as the glass; let your mind empty and concentrate only on my voice. Let your mind become clear; let your body grow heavy. Your hands, your arms, your legs, your feet, your whole body is growing heavy now."

As he listened to her voice he found it easier to relax than he'd anticipated. Annie directed his attention to each part of his body, describing how each muscle was relaxing, how each limb was becoming so heavy he couldn't move it. Her voice was like a flowing river bathing him in words, seeping into his consciousness, leading the way, subtly assuming control. As the tension drained from his body he realized how worried he'd been recently; worried about Joanna's disappearance and the dreams and the alien consciousness that seemed to take control of his mind during the nightmares.

Annie's words continued to caress him. "Now your eyelids are growing heavy, as if each eyelash is made of lead, they're so heavy that no matter how hard you try you can't keep your eyes open; no matter how hard you try, your eyes are closing; you can't keep them open; your eyes are closing now . . ."

Paul felt the drowsiness induced by her voice but even as his eyes closed he felt his rational mind rebel. Like the quick flex of muscle, resistance rose inside him and his will tensed to oppose her suggestion. Then he remembered what Annie had said at lunch. He could resist—he could feel it—but what was the point? He needed the information locked away in his subconscious and the key to opening that door lay in relinquishing control. He took a deep breath, let it out slowly and let her words take him.

"Your arms are heavy now. Your arms feel like they are made of lead. You want to raise your arms but you can't. Your arms are made of rock, part of the earth, immobile and so heavy you can't move them."

She led him once again to each part of his body, weighing it down, making it part of the earth, freeing it from his mind. He was immersed in darkness, the room bounded only by her voice, which came without pause, leading him, lifting and falling in a gentle rhythm, massaging him with sound, weaving an invisible cradle of words, strong, gentle, secure, taking him deep into himself, beyond the boundaries of conscious thought to the hidden, shadowed regions of his subconscious.

"Your eyes are closed but you can still see the glass ball floating in your mind, clear and white and transparent. I want you to imagine that the glass ball is your memory, and it's opening now, expanding to include you inside it. You're inside your memory now and it's stretching out, like a long white hallway with many doors, a long white hallway stretching back to the time of your birth. Can you see the hallway, Paul?"

Watching his face closely, Annie knew that this was a critical juncture. Paul Stafford had a strong personality, one that might reassert control if called on to respond actively. The trance might be broken, but Annie had no choice. She had access to the subconscious now, but the information had to be brought outside, into the open, and only Paul could do that by speaking to her.

"The long white hallway, Paul. You're standing at one end of the hallway, which is your memory. Can you see the hallway? Tell me if you see the hallway?''

His lips quivered, then parted as he spoke in a lethargic voice. ''Yes.''

Annie smiled and clenched her fist with excitement, but she kept her voice calm.

''Good. We're going to go back now, Paul. We're going to go down the hallway, backward in time. We're going back to the last nightmare, the last time you dreamed of death. You're going down the hallway, backward in time, to the last vivid dream, the last nightmare in which someone died. You're getting close to that dream now, you can see the face of the victim.''

Paul's face twitched. It was an uncomfortable memory.

''All right, Paul, I want you to tell me where you are in this dream. Where are you?''

''An apartment.''

''And where is the apartment?''

A pause, then, ''Paris.''

''Do you know the name of your victim?''

''Yes.''

''What is the name of your victim?''

''Lisle Beaumier.''

His answers came slowly and sometimes reluctantly. But one by one, they reviewed each of the murders. Annie avoided the actual details that caused Paul obvious discomfort and that she feared might break the trance. Instead she concentrated on Paul as the killer, on who he was, why he was there, what his name was. She was looking for clues to his identity, but in this she was disappointed. ''Who are you now?'' she would ask. His answer was always the same. ''Paul Stafford.'' ''And in this dream? Who are you in this dream?'' ''I am . . . me.'' ''Why have you come to kill Jurgen Manheim?'' ''I don't know . . .''

It was frustrating. Paul had turned out to be a better subject than she'd anticipated but the only new details she uncovered had to do with the physical description of the sites of the murders. There was nothing new about the killer, whom Paul identified with so fully that his answer was always the same: the killer was him.

She wondered if Maurice Singer was right and the whole thing was an elaborate KGB ruse. If so, it seemed complicated beyond belief and without apparent purpose. Unless it was to assess how seriously the CIA was pursuing ESP research. The Russians had a long-stand-

ing interest in paranormal psychology and the KGB sponsored a number of research projects. Was it possible that Paul was fed details of
KGB hits with the intention of becoming the subject of a CIA investigation whose details he could later report to Moscow? Maurice might
think so, but Annie couldn't believe it. Or didn't want to believe it,
she corrected herself. She was also well aware that there was an
attractive quality about Paul Stafford that made her want to believe
him. At the same time she was a professional, and knew the difference between an emotional response and intellectual judgment. Her
faith in her abilities remained strong.

They had returned now to the first dream, in which Dan Kelso had
drowned when thrown from a ferry crossing the English Channel. As
with the other dreams, the new details that Paul remembered were
inconsequential, like the name of the ferry and the color of Kelso's
jacket. About his identity as a killer, the answer was still the same: it
was him. Annie was about to end the session when a routine question
brought an unexpected answer.

"And Dan Kelso was the first time you dreamed like this?"

"No."

The answer stunned her.

"You dreamed of killing someone else?"

"Not . . . not killing."

"But this kind of vivid dream? You've had it before?"

"Yes."

"In a different context than killing someone?"

"Yes."

Adrenaline made her light-headed; it took all of her self-control to
keep her voice calm.

"All right, Paul, I want you to go back now, let yourself float
backward to that earlier time, when you had this same kind of dream.
You're floating backward and you see the details emerging. The earlier time is coming closer, becoming more clear. And now you're
back, you're in that earlier dream, back before Dan Kelso, back in
that earlier dream that has the same vivid quality as the others . . ."

Paul's face tensed and his arms moved, pulling close to his chest
as if seeking protection. He was actually shivering.

"Paul, tell me what you're dreaming. What is it?"

"Hurts."

"What hurts, Paul?"

"Leg. Shot in the leg."

"You shot someone in the leg?"

"No, shot me. Guards . . . I ran but . . . ah, my leg . . ."

"What guards? Who shot you, Paul?"

"Russian . . . Russian guards." He shivered again.

Annie's mind was racing to keep up. Shot by Russian guards? How, why, where, when? She had a thousand questions but forced herself to proceed calmly.

"Where are you, Paul? In the dream, do you know where you are?"

"Yes."

"Where? Where are you?"

"Berlin."

"How old are you?"

"Eight . . . years old."

For a moment Annie was speechless. They had regressed to Paul's childhood. Eight years old. Then she remembered something else: Paul's history. The information she'd read in the file. Paul was five when the family left Germany. When he was eight years old, they were stationed in Fort Sheridan, Texas. Either he was lying or—

The apparent answer struck her like a physical blow. The telepathic sensitivity wasn't new, he'd had it since childhood. He was sensitive to other people's thoughts, to their experiences, to incidents in their lives. To someone's life in Germany when he was eight and living in Texas.

Paul groaned and Annie continued quickly.

"What else happens, Paul? After the Russian guards shoot you, then what?"

"A man. A man reaching for me. Then kicks . . ."

He grunted with pain and a tremor passed through his body. For a moment Annie was afraid she'd lost him, but the trance held and he stopped shivering and relaxed.

"Was that the end of the dream, Paul?"

"Yes."

"And did you wake up?"

"I . . . don't know."

"But the dream stopped?"

"Yes."

"And was that the first time you had these vivid kind of dreams?"
He didn't answer. "Can you hear me, Paul?"

"Yes."

"Was that the very first time you dreamed like that? So vividly that it seemed as if someone else had taken over your life?"

A faint muscle spasm disturbed his features.

"Paul?"

"I . . . don't know."

"Listen to my voice, Paul. I am your guide. Let my voice fill your body, fill your mind; my voice is like a bubble, a soft bubble all around you, protecting you, leading you back, leading you back to the earliest dream, the first nightmare where you dreamed of something outside yourself. We're floating backward, backward to that earliest, very first dream . . . back and back and back . . . Now you see that first dream emerging from the mist; the details become clear and you're in the first dream. You're in that very first dream. Tell me what you see, Paul. What do you see?"

For a moment Annie thought he hadn't heard her. Then his hands flew up, pressing flat as if he was against a wall, and his face turned to one side. He cried out.

"Nein! Nein, Tante Inge!"

"Paul—?"

"Bitte! Bitte!"

And he came out of the trance, sat upright and looked around wildly.

"It's all right," Annie said quickly. She reached to touch his arm but he drew back.

"Paul," she said gently, "you're awake now. You're all right. You're back, back in Washington. Everything's all right."

He heard her voice dimly through fear and nausea. His breathing was ragged and the blood seemed to pound in his ears. His face was clammy with sweat. Annie kept talking and finally he remembered where he was and what was happening. He let out a deep breath and smiled weakly.

"What the hell was all that?"

"Do you remember what happened?"

"I remember pain and . . ." And what? How could he explain the nameless, terrifying horror, the paralyzing helplessness and the feeling of . . . humiliation. That was it. More than the pain was the humiliation. He shifted uncomfortably, aware of a queasy feeling in his stomach.

"What is it?" Annie asked.

"Nothing."

"Don't hold back, Paul. Tell me."

"I felt sick for a moment, okay? Now can we go on to something else—like what happened and why? What did you find out?"

Annie told him about the earlier dreams, the one with the Russian guards and the last with the violent reaction that had awakened him from the trance.

"You said something in German. Do you remember?"

"No."

"Listen. I'll play it back."

She rewound the tape and played the last portion for him. Paul had the uncanny sensation of listening to someone else speaking in his voice.

"I sound like a zombie," he said.

"Shhh. Here it comes."

He heard himself shouting. The hysteria embarrassed him but the words were clear.

"No, Aunt Inge." He repeated in English. "Please."

"What about your Aunt Inge?"

Paul looked puzzled. "I don't have an aunt by that name. Not that I know of."

"You must have known somebody by that name."

Somewhere deep in his memory the name had a familiar ring, but Paul couldn't place it.

"I don't know," he said. "I left Germany when I was five."

"Think hard." She was sitting on the edge of her chair, watching him.

Paul shook his head. "I've seen the family tree. There's nobody named *Inge*."

"Then we'll go back. It'll be easier this time, now that we know what we're looking for. Do you want to get a drink first?"

Paul stared at her. "Go back to that? No thanks."

He stood up. The back of his shirt was clammy and damp.

"Look," Annie said, "I know how you feel but we can't quit now. This afternoon was a breakthrough. Now we know that the assassinations weren't the first time you received impressions from someone else. You've been sensitive since you were a child, don't you see? So you don't have an Aunt Inge, but somebody did, and that's the person whose thoughts you picked up."

Paul was shaking his head.

"What?" Annie demanded.

"No, no, the whole thing's crazy."

"It's not crazy. This has happened before. Not with this kind of regularity but it's happened. I can show you case histories—people who suddenly know—know absolutely—that something has happened to a loved one. They *experience* it as if it happened to them."

"To a loved one, yes. Not to a *killer*."

"It's not just a killer. You're sensitive to—"

She stopped in mid-sentence. Until now she had thought of his sensitivity as non-discriminating, like a quiet pond whose surface might ripple from the vibration of a distant explosion. But what if his sensitivity were linked to one specific individual? Someone whose brainwaves and thought patterns were remarkably similar to his own? In that case, the childhood memories might be those of the killer when the killer was young.

"You might be right," Annie said, a new note of excitement edging into her voice. "That's all the more reason to go back. Childhood memories may give us more of a clue than the murders."

"No."

"Paul—"

"You don't understand. This is worse than your worst nightmare and it's all mixed up with feelings of humiliation and self-loathing and disgust and a kind of nauseating fear that you've never experienced—that I've never experienced before. There's no way I'm going to put myself through that again."

He turned away but Annie grabbed his arm.

"You *can't* stop now. Don't you see how important this is? You're the first case of telepathic communication that has a chance of being scientifically proved. We have got to find the person whose experiences you've apparently been receiving, even if it's painful."

"What if we go back and I experience something that pushes me over the edge? I mean, that changes me, makes me crazy? What the hell then?"

Annie gave him a professionally reassuring smile. "That won't happen." (Was she sure?)

"How do you know?"

"You have to trust me."

"Why? Because we're such great friends or because you wouldn't jeopardize a key element in the first scientifically proved case of mental telepathy?"

Her smile became conspiratorial.

"Let's say a little of each."

"I'll bet you've already got your bio ready for the article in the New England Journal of Medicine."

"It's important, Paul. It really is."

He nodded, knowing that sooner or later it had to be done. He had to find out whose thoughts, whose life was echoing inside his own.

"I'll let you know."

"When?"

"Call me tomorrow."

Driving to the *Herald*, Paul felt isolated, cut off. The world beyond the windshield was familiar but distant. He was a freak. He was, it seemed, part of somebody else. The experience under hypnosis had led him to another reality, someone else's reality; a small kernel of that alien consciousness stayed with him, dividing and somehow diminishing him. He felt compromised, soiled, as if he had something to hide. It was a damn unpleasant feeling.

His mood didn't improve when Bernie Stern, the managing editor, called him into his office to compliment him on the Rockland-Birdwell story and then told him they were going to delay publication for a month.

"Delay? I thought you wanted to run it next week."

Bernie rolled the stub of a cigar between his lips. He was a short, thickset man with a cottage-cheese complexion and white curly hair perpetually in need of washing. He affected the look of a hard-boiled "front-page" newsman by rolling his shirtsleeves and wearing a vest rather than a jacket.

"I thought we better have the raw data checked by an independent scientist."

"What's all this? You don't trust my sources?"

"If it's wrong, Rockland-Birdwell sues us, not your sources."

Bernie was chewing his cigar a little too vehemently. Something else was going on here.

"Meaning what? You talked to the Mayhues?"

"You cynical bastard," Bernie said.

The Mayhues owned the paper. It seemed as though the more successful the *Herald* became, the more conservative the Mayhues became.

"Independent contract, Bernie. You don't want it, I take it across the street."

"Hey, hey." Bernie looked hurt. "No need to get down and dirty. We're running it. Next month, after the Mutual Defense Treaty's been signed, that's all. You wouldn't want to weaken the U.S. bargaining position for a story that can just as easily wait a month."

"Sure," Paul said. "Forget the ethics, screw the Russians. Great way to run a paper."

He wandered off without waiting for a response. There were days that he enjoyed a mock battle with Bernie but today wasn't one of them.

At his desk Paul reviewed the transcripts of an interview with a naval engineer. When he reached the end of the page he could remember nothing. His mind was still on the hypnosis session and the words that Annie had played back, his own voice speaking to him from his childhood.

He got out his address book and dialed the number of the Umbrella Tree Country Club in Fort Lauderdale. A cheery-voiced receptionist answered and Paul asked for the accounting department, where his mother worked. Maybe his mother knew who *Tante Inge* was. At this point he was willing to try anything to avoid another ordeal like the one he'd just been through.

"Paul? Where are you? Are you here?"

"No, mom. Still in Washington."

"Are you coming down?"

"I don't know. Listen, mom, I've got a question for you. About the family. Did we ever have a relative named *Tante Inge*?"

A long silence.

"Mom. Are you there?"

Her voice, when it came, was a whisper so filled with anguish that Paul could hardly recognize it.

"*Ich bitte um Vergebung,*" she moaned. "*Ich bitte um Vergebung.*"

Forgive me.

"Mom?"

She kept repeating the words, more and more upset. Paul tried to interrupt but she paid no attention; her voice rose to a wail on the other end of the line.

"*Ich bitte um Vergebung.*"

"*Mama,*" but it was no use. She didn't hear him. Her voice reached a crescendo, the phone clattered to the floor. He could hear her sobbing but she wouldn't answer. He flicked the disconnect button, hoping to get an operator. Instead the line went dead.

He hung up and dialed the number again. When the receptionist answered, Paul tersely explained what had happened and told her to send someone to see that his mother was all right. It turned out that the assistant manager had already gone to help her. Paul waited on the phone for ten minutes, receiving occasional reports of what was happening. Finally a doctor came on the line.

"She was hysterical, Mr. Stafford, but I gave her a sedative and she'll be all right. We have someone to take her home."

"I don't want her left alone."

"No, of course not. I understand her daughter's been notified. A Mrs. . . ."

"Steinberg."

"Yes. Mrs. Steinberg will be there so I don't want you to worry. The important thing is not to upset her again. If you can guard against that—"

"I had no intention of upsetting her."

"Yes, well, just so you understand the situation."

What Paul understood was that the name *Tante Inge* terrified his mother as much as it had him.

He drove home and grabbed his getaway bag, an Italian leather satchel filled with everything he needed for quick trips. By five o'clock he was on Piedmont's Flight 87 to Fort Lauderdale.

As was the CIA man following him.

CHAPTER

9

THE EVERGLADES WERE BURNING WHEN PAUL LANDED in Fort Lauderdale. It was dusk and the sun glowed a desperate orange through a gunmetal haze that hugged the western horizon. Paul rented a car, rolled up the windows and turned on the air-conditioning. Bugs accumulated on the windshield as he drove down endless freeways bordered by tall palms and identical shopping centers.

Before leaving Washington he had phoned his sister to see if his mother was all right.

"She's resting now," Ceci assured him. "But she won't tell me what happened. She says you know."

"I'll tell you when I get there."

Now as he pulled into the parking stall marked "Visitors," he wasn't sure what to tell her. Would she believe that he dreamed of deaths or that he was in some sort of telepathic contact with a killer? Would she believe that under hypnosis he'd experienced a trauma associated with the name *Tante Inge*, unfamiliar to him, but a name that made his mother hysterical? Would *anyone* believe it?

As it turned out, Ceci was so eager to get back home that she didn't press the issue.

"Bob called a few minutes ago," she said as she led him into the apartment. "The kids are driving him crazy. He had to leave work early to pick them up. We were afraid mom had a heart attack or something. Anyway, I'm glad you're here."

Ceci was tiny like her mother, but had soft round features more characteristic of dad's side of the family.

"How is she?" Paul asked.

"Asleep now. I really think she's all right, Paul. You should have waited. You didn't have to come all the way down here."

Ceci began collecting her things. The apartment was a small one that mom had moved into after the divorce—a single bedroom with living room separated from a tiny kitchen by a narrow counter. A sliding glass door opened to an outdoor patio overlooking a man-made lake. Except for a white spinet piano in the corner, the furniture looked as if it had sprung to life from a Sears & Roebuck catalogue. Paul had never understood his mother's compulsion for economy, which resulted in undistinguished, ill-made goods that wore out twice as quickly as something only marginally more expensive.

He went to the bedroom and peered in. Mom lay curled on her side, her white hair adrift on the pillow, lips parted slightly, the sound of her breathing lost in the low hum of the air conditioner. On an end table next to the bed stood a familiar photograph of mom and dad on their wedding day. She held Ralph's arm and was gazing up at him while he stood tall and confident in his army uniform smiling at the camera. Their attitudes defined the relationship, Paul thought— mom dependent, dad carelessly confident.

"He gave me a new life," she once told Paul when he criticized his father.

Now he'd given her another new life, a lonely, empty one. But mom was still grateful and would allow no criticism of the man she married. Paul realized he was less generous. He tended to hold people to fairly strict standards, and as far as he was concerned his father had failed in his obligation to the marriage. Ironic, considering the state of his own marriage. Had he set impossible standards for Joanna?

He shut the door and returned to the living room. Ceci was on the phone, promising Bob she'd be right home to put the kids to bed. After she hung up she invited Paul to come over for a barbeque.

"As soon as you know your schedule," she said. "The kids would love to see you again.''

She dug her car keys from the purse and added as an afterthought, ''How's Joanna?''

''Still working at the gallery.''

Ceci was in too much of a hurry to notice the tightness in his voice or that his answer was an evasion. After she'd gone Paul stood in the living room and thought more about Joanna. Suddenly he very much wanted to talk to her, to share his worry about his mother and his real fear that falling asleep would make his mind vulnerable to some unknown presence. He most wanted and needed her now not so much as a wife or lover but as a friend.

On the off-chance that she'd returned he called home. He got the answering machine. ''This is Paul and Joanna Stafford. We're not available right now but if you leave your name and number we'll get right back to you.''

Paul was about to hang up but changed his mind.

''Jo? Are you home? Listen, if you're there, pick up the phone. I'm at mom's place. I came down this evening and I need to talk to you so if you're there . . . or you get this message, give me a call.'' He stopped talking and listened. After seven seconds the voice-actuated tape shut off.

Frustrated, he felt an irrational anger. Where the hell was she? She said in her note that she'd call in a couple of days, so why hadn't she called? Why wasn't she around when something important was going on, when it counted?

He sat down and turned on the television. He was looking for something to put his mind on ice but the sitcoms annoyed him with their intrusive laugh tracks and the only movie, an over-earnest drama about teenage suicide, bored him. His mind kept returning to Joanna and to the magic of their first meeting . . .

She had been working with a relief agency helping victims of the famine in Ethiopia. Paul's first glimpse of her was in front of a Safeway store, carrying a sign and soliciting food. The sign had a photograph of an Ethiopian child, arms and legs thin as toothpicks, ribs like a birdcage and a stomach distended from malnutrition. The caption read, ''Safeway Won't Feed This Child, Will You?'' The photograph was one of his.

''Have you got a release for that?'' Paul asked.

It wasn't much of an opening line but in the next five minutes Joanna managed to convince him to donate a dozen more photographs and two weeks later, when she and a team from the relief agency took the first planeload of food to Ethiopia, Paul went with them and covered the story. Their romance blossomed in the desert, and on the way back they spent two days together in Paris.

Joanna was a continual surprise. The first time they made love she became a different person, strangely shy and reticent. Afterward she lay shivering in his arms. Thinking she was cold, Paul pulled the covers over them, but it made no difference. Holding her, he felt the texture of her skin, dimpled with goosebumps.

"I'm sorry," she said "The more important it is, the more I'm afraid."

"Afraid of what?"

"Of you. You scare me."

She was dead serious.

"I won't hurt you."

"I don't mean physically."

"Then what?"

"That with you—if I let go with you I'll never come back"

"You'll come back. You'll still be you."

She touched his cheek, her pale blue eyes with tears now. "But I don't want to come back; that's what scares me."

Cautious in love and reckless in life, Joanna was different from any woman he'd ever known. He fell asleep thinking about her, and in restless dreams saw her standing naked on a diving board about to dive into a pool that held no water. Paul yelled a warning but Joanna just waved and smiled. He ran toward her but she paid no attention. She vaulted high into the air, jackknifed cleanly and descended to the pool, now filled with water. He saw her pale form flickering beneath the waves; then she broke the surface and swam easily away, laughing, as Paul stood stunned and shaken, staring after her.

The smell of coffee woke him up. He sat up and looked around. In the kitchen his mother was moving noiselessly, carefully taking silverware from the dishwasher and putting it in a drawer. She wore yellow slacks and a floral top. When she saw Paul she smiled.

"I tried not to wake you."

"What time is it?"

"Almost nine. I phoned the club and told them I wasn't coming in today. It isn't every day I have a visit from my son." She acted as if his visit were the most normal thing in the world.

Paul stood up and ran a hand through his hair. His neck was stiff from his night on the couch.

"There are fresh towels in the bathroom. And I'm making peach pancakes for breakfast. You still like pancakes, don't you?"

She kept puttering, paying no attention to his reactions. He went into the kitchen and stood watching her.

"Mom, are you all right?"

"I'm fine. Go ahead now. You get cleaned up. Go, go."

She turned him around and pushed him gently toward the bathroom. Whether she was trying to ignore what happened yesterday or simply wanted to delay discussing it, he couldn't tell. But he left her alone for a few minutes while he washed up. When he came back she was on the patio, setting places for breakfast.

"It's such a nice morning," she said. "I thought we'd eat out here. Sit, sit. I'll bring coffee."

She bustled off to the kitchen but Paul sensed the nervousness beneath all the activity. When she brought the coffee he took her wrist and insisted she sit down.

"We have to talk, mom."

"Paul, the batter's ready." She tugged against his grip like a trapped bird, eyes darting over his shoulder, as though seeking escape.

"We have to talk about this Tante Inge."

"No." She yanked her arm free and stared at him, then turned and walked across the grass toward the lake. Paul followed. She sat down on one of the concrete white benches bordering the water and stared into the distance. Half a dozen ducks swam toward her, honking. Paul came up behind her and began massaging her shoulders. At first she tensed under his touch but after a few moments she relaxed. When she finally spoke her voice was flat.

"How did you find out?"

"I didn't find out. That's why I need to talk to you."

"You know her name."

"I had a dream. A bad dream, and Tante Inge's name came up." She turned to look at up at him.

"But you were so young. How could you remember?"

"Who was she, mom? Who was Tante Inge?"

"Not your aunt. That was just . . ." She looked away. "Just a name you called her. A name she wanted all the children to call her."

"Who was she?"

"Her name was Inge Heusner. She was Satan come to earth, a depraved thing who"—she shuddered—"who killed your brother."

Paul's hands stopped.

"My *brother?*"

"The two of you. Twins. Karl and Paul."

Paul's shock was complete. The world seemed to fall away as his senses turned inward; trees, lake and grass became mere pattern while sounds were attenuated, distant, as if he were swimming underwater. *A twin brother?* A brother named Karl? Annie's words came back to him: *emotionally close.* With a dizzying shift of perspective Paul realized that his brother was not dead. Somewhere in the world there was a shared consciousness, another part of himself. A twin. A brother . . .

He became aware of his mother's voice.

" . . . sacrificed him. I gave Karl's life in exchange for yours."

"He's not dead," Paul said.

She turned to look at him, her eyes filled with hope, and horror.

"Not dead? What are you saying?"

"I know it. I know he's not dead."

"How? How can you know that?"

"Because I've had these dreams, mom. Dreams that aren't just dreams—they're real events, things that are happening—not to me but to *him.*"

"Dreams? No, you don't know what happened. You don't know . . ."

"Tell me, then."

She shook her head. "I *can't.*"

"Does dad know?"

"No one knows."

"But why? Why didn't you tell anyone?"

"I couldn't."

"Why not?"

"Because . . . because I *gave* him to her." She stood up. "It was my fault. I gave him to her and she . . . she took him to that place where they . . . they . . ."

Her lips moved but the words wouldn't come. Her features were twisted, as if she were suffering some kind of seizure.

Paul got up and held her. "It's all right, it's all right," he said quickly. "Take a deep breath. Come on now, a deep breath.

That's it."

When she was breathing normally he told her he was hungry and let the subject of Inge Heusner slip aside while they ate breakfast on the patio. She needed time to recover; he needed time to figure out an approach that wouldn't upset her.

The air grew warm and the sky took on a mid-morning haze. When they were finished she broke the leftover toast and fed it to the ducks. She called them each by name, admonishing one not to be so selfish, encouraging another to come and get its fair share.

He waited until she had finished and returned to the table, her face flushed, before he said softly, "We have to talk about her, mom. I have to know."

Her smile died and she looked away but in her eyes there was resignation now as well as sadness. After a moment she said, "Will you promise not to hate me?"

"You know better than that."

She nodded, accepting his promise without believing it. "Come, then. Come inside."

In the living room he waited while she went to the bedroom and returned a few minutes later with an old cigar box tied with twine. The cigar box was made of wood and the label was in German.

"In here is my shame," she said. "But first you must try to understand how it happened."

She closed her eyes and took a deep breath. When she spoke, her voice was low and tinged with a bitterness that Paul had never heard before.

"No one can imagine what it was like after the war, Paul. Berlin was—there was nothing left. All ruins. No streetcars, no sidewalks, only paths through the rubble. My mother and father had died in the bombing, and Erich—your father—was lost on the Eastern front. He never heard the news, his twin boys. So I was alone, a young mother with two babies. We lived in one room, a kitchen without water or electricity, but we were lucky. We had two wool blankets and the windows were unbroken.

"This was the first year of the occupation and there was not enough to eat. The harvests had been ruined by the invasion, and people were starving. In November, before the ground froze, we watched the soldiers dig mass graves for all those who were expected to die during the winter. Every day I wrapped you and Karl in a blanket and waited outside the army base for them to bring out the garbage. The garbage was in special containers, metal barrels labeled 'Food For The Master Race.' The Russian soldiers thought this a fine joke. Food for the Master Race.''

Her eyes narrowed at the memory and she paused, lost in thought. Paul had a sense of the strong will she must have had as a young woman.

"I remember," she said. "We beat the cans with sticks to drive out the rats. Then we took what was left."

"What about *her?*"

She looked away, took a deep breath. "Frau Heusner lived in the cellar of our building. She lived by begging. Each morning we watched her leave, dressed in rags and carrying a cane. Each evening she returned with food and occupation money and maybe a pair of shoes to barter or a coat to sell. Sometimes she came back with American cigarettes, and this amazed us all. In those days, one American cigarette was worth a month's salary, so everyone envied Frau Heusner and wondered how it was she was so successful in a city where so many beggars starved. Frau Heusner just laughed and said that God answered her prayers.

"One day I discovered her secret. I was in a new neighborhood looking for work when I saw Frau Heusner on the street. She was dressed in her usual rags but there was something new. She wore dark glasses and walked slowly, tapping the street with her cane as if she was blind. So that was her secret, I thought. She got extra sympathy by pretending to be blind.

"Later, I told her what I'd seen and was surprised at her reaction. She grew pale and asked if I'd told anyone else. When I said no, she swore me to secrecy, telling me she was afraid of being arrested. I thought it was funny because the police had so many serious problems that they wouldn't bother about somebody impersonating the blind. But Frau Heusner was very scared so I promised not to tell. I often wonder what would have happened if I *had* gone to the police, how many lives would have been saved. How many lives . . .'' She stared vacantly at the wall, then looked up slowly. "When I look at you, I see him, too. It's always been that way."

Paul nodded, wanting her to continue but afraid to press the issue for fear that it would upset her again. "It must have been difficult," he said carefully.

"It got worse when winter came," she continued. "That's when you got sick, very sick, with fever and chills and even coughing blood. It was terrible to see. You were so young, helpless, and nothing I did was any help. So I went to the hospital and the doctor told me that you had pneumonia and you would die without antibiotics. There were no antibiotics in the Russian sector so I had to go to the American sector, but to do this you needed a special pass. It took all day, waiting in line, and when they issued the pass it was only for you and me. 'The other one's not sick,' they told me. They didn't care about the German people, whether we lived or died, you see? So it was only you and I who could go, and that's when I went to Frau Heusner. I was forced to, Paul. I couldn't let you die."

"And Frau Heusner took care of Karl?"

Mom nodded. "She had been kind to us. She used to bring things, little things, sometimes food, sometimes a piece of clothing—once she brought yarn and I knitted caps for the cold weather. Both you and Karl, matching caps. Frau Heusner joked about taking one of you with her when she went begging. She said the Russian soldiers had soft hearts for blind mothers and little babies. That's why I thought it would be all right, you see? To leave Karl . . .

"Of course, we were only going for the day, that's what I thought. I thought we would get the medicine and return, but when the doctor saw you, he put you in the hospital. They were afraid you would die, so they gave you oxygen and I stayed with you. It was six days before we went home. I went right away to Frau Heusner, but the police were there in her room waiting for her. The police told me what happened."

Mom bowed her head as if in prayer, then slowly untied the cigar box. Her fingers trembled. Finally he would know what was so terrible that his mother couldn't even speak the words to tell him.

The twine fell away and she lifted out a newspaper clipping, yellowed with age. Without unfolding it she handed it to Paul.

"This is my sin," she said.

The paper was brittle and tiny pieces fell from the edges as Paul unfolded it. The clipping was undated and in German. The article was headlined, "Helpful Citizens Butchered in Pankow." Paul read on:

> Police in the Pankow district discovered human remains in a blackmarket butcher shop located at 21 Uferallee. The shop is owned by Hans Furtz and his cousin, Rolf Jaspers. Both men have been arrested. An accomplice, Inge Heusner, is still at large.
>
> The gruesome discovery came to light after police

were contacted by Marie Naumann, 28 years old, of Weisensee. Naumann said that she came to the aid of a blind woman, later identified as Inge Heusner, who appeared to be having difficulty finding her way to Pankow, where she was to deliver a letter. Naumann offered to perform the errand for her but became suspicious when she glanced back and saw Heusner making her way down the street as if in full possession of her faculties. Police later confirmed that Heusner was not blind and had for some time been engaged in luring people from adjacent districts to the Pankow shop, where they were murdered.

Her suspicions aroused, Naumann went to the police, who in turn accompanied her to the butcher shop. One of the owners, Furtz, escaped by running out the back door but was later captured at home. Jaspers was apprehended on the premises. A search of the basement revealed two partly dismembered bodies.

Police said that the shop had been in operation for many months and that the actual number of victims may never be known. Apparently all victims were recruited from outside the district so as not to arouse suspicion. A chilling postscript to the incident was the message contained in the envelope Miss Naumann was to deliver to Furtz and Jaspers. In Inge Heusner's handwriting the message said: *This is the last one I will be sending today.*

Paul finished reading and looked up. His mother could only stare at him, as though waiting for judgment.

"Someone saw her there," she said, her voice hoarse and barely audible. "With Karl . . . But I kept hoping, I kept looking . . Oh my God . . . "

The tears came, and Paul, in a daze himself, went to her. She shrank back into herself at his approach. He sat beside her, cradling her like a child, wanting to take her pain but not knowing how.

"It's all right," he said, an empty phrase, which brought no comfort.

She began whispering, over and over, like a litany, *"Ich bitte um Vergebung, ich bitte um Vergebung."* Forgive me, forgive me.

But it wasn't his mother who needed the absolution, Paul was thinking. It was Karl, his twin brother . . . It was Karl who had killed six people and made Paul an unwilling accomplice. He would wait to tell his mother more. It would hardly ease the pain to discover this new horror, that her son Karl had somehow survived only to become a sadistic killer.

The memory of his dreams sickened him even more now . . . the possibility of it happening again made just the idea of sleep a terrible threat. It must not happen again. One way or another, Paul had to stop his brother from more killing.

But first, he had to find him.

CHAPTER

10

THE LOCAL AGENT'S NAME WAS TANZER. HE SAT IN
the cafeteria of Frankfurt Airport drinking coffee and paging through
an Italian magazine filled with photos of naked women with glistening wet breasts sunning themselves at a seaside resort. In his pocket
was a FAX copy of a photograph of the man he was to follow. The
man's name was Paul Stafford.

The assignment had come at the last minute. His American case
officer had contacted him before dawn, waking him from a restless
sleep, and Tanzer had the distinct impression that he was not the first
choice for the job. Tanzer had first worked for the Americans as part
of an operation that uncovered a ring of high-technology bandits ille-
gally shipping electronic equipment to the Soviet Union through Swe-
den. Since then there had been only routine assignments like this one,
in which he merely made reports without knowing anything about the
operation.

The public address system announced the arrival of Lufthansa
Flight 465 from Miami. Tanzer finished his coffee, lukewarm by
now, rolled the magazine and thrust it into his overcoat. He made his

way to the customs area where he stood near a pillar at some distance from the crowd of people who gathered at the railing outside
the opaque doors. How many of them, Tanzer wondered, were meeting friends from Miami? And did girls from Florida have bronze skin
and bleached hair like the sand-spangled girls in the magazine?

He had no chance to find out; Stafford was among the first to enter
the terminal. From the way he looked around to get his bearings,
Tanzer guessed that his target had never been here before. Stafford
carried a single overnight bag and his clothes were wrinkled from the
long flight. As he walked away Tanzer checked the time and wrote it
down in a dog-eared notebook, then followed Stafford to the Pan Am
counter, where his quarry joined the ticket line. Leaving so soon,
Tanzer wondered?

This made things more interesting. They were going somewhere.
Tanzer was glad that he'd had the foresight to bring his passport.
Already he was considering how he might pad the expense account.
A trip outside Germany required authorization but this didn't bother
him. He knew that he could plead lack of time and the Americans
would pick up the bill. They always did. After all, unhappy agents
made bad security risks.

Tanzer hoped that Stafford would buy a ticket to Italy. He had
friends in Rome and he was in the mood to rent a car and chase Italian girls in short skirts riding motorscooters. Instead, his quarry got
in line to buy a ticket for the Berlin shuttle. The shuttles left hourly
but the next one, the eleven-thirty, was all booked. Tanzer was in an
adjoining line, close enough to hear the agent explain the situation
and to watch Stafford buy a ticket for the twelve-thirty flight.

Tanzer was in a slow line, and his target had disappeared by the
time he got his ticket. He worried that this was a ruse designed to
lose him, but Stafford was waiting at the boarding gate when he got
there. Security precautions were especially stringent for the Berlin
shuttle. Only ticketed passengers were allowed into the waiting area,
which was separated from the terminal by bulletproof glass walls. All
luggage was x-rayed and inspected and entry to the area was carefully controlled. A security guard ran an electro-magnetic wand over
Tanzer's body before passing him into the waiting room, where Stafford stood staring out the window at the plane.

The eleven-thirty passengers were in the process of boarding. Most
of them were businessmen in shiny shoes and expensive ties. Tanzer
sat down across the room from Stafford, pulled out his magazine and

prepared to wait an hour. It was too bad they weren't going to Italy. Once, on the island of Capri he had made love to an Italian woman in a swimming pool who had slipped beneath the water to suck him off. Tanzer loved Italian women.

The passengers had finished boarding and the agent behind the desk made an announcement over the loudspeaker, something about standby passengers. Tanzer was only half-listening.

". . . passenger Stafford and standby passenger Fuchs."

Tanzer looked up with alarm. Stafford and half a dozen others were being allowed to board the plane. Immediately he realized what must have happened: Stafford had put his name on a standby list when he arrived here at the boarding gate. With a quiet curse Tanzer put the magazine away and ran to the ticket agent.

"Wait, is there any more room?"

"The flight is full, sir."

The last person, a middle-aged lady with a huge plastic shopping bag, was at the entrance to the ramp.

"Excuse me, madam," Tanzer called after her. "I'll pay double the price for your ticket."

She shook her head with a frown, barely glancing at him, and kept walking. The agent shut the door behind her. He had lost Stafford.

Tanzer didn't want to give up the assignment, so he spent fifteen minutes trying to find another flight. He even called two charter companies, knowing full well that his American contact wouldn't approve such an expenditure but taking down all the information anyway as a way of demonstrating his resourcefulness. Then he called a special number and left a message. He waited another ten minutes by the pay phone before his contact returned the call. As he expected, the assignment was scrubbed. They would use somebody else in Berlin. Tanzer went to the bar, got a beer and spent the rest of the day considering his bad luck.

Paul was not aware that he was being watched. He hadn't noticed the man who followed him to Miami, and he hadn't noticed Tanzer in Frankfurt. He had put his name on the standby list at the suggestion of the ticket agent, and the fact that he had made the eleven-thirty shuttle was a matter of luck. Now he was too busy analyzing the difference between Germany and the United States to wonder if he was being watched.

Stereotypes, he thought, were often based in fact. The German propensity for order and efficiency was apparent at Berlin's Tegel Airport just as it had been in Frankfurt. There was never any doubt of where to go or what to do. Everything was well laid out and well marked, with pictographs and arrows pointing the way to taxis, restrooms, police, currency exchange, buses, baggage—anything a traveler might need to know and always in the most rational place to look. The Germans were nothing if not well organized, and it was this organization that Paul was counting on to help him locate Inge Heusner and his newly discovered brother. Specifically, he was counting on the *anmeld*.

Anmeld was a German word that meant to register with the police. Each German citizen was required, within thirty days of moving to a new address, to stop at the local police station and notify them of his name, occupation, address, date he took occupancy and the number of people living in the dwelling. The *anmeld* was where Paul meant to start the search for his brother.

He took a taxi to the Hotel InterContinental just off the Kurfursten-damm on Budapesterstrasse. Like most of the new buildings in Berlin, the hotel saved its personality for the inside. The lobby featured marble floors with oriental rugs and walls that formed a back-drop for ferns that tumbled out of angled skylights. A sign welcomed attendees of the Fifth Annual Medical Technology Congress, and on the lawn outside, a large white circus tent had been erected as an exhibition space.

Paul stepped up to the front desk. "When do the elephants get here?"

The clerk, a somber balding man whose remaining hair was parted just above his left ear, stared at him with a blank smile.

"Bitte?"

"The circus tent," Paul nodded outside. "When do the elephants arrive?" The clerk turned slowly to look.

"Never mind," Paul said.

The man stared at the tent, blinked, then loosed a bark of laughter that ended as quickly as it began.

"Yes, good, good," he nodded to Paul.

As he filled out the registration form, the clerk kept glancing at the tent, pursing his lips and nodding with approval. Paul wondered how nightclub comics made out in Berlin.

In his room, he unpacked his getaway bag, an eclectic collection of everything he needed for a quick assignment: two shirts, one a short-sleeve knit and the other a long-sleeve dress, a tie, dress slacks, shorts, three sets of underwear, tennis shoes and down vest. Hardware was a Sony micro-cassette recorder with a dozen micro-cassettes, the Ricoh FF-90 with six rolls of 1,000-speed Kodacolor, three sets of batteries, two Parker T-Ball jotters and a spiral notepad. Also a leather toilet kit, a gift that Joanna had bought in Ethiopia. She hadn't known it was elephant hide and he still remembered her quick tears when she found out. Her vulnerability to abstract tragedies had been one of the things that charmed him.

Paul pushed his thoughts of the past aside, kicked off his shoes, punched up the pillows and sat down on the bed with a phone book. A quick call to the mayor's office told him there was no central record repository in Berlin; each police district maintained its own registration. Records were available to authorized researchers, which included credentialed journalists. There would be no problem checking the twelve West Berlin districts.

"What about Pankow?" Paul asked. It was the district his mother was living in when she put Karl in Inge Heusner's care.

"Pankow is in the Eastern sector," the woman told him. "You will have to discuss with them their procedures."

Discussing procedures with East Berlin wasn't so easy. It took half a dozen calls to half a dozen offices to discover that only authorized personnel could check police records. There was a Bureau of Displaced Persons that might be able to locate Frau Heusner—if she was still alive and if Paul could afford to wait a few years for them to find out. What if Paul wanted to look through the records himself? Yes . . . it was impossible. He could make a request. Certain forms to be filled out, police background checks made, clearance from proper authorities . . . it could take some time. It could take a *long* time. Was there an address where Paul might like the application forms to be sent?

It was the "yes but no" game that every bureaucrat played. Paul was used to it. That's why he'd come in person rather than called or written from the States. Calling and writing got you front-door answers; what he needed was back-door solutions. He got out the *Herald* contact sheet and called Ray Tregerdemain.

Ray was a stringer working out of Berlin. Paul had met him a few years back at a Washington Press Association Awards ceremony. Tregerdemain's mother had died and he'd come back to the States for her funeral On the return trip he stopped in Washington to see an old friend and somehow wrangled an invitation to the ceremony. He had spoken to Paul at some length, mistaking him for an overseas editor named Stanford. Later, Paul saw him at the *Herald* office and after that his byline began appearing on the odd Berlin story—the ones that weren't pulled straight from AP, UPI or Reuters.

An answering machine gave a John Phillip Sousa introduction and then Ray Tregerdemain's recorded voice began explaining that he was on assignment but would get back to the caller right away. Halfway through the announcement another voice interrupted.

"This is Tregerdemain. I'm here, I'm here. Wait a minute and I'll—"

There was a yelp from the tape machine and the line cleared.

"Yes, yes? Hello?"

"Ray Tregerdemain?"

"That's right."

Paul introduced himself, referring to their earlier meeting. It took Tregerdemain a moment, but when he remembered his tone took on a new enthusiasm and he began speaking English.

"The WPA ceremony," he repeated. "Right, right. And I thought you were what's-his-name, that other guy—"

"Jerry Stanford."

"Stanford, sure. Hey, good to hear your voice, Paul. What's going on? You working a story in the embattled city or what?"

Paul explained briefly that he was trying to locate his brother, born Karl Weiss, who had disappeared in 1946. Ray seemed disappointed that the *Herald* wasn't doing a piece on Berlin but his interest picked up when he heard that Paul was looking for his twin brother.

"I need a way into East Berlin police records," Paul finished. "You have any ideas?"

"Yeah, lots of Westmarks."

"How many and to whom?"

There was a pause, then more slowly, "You're serious?"

"I'm serious about knowing the options. If bribes are one way to go, give me some idea of how much. That doesn't mean I've got the bucks to pull it off," he added, sensing that Ray might be as much opportunist as journalist.

"Okay, Paul, how's this . . . I'm in the middle of sixteen things so let me dump everything and meet you in an hour at the Journalisten-Club. How does that sound? Give me a chance to see what I can come up with, okay?"

They made the arrangements and Ray gave him directions. Paul made two overseas calls: one to tell the *Herald* that he would be out of the office until Monday, the other to his answering service to see if Joanna had called. She hadn't. The only message was from Annie Helms, wanting to set up a time for their next session. He considered calling her but decided against it. He figured it was best not to involve the CIA. At least not until he found Karl.

Hugh Roark had hoped to have a cup of coffee and call Annie Helms before facing Maurice, but the younger man spotted him in the hallway and came bounding after him.

"What's the word?"

"Not great."

"He slipped, right?"

They passed a file clerk, and Hugh waited until the man was out of earshot before responding. "The agent didn't know. It could have been an accident."

"An accident? How?"

The two men entered Hugh's office, which had been carpeted recently and still smelled of new rug. Hugh was sensitive to smells and it bothered him that in the new buildings you couldn't open the windows.

"You want some coffee?"

"No thanks. What happened?"

As he explained, Hugh opened his drawer, took out a handmade cup in the shape of a Chinese devil's face, and poured coffee from a silver thermos.

"Stafford landed in Frankfurt and took the Pan Am shuttle to Berlin. The eleven-thirty was full so he ticketed the twelve-thirty. The agent did the same, but apparently when Stafford checked in for the flight he signed up for the standby list."

"Apparently?"

"Our man didn't see him do it. He was back in the security line when Stafford reached the check-in counter."

"What about Berlin?"

"You know Berlin. Frankfurt contacted them but they wouldn't authorize a direct. By the time I got a back channel from Langley it was too late. The plane was on the ground."

Maurice waved his hand in disgust. "He's gone, he's gone."

"I'm not so sure."

"Come on, Hugh. He's playing Parcheesi in the Kremlin by now."

Hugh took off his coat and hung it on a hanger. Relax, he wanted to say. Don't make it personal. "We've got no proof," he reminded his partner. "If he wants to go over, we can't stop him."

"Then why tail him at all?"

"Because I don't think he's going over. I think he's after that relative he told Helms about. The aunt he remembered."

"It must be contagious," Maurice said.

Hugh ignored him and leaned to the intercom. "Gayle? I need Annie Helms in medical."

"You two have the same disease," Maurice persisted.

"What's that?" Hugh asked, knowing what was coming.

"Gullibility."

"What would you have done?"

"Arrested him, sweated him, turned him. If that didn't work . . ." Maurice shrugged. "He wouldn't be much of a threat in a wheelchair."

"Maybe you should have joined the Green Berets."

"Or the KGB, like our boy Stafford."

"He didn't do the killings," Hugh said.

"Then he knows who did."

"Not yet."

"Then why would he—"

"To find the killer," Hugh interrupted. "I think that's why he went to Germany. And that's why we're tailing him."

"To *warn* the killer."

"I don't think so."

Maurice opened his mouth to argue the point but the expression on Hugh's face changed his mind. He shrugged. "Okay, it's your call."

That's right, Hugh thought as he waited to talk to Annie Helms. It's my call. And my ass if I'm wrong.

CHAPTER
11

PAUL HAD TIME TO SPARE BEFORE MEETING RAY TRE-gerdemain. Rather than sit in the hotel room, he went outside and wandered away from the crowded Budapesterstrasse into the adjoining neighborhood where the streets were smaller and more of the pre-war buildings were in evidence, broad brownstone apartments with cob-blestone walks. Here, for the first time, he was struck by a vague sense of the familiar.

After fifteen minutes of aimless wandering, he made his way back and passed through an area of expensive restaurants, trendy night-clubs and a brightly-lit casino. The nightclub flanking the casino was named the Wyoming and featured a sign that caught his attention. It was purple neon, a bucking bronco in two positions, each one alter-nately illuminated. Watching the sign, Paul was struck again by a feeling of familiarity. He'd seen this sign before or one very much like it. He was half-tempted to go inside but it was getting late so he filed the Wyoming away for possible future reference.

The feeling of déjà vu faded as he entered the crowded Breit-scheidplatz, where undistinguished concrete buildings sat like interlopers on streets whose history stretched back five hundred years. The few pre-war buildings that remained often stopped abruptly in a wall of plaster where their neighbors had been destroyed in the war. It was a city of architectural incongruity and it came as no surprise that the Journalisten-Club was located above a Burger King.

Paul signed the guest register and sat down to wait for Ray. The place reminded him of a private men's club and was divided into two areas, a lounge and a dining room, both serviced by young waiters who probably wanted to be reporters. Two couples were having an early dinner but most of the action was in the lounge, where groups of men and a few women sat in conversation, leaning toward one another, stabbing the air with cigarettes and nibbling nervously at peanuts and potato chips.

Ray Tregerdemain showed up ten minutes late. He was heavier than Paul remembered and it looked as if the weight was recent. Ray's shirt and coat seemed tight, as if left over from an earlier edition of his body. He was breathing heavily and looked around the room with a worried expression. When he saw Paul, he relaxed.

"Hey, there you are," he said in a voice that carried across the room. "Long time, no see."

Ray weaved through the crowd with a delicate grace that Paul wouldn't have thought possible considering his bulk.

"Didn't mean to keep you waiting," he said as the two men shook hands, "but the phone rang and one thing and another."

He sat down heavily. The exertion of climbing a single flight of stairs had sweat glistening on his forehead. He called to the waiter in a loud voice and, after a glance at what Paul was drinking, ordered scotch and water.

"Make it a double," he called after the waiter, then favored Paul with a conspiratorial smile. "You need a kick in the butt to take this place seriously. All the heavy hitters come out in the evening. That's Alex Sandor over there. Not his wife, though. 'Business associate.' " Ray kept up a running commentary until his drink arrived. Then he returned his attention to Paul and raised his glass. "As our American doughboys say, *Gut Kopf.* "

He downed half the drink and set down the glass with a sigh of satisfaction and a shudder. Ray's warm, friendly smile was sabotaged by eyes that were bloodshot and bordered by skin that sagged like a hopeful bloodhound's. A lush, Paul thought. He wondered how much help Ray was going to be.

Becoming aware of Paul's scrutiny, Ray smiled sheepishly. "Journalist's lunch," he said, indicating the drink.

Paul nodded. "What about the *anmeld* records? You got any
ideas?"

"One or two." Ray took out a soiled handkerchief and wiped his
brow, hunching forward to stuff it back into his pocket. "First let me
make sure I've got it straight. You're looking for your brother—twin
brother, that is—who got lost in February of forty-six with some
woman taking care of him. Name of brother was Karl, Karl . . . no,
don't tell me. I've got a system." He squinted with the effort.
"Weiss! Karl Weiss. Let's see, lost in forty-six with a caretaker
woman some years his senior by the name of of Inge Heusner! Name
of district they disappeared from was Pankow! How's that?"

"How do I get access, Ray?"

Ray's attention had shifted to a man with silver-gray hair, a newcomer who was on his way to the dining room. Ray jumped to his
feet.

"Herr Fricke," he called. "*Grüss Gott.* This is Paul Stafford,
from the Washington *Herald.* The man who won a Pulitzer a few
years ago."

"Ah," said Herr Fricke, turning with a polite smile.

"Paul, Herman Fricke, editor of *Berliner Zeitschrifte.*"

Paul stood up and shook hands. It was evident that Herr Fricke
had as little interest in meeting him as he did in meeting Fricke.

"Paul's working on a little *Kriegserleidnis* about post-war refugees
and I'm doing what I can to fix him up with sources."

"Actually," Paul said, "the story's about the resurgent Nazi
movement in Berlin."

Fricke's smile faded.

"There are no such groups—none that can be taken seriously by
serious people. If you'll excuse me . . ." He moved on to the dining
room. Ray took half a step after him. "He's joking," he called. Herr
Fricke pretended not to hear. Ray turned to Paul. "Are you crazy?
You'll ruin my reputation with these people."

"Have you got one left, Ray?"

Ray took a quick breath and blinked as if someone had thrown ice
water in his face. For a moment Paul thought he might get angry.
Then his gaze faltered and he looked away. "That's okay," he mumbled. "No harm, no sweat."

Ray sat down and reached for his drink. The glass was empty but he lifted it to his lips in a sort of reflex action. After a moment he said, "Is it that obvious?"

"What's obvious is that you're trading on my reputation. See and be seen at the Journalisten-Club, is that it?"

"You don't pull any punches, do you?"

"What is it, Ray? The work or the booze?"

Ray winced. "I'm not a basket case, Paul. Not yet, anyway."

"So what's the problem?"

"There are *no* problems, that's the problem. Nobody's interested in Berlin, nobody cares about the Wall, it's a dead issue. Oh, sure, occasionally some protester will go over and pee on the Wall and the *Grenzpolizei* will kick the beejesus out of him, but even then it's only worth a column in Berlin. The rest of the world's got its own problems. Meanwhile the East is busy turning itself into a communist Disneyland in exchange for tourists' dollars. Last summer things were so slow I worked for this Theissen Tourist Agency taking busloads of tourists to the Wall and reciting statistics about how many people were killed. After a while I got bored and started making the statistics up. *Ten people killed crossing the Wall here. Twenty people killed. A family with three children.* The next time it was six children and a dog. Then the youngest girl went back to get the dog and they shot her. A little girl named Heidi. I was a smash. The next day I get to the same spot and there's this couple from the day before with flowers they're going to leave in memory of Heidi." Ray shook his head. "I quit the next day. I couldn't stand it."

The waiter materialized, collected their glasses and asked if they wanted another. When Paul refused, Ray gave him a troubled look.

"You sure you aren't on an expense account?"

"Private business."

Ray turned to the waiter. "Make it a single."

After the waiter was gone Paul said, "Are you going to be any good to me, Ray? Because if not . . ."

"Okay, okay, there are a couple of ways to go. First, as an accredited journalist you can be working on a *Kriegserleidnis*. That's very common over here. Some noble German saved somebody's Jewish father or mother and now they're trying to find this savior to thank him. Even the East Germans will cooperate on something like that—as long as it's not an anti-communist slant. So in your case we make Inge Hausner an anti-fascist hero who saved some poor communist from the Nazis; some big boy in a baggy suit, Walter Ulbricht maybe, first leader of East Germany and hero of the Berlin Wall and all that . . ."

Paul was shaking his head. "A story like that wouldn't hold up if they investigated. Besides, I'm assuming she changed her name when she moved."

"Changed her name? Why?"

Paul took out his wallet and removed the folded newspaper clipping that his mother had given him.

"She was implicated in a murder conspiracy. That's why she disappeared in the first place."

He handed the clipping to Ray, who read it with growing interest. "Even better than a *Kriegserleidnis*. Except it doesn't say anything about your brother. How do you know he was with her?"

"My mother left him with her."

"Great, so how do you know he wasn't one of these human hamburgers? If you pardon my French."

Paul didn't want to talk about the nightmares or the killings, particularly with Ray Tregerdemain.

"I don't," he said. "But the *anmeld* records should tell us."

"Not if Inge Heusner became Kathy Nicekraut, which wasn't all that difficult back them. All she'd have had to do was walk into a refugee camp and say, 'Hi, I'm Kathy Nicekraut, one of the friendly *Deutschvolk* who got kicked out of Poland and I've been walking for a couple of months and lost my identity papers, sorry' . . ."

"*Inge* Nicekraut," Paul corrected.

"Why *Inge?*"

"I'm assuming she kept her first name but changed the last."

"How do you figure that?"

Paul shrugged. "Somebody once told me it's easier for people not to forget who's talking to them if they keep their first names." Actually, a low-level hood who'd acted as a source for him on a story had told him so.

The drink arrived and Ray busied himself nursing what he assumed would be the last drink he could charge off Paul. Around the room some of the groups had moved into the dining area while outside the window, streetlights were beginning to flicker into life.

"Question," Ray said. "How in the hell can you track down little Miss Inge if she changed her name?"

"Well, I know when she disappeared," Paul said, fingering the clipping. "So never mind the name, just check all records for the week of February ninth, a woman thirty-five to forty years old with a child between a year and two years old.''

"Between a year and two years old? The kid was born the same day as you, wasn't he? You're twins, you said.''

"She could have changed the birth date.''

"She could have changed a lot of things. How do you know she didn't take off for Dresden or Leipzig? What makes you think she stayed in Berlin?''

"It's the logical place to start.''

Ray shook his head sadly. "I should have ordered a double,'' he said. "You've got nothing, you know that? She might or might not have left Berlin; she might or might not have taken your brother with her; she probably changed one or all of her names and his names; she might have moved in with a friend or even slept on the streets for a couple of years—''

"I don't need you to tell me the odds, I need help. So we go with what we've got . . . Week of February ninth, a woman between thirty-five and forty with a child between age one and two.''

Ray pulled back for a moment, like a turtle sinking into its shell. "Can we get another round?''

"Can I get an answer from you?''

"Ray Tregerdemain has more angles than a clubhouse politician. I've got a contact at Humboldt University. It's just hard to talk when my mouth is so dry.''

Paul flagged the waiter and ordered another round. "Okay, what about Humboldt University? That's in the East, right?''

"As Adolf said, 'The destiny of the Fatherland lies in the East'—''

"Humboldt, Ray?''

"In the East, right. Has a great reputation, not exactly the party school it was in the twenties but academically still top of the line. Got some great professors. One of them's a buddy of mine, Julius Schiller. Julius is the kind who actually believes the key to one big happy world is communication. Has me come once a semester to give a little lecture on 'Journalism as Practiced in the West, or How Ethics Takes a Back Seat to Entertainment.' I get them all jazzed up and afterward we go to the local Kneipe and argue over beer. That's an interesting thing about commie countries . . . the written word still matters so goddamn much. A typewriter's a gun and words are bullets.''

"Meanwhile,'' said Paul, "how does your professor help us access to *anmeld* records?''

"Not us, him. We let him do it. Julius happens to have a brother in the foreign office. One of the original commie kids who helped build the Berlin Wall. Still got cement under his fingernails. Anyway, he's a mucky-muck official and that makes life easy for Julius. He comes in handy in cases like this—no politics, just good old-fashioned fact-checking, research and red-tape cutting. Mr. Julius Schiller, brother of Comrade Rolf Schiller, Order of Stalin's Nosewart and all that? Yes, sir, step right up, take any old *anmeld* record you want, take it home with you if you like and remember to say 'hi' to your brother for me.'' Ray chuckled, coughed. "Human nature. They can put a wall around the city but they can't put a wall around human nature.''

Paul was willing to pay for services rendered. He knew from experience how time-consuming checking records could be.

"All right,'' he said. "How do I meet him?''

"You meet him?'' Ray looked surprised.

"I don't want a middleman, Ray, but I'll give you a finder's fee if he works out. And I'll need help on this side of the Wall. There's twelve districts over here and she might just as easily moved west as east. I can use a researcher, if you want the work.''

"I don't know, let me check my schedule.'' He pulled out the neck of his shirt and peered down at his stomach. "Nope, not too busy next week.''

Paul half-smiled. Ray Tregerdemain might not be Woodward or Bernstein but Paul couldn't help liking him. They arranged that Ray would make contact with Julius Schiller and call Paul at the hotel by noon the next day. In the meantime Paul would make a list of districts in the West, dividing them into those he would cover and those Ray could handle.

"It really would make a good *Kriegserleidnis,* you know,'' Ray told him as they left the club. "Brothers torn apart by war reunited and all that.''

"*No,* Ray. Don't even think of it.''

"Up to you, but I hate to see a good story go to waste . . .''

The night had brought a change of character to the Kurfursten-damm, the main street that Berliners casually called the *Ku'damm.* The glass display cases that occupied prominent positions along the sidewalk were no longer the focus of attention for shoppers but had become illuminated islands streetwalkers posed against.

"Asphalt swallows," Ray said. "They've each got their own spot. I saw a fight once when some new kitty tried to take another's place. Better than professional wrestling, let me tell you."

Ray kept up a running commentary as they walked. He was meeting friends at the Europa Center casino, which was on the way back to the InterContinental. The drinks had boosted his natural energy and he walked briskly, head swiveling back and forth, a visual sniper taking potshots at the city.

Outside the gleaming arcadelike entry Ray hesitated, asked Paul if he wanted to come along.

"No thanks," Paul said. "I want to poke my head in there."

Ray followed his gaze to the Wyoming, where the neon bronco was kicking up its heels.

"You'll poke more than your head if you go in there."

A shriek of laughter obscured his words. Two couples had emerged from the casino, joking and stumbling against one another as they waited for their car. The men were obviously businessmen and the women just as obviously the evening's entertainment.

"They call him *die Schlange!*" the younger man said.

The girls tittered.

Paul started back toward the Wyoming but Ray took his arm.

"One more thing," he said. "How about a little advance on that finder's fee? I mean, I've got a couple checks coming in but you never know. The mail and everything. Fifty marks, say? You mind?"

Headlights swept across them as a long white limousine pulled into the driveway. Paul and Ray stepped up on the curb to clear the way.

"It'll come out of research," Paul told him.

"Fine, great. You're a lifesaver, old buddy."

As he got out the money Paul was only vaguely aware that the sounds of merriment had died away. It wasn't until Ray said, "Hello there, honey," that he looked up and saw one of the women, a waiflike oriental in a silk miniskirt, coming toward them. She was staring at Paul with fierce concentration.

"Hey, Kristy," the older man called.

Paul noticed that the back door of the limousine was open and that the other couple was staring out in mild surprise. He was aware of the older man standing on the other side of the car, his frowning image reflected in the polished surface of the roof, sparkling beneath dozens of tiny lights that bordered the awning. But only at the last moment did he realize that the girl's face had become a mask of fury.

And then she hit him.

CHAPTER
12

HER HAND EXPLODED ON HIS CHEEK. PAUL STEPPED back and raised an arm to protect himself. The girl, Kristy, came after him, flailing away with such fury that one of her blows knocked the money from his hands and Ray, who had just grabbed her arm, let go to run after the bills.

"Pervert bastard," Kristy was screaming. "You don't treat people that way, damn dirty pervert . . ."

She was so enraged that Paul had a hard time getting hold of one of her wrists. Meanwhile the doorman came running. He wore a maroon tuxedo with a matching top hat that tumbled to the ground when he grabbed the girl from behind. She struggled against him and he leaned back, lifting her from the ground. Instantly all the fight went out of her and she collapsed in sobs.

The doorman's concern was Paul. "Are you all right, sir?" His face was partially obscured by the girl's black hair.

Paul nodded. There was a ringing in his left ear from the first blow and his neck stung where the girl had scratched him but otherwise he was okay.

"I'm fine," he said, straightening his jacket. The doorman lowered the girl to the ground and took her by the arm. "We'll let the police take care of you, Miss Crazy." He recovered his hat and began leading the girl back to the casino. The white limousine had disappeared, its occupants not wanting to become involved in any trouble. Even the girl's companion had deserted her.

"Wait a minute," Paul said. "It's nothing serious. Why not let her go?"

"If I were you I should make a complaint." The doorman had the wide, flat face of a farmer and spoke with the moral certitude of a preacher. "You were not with the woman. I can attest to that."

"No, that's all right. I just want to talk to her."

"Eat shit," the girl said. She had stopped crying and stood glaring at Paul.

The doorman turned on her, took her by the shoulders and shook her. "You want the police?"

"I don't care," she mumbled.

"Let her go," Paul said.

Reluctantly the doorman let go of the girl but admonished her never to come there again. She was prohibited, *unerwünscht*.

As soon as she was free, the girl straightened her dress, watching Paul warily. Ray approached with a handful of bills. "How much did you have?"

"I don't know." The girl began to move away and Paul followed "Wait, damn it, I want to talk to you—"

"Go *away*, I'm legal Berliner, you don't *touch* me."

She turned and began walking toward the Ku'damm. Paul and Ray caught up with her.

"You think you know me, don't you?" She ignored him and walked faster.

"I have to talk to you."

She turned to face him. "You leave me *alone*, I'm legal now."

"You're mistaking me for someone else," Paul said slowly. "I want to know who. I want to know when and where you met him—"

"It was *you*."

Ray stepped forward and said in a conciliatory voice, "Tell me, honey. You tell me what he did."

"What for?" she said with disgust. "You're probably a pervert, too."

Paul held up five bills. "Fifty marks to tell me—or him—what happened.''

Ray whispered, ''Just don't give her *my* fifty marks.''

The girl insisted that they follow her to Breitscheidplatz, which was bright with lights from a film crew that was shooting a commercial at an outdoor cafe. Thick black cables snaked their way from a generating truck to an area bordered by a crowd that merged into mass silhouette. At the other end of the plaza stained-glass squares of the Kaiser Wilhelm carillon tower glowed transluscent-blue against the night sky, and on the rooftops of surrounding buildings names of businesses marched in tall neon letters interspersed with gleaming company logos.

The girl stopped at a fountain where water tumbled from a marble dome over stone sculptures of figures embracing. She perched on the low wall that enclosed it, lit a cigarette and tossed the match into the water. When she spoke she addressed Ray rather than Paul. Listening to her, Paul found himself with conflicting emotions, excited by the concrete evidence that his brother existed, repelled by what Karl had done.

The girl told them that two years ago she had been brought from Thailand to work in a brothel. She arrived with fifteen other girls, all from Asia. They worked for three months and then returned home. The day before they left the girls were told that a very important man was coming, a man with specific tastes. He didn't like makeup or high heels or sexy clothing. They were to appear before him fresh, clean, like schoolgirls.

Most of the girls were excited. The great hope was always that an important man, a rich man, would take a special fancy to one of them and make her his mistress. This was called ''going private.'' There were rumors that such things had happened before, that Asian women had been put up in apartments and given resident permits. So excitement ran high on the day that the man arrived. Of course, some of the girls felt naked without makeup and tried to sneak a light blush or a faint lip gloss, but Madam Tran, who ran the place, had a sharp eye and made them wash it off. There would be no makeup.

''Then *he* came,'' the girl said, pointing to Paul. ''And nobody knows what kind of harm he has in his heart, so we are all smiling and each one he looked at until he chose me. 'You're so lucky,' my friend Lani told me when he pointed to me. But I'm not so lucky because he hurt me with the enema stick. I said 'no' because I don't like that preference. I told him, some other girls it's okay for that kind of thing. He should choose them but he wouldn't listen. Instead, he tied up my hands and feet, and then the boiling water came. He *hurt* me." She turned to Paul and pointed. "*He* did that. You *know* you did . . ."

Paul felt himself drawing away, trying to become detached the way he did when he was in the field. It was the only way he could listen to her story, which evoked memory of his dream, or whatever it was. "Where did this happen?" he asked quietly.

"You know very damn good where it was."

"Please tell me anyway."

"At Vanilla Rose Club, you pervert—"

"Ahh," Ray said. "The Vanilla Rose."

"You know it?"

"A specialty whorehouse supplied by a couple of ex-G.I.'s and run by a guy named Otto Wenzler. Very decadent *and* very expensive. Your brother's got to be living in the West. Visitors from the East can only bring in fifteen Eastmarks. Not enough to buy a watered Coke in a place like the Vanilla Rose."

While they spoke the girl busied herself with her hair, brushing it in swift businesslike strokes with a gold-flecked pink brush. Now she tucked the brush into her purse and asked for her fifty marks. Her eyes were already scanning the plaza, looking for her next client. Paul asked more questions about Karl—about himself as far as she was concerned—but the girl knew nothing more. He gave her the fifty marks and took a picture with the Ricoh—which surprised her and brought forth a string of over-the-shoulder obscenities as she walked away.

Paul stared after her. "She wouldn't believe it wasn't me," he said.

"You sure you haven't been to Berlin before?" Ray asked in a tone of mock skepticism.

Paul gave him a black look.

"Kidding, kidding," Ray said quickly

Paul turned and began retracing their steps. Ray hurried after him and the two walked in silence. Finally Paul said, "The Vanilla Rose. Give me some background."

"Kind of an international consortium," Ray said, relieved to be on a neutral subject. "The G.I.'s get the girls in Asia—Thailand, Vietnam and the Philippines mostly—bring them over here on Interflug for a sixty percent savings off Pan Am."

"Interflug? They come in through the East?"

"You got it. That's where Otto Wenzler comes in. He's got contacts East and West, the original Berlin swami, knows all, hears all, sees all. Originally a street kid, came out of the rubble gangs but you'd never know it. Very pretentious fellow, very much involved in social functions—theater, opera, Berlin Philharmonic. Regular Tuxedo Joe, but you turn him over and up pops the major domo of specialty whorehouses. Meaning very young girls. The kind who look like daddy's little daughter—none over five feet, hardly any tits, supposed to look thirteen although their passports say they're sixteen and their eyes say they're thirty. Anyway, they're all professionals, all presumed volunteers and they make more money in three months than they can make in three years back home so nobody complains. The kids are happy, daddy's happy, and Otto Wenzler's very rich."

They had arrived back at the casino. Paul gave Ray the advance he'd asked for and told him to call him at the hotel in the morning.

Ray stuffed the bills into his pants pocket and slapped Paul on the arm. "Don't worry," he said. "Now that we know he's real, we'll find him."

After Ray disappeared Paul had the doorman call a cab. As they waited, the man offered sympathy for the earlier incident.

"You were generous not to press charges, sir."

Paul shrugged.

The doorman stepped close and spoke in a low voice. A lacework of broken veins discolored his sunken cheeks and his watery blue eyes invited Paul's confidence.

"She was a foreigner, of course. They have no respect, these new ones. In the old days such a thing would never happen. But now? Too many *Ausländer, ja?*"

"Right," Paul said. "Give me a good old-fashioned German whore any day."

The doorman's complacent smile faded as a taxi arrived and Paul hopped in.

"The Vanilla Rose," he told the driver. "You know where that is?"

"Do I know where my mother lives?"

The cab shot forward, cutting off a Fiat that proceeded to tailgate them for the next three blocks, blinking its headlights.

The Vanilla Rose was located in Neukoln, a working-class district adjoining the Wall. On one side of the street were small neighborhood shops, most of them closed; on the other side, a canal with dark water glistening beneath overhanging trees. At first glance the Vanilla Rose seemed like a poor candidate for a bed of iniquity. No light came from the shuttered windows, but a porch light shone brightly over the entrance and a stained-glass rose worked into the mahogany door glowed with light from inside.

Paul looked for a bell, there was none. He opened the door and stepped into a small anteroom, dimly lit. Directly ahead there was a short hallway with a carpeted stairway at the end. From beyond an archway on the right, music, laughter and light spilled into the hall. There was another door on the left, and it was here that a Vietnamese woman wearing an elegant Bao Dai appeared. She was a type that Paul remembered from the war, her smooth skin stretched tight over a patrician face, thin lips made larger with red lipstick, flared eyebrows drawn in dark pencil like a raven's wings outstretched in flight.

"Madam Tran?" Paul asked.

He expected her to be surprised that he knew her name. Instead she surprised him.

"Good evening, Herr Alexander. Are you joining us for pleasure or are you here to see Herr Wenzler?"

"What?"

"Are you here on business or pleasure this evening?"

His surprise must have shown on his face. Madam Tran cocked her head to one side. "Is something wrong, Herr Alexander?"

"Nothing, nothing . . . I just—I'm fine."

"So. You are here to see Herr Wenzler?"

"Is he here?"

Again the quizzical look.

"Doesn't he know you're coming?"

"I'm pretty sure he doesn't."

"Let me call and see." She indicated a settee beneath the stairway. "Please."

Paul walked to the settee but rather than sit down he stepped into the parlor, where the air was thick with cigarette smoke and perfume. What unnerved him were the girls. Girls on the verge of puberty who looked as if they'd gathered for a slumber party. They wore pinafores and little chemises and skimpy teddies and knee socks and smocks.

He saw a girl on the couch who couldn't have been more than ten. Amber-skinned and blonde, she wore lacy panties and a rose silk camisole. Her slight build was a child's. Slender hips and legs, delicate shoulders and arms with barely a hint of breasts beneath the luminous folds of the camisole. The man next to her had taken off his jacket and loosened his tie. His shirt was partly unbuttoned and the top of his undershirt was visible. He had a florid face and receding hair and, as Paul watched, he lifted the girl and put her onto his lap. She squirmed, as if trying to get away. He leaned forward, encompassing her like a huge bear.

Without thinking Paul moved toward them. He knew where he was, he knew this was the Vanilla Rose, but the gross discrepancy between the man's heavy flaccid body and the girl's flawless delicacy repelled him. The girl was too young; she just couldn't know what she was doing . . .

As he crossed the room, another girl greeted him in an oriental wind-chime voice, but Paul ignored her. His attention was fixed on the blonde girl. By the time he reached the couch, his fists were clenched.

Twisting on the man's lap, the girl became aware of Paul and looked up. Instantly the impression of innocence was shattered. The girl had a lascivious yet elfish face. Her lipstick and eye makeup were matching shades of purple, her false eyelashes were silver. Close up, Paul could see that her hair was dyed and her skin did not have the childish purity that he had imagined.

"Hi, honey," she said. "You wish to wait for me?"

"Hey," the man protested, "not my little birdie. You're mine for the night, little birdie." He nuzzled her neck and the girl giggled.

Paul felt foolish—and sickened.

Madam Tran returned. "Herr Wenzler is at home," she said. "A reception of some sort; you will see."

She led him down a hall and ushered him out the back door. As Paul stepped past her, Madam Tran sniffed. "You smell like an American tonight, Herr Alexander."

He looked at her in surprise. His Berlin accent, he knew, was pure. Madam Tran smiled. "Mennen Aftershave. You didn't think I'd notice?"

She closed the door, leaving him at the edge of an irregularly shaped cobblestone plaza bordered by the backs of homes and apartment buildings. Two streetlights threw double shadows from a lone tree in the middle of the plaza. From open windows came suburban sounds: people eating dinner, a child crying, someone playing piano,

the sound of radio and television. Strange juxtaposition, the Vanilla
Rose next to these average, everyday homes. Paul wondered how he
was supposed to know which one was Wenzler's.

His problem was resolved a moment later when a porch light
blinked on near an atrium across the plaza and a man appeared in silhouette and called into the darkness.

"Herr Alexander?"

"Coming," Paul said.

At least he knew for certain his brother's last name now. Alexander. Karl Alexander. A madam and a whoremaster had established
that much.

As he approached, details began to emerge. The harsh porch light
glistened off coal-black hair and threw shadows over mannequinish
features. The man stepped back, holding open the door for him. He
was well-built, over twenty-five, dressed in a tuxedo. As Paul passed,
he noted that the man was wearing a sapphire stud in one ear.

"We're having a reception for Ernesto Guianni," the man said, a
slight hint of reproof in his voice. "If you don't mind, Otto asks that
you use the servants' stairway."

So this was not Herr Wenzler. This was, what? The doorman? The
aide-de-camp? The companion?

From down the hall came the sound of voices and wineglasses and
laughter; a reception in full swing. Someone was playing the piano,
and Paul heard the unmistakable voice of Ernesto Guianni raised in
song. It was a Jekyll and Hyde situation . . . Wenzler hosting this
reception for a famous opera singer while teen-age prostitutes writhed
in mock passion less than a block away.

"This way, Herr Alexander."

His escort led Paul through a narrow door and up a circular stair-
case to the second floor, where they stepped out into a wide, thickly
carpeted hallway. Track lighting focused pools of light on what
looked like original artwork. Obviously Wenzler was involved in a
lot more than the Vanilla Rose.

With his fingers trailing through the air, the man went to a carved
oak door, knocked twice and entered. Otto Wenzler sat at a desk
arranging a line of cocaine on an upturned mirror. He wore a tuxedo
with a silver cummerbund. His blond hair hung pale and damp
around his neck and everything around him, from the jeweled ring he
wore on his little finger to the bronze statue on the desk, was meant
to impress.

Wenzler glanced up and nodded. "Thank you, Helmut."

Not knowing how well he was supposed to know Helmut, Paul simply nodded a polite goodbye. As soon as they were alone, Wenzler said pleasantly, "I detest surprises, Karl. Particularly when I'm entertaining."

"I'm sorry." Paul said, wondering how long he could keep up this impersonation.

Wenzler blinked in surprise, moving his head in a nervous, staccato fashion.

"A red-letter day!" he said. "That's the first time I've ever heard you say you were sorry for anything. You must be getting old, Karl, coming here like this, taking such risks . . ."

He pulled a large gray envelope from the drawer and tossed it across the desk. "I suppose you want these."

With the eerie feeling that he had stepped out of his own clothes and into those of a stranger, Paul picked up the envelope.

"I'd offer you a line," Wenzler said, "but I know you confine your vices to a different arena."

Placing one end of a glass tube to his nose, Wenzler inhaled the cocaine, first one nostril, then the other. Paul barely noticed. He unwound the red twine holding the flap shut, reached inside and took out two passports, one a familiar American blue, the other the dark green of West Germany. Opening each in turn, he found two matching driver's licenses, American and German. The names on each were different but it wasn't the names that caught his eye, it was the face—his own face—pictured in photographs that he knew had never been taken. Not of him.

It was like looking into a tiny, wallet-sized mirror. The hair was a little shorter, combed differently, but other than that there was no difference. But studying the photo more closely, it seemed to him that there was something different about the eyes. Not their size or shape but their expression. Alien, not him.

He held in his hands the proof of his brother's existence. He was only vaguely aware that Otto was telling him about the performance that night; that it had been opening night and that the reception for Ernesto Guianni had lured even those of Berlin's social elite who normally snubbed him. After a moment, Otto stopped.

"What is it? Something wrong?"

Paul said, "This is my brother." The impersonation couldn't go on, he couldn't manage it. He'd have to take his chances on the truth.

"Who?"

"The man in the passport. It's not me, it's my brother."

Otto held up a cautionary hand. "Don't tell me, please. I only like to know secrets of the kind that make other people uncomfortable. Your secrets, Karl, are the kind that would make *me* uncomfortable."

"Mr. Wenzler, listen to me. I'm not the man you think I am. I'm not Karl, I'm Paul Stafford, his twin brother."

"Of course," Otto said with a sardonic grin. "And I'm the Queen of England with a frog up my ass."

He snickered and slid the drug paraphernalia back into a drawer. Paul stepped forward and held the passport photo next to his face.

"I'm serious. I'm not this man. I'm Paul Stafford—this man is my brother. I came to Berlin to find him and I need your help. Do you understand?"

Otto looked him carefully up and down. "You are not Karl Alexander?"

"My name is Paul Stafford. I'm an American. Here." Paul pulled out his wallet and flipped it open to display his driver's license and *Herald* I.D. card.

"Karl is my brother. We're twins but we were separated when we were young. I never knew I had a brother until a few days ago. Now I need to find him. I've got to know . . ."

A hooded look came into Wenzler's eyes.

"May I have those back, please?"

He reached for the passports but Paul moved away.

"In return for telling me how to get in touch with my brother."

"I believe you. You are not Karl. If you were, you would know better than to try and hold me up."

"Just a trade. My passports for your information."

"*Your* passports? Those belong to me."

"Not any more—"

Wenzler reached into his desk and pulled out a pistol. A lady's gun, a 25-caliber chrome-plated Beretta, but it could put holes in a man. "And now, whoever you are," Wenzler said, "I think you will give me the documents." As Paul moved to hand over the passports the door opened and a woman in a jeweled evening gown came into the room.

"You have sixty seconds to come downstairs," she announced airily. "Ernesto is doing the aria from *La Traviata*."

The woman was about sixty, imperious and a little drunk. Her dark hair was pulled tightly back and tucked beneath a tiara. Otto hastily slid the gun inside his jacket.

"I shall be right there, my dear Helena."

"You know he won't sing without you there. *Wo ist Liebling Otto?* he keeps asking. He thinks you're snubbing him, but I told him that was just your way, sneaking off to your little debaucheries."

At which point she turned to Paul, looked him up and down. "You are a debaucherie, aren't you? Or are you a servant?"

"Countess, if you please—" Wenzler began.

"A guest," Paul said. "And I'd love to hear Signore Guianni sing the aria."

He moved toward her. Behind him, Wenzler called, "Mr. Stafford, we have business . . ."

Paul turned at the door. "I think the countess is right. Art before business." And he offered her his arm. "Sir Cedric Stafford. Shall we?"

The woman touched her chin to her shoulder and regarded him with amusement.

"We shall find out," she said. "Come along, Otto."

The countess took Paul's arm with ring-encrusted fingers and allowed him to lead her down the hallway.

"Are you really British?" she asked.

"Right now I am."

"Ahh, I knew it. Your teeth aren't bad enough to be British. They breed wonderful dogs and horses but have coal miners for dentists."

Paul decided that the countess wasn't as foolish or tipsy as she appeared.

Wenzler caught up with them midway down the hall and grabbed Paul's arm, stopping them.

"One moment, please. Excuse me, countess, but this man has something of mine."

She raised an eyebrow. "Does he? How exciting. What is it?"

"This," Paul said.

He pulled out a passport, flipped it open and held it toward the countess so that she could see the photograph without reading the name. At the same time he leaned close to Wenzler.

"You be the judge," he went on. "Is that me or Herr Wenzler?"

Wenzler lunged at the passport but Paul pulled it away. "Let the lady judge."

"Don't be rude, Otto. It's our Sir Cedric's picture, no question. Now come on, Ernesto is waiting." She pushed between them, took each by the arm and led them to the top of a stairway that descended in two circular flights, mirror images of one another, one to the left and one to the right. Below, in a richly appointed foyer, a dozen people in formal evening clothes stood sipping champagne and waving jeweled wrists. A waiter in a pink jacket with a black carnation in the lapel offered drinks from a silver tray.

As they descended, Wenzler craned to see into the drawing room, looking, Paul guessed, for his partner Helmut. Rather than wait for the two of them to get together and figure out how to deal with him, Paul abruptly pulled away at the bottom of the stairs.

"I left the car in a no parking zone," he said. "Be right back."

Followed by the countess' protests and Wenzler's murderous glare, he ducked through the crowd to the front door. As he brushed past a surprised doorman he had one final glimpse of Wenzler pointing him out to the man called Helmut. Then he was on the street, running. At the end of the block he turned right, kept jogging and changing directions until he was sure that nobody was following. Then he went to a pay phone and called Wenzler.

"How's the party going?" he asked.

"You must be brothers," Wenzler said, ice in his voice. "You both take chances with your lives."

"Don't worry about it. If Karl wants his passports, tell him to get in touch with me. I'm in Room 317 at the InterContinental."

In the background Paul could hear the aria.

After that, matters moved with German efficiency. By the time he got back to the hotel a message was waiting: "Your brother will meet you at the Spree Bowl, Peoples Republic Plaza, GDR, at noon tomorrow."

Paul read the note twice. In his room he went to the window and looked out. The circus tent glowed a milky white in the yard below. Beyond it, the blackness of the Tiergarden and beyond the Tiergarden, East Berlin, dark and somber except for its modern television tower topped with a silver globe that hung like a metal moon over the divided city. The GDR. East Berlin. Where he would find Karl Alexander. A killer. His brother. His blood.

CHAPTER
13

THE PALAST DER REPUBLIK WAS A FIVE-STORY CON-
crete and glass building situated where the baroque Hohenzollern pal-
ace once stood. Its primarily function was as the home of the East
German parliament, but for no apparent reason the ground floor also
contained a disco, a nightclub and bowling alley, all of which overlooked the rock-embanked Spree River. The entrances were visible
from the opposite side of the river, which was why Karl Alexander
chose this spot to meet his brother. He sat in his car, monitoring the
entrance to the Spree Bowl through binoculars.

Through the large picture windows, Karl could see the bowlers
going through their slow-motion three-step and the spectators who sat
off to one side drinking beer and eating pizza. A group of tourists
passed, obscuring his vision. Karl lowered the binoculars and waited
for them to take pictures of a slow-moving barge and its bare-chested
bow helmsman. It was almost twelve . . .

Karl had been shaken by the phone call from Otto Wenzler. The
man's obvious distress bothered him as much as the news itself. Otto
wasn't the type to panic.

"I thought he was you," he kept repeating. "I was sure of it."

"Calm down, Otto."

"I prefer to be upset. I don't deal in dirty passports any longer, Karl. It's ridiculous for a man in my position. I do it only as a favor to you."

"Can you get me replacements."

"Aren't you going to meet him?"

"If I do it's to recover the photos. The names are blown. I need replacements, all right?"

"By Wednesday? These are originals, you know. Its not so easy."

It was never so easy with Otto. Since difficult things cost more, everything with Otto was difficult. They had known each other since childhood, when both were members of the same rubble gang. Then Karl began his life with Uncle Alex and lost contact with Otto. Fifteen years later Otto's name appeared in a Stasis file; he was picked up trying to smuggle a professor and his wife into West Berlin. Karl offered him amnesty. All Otto had to do in exchange was to infiltrate other flight-helper groups and tip off the Stasis.

It was the beginning of a long-standing association whose emphasis shifted over the years from the political to the private. Karl's aid in smoothing the transit of the Vanilla Rose girls was just one of a number of business relationships. It was less risky than Otto supposed. The East German authorities had little interest in stopping a practice that proved that capitalism and degeneracy went together.

Because it was such short notice, Karl agreed to pay double the price for replacements. When he agreed so quickly Otto's curiosity was aroused.

"Just what kind of operation is this?"

"You know better than to ask."

"You mean I know better than to ask *you*?"

Karl spoke quietly and clearly. "Otto, if you so much as make an inquiry, someone will bury you in the Spree . . . Now tell me about this man. Could he have been an imposter?"

"I don't see how." Otto's tone was abrupt, showed his hurt. He didn't like threats. But he took this one from Karl.

"Plastic surgery?"

"No, no. He fooled everyone. Madam Tran, Helmut, me. Even when he told me, I didn't believe. If this man is not your brother, I'll kiss the cross and become a priest . . ."

His brother. Karl lay awake that night, his emotions running high.

If Paul Stafford was an imposter, then he was in trouble. Only one organization had the skills and resources to perform a facial reconstruction so complete that it could fool Otto: the CIA. Had they discovered who was responsible for the assassinations and sent someone to capture or kill him? If so, why the elaborate deception? Why the oblique approach?

Unless it was the KGB.

The thought truly chilled him. What if the Redeye plot had been discovered? Uncle Alex betrayed? He had said that there were others involved. The map of the Bayonne Terminal, the cargo manifest and the Sony-disguised CIKOP-34F—all these had come from a source inside the KGB. And what about the girl, Marina? The one who was to sabotage the infra-red defense capability on the General Secretary's aircraft. Had she been caught? Broken?

No, Karl thought, if the KGB knew he'd already be dead.

Which brought him back to the possibility that the man Paul Stafford was actually his twin brother. The idea gave him a chill. He had to be careful. He had to make certain. If Paul Stafford *was* his brother, then the visit must be an innocent one, the timing accidental. But if he was an imposter . . . if he was an imposter he would soon be a dead one. And if he was his brother . . . Well, one thing was certain . . . whoever he was, Paul Stafford could not be allowed to interfere with the Redeye assignment.

Karl glanced at his watch. Five minutes after twelve. The man was late. He would give him another fifteen minutes and then he would call Otto.

Paul had actually gotten up early. He'd eaten a heavy German breakfast, pored over a map to the city and caught the eleven-thirty S-Bahn to the Friedrichstrasse Station. The station was inside the Eastern sector but since the trains went only to the West, little effort had been spent in maintaining the place. The atmosphere was gloomy and not improved by the dour guards who roamed the long platforms in their rumpled gray uniforms or sat watching from crosswalks high above the tracks, profiled by grimy glass walls, cradling rifles in their arms. A worker's paradise, Paul thought. For guards.

The border formalities took longer than he expected. He had to stand in line before entering a narrow stall where a sad-eyed official sold him a one-day Cinderella visa—he had to be out of East Berlin by midnight or face arrest—and then join another line to exchange twenty-five Westmarks for an equal number of grossly inflated East-marks. By the time he reached the street he was running late.

He took a taxi down the Unter den Linden, surprised that so many of the once-elegant buildings still showed bullet scars from the war. The famous tree-lined boulevard was made melancholy by the host of rooftop statues looking down from above, marooned in mid-air, searching for their lost city.

Paul's excitement rose as they approached the Palast der Republik. He hoped Karl would be waiting when he got there, but it didn't sur-prise him when he wasn't. He was probably a careful man, unlikely to show himself unless he felt safe. As he waited he wondered if the threat of CIA exposure would force Karl to stop the killings. He hated to think of his brother as an assassin, but the false passports and driver's licenses proved Karl was involved in clandestine activi-ties, and any doubts he'd had about Karl's responsibility for the CIA killings were gone. There was only one explanation for his dreams— the one Annie Helms had proposed. He could imagine her excitement if she found out he had a twin brother, but whether or not he would tell her would depend on Karl . . .

The rumble of bowling balls and clatter of pins seemed an odd counterpoint to what had brought him here. Paul sipped his coffee, tried to control his impatience. It was possible Karl feared a trap and had decided not to meet him. But finally a waiter approached and told him that he had a phone call. Paul got up and went to the counter, where a red-haired girl handed him the phone.

"Hello?"

"Paul Stafford?"

It was like listening to an echo of his own voice.

"It's me. Are you Karl?"

"Yes. I prefer to meet you outside. You have no objection?"

"Anywhere you want—"

"All right, then. Leave the Spree Bowl, turn right and when you reach Rathaus-strasse, turn left. Keep walking on the left-hand side of the street. I will pick you up."

Paul gave the cashier two marks and went outside. It was almost twelve-thirty and the sidewalks were beginning to fill with business-men and secretaries on their lunch breaks. One couple sat on a grassy embankment overlooking the river and ate sandwiches from a paper bag. A group of teen-agers in a parking lot performed skateboard tricks. There was no sign of Karl.

Paul followed the instructions, crossed the Spree and headed toward the old town hall, the Rotes Rathaus. He'd gone a block and a half when a white Mercedes 280 E detached itself from the oncoming traffic and came quickly to a stop beside him. The driver leaned over and opened the door.

His hair is neater was Paul's first thought.

In the first moment of recognition, their eyes caught and Paul saw in Karl's face surprise, suspicion, pleasure, distrust and . . . fear? Or were these his own feelings? For a moment Karl's features seemed blurred by emotions, and then the moment passed, and Paul was staring at a man who looked exactly like him and not like a murderer at all.

"Get in," Karl said.

Paul slid inside and shut the door. Karl quickly drove off.

"Why all the precautions?"

"In case you were followed."

"By whom?"

No answer. Karl swerved quickly to the inside lane and turned left. Two more blocks he turned left again, down a side street blocked at the far end by a construction project. A tall crane loomed over a concrete foundation surrounded by steel girders and bordered by a chain-link fence, open to permit access to work trucks.

Barely slowing, Karl turned into the construction area. The car bumped up over the dirt-packed curb and headed for a gate on the opposite side, leaving a trail of dust in its wake. Workmen paused and a man in a hard hat got out of a rusty trailer and shouted after them. Karl paid no attention. A moment later they had regained the street on the opposite side of the project.

"More precautions?" Paul said.

"My work with the government makes such measures necessary. It is all right now."

"Just what is your work with the government?"

"I'm an instructor at the Eichwalde Combat School. Commando training, you would call it." Karl gave him a sidelong glance. "Otto said you were an American."

"I am."

"You speak German like a Berliner."

"I lived here until I was five. My mother and I still speak it."

"Your mother is alive . . . ?"

"*Our* mother is alive."

Karl looked startled.

Paul said, "You didn't know?"

"No."

"That's how I found out about you."

"I was told she was dead . . . killed by an American bomb."

"Told by who? Tante Inge?"

Karl's reaction couldn't have been greater if Paul had tossed a live grenade on the floor. He turned toward him, the car swerved across the road and back again as he fought to bring it under control. He pulled over and stopped the car. His hands gripped the steering wheel so tightly that the muscles in his forearms bulged. When he turned to Paul his face was deadly pale.

"Who are you?"

"Doesn't the face tell you?"

"How could you know about her?"

"Tante Inge?"

Karl winced, and Paul thought, my God, he's more upset than mom was. He told him the story of their early separation, leaving out any mention of the CIA or of the dreams. At one point Karl became agitated and broke in:

"You're sure?" he demanded, "You're *sure* she was not my aunt?"

"According to mother she was a downstairs neighbor. All the kids called her *aunt.*"

"Not my aunt," Karl muttered.

"You thought she really was?"

"I was a child. What could I know?"

"Where is she now?"

"She's dead."

Paul realized he had been trying somehow to reconcile the CIA killings with the man sitting beside him, this person made in his own image, this person linked so intimately to him, whether he liked it or not. Until the mention of Inge Heusner it had been nearly impossible. Now, seeing the change in his brother's expression, there could be no more doubts. Karl's eyes narrowed, his lips compressed, his clenched teeth accentuated the jaw. There was hatred there—hatred and a remorselessness that seemed to chill the air around them. Yes, Paul thought, he's capable of it, all right. He's capable of murder. His twin, from the same genes—he pushed *that* out of his mind.

Karl returned the conversation to the details of their separation.

What seemed to bother him most of all was why their mother hadn't tried to find him.

"She did," Paul said. "She looked for months. She kept going to the police—"

"The police," Karl said derisively. "What could they do? We were hiding from the police—"

"She thought you were dead, Karl. Someone saw Frau Heusner take you into the shop. Mom thought they had . . ."

"Butchered me?"

Paul nodded.

Karl looked away, his expression seemed to soften. "Still," he said, "she should have said something later. To you. To her husband and her family."

"She was ashamed."

"Of me?"

"Of what she'd done. Of what she thought happened to you."

Karl nodded, but Paul sensed the answer didn't really satisfy him.

"And where is my . . . my mother?"

"She lives in Florida. A little house on a man-made lake. She and dad—my stepfather—are separated."

"All these years I thought she had been killed in the bombing," Karl said in a distant voice. "I used to dream about her. I never knew her face but I dreamed that she covered me with her body and saved my life." He gave Paul a sidelong glance "But it was you she saved."

"What?"

"She took you to the hospital; she left me behind."

Stunned. He thought Karl would be happy to know about his mother. Instead, he blamed her. He had his own guilts, he realized, about being the one their mother had saved and his reaction was as much defensive as it was in defense of his mother when he said, "She was nineteen years old. You can't blame her for what happened—"

"*I* was fourteen months."

As if that settled the matter, Karl started the car and moved back onto the highway. Paul was about to argue that nobody could entirely protect another person, when he remembered hearing those same words before. Not from his lips but from Joanna's in response to something he had said. And what had he told her? That there were no excuses in raising children. The arrogance of it brought a quick sting of regret.

Karl was asking him something but Paul had missed it. "What?"

Karl gave him a curious glance. He had regained his composure. "How did you find Otto Wenzler?"

"A girl, a hooker," Paul said.

"What girl?"

"Her name was Kristy. From Thailand. She tried to beat me up last night. It seems that she once worked at the Vanilla Rose, and when she saw me on the street she thought I was you. It seems you play rough with the girls." An understatement, as he knew from the dream.

"And from this girl you learned about Otto?"

"No, from Otto I learned about Otto. When he realized his mistake—that I wasn't you—he got nasty and pulled a gun."

"Which you ignored?"

"We were interrupted. Fortunately."

"Yes, you seem to have fortune on your side."

"Not always," Paul said.

"When not?"

There was an eagerness to the question that made Paul uncomfortable.

"I guess I've had my share of disappointments."

"Oh. Disappointments."

Again the defensive feeling. "I suppose getting out of Germany was lucky," he said. "The army was a secure life, we had good housing, clothes, plenty to eat—all the good old American perks."

"When you were a child did you have a bedroom of your own?"

"Most of the time."

"And when you shut the door, would they leave you alone?"

"Who?"

"Your mother, your father, everyone."

"I guess . . ." A strange question. "What about you? Where did you live?"

"Berlin," he said and quickly switched the subject to America, about which his curiosity seemed insatiable. Paul in turn wanted to find out more about Karl but sensed he'd better go easy. He was still a shock to Karl, and he was, after all, dealing with an explosive personality.

So as they drove on, Paul mostly answered questions about his childhood and career as a journalist. He showed his discomfort over

Karl's questions about Joanna, how they'd met, why Paul hadn't married earlier. Karl was watching him closely now, and Paul realized why . . . he had discovered an area of uncertainty, an area where Paul felt defensive. He had zeroed right in on it. Paul had done the same thing in interviews, looking for a crack through which he could get at the person behind the persona.

Paul tried to get back the control of this bizarre meeting. "You know I came here to find out about you, about your life. You've been digging into me and my past—"

"So I am like you, then."

Not exactly, he thought, I'm not a killer. He asked if Karl was married.

"I have one wife and three children; two girls and a boy."

One wife and three children. As if they were objects, not people.

"Does your wife work?"

"Sometimes she teaches swimming for the Young Pioneers." All very matter-of-fact, as if Karl was reporting facts for a census taker. No matter how Paul tried to dig below the surface, Karl resisted. He either had no strong emotional ties to his family or he kept them well guarded.

They turned off the main highway and entered Treptow Park. Dappled sunlight filtered through the trees, flew up the hood and over the windshield. The road curved gently as it rose to the crest of the hill overlooking a lake with a small harbor dotted with sailboats and canoes. As they approached, an open-decked sightseeing boat began backing away from the pier.

They parked the car and went to an outdoor cafe where a youthful trio was singing folksongs in rudimentary English. Each table was sheltered by an orange umbrella that shuddered and flapped in the breeze. The place was alive with conversation, music and children playing at an adjacent playground.

"Do you have a picture of her?" Karl asked as soon as they were seated.

For a moment Paul thought he meant a picture of Joanna; then he realized Karl wanted to see his mother. He took out a photo of mom and Joanna and himself taken a few years ago. Karl inspected it.

"You can keep it if you want."

With barely a nod, Karl slid the photo into his coat pocket. A waiter appeared with menus and did a double-take.

"You must be twins," he announced.

"Why would you say that?" said Paul, straight-faced.

"Well, because otherwise—" the man finally realized Paul was joking, raised his eyebrows, puffed out his cheeks and laughed. "Otherwise I drank too much last night."

Karl ordered them both something called a *Berliner Weisse mit Schuss*, a bubbling local concoction of white beer with a dash of raspberry syrup. When it arrived Karl held up his mug for Paul's inspection.

"Cheap champagne," he said, and actually smiled. They drank. Later Paul would remember there had not been a toast.

CHAPTER

14

THE BEER AND THE WARM SUN RELAXED PAUL enough to make him aware of the strain he was under. Dealing with a physical duplicate of himself was more of a strain than he'd thought it would be. Especially when he allowed himself to think that this duplicate, his brother, was an assassin. He considered saving the question of CIA killings for another day but forced himself to push ahead. To know himself, to understand himself, he had to at least understand his brother.

His chance came when Karl became distracted by something behind him. Paul turned to look. A family had just sat down at a nearby table, a man and his wife and a couple of kids. One of the little boys was pointing toward them. When Paul turned, the mother slapped the child's arm gently and leaned down to whisper in his ear.

"Those people are looking at us," Karl said, tight-lipped.

Paul shrugged. "So what?"

"It doesn't bother you?"

"Why should it?"

"I am not entertainment."

Paul picked up on it: "You should tell them what you do for a living. They wouldn't think that was entertainment."

Karl had been toying with some coins on the table, stacking them in a neat cone according to size and running his fingers up and down the edges. Now his hand froze.

"You mean my teaching?"

"I mean Kelso, Manheim, Durning, Wilson, Schrader and Beaumier."

As he spoke the names it seemed to Paul that Karl's personality contracted, pulled away from the body leaving a shell with two empty eyes gazing at him.

"Whom do you work for?"

"I told you: The Washington *Herald*."

"You know what I mean."

"You mean do I work with the CIA? As of this moment, no. As of tomorrow, maybe. That could depend on you. I know what you do, Karl. I know you're some kind of contract killer, probably for the KGB . . . You're also my brother, more important—you're my mother's son. The CIA doesn't know about you yet. I might be convinced to let it stay that way. On one condition—no more killing."

Karl seemed not to be breathing. And Paul suddenly realized something else he'd pushed out of his mind: this man could decide to kill *him*.

"You say the CIA doesn't know," Karl finally said. "But you know. How is that?"

It was time for the truth. Paul took a deep breath and told him about the dreams, about the stories in Black Cat Magazine and about the CIA men coming to see him. Karl just looked at him. When he showed him a couple of back issues of Black Cat he'd brought along and told him to note the date, Karl said, "A man can have anything printed, with the help of the CIA. Why else would anyone publish such . . . dreams?"

"Nightmares. Names and particulars. It's not pleasant. But you know that—or maybe you don't. Maybe you like killing, I don't know."

Karl shook his head, sat back in his chair, and toyed with the coins. At least he's nervous, Paul thought. Which gave him some hope that maybe he could break through the defenses and get a look at the man underneath. He had to do that if he was ever going to begin to understand how a man made in his own image, whose genes and parents he shared, could commit murder. And to reassure himself that he was not that kind of man.

Karl followed Paul's glance and became aware of what he was doing, running his fingers over the stack of coins. He slipped them into his pocket, not pleased at this outward sign of his inner feelings. He was not prepared to deal with a brother who also knew about his wet assignments for the KGB. And he rebelled at accepting *dreams* as an explanation for this knowledge.

"If it's any help to you," Paul was saying, "I didn't believe it myself until mother told me about you."

"I would prefer to speak in English," Karl said.

"You're a man of many talents."

Hearing Karl now speak English gave Paul chills. The uncanny similarity between them was reinforced: this man, his brother, who spoke with his voice, now used the same words and sounds and meanings that he used.

Continuing in English, Karl leaned forward and said, "How do I know you are not with the CIA right now?"

A good question and Paul had no answer. "Can't you tell when I'm telling the truth?"

"Can you tell with me?"

Good questions again. His answer wasn't, except it was true. "I hope so."

And I hope not, Karl thought. It made him uneasy to have this person, a double in appearance, sitting there, watching him, analyzing him . . .

"The CIA could have given you details of the killings before you wrote those stories."

"They didn't."

"It makes more sense than dreams."

"You made most of them look like accidents, remember?"

"The CIA is not stupid. They may guess what they cannot prove."

So now he finally admits it? Paul leaned forward. "Dan Kelso: you hit him in the stomach before you threw him overboard. Could they guess that? The girl, Lisle Beaumier—what was it you said? '*I want to lick you dry*'?"

Karl was on his feet, disbelief, even fear on his face.

"The dreams," Paul said quietly.

Karl nodded, forced to believe now.

"That's how I know about Tante Inge."

He sat down. "You said . . . I thought your mother told you."

"She did. But only after I had been hypnotized and remembered dreams I'd had as a child. Dreams about Tante Inge."

"You know what she did?"

"Not the details. But I know she scared hell out you, made you sick with fear—at least that's how I felt when I relived the experience."

Strangely, at mention of Tante Inge, Karl's self-control seemed to reassert itself. "Tante Inge," he said. "Would you like to know what happened when you and your mother—when *my* mother—abandoned me? Do you want to know? Come, then. Know everything, brother."

He stood up, went to the cashier and put a handful of bills on the counter, walked off. Paul caught up with him, and Karl set the fast pace, eyes straight ahead. As they walked he told Paul the story of his childhood. The words poured out in staccato fashion, so fast and drenched in bitterness that Paul could barely understand.

"She sold me, you understand? While you were in America going to school and watching movies and playing childrens' games Tante Inge was bringing men into my bed. She said that one of them might be my father, that we would test to see how much they loved me. There was a record she had—the song 'Lili Marlene'—and she played it over and over while the men came into the bed and used me for their pleasure. Played with my genitals. Smeared me with oil and butter, pushed their fingers into me, pushed themselves into me. Sometimes a woman was there, sometimes Tante Inge, all together. While you were eating ice cream I had to eat them. What came proved their love, that's what Tante Inge said. 'Drink your man's milk or no food tomorrow.' That was love. And the money she used for liquor and perfume. One of the men gave me a book, an illustrated version of the *Odyssey*. I was locked in the apartment, that book was my freedom. She took it from me, threw it away. An infraction of the rules. I was to have nothing."

He walked even faster, as though propelled by the flood of hated memories. Paul stayed half a step behind. It made it more difficult to catch Karl's words, but he sensed that during this outpouring Karl didn't want to—couldn't—meet his eye. Not until the end of his recital did Karl stop and turn to face him.

"So you understand now? The world turned its back on me. *I - made - my - self!*"

Karl paused, added, "And you have no right to judge."

They had come alongside a wide meadow with a soccer field on it. Abruptly Karl threw his jacket to the ground and started running. He headed across the meadow to the soccer field, turned right and followed the perimeter, running fast, arms pumping, head back.

Paul sat down on a bench, shaken by what he had just heard. The utter depravity of Karl's childhood sickened him even as it offered a measure of understanding of Karl's later ruthlessness. Understand, but not justify. Nothing would do that entirely, but Karl's childhood went a long way toward it. The child savaged by Tante Inge and her clients had become a killer. Karl's future had been traded for Paul's health, and now years later innocent people were paying the price. More than ever Paul felt he had to stop the killings, for Karl's sake as well as his own . . .

Karl ran until he was exhausted, then stood doubled over with his hands resting on his knees as he fought to regain his breath. Paul took his coat to him. Karl straightened and took it.

"Come," Karl said, "I will take you back to West Berlin."

He was still breathing heavily. The two men began walking back toward the restaurant.

"You don't have to do that," Paul said. "Just drop me at the S-Bahn."

"It's not for you I'm going. My wife went shopping at the KaDeWe this afternoon. You know it? The big department store?"

"I passed it the other day."

"Magda goes once each month to the Western sector. We have dinner and attend the theater. If you will not mention our discussion this afternoon, you may meet her."

Paul hesitated. After what he'd heard, and already knew, he didn't altogether trust this brother. Noting his reaction, Karl smiled and said, "Unless you think I'm going to shoot you and dump your body in the Spree."

"I'd probably know it if you were."

Except he didn't believe that. He wasn't a mind reader. The only impressions he'd ever received from Karl were actual perceptions as Karl lived them. And even then it only happened when he was asleep and Karl was in a highly charged emotional state. He wished he *could* read Karl's mind, he would have felt considerably more secure.

When they returned to the restaurant Paul took out the Ricoh and asked a waiter to take a photo of the two of them. Karl objected. "I let no one take my picture.''

"It's for our mother. I want to prove you're alive.''

Karl's eyes hardened, and for a moment Paul was certain he would refuse. Then there was a subtle shift of expression and he gave in. The waiter had them stand at the entrance to the restaurant. He even had them strike an identical pose and insisted that Paul comb his hair back to match Karl's.

Before they left, Karl stopped at a concession stand and bought two packs of breath mints. Paul, wondering how he would ever be able to convince Karl to stop the killing, paid no attention to the nervous, smiling man behind the counter. As they walked to the car Karl offered Paul a pack of mints.

"Would you like one?" Paul took it and thought no more about it.

After the two men had gone, the man at the concession counter locked his shop and went to a pay phone. He took out a piece of paper and dialed the number written on it. The number was in West Berlin.

"Yes?" an unfamiliar voice answered.

"I have a message from K."

"Go ahead.''

"He bought two packs of the mints.''

"Two?''

"Yes.''

"Is he leaving now?''

The little man peered around the booth toward the parking lot.

"Yes, he's just gone.''

The line went dead. The concessions man fingered the twenty marks that he had received earlier that morning from the mysterious K. Twenty marks for a simple phone call. Too bad he couldn't duplicate the money in the same way that K seemed able to duplicate himself.

Smiling at this clever thought, the concessions man returned to his shop.

Paul returned to the CIA killings on the way back. At first, Karl seemed amused by his concern.

"They are all agents or spies or traitors. Why care about them?''

"Because I *know* when you kill. I have to live it *with* you. The crack of a spine breaking, the look on their faces, the last sound of a dying man. I feel like I'm doing it, you understand?''

"And what will you do if I refuse to stop?"

"Tell them."

"The CIA?"

"I won't be a party to murder, Karl."

Karl surprised him then. "I can understand that . . . I will talk to my superiors."

Paul should have felt relieved but despite Karl's last statement, his earlier reference to dumping Paul's body in the Spree River was not forgotten. He remained alert to every change in direction, and not until they approached the barrier on the eastern side of Checkpoint Charlie did he begin to relax.

While one of the East German *Grenzpolizei* stuck a mirror under the car another asked to see their papers. Karl flashed an identification card, and the guard, a husky young man who looked more like a farmer than a policeman, immediately straightened.

"Yes sir," he said. "And him?"

Karl handed him Paul's visa. The guard became uncomfortable. "Excuse me, sir, but this man came from the S-Bahn Friedrichstrasse station. He must return that way."

"He's returning with me."

The guard cleared his throat. "But the official regulation states—"

"If I have to get out of this car and call your superior," Karl interrupted coldly, "you will lose your job."

"One moment, sir." With a worried glance at the other *Grenzpolizist,* he ducked back inside the station.

Karl was obviously impatient at the delay, his index finger tapping nervously on the steering wheel. They sat beneath a covered plaza with stalls on either side, each facing a red-and-white-striped barrier. There was a fenced pedestrian crosswalk and beyond that no-man's-land, the wide strip of graded and raked earth that worked its jagged way round the western half of the city.

The young guard reappeared with an older man who was all crisp efficiency and accommodation. He leaned down and spoke to Karl. "Don't worry, sir. We'll take care of everything."

The red-and-white barrier was raised, a red light turned to green and they drove a hundred yards to the American side, where the U.S. Marines in full dress uniforms ignored them as they passed.

"You don't stop on this side?" Paul asked.

"Your American forces refuse to recognize a separate Berlin so they don't consider this a border. Those guards serve only the military personnel of the occupation armies.''

Paul nodded, feeling much better now that they were back in the American zone. They agreed that Karl would call tomorrow after talking with his superiors about a new assignment.

They turned into a multi-level parking garage at the KaDeWe, drove to the third level although there were a few parking places available on the second. Paul paid no attention. Why should he? He was on home territory again. He also paid no mind to the parking slot that Karl chose, bordered as it was on the driver's side by a wall and on the other side by a Volkswagen Camper.

"Until tomorrow, then," Karl said.

He offered his hand. As Paul took it the rear door opened and the car rocked as someone sat down.

"I'm sorry," Karl said, tightening his grip, leaning over and pinning Paul against his seat.

Paul instantly threw himself forward and up and might have been able to break free except for the seatbelt he hadn't yet had a chance to unfasten. From behind, an arm came around his neck and a white cloth covered his mouth.

He tried to shout but the sound was muffled and he knew it was no good. These were professionals, no one would hear. He kicked and twisted, trying to get his arms free. When he gasped for air he could tell that it wasn't chloroform they were using, it was something less smelly and more powerful.

A strange dizziness took him, and the last thing he heard, as if from a great distance, was Karl's voice, this time close to his ear, saying, "Go easy . . ."

And then darkness.

CHAPTER

15

THERE WAS NO WAY TO PREDICT AMERICANS, THE desk clerk at the InterContinental decided. Some of them wanted to be treated like kings, while others were insulted if you didn't act as if they were your best friend. Take the man in 317, Paul Stafford. When he checked in, 317 insisted on joking about the exhibition tent on the lawn. A casual man with a sense of humor. And so today, when 317 came to check out, the clerk returned the humor with a reference to the elephants and what kind of a response did he get? 317 looked up with a frown and asked, "What do you mean?"

"Nothing, sir."

"You must have meant something."

"Yes, sir. I was referring to your humorous remark the other day concerning our exhibition tent."

317 glanced outside, then gave him an empty smile.

"Oh, right . . ."

No, wrong, the clerk decided. Obviously, 317 was in no mood for familiarity. Just no predicting, or pleasing, Americans . . .

*   *   *

150

There had been no choice, Karl told himself as he waited for the elevator. Too much had happened too fast. He needed time to think things out, check facts. He needed time but there was no time. In three days he would leave for America. In three weeks the General Secretary was scheduled to land at Andrews Air Force Base. He had to be ready and there was no time to negotiate with his new-found brother. Paul's existence jeopardized the Redeye mission. There had been no choice.

When the elevator arrived a group of businessmen sporting name tags got out. Karl stepped inside, pushed the button to the third floor and checked his appearance in the mirror. The jacket, the jeans, shirt and shoes all fitted perfectly. He'd washed his hair and combed it in a freer, more casual style, and the disguise—if it could be called that—was complete. "Paul Stafford" would now gather his belongings, check out of the hotel and disappear.

Paul's room was like any other fancy hotel room, right down to the two pieces of foil-wrapped chocolate, one on each pillow, with little cards wishing each guest a good night's sleep. Outside the glass door to the balcony the top of the circus tent was visible. Karl pulled the drapes and then remembered: he was Paul Stafford, not an intruder. It was his room. No need to worry if anyone saw him.

His first task was to recover his false documents Paul had gotten. He began searching the dresser. The first drawer contained a sight-seeing guide, hotel postcards and a room-service menu. The second was stuffed with tee-shirts and underwear. As he started to run his hand along the bottom of the drawer a movement in the mirror caused him to freeze.

The door to an adjoining bedroom had opened and a man stood watching.

"Looking for these?" the man said. He held up the two passports.

Karl turned around. So his fine new brother had deceived him. Paul had said he had come alone and Karl had believed him. The man in the doorway looked CIA—the crew-cut hair, the clumsy American clothes—just like the American civilians who flooded Berlin in the nineteen-fifties.

"I told Maurice you were innocent," the man was saying. "Annie Helms thought so too. It looks like he was right and we were wrong."

Careful now, Karl thought. He wasn't blown—not yet. This man thought he was Paul, now he really had to play the part. What had

Paul told him about the CIA? They had come to him, suspicious. He met with them only a few times. And this man was one of them. He wished he had gotten more information from his brother.

"This is my room," he said coldly, buying time while he searched his memory for anything else that might help him.

"But not your passports," Hugh Roark said. "And not your driver's licenses. We checked; they're stolen. And before the police get here I'd just like to know one thing—what were you going to use these for?"

Karl judged the distance between them. Twenty feet. If he could get a little closer . . .

"Those are jokes," Karl said easily. "Look, you can tell on the back . . ."

He came forward but the CIA man slid his hand beneath his coat and came out with a gun.

"Stop there, Paul. I don't trust you anymore."

I'm not Paul, Karl felt like shouting. Caught in a trap set for his brother . . . The police had been called, the man had said. If he was arrested they would find his real I.D. The entire Redeye mission would be threatened, maybe compromised. He decided to brazen it out. Hope for an opening . . . "This is ridiculous. I'm getting the manager—"

"Paul—"

"Those are jokes, I can prove it."

How, he had no idea as he moved to the door. At any moment he half-expected to hear a sharp explosion, feel the bullet tear into his back. Except an educated instinct told him that this was not a man who would shoot another in the back. He was, after all, a professional, and he thought he was dealing with a "civilian," even if a guilty one . . .

He kept talking, keeping his hands in full view. The CIA man didn't move. When he opened the door he knew why. Another man, younger, blocked his way. This man also had a gun in his hand, and a smug sort of smile on his face.

"Back you go, Paul," he said, shoving the gun toward Karl's solar plexus.

Karl's reaction was a reflex. He swiveled to one side, the barrel of the gun missed its mark and glanced off his chest. At the same time he kept his forward motion, stepped inside and clasped the man's gun arm close to his chest, slid the other around his neck. Pivoting from the waist in a *kubinage*, he tumbled the man into the room.

It happened as quickly and smoothly as a demonstration at the Combat School. Karl heard the grunt of surprise as the gunman hit the floor, and then a sharp report as the gun went off. The television screen shattered. The older CIA man went into a crouch as Karl stepped into the hall and slammed the door.

He moved quickly down the hall. A woman watched him uneasily, probably had heard the gunshot. Two police came around the corner, a man and a woman, and the look on their faces told Karl that they had heard the gunshot too. The man had drawn his gun.

Karl stopped, caught between the police and the room with the CIA. Until the door to room 315 opened and a florid-faced man peered out.

"What's all the noise—?"

"Get back inside," Karl snapped at him. "He's got a gun." And he pushed the man back and stepped in after him. Three other men were seated around a bed playing poker. Red, blue and white chips were stacked on the bed and beer cans littered the floor. Two of the men had taken off their coats and rolled up their sleeves; the third sat in his undershirt, stomach overflowing his belt.

"A gun?" one of them said, "Is that what—?"

The screen door was open. Karl climbed over the bed, scattered cards and poker chips and beer. Angry yelps followed him onto the balcony. Below, the angled top of the circus tent extended to within ten feet of the building.

Karl got up on the railing, crouched for a moment, then launched himself into the air. The tent's roof was supported by cables, and Karl aimed just to the side of one of them, hoping that the fabric wouldn't tear. Someone on the ground shouted and the world raced upward at him.

The impact wasn't too bad but his right ankle caught on the fabric as he slid. There was a twinge of pain and then he was rolling down into the trough as the tent dipped to take his weight.

He dropped to the ground next to people still staring at the sagging roof. It seemed some sort of reception was going on. Men and women posed in evening clothes, drinks in hand, cheese and crackers in the other. A table next to him was covered with glasses of white wine. Karl moved forward, felt a sharp pain and stumbled against the table. Glasses banged in a medley and overturned. The bartender looked at Karl in alarm.

"Did you fall, sir?"

"There's a man with a gun up there," Karl said. "I'm getting the police."

Ignoring the pain in his ankle, Karl moved inside the lobby. Behind him, he could hear the news spread: *a gun? who said a gun? what's going on?*

Karl walked as quickly as he could. With each step the pain in his ankle seemed to increase. Running was impossible. He needed a car, but first he had to cross the lobby without being spotted. Any moment he expected the elevator doors would open and the police or the CIA men would rush out. He forced himself to act nonchalant. Behind him, he could hear the men from the poker game yelling down at the crowd.

He reached the entrance and then was outside. Two vehicles were in the driveway: a taxi and a black limousine. The taxi's passenger was still counting out his fare. The limo was empty but the trunk was open and the chauffeur was unloading suitcases.

In the lobby someone yelled, "Stop him . . ."

Karl crossed to the limo. The driver's door was open and the keys were in the ignition. He slid inside and turned the key.

"Hey—"

The chauffeur came at him and when he realized the car was moving he grabbed a rear-door handle, running frantically as he tried to get his legs beneath him, then stumbled and fell. Karl was at the road now, yanked the wheel to the left and headed east on Budapester-strasse. Two hundred feet ahead the road curved to follow the Tiergarden. Beyond was the Landwehrkan canal and side streets he could lose himself in—

Three pops in quick succession. In the rearview mirror he saw the younger CIA man in the middle of the street, legs spread, gun pointed at him. Just before Karl rounded the curve the man dropped to one knee, fired twice more. Matching holes appeared in the rear and front windows, and then he was around the corner and out of sight.

Karl smiled, and the smile froze on his face. Ahead of him three cars stopped in the middle of the road. A moving van trying to back into a driveway had blocked the road. What sidewalk remained was too narrow for the limousine. Karl yanked the parking brake. Tires screeched as the heavy machine swept one hundred eighty degrees in a bootleg turn. In moments he was headed in the opposite direction, back around the corner, back to the hotel. The CIA man was walking away when Karl reappeared. Startled, he turned around, dropped again to one knee and took aim. Karl turned directly toward him and slid low in his seat. He was protected by the engine now but couldn't see the road so he steered toward a distant building in line with where he knew the shooter was. Two more shots, and two more holes appeared in the windshield, one of them where his head had been.

As the wheel hit the curb Karl turned left to regain the road. He straightened up, but as he had anticipated, the CIA man had already dived to one side to avoid the car. He caught a glimpse of the man running in a low crouch across the lawn. In front of the hotel the policeman had moved into the street, where he stood like a sentinel with his hand raised, signaling Karl to stop as though he was a traffic cop. Karl sounded the horn and accelerated. *Move, damn you.* But the man held his ground. Karl swerved back and forth to unnerve him, sounding the horn all the way. There were no cars coming from the opposite direction and when the policeman didn't move, Karl waited until the last minute, then swerved to the other lane. He meant to pass close to the man, to scare him, but when at the last moment the man tried to leap aside, he picked the wrong way to go. The right fender struck him, threw him aside and sent his hat careening off the windshield. In the rearview mirror Karl saw him land heavily on the grass bordering the sidewalk.

And then he was past the hotel, in the clear. At Nurnbergerstrasse he turned left, after a block turned right, then left, then right again, back and forth until he was swallowed up in the vast labyrinth of the city.

He drove to the Yorkstrasse U-Bahn, where three subway lines crossed. After wiping his prints off the limousine he took the number 7 train southbound. On the subway he had time to inspect his ankle. It was already swollen, but not too badly, he thought. A good soaking and elastic bandages should suffice . . .

Now that it was over he felt limp, exhausted. Too many revelations, too much happening at once. He shut his eyes, breathed deeply, calming himself, clearing his mind. For a moment he thought of calling Uncle Alex but decided against it. The Redeye mission had not been compromised—the CIA men thought he was Paul and Paul was safely out of the way. Everything could proceed according to plan. In fact, he might be able to use Paul's identity to his own advantage. By the time Karl reached the Neukoln–Rathaus station, he at least felt in control of the situation.

Back in his own car, Karl considered whether or not to bypass Checkpoint Charlie and return through one of the three border stations at the western edge of the city. These exits served the highways that led to West Germany but it was a half-hour drive to the nearest one. Checkpoint Charlie was only minutes away. There hadn't been time to circulate Paul's picture, and if there was an alarm out the police would be looking for a stolen limousine rather than a Mercedes.

Checkpoint Charlie was a U.S. military facility and only military vehicles were required to stop. There were no barriers blocking his way, and when the white-belted American soldier in full-dress uniform saw Karl's East German license plate he ignored him. A moment later Karl was back on East German soil.

Whether his brother had tried to trick him or had been tricked by the CIA, he didn't know. It didn't matter. He had learned long ago that the difference between success and failure in a mission often hinged on his ability to adjust to unexpected circumstance and to turn a threat to an advantage. He touched his brother's passport, resting securely in his pocket. Brother Paul's unexpected appearance had already become an advantage.

In the United States, news that Paul Stafford had been involved in a car theft and hit-and-run was considered of minor importance on a day that included a hijacking and an attack on an American warship in the Suez Canal. It got only a one-column mention on the back page of major American newspapers and no air time at all on network television. The Washington *Post*, an exception, did run a headline on the second page: "Herald Reporter Accused in Car Theft."

At the *Herald* Bernie Stern found himself fielding questions about Paul for which he had no answers. Everyone wanted to know what Paul was doing in Germany, why he'd stolen a limousine and whether or not he was back in the States.

"He's not working a story," Bernie told them. "He hasn't canceled his weekly meetings. I don't know what he's doing. I know nothing."

It wasn't the kind of answer that pleased Joyce and Tony Mayhue, publishers of the *Herald*, whom Bernie contacted as soon as the story came over the wire. In a voice that managed to sound at once lilting and strident, Joyce said, "Working a story or not, he represents the *Herald*."

Bernie refrained from reminding her that he had advised against giving Paul an unrestricted contract, predicting that it would encourage an attitude that was already too cavalier. Nobody denied that Stafford was a top investigative reporter—intelligent and resourceful and persevering—but he was *also* egotistical and independent to the point of insult, qualities Bernie felt would be aggravated by an independent contract. But the Mayhues had overruled him and this was the result. All that Bernie could do was call Paul's house and leave messages asking for him to get in touch as soon as possible. He had few illusions that the messages would have effect.

The person most immediately affected by the incident at the Inter-Continental was Ray Tregerdemain. After he and Paul had parted outside the casino, Ray joined some friends that included Nanci Van Zandt, a Dutch woman of thirty-six with whom he occasionally enjoyed nights of such erotic creativity that for days afterward he was filled with amazement at his good fortune. Because of her, he didn't arrive home until late the next morning. Paul's message was waiting on his machine:

"Ray, Paul Stafford. I went to the Vanilla Rose last night and talked to your friend Wenzler. He gave me a line on my brother. Got a meeting on the eastern side this morning so hold the *anmeld* investigation until further notice. Check with you when I get back."

The message left Ray with mixed feelings. On one hand the story of the two brothers piqued his curiosity and he was eager to learn the outcome; on the other hand he'd spent most of the fifty marks and was afraid Paul might want the money back. So he waited to see what happened, and the next day heard over the radio that Paul Stafford had stolen a car and run into a policeman, breaking the man's hip.

Ray called a friend in the police office and learned that the police had gone to the hotel to investigate a case of false travel documents, that the case was being coordinated through police headquarters at Schoneberg and that the U.S. government was somehow involved. That last was only rumor. Ray called both Schoneberg and the American consulate and got the same "no comment" from each of them.

"Something is fishy in Denmark," Ray sang softly to himself. He sat in his basement apartment, slow thoughts gaining momentum as he considered the possibilities. If Paul Stafford had false passports, why? Either he was involved in some sort of illegal activity—drugs, gun-running, currency exchanges—or he planned to use them to get his brother out of East Germany. That seemed the most logical explanation: the false passports were for his brother and something had gone wrong. Maybe he'd been discovered at the border with the passports, escaped and gone back to the hotel, where the police were waiting. That made sense. And then he'd made things worse by stealing a limo and running down a policeman.

Ray shook his head. That made less sense. Paul Stafford might not care about legal niceties where his hunt for his brother was concerned, but he wasn't stupid. False passports would be an easier rap than car theft and hit-and-run. Particularly if he built up the humanitarian angle of getting his poor, oppressed brother out of East Berlin.

He went to the refrigerator for a bottle of pale local beer known as *Berliner Weisse*. The refrigerator was as cramped as the apartment; the rubber seal around the door had long since deteriorated and the interior walls dripped continually with condensation. Everything about his life had become cramped, depressing. He needed a breakthrough story to reverse his lousy luck. *He needed to find Paul Stafford's brother.*

An inspired idea. He'd promised Paul that he wouldn't do a *Kriegserleidnis* but that was before this most recent shit hit the fan. Besides, the new angle was more hard news than human interest. If he could track down Paul's brother, identify him, maybe even set up an interview, he'd have what he needed to do a story that would command international attention. "Journalist a Fugitive Trying to Save Twin Brother"—he could imagine the headlines.

He took a yellow pad and pulled a chair up to the kitchen table—chipped Formica top, metal legs discolored by rust. He wanted a new kitchen table, a new apartment—a new everything.

He made a list of the newspapers and magazines most likely to be interested in his story, then assigned numbers indicating order of submission according to rates and how likely they were to want the story. Too bad Paul hadn't killed the cop. It would have made a stronger story.

But he was getting ahead of himself. All he had right now was Paul's story of a twin brother—no proof—and his own guesses. Diddly-zilch. He picked up the phone and called Otto Wenzler.

"Residence of Herr Wenzler," a male voice answered. Ray asked to speak to the man and was told that Herr Wenzler was busy. Ray then mentioned Paul Stafford and Wenzler got unbusy, came to the phone.

Ray smiled and began his pitch. "Ray Tregerdemain, Mr. Wenzler. I'm a freelance journalist doing a story on Paul Stafford, the American who was involved in a hit-and-run accident outside the InterConnie? You know what I'm talking about, right?"

"I don't read newspapers except for the arts page."

"Yeah, right, me too. Point is, I happen to know that Mr. Stafford talked with you the day before the hit-and-run. I also happen to know that you told him where to find his twin brother. What I'd like from you is the same information: where do I find the brother?"

"I don't know what you're talking about, Mr. Treasuredome."

"Tregerdemain. And you can't insult me off this story, Mr. Wenzler. Bulldog Ray they call me."

"I repeat, I don't know what you're talking about."

"That's your statement for publication? I'll quote my tape recording from Stafford that says he's seen you and your response is, quote, I don't know what you're talking about, unquote. Have I got that right?"

"Yes."

Ray could feel his quarry, and his big chance, slipping away. He needed something Wenzler would respond to. A man involved in so many shady dealings must have—

Suddenly he remembered what his informant had told him about the false passports. Was it possible that Paul hadn't brought them from the States but got them in Berlin? From Wenzler? Ray decided to gamble. "Mr. Stafford said something else. He said you were the one who provided the false passports. Have you got any statement to make on that?"

Silence, and Ray felt a rush of excitement. Was it possible? Had he actually guessed right, that Wenzler *had* provided the false documents? If so, he had Wenzler by the balls. "Listen," he hurried to follow up, "this story is either going to end with Paul's brother or with you and the fake passports. Personally I'd rather find his brother, but if you won't link me, then you end up at the end of the line; you see how it goes? You help me and I help you."

"How many people," Wenzler said slowly, "know about Stafford's allegation?"

"Nobody. And nobody will if you pass me on to his brother."

"Just for the record, Mr. Tregerdemain, the allegation is absolutely false."

Just for your record, Ray wanted to say, I'm not recording the conversation. Although now he wished he was. "Nobody's going to hear about it, Mr. Wenzler, I guarantee you that. You can ask anybody. I've been in Berlin a long time, it's my beat, and I always protect my sources."

"I intend to check. If I'm satisfied I'll see what I can do to help about the man you're looking for. I'm always cooperative with the press if possible. Where will you be this afternoon?"

"I've got an interview this morning," Ray lied, "but I should be back here by three."

"Give me your number, I'll call you."

Ray did, and Wenzler said he'd call between three and three-thirty.

Ray smacked his hands together after they hung up. His lucky guess about the false documents had paid off. Wenzler's reaction told him the smart guess was a fact.

"Mr. Bullseye," Ray said aloud, more pleased with himself than he'd been since he managed a five-minute interview with President Kennedy in 1963. Not even the overcast skies that made the apartment particularly gloomy could dampen his spirits. He sat down with the yellow pad and again began to make headlines for his story. In his euphoria it did not occur to him that his stroke of genius had altered his relationship to Otto Wenzler—from minor irritant to serious threat.

CHAPTER
16

PAUL DREAMED HE WAS FLOATING IN AIR, STARING down at himself from the sky. He was alone, lying on a bed dressed only in a hospital gown. There was a room around him with pink walls and no windows and the only furniture was a wicker table beside the bed. He tried to open his eyes but his eyes wouldn't open; then he realized his eyes *were* open and he was lying flat on his back and somehow watching himself from the ceiling at the same time. A feeling akin to vertigo washed over him until he realized that the ceiling was covered in mirrors and he was staring at his own reflection.

He struggled to sit up but something resisted his movement. Thinking that he was tied down, he looked for the ropes that held him. Time slowed and stretched and he became aware that he'd been staring at his arms for a long time, and even as the realization occurred it happened again and he had been staring at his arms for a long time, looking for ropes that weren't there.

Paul struggled into a sitting position. He was weak and dizzy and even the slightest movement took tremendous effort. He thrust his feet over the edge of the bed and stood up. The room tilted and nau-

161

sea engulfed him. He took one step forward before his knees gave way and he collapsed. For a long time he lay with his face against the floor, staring at the legs of the bed. When he felt stronger he attempted to stand again but the same thing happened. Finally he decided he had been drugged.

At least this realization put his helplessness into perspective. On hands and knees Paul crawled around the room looking for a way of escape. There were two doors. One led to a small bathroom and the other, metal, was shut and locked. Because there were no windows in either room and because the linoleum floor and brick walls were cool to his touch, Paul guessed he was in basement. But where? Karl's house? Would anyone hear him if he called out? He tried yelling, and the sound he heard scared him. It was slurred and unintelligible, the sound of a mental defective.

There was a rasping sound, the sound of a key in a lock. Paul got his feet, stumbled, sat down heavily on the bed. The door opened and Madam Tran came into the room followed by Helmut, the man who had taken him to Otto Wenzler's study. Madam Tran wore her elegant Vietnamese costume, the Bao Dai, just as she had when Paul met her at the Vanilla Rose. When she saw that he was sitting up, she gave a satisfied nod.

"You awake now. Good."

She brought the tray to the wicker table beside the bed. Paul tried to talk but his tongue felt like clay and the words came so slowly and garbled that even he couldn't understand them.

"No, don't try to talk," Madam Tran told him. "You can't say nothing anyway. First go to the bathroom, then you eat."

She turned to Helmut, who stood in the doorway wearing pleated slacks and a light sweater with the sleeves rolled up. He looked unhappy. The hallway behind him was silent and empty.

"Go ahead," she said. "Take him before he eats."

Helmut came forward and reached for Paul's arm. As he did Paul tried to get up and push past him, but by the time his muscles responded Helmut had him on his feet and was half-carrying, half-dragging him across the room. Paul made an awkward attempt to jam his elbow into Helmut's side. There was no force to the blow but it did manage to make Helmut angry.

"Scheisskopf." He turned Paul around and shoved him back on the bed.

"He doesn't want my help," he said to Madam Tran. "You take

care of him." And Helmut left the room.

Paul rolled to his side, saw Madam Tran shaking her head sadly.

"See what happens," she said. "You don't cooperate, you get treated bad."

"*Get away*," he yelled, but the words echoed only in his mind. From his lips came only slurred nonsense.

Madam Tran stood and picked up the tray.

"You a baby now," she said. "You better learn that quick."

She shut the door and locked it, leaving Paul alone with his helplessness and his rage.

Karl arrived in Washington, D.C., with a new passport, a new driver's license and a new name. As Ron Tednick he rented a car and spent two days with a real estate agent inspecting vacation rentals within a ten-minute drive of Andrews Air Force Base. The one that suited him was a farmhouse on Toons Creek Road. On the crest of a hill overlooking the Patuxent River, it sat well back from the road on two acres of land and was, as the agent Rita Gaylord assured him, "within walking distance of the river."

Ms. Gaylord was an attractive woman in her mid-thirties. The first day he met her, she was wearing a pants suit that showed off her trim figure. The next day she wore a light, clinging summer dress. She was a well-manicured woman with perky features and luxurious, streaked hair swept back in a wave. And she was happy to be of service to Ron Tednick, a divorced father whose children were coming to visit him for a month.

"How old are your children?" asked Rita.

"Eleven and nine," Karl said, choosing ages too old to draw on walls and too young to throw wild parties. His wife, he said, lived in California and he worked for the National Security Agency in Washington. His parents were coming from Philadelphia to be with him and the children and he wanted a large place for them to spend the month.

Karl enjoyed spinning out details of a fabricated life. Pretending to be someone else offered him a strange freedom. For once he could be a part of normal society, an average man, secure, faceless.

Rita Gaylord didn't think of Ron Tednick as an average man. His athletic body and good looks attracted her, and she attached no stigma to his divorce. She was divorced herself. Rita put a lot of energy into finding just the right place for Mr. Tednick. She also offered to show him a beach south of Annapolis.

"It's an out-of-the-way place," she said. "Great sand, a great place to take the kids."

Karl declined the offer. The last thing he wanted was someone getting close. That was why he'd chosen the Toons Creek house: it was private, close to Andrews Air Force Base and had an adjoining building that had once been a stable. The stable had been renovated and the bottom floor was now a garage and work area while the top floor contained storage space filled with articles the owners of the house didn't want to trust to tenants.

They signed the rental agreement at Rita's office and Karl gave her a cashier's check for two thousand dollars. Turning it between a thumb and forefinger, Rita said, "Maybe you should have a house-warming party before your children arrive."

"No thanks," Karl said. "I like privacy." Now that the house was his, he could afford to be blunt. He already regretted telling her that he was divorced. A wife with terminal cancer or Alzheimer's disease would have been a safer story.

Once settled, Karl began putting together the elements needed to accomplish the Redeye mission. He divided his mission into three preliminary operations: finding a launch site, stealing the Redeye, and implicating a third party.

The first operation was more difficult than he had anticipated. Andrews Air Force Base was bordered on the north and south by housing developments and shopping centers and on the south and east by industrial parks, farms and a trailer court. Unfortunately, the approach path of the General Secretary's aircraft was over the most populated areas, and this made the risk of being seen unacceptably high. He couldn't just step out of the car and stand on a street corner with a Redeye missile over his shoulder.

At first he considered using the roof of a house or a store. This would give him a clear shot at the *Ilyushin*, but could he gain access to a roof of a building without alerting its occupant or owner? He investigated renting a house but none was available in the area beneath the approach path. The more he thought about it, the more flaws Karl found in the roof idea. If he did find a place how could he be sure that the police didn't routinely check all recently rented property below the approach path? And how could he get his scapegoat, the person who was to be blamed for the General Secretary's assassination, to rent the house? What about helicopters? On a roof, he would stand out as clearly to them as they would to him. And if he could overcome all those problems, how would he know which place to rent when he couldn't know what runway the General Secre tary's plane would use until the day it arrived?

Ultimately it was the consideration that the runway would depend on which way the wind was blowing that inspired Karl's solution. What he needed was mobility, mobility and camouflage—an innocent-looking vehicle that would hide him even while he pulled the trigger; something with an opening through which he could fire the Redeye. Fortunately, the American mania for traveling without leaving home provided just such a vehicle: a Winnebago.

Karl was pleased with himself. Instead of worrying about one or two fixed launch sites, the motor home opened up a number of possi bilities. He could park on a neighborhood street or go to a shopping mall or a school or a church or even pull to the side of a freeway and fake a flat tire or engine trouble. And with a skylight he could fire the missile from inside, eliminating the possibility of accidental or chance witnesses.

The only real difficulty he had was finding a motor home with a skylight-escape hatch. It was a luxury option that didn't come with most rental vehicles, and he didn't have the money to buy a Winne-bago outright. Uncle Alex and his group did not have unlimited resources. They were patriots, not those favored by the Kremlin and its largess. He located what he needed at Sunshine RV in Fairfax, Virginia. A chubby salesman came with him on a test drive and gave Karl a rhapsodic account of his own family's vacation in a motor home. It was a lumbering, clumsy vehicle but it was everything Karl needed.

The second operation, stealing the Redeye, first required a physical inspection of the Bayonne terminal. For this Karl needed the services of his brother. He rehearsed his story, then phoned the Military Ocean Terminal, asked for the public affairs officer, was handed to a Major Irene Fellows.

"Major Fellows . . . my name is Paul Stafford. I'm a reporter for the Washington *Herald* and I'm working on a story about the Military Sealift Command. I would like to make an appointment for an inter view."

"I'll see what I can do, Mr. Stafford. Give me the specs again. This is a story for the Washington *Herald*?"

Karl expanded on his theme. He felt an odd delight in pretending to be Paul Stafford, the prize-winning journalist. It turned out that Major Fellows had read a story of Paul's—something about the rebellion in Afghanistan. Karl made a mental note and later, when he was in the library, he looked up all of Paul's articles and read them. They were well done, Karl decided, but ultimately came to nothing. The world responded to actions, not words.

His brother's life continued to hold a strange fascination for him. He drove past the Arlington house and was surprised by its size. It was a two-story brick home with a turret at one corner. On one side of the house was a screened-in porch and on the other an attached garage. The front yard, big as the house itself, was dominated by a huge maple tree.

It was Karl's first evidence of just how successful his brother was. Later when he was in D.C. he stopped by Farragut Square and stood in a Crown bookstore across from the *Herald* Building. He imagined Paul going to work there each day and tried to guess which of the nearby restaurants his brother frequented.

These excursions to the site of his brother's haunts were brief. Most of the time he spent in the library researching American fringe groups and radical movements. What he was looking for was a violently nationalistic organization in desperate need of money.

He found it in the Rank, a white-supremacist group based in Houston, Texas. Its leader, Grant Harkness, had been convicted along with two others of killing a radio talk show host by sending a bomb through the mail. The three men were currently appealing their convictions. One of the articles described a fund-raising auction at which maps of the world were sold with new borders drawn along racial lines. These were the sort of people Karl was looking for, zealots and believers in bizarre causes. There must be others like Grant Harkness. Within the Rank he felt he would be able to find a man gullible and hungry enough to rent the Winnebago.

Ray Tregerdemain met Otto Wenzler at the Berlin Zoo. It was five o'clock. The skies were overcast and a chilly mist dampened the pavement and caused Ray's nose to run. He dabbed it with a handkerchief as he made his way to Zellerbach Hall, where a reception for the Friends of the Berlin Zoo was in its final stages. Wenzler was at the reception and Ray was to meet him outside the Hall at a quarter past five.

As he hurried along, Ray felt the familiar tingle of excitement at the prospect of an important story. According to Wenzler, Paul's brother was a GDR communist party member with aberrant sexual tastes. In exchange for anonymity, Wenzler was to give him the name of the brother and four other East German heavies who had visited the Vanilla Rose. This was more than Ray had hoped for. This might open the door to an exposé about East German officials who visited West Berlin bordellos. The world press would eat it up. Especially tabloids.

Ray could feel the story unfolding, building. More than one story, really, and that made him feel more secure. Paul was probably back in the States, maybe doing a piece on his brother. Well, now Ray would have his own slant, could put his own spin on it. If Paul came out with the story of his brother or even the InterContinental Hotel incident, Ray could develop the sex-and-politics angle into something all his own. *Special to the Tribune by Ray Tregerdemain*. He'd have a byline on the wire by the end of the month.

Because of the rain, most visitors were leaving. Only the animals seemed oblivious to the weather. Ray turned up the collar of his overcoat, adjusted the angle of his corduroy touring cap and jammed his hands into his pockets. When he got to Zellerbach Hall he waited in the lobby for Wenzler to appear. Inside the hall a string quartet playing classical music served as a background to the noisy chatter of well-to-do attendees who had donated money for the new aquarium. Ray caught a glimpse of them whenever the door opened. They didn't look like the kind of people who visited zoos; they didn't look like the kind of people who visited anywhere without an engraved invitation.

Wenzler came into the lobby engaged in animated conversation with an older couple. He was wearing a dark, well-tailored suit, a silk shirt and tie, but his long flowing hair and thin body reminded Ray of an aging rock star. When he spotted Ray, Wenzler made a casual gesture behind his friends' backs, acknowledging Ray's presence and cautioning him to stay away.

Ray slipped outside and waited. A few moments later, Wenzler came out alone. Now he was wearing an overcoat and carried a briefcase in one hand and umbrella in the other.

"You are Mr. Tregerdemain?"

"That's me."

"Follow me at a distance, please."

Ray started to ask where they were going but Wenzler was already heading down a wide cobblestone walkway toward the sea-lion enclosure. The overcast had grown so thick that wrought-iron streetlamps were on, their gold light gleaming dully from rain-slick stones.

Ray followed about twenty feet behind. The few people who were on the path were heading in the opposite direction, toward the main gate. The bark of sea lions grew loud as they approached. Wenzler went into a low concrete building—public restrooms—and Ray followed.

The restroom was deserted. There was a gutter at the base of a urine-stained wall that led to a cigarette-clogged drain. A row of empty stalls faced six sinks beneath a flickering neon light. After checking to make sure no one was in the stalls, Wenzler set his briefcase on a sink and took out a metal detector that looked to Ray like the sort of thing security guards used in airline terminals

"You don't mind, I hope," Wenzler said.

"You think I've got a gun?"

"Or a transmitter or a tape recorder. Please."

He had Ray turn slightly while he ran the metal loop up and down his legs, along the small of his back, under his arms and along his chest. The machine beeped twice, once for his massive key ring with its Swiss army knife, the second time for a small microcassette tape recorder in his vest pocket. Wenzler wanted to inspect each item. When Ray showed him the tape recorder, Otto asked him to take the tape out.

"What for? It's not on."

"This way we shall be sure."

Ray hesitated. He didn't like the smell of the restroom or the way Wenzler kept after him. Still, he had to take some chances if he was going to get a story that would bring back his reputation.

He took the cassette out of the recorder, trying for bravado to boost his confidence. "It's not like we're trading Gary Powers for Colonel Abel, you know."

"It's closer than you think," Wenzler said. "Do you know the name Erich Loerke?"

"Sure, the deputy chairman of the Volkskammer. You're saying *he's* been to the Vanilla Rose?"

"Just so."

Ray let out a low whistle. The Volkskammer was East Germany's legislative body and Erich Loerke was one of its leaders. Loerke was one of the new generation of politicians rapidly achieving positions of prominence.

Wenzler said, "Now you see the reason for my caution. A man becomes more desperate and dangerous the more he has to lose, and Deputy Chairman Loerke has a great deal to lose should this information become public."

"If there's proof," Ray reminded him, but his blood was already racing.

Wenzler nodded toward his briefcase. "In here."

"Let me see?"

"Do I have your assurance that my name will never be mentioned?"

"I told you that before. If you checked me out you know I can be trusted."

"Oh, I checked you out," Wenzler said. "But I like to watch a man's eyes when he talks to me. The telephone is the world's great deceiver—you could tell me you're an animal lover while pulling the wings off a sparrow."

You are one evil fruitcake, Ray thought . . . "Well, now that you know I'm not a spy, let's get out of here. I don't like the smell of this place." In more ways than one, he added to himself.

Without waiting, he went to the door, but not until he was outside beneath the awning and surrounded by the smell of damp leaves and wet concrete, did he relax. Wenzler joined him as a young couple passed, laughing, arm-in-arm, paying no attention to the light rain.

"Ahhh," Wenzler breathed deeply. "Much better out here."

"What about Paul Stafford's brother?" Ray said. "You were going to give me his name."

"Rolf Schmidt, a banker. He has been to the Vanilla Rose on numerous occasions. His sexual preferences run to bondage and S and M and he makes no distinction between fantasy and reality. The result has been some less than savory episodes in which the girls have been damaged."

"Yeah, I know. I met one of them Saturday night. Kristy . . ."

Wenzler raised a negligent shoulder. "So many girls, so many names, who can keep track?"

Ray's attention had already returned to Erich Loerke, a much more important story than Rolf Schmidt.

"What about the others?" he asked. "You said there were six other party members who got their rocks off on this side of the

Wall.''

Ray deliberately inflated the number but Wenzler caught it.

"Four others."

"Are any of them as prominent as Loerke?"

"I'm sure they will be after you sensationalize their exploits."

A balloon vendor wheeling a tank of helium passed them. Rain dripped from his felt hat and the balloons that struggled after him were huddled and bent like old men. Wenzler moved out from beneath the awning and began walking.

"Wait a minute," Ray called, following him. "What about the proof?"

"All in good time. First I want to see if my coat is dead."

"Your what?"

"Are you aware," said Wenzler, "that you can buy dead animals from the zoo? Perhaps there is another story for you. I am interested in a sick polar bear. I will pay to have it made into a fur coat. Two thousand marks—expensive, perhaps, but how many people in the world can wear the white fur of a polar bear?"

They had reached the polar-bear enclosure where a lone man in a yellow rain slicker was taking pictures of the bears. A three-foot-high wall surrounded the area; on the other side, twenty feet below, a wide moat surrounded a rocky island where the bears went about their business, oblivious to both visitors and rain. Wenzler went to the wall overgrown with ivy and began counting the bears.

"If there are thirteen bears, one is mine," he said. "How many do you count?"

Ray was uninterested in the bears but turned and counted, wondering which one would appear in the society pages next winter wrapped around Otto Wenzler.

The bears were like huge snowmen on the brown rocks. One of them sat on its haunches, scratching like a dog, another broke into a lopsided but oddly graceful run as it loped briefly after its mate. Still another was in the water, head high, snorting noisily as it swam. Ray counted only nine but it was impossible to see what was on the far side of the rocks.

Wenzler turned to him. "How many?"

"I count nine."

"Excuse me, sir." A voice behind him.

Ray turned to find the man who had been taking pictures standing next to him. Holding out his camera, the man said, "Could I trouble you to take my photograph?''

Ray was annoyed but what could he do? Say no, I don't want to take your stupid picture? He glanced around but there was no one else to do it so he reluctantly held out his hand for the camera. As he did, from behind something stabbed his neck and a jolt of electricity caused his mouth to snap open, his muscles to convulse.

Ray collapsed. His body felt numb, burning as though stuck by a thousand pins. A buzzing was in his ears and a gagging taste of metal was in his mouth. Through the haze of pain, he saw Otto Wenzler standing above him. In his hand he held a black plastic device with two sharp metal probes extending from it. Electrical connectors, Ray dimly realized.

It was like looking at the world from the bottom of a well. He saw Wenzler slip the device into his coat and kneel beside him. Ray wanted to tell Wenzler that he was not a brave man, that he was a coward, that he could be scared into silence. He had nothing to prove, he could get by without the story about forged passports or Erich Loerke and the Vanilla Rose. None of it mattered. I don't care, I'll stop . . . He tried to speak but his ears were clogged, he couldn't hear his own words. He wasn't even talking, he realized, the noise in his ears was only the sound of his teeth grinding.

He watched as Wenzler searched his pockets, handed over his tape recorder to the man in the yellow slicker, then removed all the little scraps of paper, receipts and notes from his wallet, leaving only the credit cards, money, I.D. cards and photographs. Ray wanted to tell Wenzler that the credit cards had expired, maybe if Otto knew how close to poverty he was he'd let him live. A foolish thought for a desperate man.

They lifted him up, the two of them, and he realized what they were going to do. He kicked out hard, barbed wire ran through his muscles, his legs wouldn't respond. They balanced him on top of the ivy-covered wall and looked around to make sure no one was in sight or within earshot.

Please . . . but the plea echoed only inside his own brain.

Tears came. Suddenly, finally, everything in his world was precious: his gloomy apartment seemed familiar and secure; his last assignment, a dumb piece on military wives in Berlin, seemed wonderful, the resulting hack story lighthearted and amusing; his nights with Nanci Van Zandt were like magic, her eager body a gift beyond measure . . .

The cement scraped his neck, he fell, and water engulfed him. He rose to the surface coughing, trying to swim. Water flooded his mouth, he tried to spit it out. He had no more control over his breathing than he did over his arms and legs. The coughing was automatic but he couldn't hold his breath, couldn't spit. Water lapped his mouth and flooded his nose.

He made one last effort to swim, and for a moment it seemed that his arms and legs responded weakly. Maybe the shock was wearing off. From the corner of an eye he caught a flash of white and heard a distant splash. A spreading wave reached him, momentarily covering his face as it passed. Water flooded his mouth. He lashed out, rose to the surface coughing and gasping, eyes wide.

His efforts began to take some effect, moving him away from the wall toward the rocky island where a polar bear stood with lowered head, staring at him. Something off to one side, in the water, was snorting. Ray doubled his efforts, willing his arms forward, his legs to kick. If only he could breathe. Again a wave choked him and he sank beneath the surface. His chest heaved and bubbles tickled his nose as the air left his lungs.

No.

His head was pounding from lack of oxygen, but he could feel his arms and legs responding now. He struggled to the surface. His head broke free and he took a gulp of air. As he did, something struck his leg, a downward force that submerged him in mid-breath. Water gushed thick and cold down his throat into his lungs.

His arms and legs responded instinctively. He bobbed again to the surface, chest convulsed, no longer able to cough, no air left to expel the water. And then the strength was gone and his arms and legs grew still. The world dimmed and the rain-spattered surface rose in liquid craters in front of his eyes. His last thought was that he had stumbled onto something more important than twin brothers finding each other or a car theft and hit-and-run or high-ranking communist officials coming to the West for sex—and he would never ever know what it was . . .

Oh, mama, please . . .

Ray lost consciousness before the bear's second tentative swipe disemboweled him.

CHAPTER

17

KARL WAITED AT THE SECURITY DESK AT THE MAIN gate of the Military Ocean Terminal in Bayonne, New Jersey. Outside the window a uniformed MP waved vehicles through: a snappy salute for officers, a quick flick of the wrist for enlisted men, a gesture toward the security office for anyone without I.D.

A white golf cart turned the corner and sped toward him. The driver was an army officer, a woman in her early thirties. Karl was expecting her, Major Irene Fellows, the public affairs officer, his escort for the day. After slamming her cart to a stop just inches in front of the window, Major Fellows got out and came inside.

"You're Paul Stafford?" she asked.

"That's right."

"Your editor wants you to call," she told him as she signed a visitor's log next to his name.

"My editor?"

"A guy named Bernie Stern. He seems to think you're AWOL." She pronounced it *eh-wall*. Karl tensed . . . he didn't recognize the term. "You talked to . . . Bernie?"

173

"Had to validate your credentials. We're not open to the public except on Armed Forces Day."

Karl, of course, would have preferred that this editor Bernie Stern not know about "Paul" being back, but he knew what his response would be. For some time he had been considering calling the *Herald* and making some excuse for Paul's absence; now he had to do it. He hardly wanted Paul's superior becoming concerned or trying to track him down.

The cart whined as they sped down a road bisected by railroad tracks. Major Fellows had a long, bony face but what she lacked in physical beauty she made up for with an outgoing, cheerful, even chipper, manner. She drove aggressively, weaving around workmen and sounding a high-pitched horn whenever anyone got in her way.

Karl asked how long she had been working at the terminal and barely listened to the answer. His attention was on the surroundings, on the rows of gray warehouses and tall cranes that loomed like metal spiders and moved along metal tracks to the tune of warning bells.

Uncle Alex's map of the terminal was out-of-date. Karl began making mental corrections: location and type of buildings, their age and construction, paths of electrical and telephone lines, types of locks and security systems. He also noted the attitude of the employees and general feel of the place—who blended into the background and who didn't and how security-conscious people seemed. The atmosphere was more businesslike than vigilant. Americans were, as advertised, an unsuspecting people. He was glad he wasn't on the other side, wandering around the Soviet Union trying to wangle a tour of a shipping terminal in Murmansk.

Major Fellows filled him in on the history of the terminal, how it had been used in World War II, what its importance was today, as well as a rundown on the Military Sealift Command, which, she felt, got too little credit for the job it did.

They came to a ship that was loading huge crates on pallets, and Karl expressed his surprise that everything wasn't in closed containers.

"We're a full-service facility," Major Fellows said. "We still do a lot of pallets as well as drive-on, drive-off shipments—automobiles and household goods for officers going overseas, the works. But you're right, containers are the easiest and fastest way to go. They're airtight and waterproof and we can stack them outside if we have to.

Don't even need a warehouse."

"Are they safe sitting outside?"

"Each container is locked and sealed. And if it's security cargo, it goes to Warehouse E."

Karl kept the conversation going, never focusing directly on security questions but picking up bits of information. He learned that Warehouse E was locked and alarmed and checked every hour by a security patrol. He would have liked to go inside and look the place over but there was no way to do it without asking. The most he could get was a quick look at the outside of the building as they passed by.

Major Fellows took him to inspect a row of containers stacked on the pier. They were like oversize shoe boxes measuring eight feet square by twenty feet long with full-width doors opening at one end. Karl paid special attention to the way the doors were secured.

"Is this brass?" he asked, hefting a padlock.

"Has to be. The containers are secured on an open deck. If those things were steel they'd be rusted shut by the time some of these cargos reached port."

After noting the manufacturer's name—Eagle Safe & Lock Company—Karl turned his attention to the container itself.

"How can you tell what's in this?"

"I can't. Not without a manifest to check the CDN."

"The what?"

"Cargo designation number. Right there."

She pointed to the letter-number code stenciled on the side of the containers. It was similar to the code Uncle Alex had given him for the Redeye shipment, but Uncle Alex hadn't mentioned that the same numbers were stamped on the security seal, a metal band looped through the hasp along with the padlock. The ends of the security band were crimped together where they passed through a metal ball, which made it impossible to open the door without breaking the seal.

The last stop on their tour was the Cargo Control office located on the top floor of a rust-streaked gray building that commanded a view of the entire terminal. There were half-a-dozen people in Cargo Control. Computer screens glowed green and a teletype machine occasionally clattered into life, but no one seemed particularly busy. One wall showed a map of the terminal; on another was a white Plexiglas scheduling board with names of ships, dates and warehouse codes written in grease pencil. Karl noted with satisfaction that the Redeye transport ship *Coralis* was still due to arrive on the twenty-fifth.

While Major Fellows traded jokes with a lieutenant, Karl moved to the window and got a good look at the roof of Warehouse E. He was pleased to see that there were three metal ventilators that looked large enough to climb through. All he had to do was to figure a way to remove them and deactivate the alarm system.

"What are you looking at?" Major Fellows said from behind him.

"Great view of New York," Karl said easily, turning around.

"The best on the base," she agreed. "In Manhattan people pay twenty-five hundred a month for this kind of view. These guys get it for free."

The chatter continued, but Karl's mind was already on ways of breaching the security of the warehouse, breaking into the container and getting a Redeye.

Major Fellows dropped him off at the Main Gate, and Karl drove the shoreline adjacent to the terminal, periodically stopping when he found a clear view of the harbor to make notes on a map. He crossed the Bayonne Bridge into Staten Island, where the land curved until it brought him to a point directly across from the seaward end of the terminal. In Bayonne the shoreline was given over to industry, but here it was more residential.

Finished with his reconnaissance, Karl went to a restaurant and ordered lunch. While waiting for the food, he went to the pay phone near the restroom and called the *Herald*. Since arriving in America he had attuned his ear and adjusted his accent to standard American English. In preparation for talking to Bernie Stern, Karl also brought to mind his brother's speech patterns, which were so similar to his own, and tried to imagine what kind of a relationship Paul might have with this man, his boss. It would not be a normal boss-employee relationship. Paul was some sort of prize-winner and worked independently. He decided on a tone of guarded equality and, as the English idiom went, would play it by ear after that.

The main switchboard at the *Herald* patched him through to the editor's secretary.

"This is Paul Stafford. I'd like to talk to Mr. Stern."

"*Hi*, Paul," the secretary said, startling Karl with her unexpected informality. "You're the man of the hour here. Hold on."

While he waited at the phone he became aware of his unconscious habit that his brother had noticed in the beer garden at Treptow Park. He had taken his spare change and stacked the coins in a graduated cone, quarters on the bottom, then nickels, pennies and dimes, and now he was running his fingers up and down the neat stack. Annoyed, he swept the coins off the narrow ledge and into his pocket. Nervousness was weakness.

Bernie Stern came on the line, using neither preamble nor greeting. "Stafford, what the hell is going on with you? Where are you?"

"I'm in Bayonne, something important came up—"

"Right. Like going to Berlin and stealing cars and running over German cops. Listen, you want to leave the country, let your people know you'll be missing weeklies and maybe you could even let me know, considering I'm your editor. It doesn't look too good when the only way we can find out what our reporters are doing is by reading it in the *Post*. The Mayhues are all over me about what's going on and what can I tell them? Nothing. As in 'I don't know nothing'— which I don't."

Karl hadn't realized that the incident at the InterContinental had been so well reported. "I'm sorry—"

"Wait, let me guess: You're pissed off at the delay in the Rockland-Birdwell piece so you're going to do a prima donna tap dance on company time and I'm supposed to keep time with castanets? You trying to prove a point here or just proving that you're the world's *numero uno* pain-in-the-ass hotshot . . ."

Karl could feel the panic rise. He had been wrong to call Bernie Stern. It was more than a voice he was impersonating, it was a whole relationship with all its subtleties and nuances and personal history. He didn't even know what Bernie was talking about—Rockland-Birdwell? Mayhues? Weeklies? He was lost and at any moment the editor was going to realize it.

"Listen," he said quickly, "I can't explain now but I had to go underground for a story—"

"Underground?"

Karl winced. Not the right term, not the right term. He pushed ahead. "I'm working on a story about illegal arms sales by ex-CIA officers. It could be very big."

"Very big up my ass. What are you talking about? Where'd this come from? There is no story about arms sales and the CIA. Iran-contra is history, for Christ sake."

He was in trouble, no doubt about it. The more he talked, the worse it got. The only way now was to end this conversation before the editor caught on. But Bernie's next words were like a reprieve.

"Or is it?"

His tone was different, quieter, even uncertain. And Karl began to understand better his brother's relationship with the editor. It was based on verbal jousting and mock battle—and the editor's grudging respect. Bernie's outrage and disbelief were, it seemed, the common currency between them, not evidence of Karl's failure. The pause—Karl's silence—had seemed to change the character of the interaction, tipped the scales, as they said, in his favor.

Karl picked it up. "Bernie, this makes Iran-contra a footnote. That's why I had to disappear. My life's not worth a—" he remembered another colloquialism from his training—"plugged nickel if these guys find out I'm onto them."

"Who, for Christ sake? Can you give me a name?"

"Not yet. It wouldn't be safe."

"A CIA—arms sales link? For real, cross your heart and hope to work for Rupert Murdoch?"

The jargon was still confusing, but Karl ignored it.

"It's real but I've got to disappear for maybe another month. If it's longer than that, I'll let you know."

"Wait just a damn minute. Give me a contact, give me a number."

The editor's eagerness for the story was apparent, as was his belief that the man he was talking to was Paul. Karl's earlier despair turned to exultation. He could do it. He *could* impersonate Paul even with someone who knew him personally.

"No contacts, no numbers," Karl said. "I've got to do this one alone."

"What about the cop in Berlin? What am I supposed to tell the Mayhues?"

"Tell them the CIA planted the story to discredit me. Nothing really happened in Berlin."

"Is that kosher or bullshit?"

"Uh . . . listen, Bernie, I've got to go. Someone is coming." Kosher? Another omission in his linguistic training.

"Keep in touch, damn it."

"When I can."

Karl was smiling as he hung up. Before returning the car at the airport he took a tour of Manhattan. With the aid of a map he found his way to Broadway and Forty-second Street, where traffic slowed to a noisy crawl and gangs of teen-agers ran forward to clean windshields, unasked and unwanted, then demanded money. Remembering his years in the rubble gang, Karl gave them a dollar.

He parked the car and wandered the crowded streets and littered sidewalks of New York. There was a sense of anarchy here that reminded him of the Berlin of his youth. A man in a ragged harlequin get-up stood in the middle of a street and conducted an imaginary orchestra while traffic surged around him. Another man sat cross-legged against a building mumbling to himself. In front of him were a plastic cup for donations and a skinned rabbit, head intact, spread across the sidewalk. No one paid any attention. Karl stopped and pointed to the rabbit.

"Is that yours?"

The man looked up with glazed eyes. "It's Bugs Bunny, man. Gimme a dollar and I'll resurrect him."

Karl turned away and joined the careless crowd that moved with its eyes inward, each person intent on his own business, his own problems. Even the police ignored the bums and beggars and street people, some of them clearly in distress. No socialist safety nets here. This was a city for the strong and powerful and cunning. Near Central Park rich ladies in furs dashed from doorman to taxi like sleek deer among the wolves. It was a city of prey and predator, and Karl understood it instinctively. Indeed, a feeling of exhilaration came over him, and he decided right away that he liked New York better than Moscow. Better in fact, than any city except Berlin.

Something that Uncle Alex had said about New York came to mind, something about the Nevsky transmitter: that with enough power it could cleanse this city of all life. *Sterile destruction* was the term Uncle Alex had used. It was hard for Karl to imagine that anything could overwhelm the energy and vitality of this city. He tried to picture the streets silent and empty, the gaudy marquees dark and broken, taxicabs rusting where they came to rest after plunging through storefront windows, food rotting on grocery store shelves, untended buildings with cloying air thick with the stench of decaying corpses. It was a nightmare image hard to believe had he not seen the experiment with the dog and the T-54 tank.

He would have liked to stay longer in New York, but he had reservations on an evening flight to Houston. It was time to investigate firsthand Grant Harkness and his radical organization, the Rank. It was time to find an American who could credibly be blamed for the Redeye mission . . . for the destruction of the General Secretary's plane and the death of all aboard it.

For Paul, the worst part of captivity was the humiliation. His muscles had no more strength than a baby's, his coordination almost as rudimentary. Vertigo and nausea overcame him whenever he tried to stand, so that like an infant's his world was defined from the floor, from his hands and knees.

They didn't bother to guard him, didn't need to. Madam Tran came three times a day to feed him, and Helmut came twice a day to manhandle him into the bathroom. His injections came with the evening meal. Madam Tran would push him onto his side, pull up the hospital gown and shove the needle into his buttocks. She didn't need Helmut to help her, not after the first time, when Paul had fought her and the needle had broken off in his flesh.

Madam Tran had been furious. "Damn you, cow-dung man!" She fetched Helmut, who came with a pair of pliers and sat on Paul's back while he pulled the needle free, causing as much pain as possible.

"You want to make trouble for us, *ja*?" he said. "Don't want to take your medicine?"

The needle came free but Helmut didn't get off his back. Instead he leaned over and put the point of the needle against Paul's testicles.

"Maybe we should give the injections here. How would you like that?"

Paul gritted his teeth, kept silent. "You going to be a good boy now, *ja*?"

He flicked the needle sideways, pricking the soft skin. Paul flinched.

"Enough," said Madam Tran.

"No, he likes it, don't you?" Again the flick of the needle.

"He's in *my* charge. You don't hurt him bad until you have permission from Herr Wenzler."

Helmut climbed off Paul's back. "The next time he causes trouble let *me* give him an injection. He'll be good then. Very good."

Paul rolled away, weak, trembling. He wanted to strike out, smash Helmut's face.

The two of them moved to the door, paying no attention to Paul.

"I don't need you no more," Madam Tran told Helmut. "If he tries trouble I can just increase my dosage."

Paul's anger fueled his attempt to get off the bed. He stumbled to his feet and stood half-crouched, clutching the mattress for support. The two of them turned to look at him.

Helmut grinned. "Oh, he wants to fight."

Paul tried to tell him where to stick it, but his tongue was thick and his words were slurred.

Helmut came toward him. "What's that? You want to say something?"

The face danced in front of him, misshapen, taunting. Paul hit out with his fist, but his muscles were spastic and the effort only unbalanced him and sent him sprawling to the floor. Helmut nudged him with his foot, taunting him to get up, easily avoiding Paul's clumsy attempts to grab his leg . . .

Later, after they had gone and his anger faded, Paul realized he was only risking having the dosage increased, which would turn him into a zombie unable even to crawl across the room. He wondered briefly what they were using on him? Phenobarbital? Some kind of barbiturate . . . Whatever it was, the drugs held him captive as much as the locked room.

He decided his best, his only option, was to cooperate. He ate his food, ignored Helmut's taunts and handling, even turned dutifully to one side when Madam Tran gave him the injection. He would bide his time until he could collect his energy and find some way to escape. Meanwhile, the days and nights flowed one into the other, forming a white haze in which he drifted, drifted, drifted . . .

CHAPTER

18

IT WAS HOT AND HUMID IN HOUSTON, TEXAS, NOT
what Karl had expected. His picture of the American West came
from movies and television, a land of flat mesas and painted deserts
and tubular cacti standing tall against a wide sky. Well, at least a lot
of the men wore cowboy boots and Stetsons.

He bought a street map, rented an air-conditioned Thunderbird
whose steering and handling disappointed him, and drove to the Fed
eral Court House on Rusk Street. Houston, with its downtown cluster
of slab-sided silver-windowed buildings, felt more alien to him than
Washington, where the tops of monuments and church spires still
dominated a peaceful horizon.

Karl took an elevator to the fifth floor, where a young black
woman wearing handcrafted Indian jewelry helped him locate the case
number of *United States versus Harkness* and then delivered a transcript of the trial in two volumes. Karl joined two law students at a
long table hunched over their research. Locating the names he wanted
was easy enough: in back of the transcript was an index of witnesses
and exhibits matched to page numbers. Karl turned to the testimony

of each witness and wrote down the names of those associated with the Rank.

Two hours later he had a list of seven possibilities and proceeded to look up the names in the Houston phone book. One name was missing, another he discarded after seeing how many people were named "Johnson." He ended up with five addresses, which he located and marked on his map. After lunch he drove to each address. Those who lived in well-tended suburbs with second cars or children's toys in evidence he dismissed, while those who were in depressed areas or whose homes looked in need of repair he carefully noted.

One man, George Lish, lived on the outskirts of Houston in an area of old farms and new housing developments. His home and business were on the same property, half an acre of land bordered by tangled timber and humming power lines. The sign on the chain link fence said "Lone Star Dog-O-Rama: Boarding and Obedience Training." Beneath the letters a crudely rendered German shepherd growled at the world. The same sign was on the door of a pickup truck that sat in the driveway of the house. Clearly business was not booming for George Lish.

Karl checked into a Holiday Inn and further narrowed the selection by calling each person and asking for the wife. George Lish's response pleased him most of all. "There ain't no Mrs. Lish," he grunted, and hung up.

Karl placed a *1* beside the man's name. He remembered from reading some of the testimony that George Lish was one of the founders of the Rank but that he now served only on an advisory council. Not a bright man, not a prosperous man and not a married man—a near-perfect fall guy.

Next morning Karl drove to the Dog-O-Rama. The reception area was as tawdry as the exterior. The furniture consisted of a plastic couch with one leg propped up by a brick and an orange coffee table covered with faded Breeder's World magazines. The pale green walls were plastered with advertisements for pet supplies. The room was empty when Karl walked in so he followed the sound of voices to the open back door.

Two men, one white, one Mexican, stood in front of one of the runs arguing in a mix of Spanish and English. Karl assumed the older man was Lish. The German Shepherd at Lish's feet bristled and bared its teeth when Karl appeared in the doorway. The two men turned.

"King," Lish yelled. "At ease."

The dog stopped barking.

"King, sit."

The dog sat down and Lish waved to Karl. "Come on over. He won't hurt you none."

Karl moved forward, keeping an eye on King just in case the dog didn't understand English.

"He's got perfect training," Lish said. "Don't you worry. He won't eat nothing I don't tell him to eat."

George Lish was a short, thickset man, about thirty. He had the body of a weight lifter and a boyish face that reminded Karl of the preacher he had seen on television the night before. Lish wore soiled, khaki shorts and a black, tight-fitting tee-shirt.

"Didn't see you come in," he said. "What can I do you for?"

"I'm Karl Muller, Mr. Lish. Is there someplace we can talk privately?"

"What about?"

"The Harkness case, for one thing."

Lish's eyes narrowed.

"You with the government?"

"No. I represent an organization whose goals are similar to your own."

"What organization?"

Karl indicated the young Mexican who was now investigating a hole in the fence surrounding one of the runs. "It's a confidential matter. Can we go into your office?"

"Berto," Lish called, "when you get that finished cut Kay-Ray's nails and check that abscess on his ear. I'll be inside."

Lish led him through the reception area to his private office, a room only slightly less depressing than the outer room. There were a couple of chairs, a desk, and a sagging bookcase beneath which clumps of dust and dog hair had grown to the size of tennis balls. A series of photographs on the wall depicted annual meetings of the Rank in which Lish stood arm-in-arm with his buddies, each of them wearing military fatigues and holding a rifle. A brown-stained Mr. Coffee sat on a small table.

"Let's get one thing straight, Mr. Muller, whoever you are, if it's about the Harkness case I don't talk unless I'm subpoenaed."

Karl understood the trap had to be baited with trust—or at least credibility—before he offered any money. Still standing, Karl spread his arms. The dog, which had followed them inside, growled.

"Why don't you search me," Karl said. "I'm not from the government. I'm not carrying a weapon and I'm not wired. Go ahead."

Lish stared at him, and gradually the suspicious look gave way to a smile. "Hell, I know you ain't carrying, otherwise you wouldn't offer."

He pushed a copy of Soldier of Fortune from a chair and motioned Karl to sit down before taking a seat behind the desk. The dog lay down at his feet. Karl put his briefcase on the floor and began his pitch.

"Mr. Lish, I'm sure you know that the Rank is not the first organization or the only one that advocates racial purity."

"Yeah, I know. We're like different chapters of the same book." He smiled, pleased with his clever phrase, which he had read in one of Rank's handouts.

"The attempt to purify America," Karl continued, "goes all the way back to the Civil War, when freed American slaves were resettled in Liberia."

"Where? New Iberia?"

"No, Liberia. In Africa."

"Oh, yeah."

"And more recently Germany attempted a purification plan."

Lish's features hardened. "What are you? Some kind of damn reporter?"

"Not at all, I am merely—"

"Well, we're not Nazis so you can forget that. We're white separatists—*Americans*, hundred percent. We don't say any one race is better than the other, just that God meant them to be separate. And we're *not* Nazis because we're not going to kill any races, including Jews. It says right there in the Bible that the Jews shall inherit the land of Canaan and that's Israel. The Germans lost the war because they went against the Bible."

"You're right," Karl said. "And they realize that now."

"Who realizes it?"

"The men who were once Nazis and escaped to South America. You've probably heard of them—the *Organisation der ehemaligen SS-Angehörigen?*"

Lish looked baffled.

"Commonly known as the Odessa."

"Oh, the Odessa. Yeah, I heard of them."

"And they've heard of you."

"Of me?"

"Your organization—you were, I believe, one of the founding members of the Rank."

"And proud of it. That's no crime."

Lish's quick changes from belligerence to suspicion to defensiveness and back made Karl wonder if he'd chosen someone a little too unstable for the role he had in mind. But along with the instability there was gullibility, and if the story he told fitted Lish's preconceptions he would, he figured, accept it.

Lish picked up a hand exerciser from the cluttered desk and as they spoke he squeezed it, first in one hand, then the other.

"Anyway," he said, "we're not part of *any* foreign bunch. People keep paintin' us as un-American, but all we're after is to keep the racial heritage of this country."

"I understand. Germany took the wrong path, it's up to America now."

"Maybe so, maybe not," Lish said suspiciously. "What'd you come here for, anyway?"

Karl now began building the foundation of lies intended to seduce Lish into his trap. He began by telling Lish that the Odessa felt a comradeship with all "organizations which share your ideals," and that it was aware of the trouble that the Rank's leader Harkness was having. Members of the Odessa sympathized with his plight and admired the strong action he had taken to silence the enemies of racial purity.

"*That's* for sure," Lish agreed. "You should have heard the stuff that radio guy came out with—all kinds of lies. Grant started getting hate mail. People were calling him at night, scaring his kids, all because of this guy on radio. And whenever Grant would call up to set him straight the guy would say some insult and cut him off in the middle of his answer. I've got tapes—you want to hear firsthand some of the crap he was putting out?"

"Perhaps later."

"Well, anyway, that's not fair, not the American way to use media to attack somebody who can't defend theirself, you know what I mean?"

Of course he did, said Karl. And so did his comrades in the

Odessa. Which brought Karl to why he had come. His people wanted
to contribute to the defense fund for Grant Harkness and wondered if
Lish would handle the money for them.

Lish suddenly became alert. "What money?"

"Five thousand dollars . . ."

Karl placed the briefcase on the desk, opened it and turned it so
Lish could see the money. The man's Adam's apple bobbed as he
looked up at Karl.

"That's for Grant?"

"For his defense fund. Would you be willing to be our conduit for
the money and insure that it reaches Mr. Harkness?"

"Well, sure if—"he paused in mid-sentence, frowned. "Yeah,
well, we're Americans, not Nazis. My daddy fought the Nazis in the
war. If this is going to tie us up with old Nazis, I don't know . . ."

"Just the opposite. We are as eager as you to keep the source of
the money anonymous. Say that you raised it from secret sources,
whatever you wish. Not necessary to mention the Odessa, although I
assure you we *are* on your side."

Lish chewed his lip and looked back at the briefcase, and Karl
quickly picked up a stack of twenty-dollar bills, slid the rubber band
off one of them and held it up to him.

"I don't see any German writing on this, do you?"

A brief smile appeared. "Well, like my daddy used to say, green
is green . . ."

"Then you're willing to handle the transaction?"

"I guess, so long as we're quiet about it. But how come you want
me to do it? Why not just give it to Grant?"

"Can I speak confidentially?"

Lish glanced around, leaned forward. "Sure, what?"

"Without casting any doubts on Mr. Harkness, we have no way of
knowing just what kind of pressure the government might bring to
bear on that man. We feel it's best, at this point, if he knows nothing
of the source of the money. What he doesn't know . . ."

Lish nodded sagely. "Sure, sure, I can understand that."

I'll bet you can, Karl thought, noting that the man could scarcely
keep his eyes off the money. It was time to close. If he had prepared
correctly, Lish would accept the next mix of truth and fiction not
only because it conformed to his preexisting beliefs but because he
stood to gain from it.

"The Harkness matter isn't the only reason I came . . . Are you familiar with the name 'Dr. Mengele'?''

"The Nazi doctor? Sure."

"Good . . . Dr. Mengele, as you may know, escaped to Paraguay after the war. He brought with him a large amount of gold and jewels. Some of this he invested, some of it still survives. When the doctor died his fortune was entrusted to his common-law wife Maria, with the instruction that she distribute it to promote the cause of racial purity. At first she didn't want to do this. Maria is half-Indian, a beautiful woman who grew up in the streets, a beggar, so money has a far greater importance for her than it might for you or me."

Lish nodded, Karl pushed on with his concoction. "For years Maria could only bring herself to give away a thousand dollars here and there, but the bulk of the estate remained intact. In fact, the estate continued to increase in value until today it is worth in excess of one point three million dollars . . ."

Lish whistled appreciatively and the dog lifted its head.

"To get quickly to the point," Karl hurried on, "Maria was recently diagnosed to have leukemia. Her doctor says she has only a few years to live, and now she wants to honor Dr. Mengele's wishes. She is a superstitious woman, an Indian, after all, and she seems to believe the reason she contracted the disease is that she failed to follow the doctor's wishes."

Lish's mind was spinning with zeros—one point three million of them.

"My job," Karl concluded, "is to find someone from the Rank who would be willing to meet Maria and discuss the dispersal of one hundred thousand dollars in the United States. To promote the cause of racial purity."

"A hundred thousand dollars . . ."

"There is only one stipulation: under no circumstances is the money to be traceable to Paraguay, to Maria Mengele or to the Odessa."

"You just want to keep it secret, that's all?"

"We *must* keep it secret. Most of Dr. Mengele's wealth was from Jewish sources—that is to say, Jewish property—all of which was assigned to the Jewish Relief Agency after the war. Some of the property is still in the form of jewels, coin collections, so on. Israel has a claim against all Jewish property not returned or compensated for. If any of the money or the property can be traced to Maria, the Israeli government may attempt to claim it, to steal it . . ."

"Oh, so it's Jewish money."

Karl held up the twenty-dollar bill again. "I don't see any Hebrew on it, do you?"

Lish smiled. "Still green from where I sit."

"All right then, all you have to do, Mr. Lish, is meet Maria and get her blessing."

" 'Get her blessing'? What do you mean?"

"She always meets each recipient in person. Indian, you know. They have to look you in the eye before they trust you.

Lish looked worried. Would this Indian woman like what she saw? Karl noted his expression, assured him there shouldn't be a problem, that from what he knew of Maria they'd get along fine. He said that Maria had just arrived in the United States. She had come to consult with the medical experts at famous hospitals. "She's in Miami now," Karl said, "but she'll be going north very soon for treatment."

Lish frowned. "She's not mixed up in drug traffic, is she? We don't hold with drugs. They poison the mind, like interbreeding poisons the blood."

Lish's unpredictable, near-random thoughts startled and worried Karl. He hoped that the man wasn't too bizarre to be credible as the General Secretary's assassin.

"Maria is a wealthy woman," he reminded Lish. "She doesn't have to traffic in drugs."

"Well, I know Miami. It's gone Cuban now and they're all tied into drugs."

"No, no," Karl said, inventing some as he went along now. "The only reason Maria is in Miami is because passenger ships don't go to Washington, and she's afraid of flying, doesn't trust airplanes. She only travels by ship and by train."

And by Winnebago, he added silently. But he said nothing to Lish about the motor home. Instead he explained that Lish was to come to Washington the next Thursday to meet Maria. This would be after she finished her tests at Johns Hopkins University—he had researched famous American hospitals that specialized in cancer treatment—but before she left for the Mayo Clinic. It would also be four days before the General Secretary's arrival on Monday, which would give Karl time for his final preparations.

Karl was pleased with himself. He felt like a chess master, moving a piece here and a piece there in a deceptively innocent fashion designed to lead his opponent into an inescapable trap. The lure of this particular gambit was one hundred thousand dollars, available in cash as soon as Maria approved Lish.

Lish's eyes gleamed at the prospect, but he forced a frown. "Who's going to pay for the trip?"

"We will, of course. You'll stay at the Marriott-Arlington with us."

"You'll be there?"

"I'll pick you up at the airport."

Lish still seemed preoccupied.

"Is that a problem?"

"Just that I'll have to pay Berto to feed the dogs while I'm gone . . ."

You greedy bastard, Karl thought. He took out his wallet. "How much will it cost?"

"I got to give him a hundred a day, otherwise he'll scab for pipe-fitting down at Lenmore."

Karl separated two one hundred dollar bills and made certain Lish got a good look at the rest.

Lish reached for the money but Karl hesitated. "You are certain you can leave here?"

"I'm your man, Karl."

You're my dead man, Karl thought.

He handed over the money and returned Lish's smile, as false as his own.

In Berlin, Paul found it almost impossible to concentrate on any single thought long enough to follow it to a conclusion. He was con-tinuously weak and dizzy, felt as if the drugs were dissolving his muscles and turning his bones to rubber. To conserve his strength he began sleeping for longer and longer periods of time. He was dozing almost constantly by the time he realized that it was the drugs that took his energy, not lack of sleep. And he was growing weaker, not stronger.

Galvanized into action by the thought, Paul slid off the bed and attempted to exercise on the floor. A single push-up was an effort and caused blood to pound in his head. He rested and did another. He managed to do three before Madam Tran brought in the food tray and laughed at his efforts.

"You think you're going someplace? Huh? Not unless you're a worm, maybe. You want to crawl under that door? Come on, now, it's time to eat."

She helped him up onto the bed. In the process his hand struck the table, spilling a glass of orange juice. Madam Tran jumped back.

"Damn no good," she said, inspecting her silk Bao Dai and the drops of juice near the skirt. She went into the bathroom, cursing softly in a mixture of Vietnamese, French and German. It took Paul a moment before he fully realized that she hadn't closed the door. If he could get out of the room, out of the building . . .

He got himself up, bracing himself against the dizziness that made the room spin. The door was twenty feet away but might have been a mile. His legs were weak, his stomach queasy. He dropped to his hands and knees and the nausea passed. He could hear the water running in the bathroom. He focused his attention on the open doorway and crawled. It seemed to take an eternity to cross the room—and when he reached the door, it closed in his face.

He turned, looking over his shoulder like an animal. Madam Tran was staring down at him, hands on her hips, the wet spot on her Bao Dai gleaming darkly.

"You spilled your food, little worm," she said. "Maybe you rather eat off the floor."

She took the tray from the table and carefully emptied the contents onto the floor. As she left, Paul grabbed weakly at her ankle but she kicked his hand aside and slipped out the door, taking the tray and utensils with her. Using the doorknob, Paul pulled himself to his feet and pounded in frustration. All that did was make him dizzy. He slid to the floor, the hospital gown bunching around his chest.

Paul clawed at the door. "Let me out," he yelled, but the strangled sounds that came from his mouth were as pitiful as his efforts. His motor skills were disintegrating, his body failing. He had to find a way out—and quickly.

Exhausted by his struggle at the door, Paul took a plastic glass from the wicker table beside the bed and crawled into the bathroom. He was not an animal. Water would be his breakfast this morning. He wouldn't eat from the floor . . .

Later, he lay in bed and stared at the spilled food reflected in the ceiling mirrors. A fly crawled over the white dome of a broken soft-boiled egg, and the toast was discolored by a puddle of orange juice. The garbage that had been his meal mocked his weakness. He tried to think, to concentrate, but the morning's exertions had worn him out. But then, as he began to doze, an idea came and he sat up, thoughts racing, and stared at the mess on the floor. The food had given him an idea about how to escape.

He lay back down, smiling, and the smile persisted even after he fell asleep.

When he awoke the food was gone, and so was the memory of his escape plan. He had forgotten.

CHAPTER
19

KARL INSPECTED EACH TOOL AND PIECE OF EQUIP-
ment before placing it in a nylon backpack. He was at a hotel in
Hoboken, New Jersey, and the equipment was spread before him on
the bed. Metal tape, gaffer's tape, surgeon's gloves, dentist's mirror,
padlock, caulking compound—the list was a long one, too long for
his liking. He preferred simplicity, but for this operation there was
no choice. He had to get onto the terminal, break into Warehouse E,
steal a Redeye missile and escape, all without leaving a trace. And he
had to do it tonight—tomorrow the *Coralis* arrived.

Karl took a taxi to a marina on Staten Island, where he had left an
inflatable boat and motor. He had bought the outfit through a newspaper ad. The boat was patched and the motor had been repainted an
ugly blue, but its looks were deceiving. He had inspected everything
carefully and made two practice runs, the first up Newark Bay to
Bayonne Park and the second into Upper Bay, around the Statue of
Liberty and back, a route that took him past the Military Terminal.

The boat would get him across the bay but he could not risk leaving it exposed on shore or anchored in the water. To make his escape

193

he had purchased an underwater propulsion vehicle, a Dacor Nereid that lay in the bottom of the inflatable boat covered with plastic. It was shaped like a torpedo with handles extending from the rear. When he bought the Nereid, it had been bright yellow; Karl had since painted it black. The vehicle was battery-operated, silent and would run for some three hours at one-and-one-half knots. Towing the Redeye would cut the speed and endurance, but Karl had made his plans so as to have both the outgoing tide and river's current behind him.

It was a mild weekend night. Nobody paid any attention as he left the marina. The tide was rising and the air was thick with the smell of brine, seaweed and mud. On the larger boats, interior lights glowed and traced rippled patterns across the black water. A motor cruiser moved down one of the slips, the sound of animated chatter drifting from its deck.

Karl twisted the throttle and the roar of the outboard dominated the night. As he moved beyond the confines of Van Kull Kill into Upper Bay, the sea began to heave. Now the Military Ocean Terminal came into view, its bright perimeter lights glancing off obsidian waves and throwing deep shadows into warehouses and streets beyond. A ship was being loaded, and Karl angled away from the activity toward a portion of the pier close to Warehouse E. Before entering the glare of the lights he stopped the motor, removed his outer clothing and shoes, sealed them in a waterproof bag he tucked inside the backpack. Beneath the clothes he wore a torso wetsuit.

He adjusted the straps on the backpack, thrust his feet into swim fins and slipped overboard. The shock of cold, oil-slick water quickly dissipated as the water warmed the inside of the suit. With a knife he sliced open each of the inflatable sections and let the boat sink beneath the waves. The Nereid, which weighed over thirty pounds on land, settled into the water with a slightly negative buoyancy. Karl engaged the vehicle and let his body trail like the tail of a kite. The water swirled and bubbled around his shoulders as the Nereid pulled him toward the pier.

There were no permanent guards along the seaward boundary of the terminal. When his feet touched bottom Karl took off his weight belt and put it in a fishnet bag he then fixed to the Nereid. He tied a fishing line to the belt and let it sink along with the vehicle to the bottom. After noting his position, he made his way to shore, letting the fishing line unwind behind him. He hid the fishing line beneath a rock, removed his swim fins and scrambled over slippery pilings and broken concrete slabs until he gained dry ground. Keeping to the shadows, he crossed the deserted terminal to Warehouse E, where he knew that a security patrol made its rounds once an hour, although he did not know exactly when.

The warehouses were bordered by deserted streets bathed in pools of light. Warehouse E had loading doors twenty feet high at one end, and next to them was a normal-size metal door inset with squares of frosted glass. Karl stood silent in the shadows, listening and watching. When he was certain that no one was around he went to the door, risking the porch light to inspect the frosted glass. Just as Major Fellows had said, there was a faint outline of metal security tape on the inside.

He moved back into the shadows and made his way to the rear of the building, where he took from the backpack a spider hook attached to a Dacron line. Using the rope as a sling, he lofted the hook onto the roof. It tumbled into the gutter and he winced at the sound. When he tugged on the rope the hook bounced free and fell to the ground. A cat darted silently out from the shadows and disappeared. Karl paused to listen, then threw the hook again. He did this four times before it caught.

Once the the hook was lodged firmly he tied the backpack to the free end, then scaled the rope. The metal gutter gave slightly when he grabbed it, and Karl prayed that whoever the contractor had been he hadn't skimped on materials. For a moment he dangled thirty feet in the air, the gutter sagging under his weight, then managed to swing a heel over the edge, rolled up and over and was on the roof.

He paused a moment to catch his breath before hauling up the backpack. Along the apex of the roof were three metal ventilators capped by hoods. Karl made his way to the one in the middle and took out of the backpack a small oxyacetylene torch and a black asbestos cuff. The oxyacetylene outfit he had bought at a hardware store; the asbestos cuff he designed himself so that the flame wouldn't show while he was working.

He positioned the cuff and lit the torch. After adjusting the flame he began to cut around the neck of the ventilator about six inches above the base. The suit was wet against his skin, and the light wind made him shiver. He was glad for the tendrils of warm air that came drifting from the torch. From his vantage point Karl could see the spread of the terminal, the harbor, and on the far shore, the city of

New York, its millions of lights casting a pale glow on the underside of low-hanging clouds.

It took just over ten minutes to cut around the ventilator. Karl placed it on its side and peered into the warehouse. The opening was blocked by iron bars. Using a flashlight and the dentist's mirror, he took a look at the underside of the bars. Shiny metal tape ran their length, each end attached to terminals in the ceiling.

With his own metal tape Karl ran an alternate path between the terminals, bypassing two of the bars, then cut the bars with the acetylene torch and placed each segment on the roof. The opening now large enough for him to fit through, he lowered the backpack to the floor, fixed the other end of the line to the roof and climbed down.

The interior of the warehouse was almost completely dark, the only light coming from the frosted windows in the metal doors. The cargo containers were stacked two and three high, each shipment in a separate area. Using a flashlight to check the Cargo Designation Numbers, Karl found QL 4416 H5. He breathed a large sigh, the Redeye shipment had arrived on schedule. Moving quickly, he cut the padlock with the torch, broke the metal security band and opened the doors.

The narrow beam of the flashlight revealed rows of dark green metal boxes separated by wood frames. Karl removed a wood brace, pulled out one of the boxes and lowered it to the floor. It was five feet long, eighteen inches wide and a foot high. The corners were rounded and there were metal handles at each end. It weighed about fifty pounds but almost half of this was from a battery charger and the box itself.

Karl flipped open the latches and lifted the lid. The smell of fresh paint and electrical wiring reminded him of a new stereo. He was looking at a metal tube about four feet long with a handgrip and eyepiece located one third of the way from the firing end. This was the launch tube; the missile itself was inside it. Karl took out the launcher and inspected it: handgrip, flip-up eyepiece, cable terminals, battery compartment. Removing the end caps, he peered into the barrel with a flashlight. The heat-seeking hemisphere of the Redeye gleamed back at him like a reptilian eye—

The sound of a car. He flicked off the flashlight and waited. Headlights washed across the frosted window and stopped. The security patrol. Karl checked his watch: twelve-forty. Instinctively he moved back against the container, knowing that it would do no good . . . if anyone came in now the operation was blown.

A man's silhouette loomed large against the frosted glass, then shrank as the man approached the door. The sound of the idling engine echoed faintly off the warehouse walls. One man called to another and laughed. The doorknob rattled once, then the shadow moved away. Moments later the engine roared and the window reflected a reddish glow as they drove off.

Karl let his breath out slowly. Now that they were gone, the adrenaline came in a quick rush; his heart raced and a prickly sensation spread across his hands.

He replaced the weapon and checked the four batteries and their charger. He would only need one battery, but the others would serve as backups. When he was finished checking the Redeye, he repacked it and set it aside. The next step was to lock and reseal the cargo container so that no one could tell that it had been opened.

From his backpack Karl pulled out an Eagle padlock, one that matched the army's model, and snapped it into place. Finding a duplicate lock had been a matter of calling hardware stores until he found what he wanted. The security seal had required a more complex although ultimately no more difficult solution. He had a new seal with the correct cargo designation code already embossed: QL 4416 H5. The blank security bands were readily available and so were the individual dies that he used to stamp the correct code. Now he threaded the band through the hasp, slid one end through the slotted metal ball and clamped them together with a crimping tool. Not until the cargo arrived in Costa Rica and the assignee tried to open the lock would anyone discover the switch.

Once the container was sealed, he brought out the caulking compound and sealed the metal box containing the Redeye. He smeared the sticky substance around the seam, applied a strip of gauze and repeated the process. The caulk had a distinctive smell that made him uneasy; he imagined it permeating the building and alerting the security guards. After finishing the job he went to the front door and bypassed the alarm system in the same way that he had earlier, using his own metal tape to trace an alternate path between terminals.

He opened the door and peered outside. The area was deserted. Moving quickly he took the Redeye around to the side of the building to a metal trash dumpster. Although the air was cool he was sweating inside the wetsuit. Rusty hinges squeaked as he lifted the lid. He had forgotten oil. It seemed there was always something, in this case nothing critical, but it annoyed him just the same.

He stowed the Redeye in the dumpster and closed the lid quickly and firmly to minimize the noise. Then, back inside the warehouse, he retraced each step, removing the metal bypass tape as he went. He scaled the rope to the roof and replaced the security bars, using gaffer's tape to secure the broken segments back in their original position. The tape was dark gray and similar in color to that of the bars. He doubted that anyone glancing up into the shadowy recesses of the ceiling would notice the difference.

Once the bars were in place he ran metal tape along the underside to reconnect the original circuit. Finally, he put the top back on the stump of the ventilator, again using the gaffer's tape. Eventually the sun and rain would dry out the tape and strong wind would topple it, but by then his mission should be accomplished.

He climbed down the rope and tugged a disconnect cord to free the spider hook. He shoved the gear into his backpack, returned to the dumpster and retrieved the Redeye. This, of course, was when he was most vulnerable. The Redeye package with its case and batteries weighed almost sixty pounds. Bending forward so that some of the weight was taken by the backpack, he made his way to the water. At one point he was crossing the street when a car appeared and turned onto the street and it was only a matter of good luck that it turned away rather than toward him. Karl cursed softly and wished again that he'd figured out a better way of transporting the missile. Something less noticeable, something with wheels.

By the time he reached the water, he was breathing heavily. Rocks slippery with seaweed lay exposed by the ebbing tide. Twice he slipped and sat down heavily, trying to cushion the Redeye case with his body. The second time the case slipped free and banged against the rocks. To Karl the sound was as loud as a rifle shot but there was no reaction from the terminal; the only sound to disturb the quiet night was the distant rumble of the crane moving along the pier and the faint jangle of its warning bell.

The cold water was a shock to his overheated body but Karl welcomed it. The water was safety. He followed the fishing line back to the Nereid, put on his weight belt and attached a rope from it to the handle of the Redeye case. With the case floating low in the water behind him, he let the Nereid take them across the narrow channel to Staten Island.

He had parked the car in a residential area along Richmond Terrace near his landing spot, a small park bordering the shoreline. The outgoing current was stronger than he'd anticipated and he had to make a heading change to the west to correct for it. Even so he missed his landfall by a quarter of a mile and ended up beneath a restaurant that sat on pilings overlooking the water. It was two-thirty in the morning.

He hid the Redeye, stripped off the wetsuit and dried himself as best he could with the thin white towel that he'd taken from the hotel and stowed inside the waterproof bag along with his clothes. The clothing soaked up what moisture the towel missed, leaving his shirt clammy against his back as he walked the deserted streets. By the time he reached the car he was shivering. He turned on the heater, returned to the restaurant and retrieved the Redeye.

Exhilarated by his success, Karl drove all night back to Washington. He slept for six hours, ate breakfast at noon and then sat down on the living room floor, the Redeye and its components spread out around him. He had memorized the instruction manual during the holiday at Zinnowitz with Uncle Alex; now he began practicing what he had learned. The launch sequence consisted of a number of operations: gyro spin-up, target ranging, uncaging the gyro, infra-red acquisition and firing. Karl practiced them over and over, and by the end of the day the Redeye felt as familiar in his hands as the steering wheel of the Mercedes.

The next step was to develop a procedure for firing the missile from inside the motor home, a task that proved more difficult than he'd anticipated. After renting the Winnebago he drove at night with the Redeye to Dulles airport and parked beneath the approach path of the incoming jets. The civilian aircraft appeared in the open skylight framed by a black sky alive with stars, but Karl found that there was no time to track them. By the time he caught the aircraft in the ranging ring, the forward edge of the hatch blocked his view. The only way he would have enough time to track, lock and fire seemed to be to stand on the roof and this he was unwilling to do. Of his four launch sites two were in suburban neighborhoods, one was at a roadside rest stop and the fourth was in a shopping center parking lot. Karl wanted to be able to remain hidden, even during launch, which meant firing through the skylight.

One solution was to modify the opening and make it bigger but this couldn't be done until after he'd duped George Lish into renting the motor home. Once that was done, he could make the modification himself or pay to have it done. If he paid someone, there was no telling how long it would take or if the person would realize that the Winnebago was a rental. The best course was to do it himself, but he hated to do anything that would draw attention to the Winnebago and he had a natural distrust of half-way measures. What if he made the opening so big that it weakened the frame? He imagined a scenario in which the roof gave way when he hit a pothole and the motor home collapsed like a dynamited bridge.

In the end Karl opted for a simpler, more innovative solution that involved a mirror and a lot of practice. The mirror was convex and when he clipped it to the forward edge of the skylight opening it provided a view of the sky behind the Winnebago. It was a distorted view, with tiny planes growing rapidly in size and ballooning outward as they passed overhead, but with enough practice Karl found that he could interpret distances just as easily as he could with the naked eye.

Using the mirror, he practiced the same procedure that he'd mastered at the house. He stood in the Winnebago with the Redeye on his shoulder, one eye at the target ring and the other on the approaching plane. He uncaged the gyro and began leading the aircraft even before it reached the skylight. As it swept into view, the acquisition signal, a thin, reedy tone, indicated that the Redeye was locked on target and that he could fire at will. Once launched, the jet's exhaust gases would act as a hot carpet, leading the heat-seeking head of the Redeye to the aircraft. Once launched, an aircraft without infra-red counter-measures was doomed.

Karl spent three nights locking on one civilian aircraft after the other, each one a trigger pull and three seconds away from destruction. He wondered how many lives passed through his hands? A thousand? Two thousand? Ten thousand? It didn't matter. Only one life was important. Only one life was the target.

His experience with the Winnebago convinced him that while ideal as a launch platform, the motor home was too slow and clumsy to serve as a getaway vehicle. He bought a copy of the local paper, the *Prince George's Journal*, and went looking for used motorcycles. In a neighborhood of permanent house trailers he met a sullen young man who had a Kawasaki KE-100 for sale.

"I wouldn't sell it," the boy mumbled, "only I'm going into the army."

He had pale skin, stringy hair and pouting lips, and Karl had trouble believing that the American army would want him.

The Kawasaki was black with red-and-orange flames dashing across its gas tank, a dual-purpose machine made for off-road work as well as the street. With a one hundred cc engine it wasn't particularly fast or powerful but it wasn't heavy and would be easy to get in and out of the Winnebago. Besides, the motorcycle only had to take him from Andrews Air Force Base to National Airport, just across the Potomac from downtown Washington.

"It's in cherry condition," the kid mumbled.

A ride around the neighborhood convinced Karl, and they quickly settled on a bargain-basement price.

When Karl returned the Winnebago to Sunshine RV, he took the motorcycle and used it to return to the Toons Creek house. It clearly wasn't made for freeway driving, so he stayed on the secondary roads, just as he would when he made his run from Andrews to National Airport.

He also bought a space-age helmet with a full face visor and spent hours riding the country roads that wandered through the wooded hills of Maryland. Twice he rode from Andrews to Washington National Airport to familiarize himself with his escape route.

It was on the second trip that he saw his brother's wife.

It was a Wednesday afternoon, and for no reason other than his continued fascination with his brother's life, Karl had detoured past Paul's house in Arlington, Virginia. Dressed in a leather jacket and full-face helmet, he wasn't worried about any of the neighbors mistaking him for Paul.

It was when he turned onto the block that he saw a woman exiting the house. Could it be her? He made a quick U-turn, drove around the corner and returned to a position where he could watch without being seen. The woman had black hair held in place by a red silk scarf worn as a headband. She wore a gray blouse with black slacks and moved briskly to an Alfa Romeo parked at the curb. When the Alfa came toward him, Karl remained where he was and with the visor down, pretended to study a map and glanced up only at the last minute to get a good look at the woman. It was Joanna, all right. He recognized her from the photograph that Paul had given him.

She seemed concentrated on something and he felt sure that she hadn't noticed him. Excited, he allowed himself to follow her across the Key Bridge to an art gallery in Georgetown, the Kawasaki making it easy to slip through traffic and keep hidden by intervening cars. When they arrived at the Gallerie L'Enfant he remembered that Paul had said his wife worked at an art gallery. Paul's wife. Joanna . . .

There was a smile on his face as he rode back to the Toons Creek house and began to speculate on his brother's life. Somehow, from Paul's uneasiness when he mentioned her, he had gotten the impression that his brother and Joanna had separated; if so, she must have returned in Paul's absence. Was she worried about Paul? Did she know that he had gone to Germany? If she called the editor, Bernie Stern, he would tell her the same story that Karl had given him about going underground to investigate the CIA and arms deals. The more he thought about it, the more Karl thought of learning firsthand about his brother's life. If he could sneak into the house while Joanna was at work . . .

But he wouldn't have to sneak; he had Paul's keys. That realization carried its own special excitement and anticipation. He could just walk up to the door and—no, too dangerous. The Redeye mission was far too important to risk for a whim. Paul's life was Paul's life and his life was his and nothing he could discover could change their separate destinies. Karl thrust from his mind the notion of going into his brother's house, but it didn't disappear . . . it took root in his subconscious, and began to grow even as he prepared to meet George Lish.

The idea of his escape returned to Paul with a rush in one of the rare moments of lucidity that preceded his daily injection. It came back to him . . . that day he spilled orange juice on Madam Tran and her first reaction had been concern about her clothes. And that was the key. Praying that she would react the same way if it happened again, Paul made his preparations.

First he filled his plastic glass with water. Since the vertigo made it impossible for him to stand, he crawled to the bathroom and back, putting the glass on the floor each time he moved ahead. When he got to the bed he put the glass against the wall underneath the wicker table. Then he lay down and practiced every movement, over and over. What he had to do was simple but his limbs lacked coordination and his muscles were weak . . . he worried that he wouldn't be able to perform the maneuver quickly enough and without faltering.

But there was no choice: he *had* to do it; somehow he had to make his body obey. It had been so long since he'd been healthy that he couldn't even recall the sensation. Had there actually been a time when he could stand without getting dizzy, walk without falling, and even run? When, if his mind said, *Do it,* his body had swiftly responded with no more concentration on the mechanics than he used in breathing?

He had to regain these capabilities to escape, but everything depended on Madam Tran and whether her reaction would mirror the previous one. When she arrived Paul saw with satisfaction that her Bao Dai was a rich gold decorated with brocade. Good. The more expensive and fancy the dress, the more likely she would react to protect it. Clothes were clearly an obsession with her.

She approached the bed as she always did, businesslike, lips pursed, one eye on Paul. As usual the syringe was on the tray beside the food, beside the glass of milk that came with dinner. Paul struggled to a sitting position and, pretending to be very hungry, reached for the tray just as Madam Tran put it down, hit the glass of milk and knocked it to the floor, splattering Madam Tran's Bao Dai.

"Damn you!"

She slapped him hard as she could. Paul fell back on the bed, ear ringing from the blow. His face felt numb and one eye was watering so that he had to keep blinking to make it focus. He could see himself in the mirror over the bed, first fuzzy, then in focus, then fuzzy again . . .

The sound of water running in the bathroom brought him to his senses. How long had he been lying there? How long did he have? Never mind, he had to act. Now . . .

He rolled to his side. The tray was still on the table, and on it was the syringe. Now came the part he had practiced. He reached out, hand shaking. The syringe seemed such a long way off . . . He levered himself up on one elbow, and the elbow gave way. He fell against the mattress, got control again, tried again . . . The syringe. His fingertips brushed the smooth glass, which moved away. He leaned further, felt the muscle in his supporting arm begin to tremble—and then, finally, he had it.

He brought the syringe close to his chest. Through the doorway Madam Tran was partly visible, her back to him, still busily, angrily cleaning the Bao Dai at the sink. Paul turned his attention to the syringe. With clumsy hands he thrust the needle into the mattress and depressed the plunger. There was resistance, it didn't seem to be moving. He pushed harder, his thumb slipped off. Cursing softly, he wiped his sweaty hand on the sheet and tried again. *Easy*, he told himself, don't try too hard, don't break the needle . . . He kept a steady pressure, and slowly, slowly the syringe emptied. When all the fluid had been expelled Paul rolled to his stomach, head and arms extending beyond the mattress so that he could reach the water glass on the floor. He put the needle into the glass and pulled the plunger. Slowly, ever so slowly, the syringe began to fill.

Too damn long, a voice inside screamed at him. It's taking too *long*, she's on her way out, hurry, for God's sake . . . He fought the panic and continued the steady pressure. The plunger moved with terrible slowness. His hands trembled; his fingers almost slipped. His head, hanging over the side of the bed, throbbed painfully. He wanted to yank the plunger back but forced himself not to . . .

And then at last it was done.

And the water in the bathroom had stopped.

He shoved an elbow under his chest and levered himself up. In the bathroom Madame Tran smoothed her wet Bao Dai and began to turn. He had to get the syringe back onto the tray. In his hurry his hand struck the underside of the table and the syringe flipped out of his fingers and skittered across the floor.

"You damn trouble . . ." Madam Tran was saying as she came into the room.

The syringe lay by itself, midway between the spilled milk and the bathroom. In a moment she would see it. In a moment she would know. Unless—

Paul lunged and struck the tray, tumbling the chicken and dumplings, the beets, everything onto the floor.

"No more," Madam Tran shouted. She came forward, avoiding the mess on the floor, and shoved him back on the bed.

"Hungry," Paul mumbled.

"You get nothing, you get nothing tonight, maggot-eaten trouble man . . ."

She started toward the door, then saw the syringe and remembered the injection.

"Hungry," Paul said.

"Shut up. Turn around."

She pushed him to his side and Paul felt the familiar sting in his buttocks. A smile tugged at his lips as Madam Tran marched out, slamming and locking the door behind her. Somebody would come to clean up the mess, but Paul didn't stay awake to find out who. Exhausted, he fell asleep, and in sleeping began to become a threat to his brother.

CHAPTER

20

GEORGE LISH ARRIVED AT WASHINGTON NATIONAL AIR-port shortly after noon on Thursday, just four days before the General Secretary was due to arrive. As the plane approached low over the silvery brown Potomac he began to pick out familiar landmarks: the Washington Monument, Arlington Memorial Bridge, the Capitol. He strained to see the Vietnam War Memorial, the monument to his own generation's sacrifice in the cause of freedom. George had championed the cause of a Vietnam memorial, only to be disappointed by the author of the winning design—an oriental girl, American by nationality but clearly foreign by race . . . clearly not from the same brave stock that produced the men who fell at Bunker Hill and Iwo Jima.

George shared with other members of the Rank a special world geography in which each continent was allocated to a certain race: blacks in Africa, orientals in China, Mexicans in South America, Jews in Israel, and Aryans in Europe and North America. This was the natural order of things and obviously the way God intended it.

Unlike some members of the Rank, George considered himself a moderate fellow. He didn't want to kill all the blacks and Jews—people were people, after all. No, he favored the "Israeli model," which meant that each race would be put back in its proper homeland. Like he always told people, he *supported* the blacks in South Africa. He was willing for all whites to leave Africa in exchange for all blacks leaving America. "A White America for White Americans." That was the Rank's slogan.

George was proud to say he had invented the slogan ten years ago when he and six others had founded the Rank. He had been the organization's first vice-president, married at the time to a woman named Bobbi who bore him three children and turned failing Dog-O-Rama into a profitable business before leaving George for a pet food salesman. Since then the Dog-O-Rama had gone into a decline, stimulated by the downturn in the Houston economy, which everybody knew was on account of the Arabs and their cheap oil.

George's fortunes within the Rank suffered a similar decline. As the memberships grew he was overshadowed by men like Grant Harkness, men with dynamic personalities, more jazzy, extreme ideas and lots better slogans. In subsequent elections George suffered humiliating defeats, although he was careful to hide his disappointment behind an outward show of good-natured camaraderie. He was demoted to serving in committees and organizing the combat games that took place once a month. He was not part of the inner circle and wasn't a member of the Action Squad that sent the bomb to the radio station. So it was with a secret and understandable thrill that he heard the news of Grant Harkness' arrest.

George smiled as he recalled presenting the Odessa's money—the half of it that he'd parted with—to Grant Harkness. He'd kept two thousand five hundred in reserve, figuring that he could double the satisfaction of seeing Grant's stunned expression if he gave the money in two separate chunks. Asked where it came from, George had smiled and said, "I have secret sources that I'm not at liberty to divulge."

He was vaguely aware that he was fooling himself, that what he was doing with the money was waiting to see if he was approved as a beneficiary for Dr. Mengele's money. If this woman Maria didn't approve him, maybe he would hold back some of the twenty-five hundred in payment for the time and effort he was spending. In fact he had already spent eight hundred dollars to pay off some pressing debts—he thought of it as a loan he would pay back as soon as the summer business picked up . . .

George's self-confidence began to ebb as the plane taxied toward the terminal. This Karl Muller, so confident and self-assured, represented a larger, secret world of foreign affairs that George only dreamed about. Why should such a man trust him? Why should Maria Mengele? By the time he stepped into the terminal he was so uneasy that he was almost surprised to find Karl waiting.

The Odessa man, as he knew him, greeted him warmly, and George's doubts began to evaporate.

"How was the flight?" Karl asked.

"The usual bullshit," George said, "Took longer to taxi to the runway than it did to get here . . . Did Mrs. Mengele arrive?"

Karl gave him a cautionary look. "We'll talk in the car."

"Got it," George said, biting off the words in a clipped, no-nonsense fashion that he hoped would make up for the obvious blunder in mentioning Maria Mengele's name in public.

In the parking lot Karl led him to a gleaming burgundy-and-silver Lincoln Continental. George felt a tweak of jealousy . . . it didn't seem fair that a Nazi organization had all this money while the Rank had to struggle to pay the printing costs of its newsletter, *Battle Lines*. If he could get his hands on a little of it . . . his thoughts were full of dreams of what he might accomplish with some real money while Karl paid the parking fee and headed north along the George Washington Parkway. He came out of his reverie when he noticed Karl's preoccupation with the rearview mirror.

"Problem?" ˙

"Someone in a yellow Jaguar. Came out behind us, turned the same way. Let's see if they . . ." Karl let the words trail off, then relaxed. "No, it's okay, they're going to the city." As he spoke they turned west on Highway 244.

"Aren't we going to the city?"

"We've got a little problem, George."

And George thought, My luck is never any good. They've found someone else to give the money to. "What's wrong?" he asked.

"Take a look." Karl handed him a Xerox copy of a telegram from Buenos Aires addressed to Karl Muller c/o the Marriott Hotel: ISRAELI M AWARE YOUR MISSION. SUGGEST PRECAUTIONS, ADVISE GL. There was no signature.

"*Israeli M?* Who's that—the Mossad?" George knew his spy fiction.

Karl give him an admiring look. "Exactly."

George glowed. "But who's GL?"

"You."

George cringed. It had never occurred to him that he was important enough to be included in a telegram, especially one like this.

Karl was saying something now about a wallet being stolen, and George forced himself to concentrate.

". . . hotel detectives couldn't find a thing," Karl said. "But then, with the Mossad after you, you don't expect them to. The point is, I was supposed to rent a motor home. You know, one of those Winnebagos with a bedroom, kitchen, everything on wheels, as they say?" He glanced at George. "You know what I'm talking about, right?"

"I think I missed the first part, sorry . . . you said your wallet was stolen?"

"From my hotel room. While I was in the swimming pool. It might have been the maid or a professional burglar *or* the Mossad. Who knows? But whichever it was, I must rent this motor home to take Maria to the Mayo Clinic. Now that we know the Mossad is onto us, she does not want to travel by train, and an ordinary automobile would not be adequate, considering her condition . . . I told her I would see if you could do it."

"Do what?"

"Rent the motor home for her."

"*Me* rent a motor home?"

"You would not have to pay for it, of course. I will give you the money: seven hundred and fifty dollars."

"But . . . can't *you* rent it?"

"Not anymore. My driver's license was stolen with my wallet."

"Maybe you could just fly out—"

"Maria is afraid of flying. I told you that."

"Oh, yeah," George said, although the truth was that he had forgotten almost everything about Maria except her one hundred thousand dollars.

"Maria tires easily, she has a special diet, she is often in pain. A motor home makes sense. It may also be a blessing in disguise. If you do her a favor, she is certain to trust you . . ."

George was alarmed by the unexpected request and the responsibility that went with it. "Well," he hedged, "what if you don't get it back in time? Or have an accident?"

"The seven hundred and fifty dollars includes insurance. As for

getting back in time, you can take the money out of the bequest if
we're late.''

George remained silent. He was trying to absorb and sort out this
new development. If he signed for the motor home he'd be legally
responsible for it. If he refused, Maria Mengele might choose someone else to handle the money. George had already awarded himself a
substantial commission and did not want to lose it.

Then he had a darker thought. He gave Karl Muller a surreptitious
glance. The man was a stranger. Could this be some kind of scam to
steal a motor home and blame it on him? How much did something
like a Winnebago cost? Thirty, forty thousand? He'd be bankrupt if
he had to pay out that kind of money . . . Of course, if she gave him
the money, the hundred thousand would pay for a couple of Winnebagos.

"Is she . . . going to give me the money today?"

"If she trusts you, you will have it in a matter of hours."

"And she's got the money with her?"

"Fifty thousand dollars is in cash, the rest is in the form of jewels
and precious metals. But, of course, if you don't want to do her a
favor—"

"No," George said quickly, "I was just thinking about the Mossad. Whether there would be any danger involved."

"To them, perhaps. Right?"

"What?"

"I have the impression that you are a man who can take care of
himself. And of those who would cause trouble for you."

Karl gave him a soldier-of-fortune grin that George returned,
faintly. Much as he liked to think of himself as a commanding presence, deep inside George suspected that he was more often the victim
of events than their master. He was beginning to have that feeling
now, of things moving too fast, of events gone out of his control . . .

But with the thought of the money to anchor his resolve, George
dismissed his fears. He would rent the Winnebago and prove his
worth. But if Maria Mengele didn't give him the money, he'd drive
the damn thing right back to the lot and tell her to forget it. Right, it
was that simple. He'd do it.

When they reached Sunshine RV, Karl said he had to call Maria
and went to a phone booth at the corner. He couldn't, of course, go
inside without the salesman recognizing him; further, it was abso-

lutely necessary for his plan that George rent the Winnebago by himself, that George be the renter of record.

Karl was pleased; things were going well. The Maria Mengele story was the most complex, and unlikely, of all the lies he'd constructed for the Redeye mission, and therefore the most vulnerable. But George Lish was running true to form. The lure of one hundred thousand dollars combined with careful ego building had overruled the man's innate caution and cowardice. Karl was proud of the telegram, which he had sent to himself at the hotel and then cut and pasted together in such a manner that the Argentine address, originally part of the message, appeared to be the address of the sender. Photocopying it had made the deception invisible, and Lish had not asked to see the original. Karl smiled as he remembered how proud the man had been about guessing that *M* meant *Mossad*—as if anyone would use such a transparent code . . .

Karl could see George through the window of Sunshine RV, filling out forms, talking to the clerk. He felt a bit like a cat toying with a mouse, letting it run a few feet and then batting it back to the center of the room to play with it once again. But now the time for play was over. He reached beneath the seat, drew out an ice pick with a shiny green handle and slipped it into the pocket of his sport coat.

The Winnebago was twenty-seven feet long, beige with a red-and-blue stripe. Karl led the way, driving slowly so that Lish, following in the motor home, could keep up. He had told him that because of the Israeli interest in Maria's movements they had moved from the Marriott to a safe house near the Patuxent River. Karl kept an eye on the Winnebago but George seemed to have no trouble with it; whenever Karl glanced his way, he gave a firm thumbs-up sign.

When they reached the Toons Creek house Karl unlatched the gate and drove on ahead, parked, and as the Winnebago came lumbering up the tree-lined drive opened the stable doors and waved it inside. George gave another thumbs-up. As he passed, Karl opened the side door and stepped inside. It smelled new inside the Winnebago, a mix of fabric, plastic and paint.

Karl came forward until he stood between the two front seats.

George turned off the ignition. "This is a great spot."

"Wait a moment," Karl said. "Before you get out, show me how this machine operates."

He slipped his hand into his pocket and grasped the ice pick as George began to point to the dashboard controls.

"Hell, this thing's a pussy rig, just like driving a car. You got a few more switches is all. This is the master electric, you check it to see . . ."

As George leaned forward to touch the electrical switch Karl could see the slight notch at the base of his skull, just above the vertebrae. He brought the ice pick into position, aiming like a matador. As he was about to strike, a horn sounded from the driveway and George turned so abruptly that the ice pick grazed his neck. He also saw the weapon.

"What's—?"

And then he saw Karl's expression, and he knew. And in that moment of comprehension, Karl struck, thrusting forward and upward, aiming at George's throat. But the Rank's combat exercises were not altogether without effect. Instinctively George parried the blow, and the pick glanced off his jaw and gouged open his cheek. He grunted in pain.

A car door slammed and a woman's voice called. "Hello?"

It was Rita Gaylord. Karl knew he had to finish this and do it quickly. Too late now to wish he had latched the gate behind the Winnebago. At any moment Rita might find them.

George had both hands around Karl's wrist, holding the ice pick at arm's length. The man, it seemed, was incredibly strong, his compact, weight-lifter's body working to his advantage in the cramped space. But he also fought badly, defensively, his eyes wide with fear, his clenched teeth visible between the torn folds of bloody flesh.

Extending two fingers of his free hand, Karl gouged George's eyes. The man let go of his wrist, trying to protect himself. Karl stepped close and plunged the ice pick into his chest. George lunged upward, hands clawing at the air, and then his eyes glazed and he collapsed onto the steering wheel. Karl reached for the body and lowered it to the floor.

"Anybody home?"

Karl stood. She was visible through the rear window, Rita coming this way. He took off his coat, which had blood on the sleeve, and stuck it under Lish's head. When he stood up she was at the back window, her hands cupped around her eyes. Seeing him, she tapped the window and waved. Karl waved back but kept his position, blocking her view of George's body on the floor between the seats. When she disappeared around the side of the Winnebago he crossed to the door and stepped out before she could enter.

"Well, hello there," she said. "Is this yours?"

"My parents own it," Karl said, closing the door behind him. "They drove down here from Philadelphia."

Rita wore tan slacks and a chartreuse cashmere sweater; in other circumstances Karl would gladly have seduced her. Now he just wanted to get rid of her.

"I've never been in one of these things before," she said.

Karl forced himself to remain calm. This was dangerous, this woman was dangerous.

"It's not mine to show," Karl said. "But let me ask them and see if it's okay to take you for a ride."

To make the point clear, he stepped past and headed to the door. Rita followed.

"You pick the day," she said. "I'll buy the gas."

Get out of here, he wanted to shout, but forced himself to speak casually. "What brings you out this way?"

"I got a box of peaches from one of those Fruit-of-the-Month clubs so I made peach pie. I thought you and your children might enjoy it. Where is everybody, anyway?"

Goddamn you, Karl thought. He was still on edge, keyed up, which made concentration difficult. Trying to remember everything he had told her before, he began fitting a new story together.

"My parents went sailing with some friends and the children are still in California. There's a legal problem of some kind about out-of-state visitation rights. I don't know if they will get here or not."

"So you're all alone right now?"

Karl looked at her. She stared back, the corners of her wide mouth upturned. She was not going to quit. She was a problem and was going to remain a problem.

He had to kill. Not Rita—that would risk a murder investigation—but himself, Ron Tednick, and the attractive image he had built up. He had to offend Rita, humiliate her so that she would leave him alone, never want to see or hear of him again. She wanted a lover? He would give her one.

"I'm not alone," he finally answered. "You're here."

"Well, then. Can I offer you some peach pie?"

"At least."

"Ahh, yes," she said in a singsong voice.

Rita returned to her car, a blue Peugeot. As she leaned across the front seat Karl could see the outline of her panties, visible beneath the slacks. She had nicely rounded buttocks. He regretted the circumstances weren't different.

They went into the kitchen, where Karl handed her a knife and she began to cut the pie. They were not talking now, but Rita wore a secret smile, even hummed to herself as she worked. Karl moved behind her and slid his hands over hers. She settled gently backward, her body warm and firm against him. With his arms around her, he lifted her hand and moved the knife away from the pie.

"Drop the knife," he whispered.

She tried to look up at him.

"Don't turn around. Just put down the knife."

"Umm, you're full of surprises."

She let the knife fall to the table. Karl guided her hand back to the pie and slowly pushed downward. Rita hesitated as she touched the crust, then relaxed. Pie filling oozed around their fingers. He lifted her hand and brought it to her face.

"Wait," she giggled, turning her head to one side.

He smeared the pie across her lips and let the messy filling fall on the cashmere sweater. She paid no attention to the sweater. Instead of resisting, she joined him, rolling her head and licking his fingers. She turned around, put her hands around his neck and kissed him, smearing the sticky filling across his lips as well.

Rita's unexpected arrival had ruined a clean kill and unnerved Karl. He felt a rush of anger—with her, with himself, with the situation. He shoved a hand up under her sweater, grabbed the front of her bra and tore it. She pulled away but her eyes remained bright.

"Wait . . ."

With one continuous movement she freed herself from the sweater and slid out of the broken bra. Her plump breasts, outlined in white, had upturned nipples. She wiggled her shoulders and sent the soft flesh dancing, watching him with a crooked smile. She was, she believed, good in bed, and she wanted him to know it.

Karl dug his fingers into her breasts and pulled her abruptly toward him. This time she winced. "Easy honey, *easy* . . ."

Putting his hands on her shoulders, he pushed her down.

"Suck me."

"Give a girl a chance . . ."

Karl pressured her to her knees and then unzipped his pants.

"I'm not hard," he said.

And he wasn't. This was not a sexual encounter, it was a defensive maneuver. He was trying to alienate her; trying to be rough without bruising her, to be offensive without assaulting her. But she was too forgiving. She took him in her mouth and began a gentle movement.

Karl's head went back, the warmth began spreading through him. And with it a familiar heady feeling.

No, this was no good, he could not let this happen. Any kind of sexual relationship with Rita would only confuse and jeopardize matters. He had to alienate her but without dangerous consequences. How? He did not want to hit her. That could lead to a police complaint. Besides, so far as he was capable of the sentiment, he liked Rita Gaylord. Another time . . . there had to be—

As soon as he thought of it he was sure it would work, if he could manage it . . .

He relaxed his mind and recalled the day he had been shot by the Russian guard, the day he had met Alexander Ikhnovsky, Uncle Alex, who had sent him here. He remembered the pain of frostbitten toes and the fear of being caught, and he used the memories to stop his body from responding to Rita's erotic manipulation.

"Wait." He took a step back, and still half-hard gave her what he had heard them call in the bordello a "golden shower." Rita scrambled to her feet.

"Hey, come on," Karl said.

But Rita yanked the cloth from the table and dried her shoulder with quick angry movements. Her breasts still bore the imprint of his fingers.

"I thought you wanted a little action."

Without answering she retrieved her sweater and stood there, breathing heavily, glaring at him. "You did that *on purpose.*" She stepped forward and raised a trembling hand, but did nothing more. Then the anger died and her eyes filled with hurt. "Why?" she said in a tiny, miserable voice, and then she was gone.

Watching from the window, Karl saw her put on the sweater before getting into the Peugeot. Gravel erupted from beneath the rear tires, and the car shot forward and disappeared down the hill. Karl was confident that she would not be back. And that she would not tell anybody what had just happened to her. He had achieved his purpose. And, strangely, felt no pleasure in it.

CHAPTER

21

PAUL WOKE UP WITH A CRY. THE IMAGE OF A MAN
with a torn face and death-glazed eyes slowly faded and he saw himself in the ceiling mirror, lying in bed, his arms outstretched to catch
a falling body.

George Lish.

He sat up, confused. It took him a moment before he remembered
where he was and what had happened. Then two thoughts struck at
the same time. His mind was clear, he was himself again. And his
brother had killed a man named George Lish. He could still feel the
weight of the body on his arms, still hear the gasp of surprise when
the ice pick pierced the heart. The memory was vivid, just as it had
been after the other dreams.

George Lish? The name meant nothing to him, but he guessed
from past experience that Lish was either a CIA agent who had
become a threat, or a KGB asset who had outlived his usefulness.
Whichever, whatever, his brother had killed again.

When Paul sat up his body responded normally for the first time in
. . . how long had it been? He didn't even know what day it was.

But at least he felt whole again. The mental fog was gone, he could think clearly. A faint dizziness told him that the effects of the drug hadn't entirely worn off. He was still weak but at least he could think, and there was still time to recuperate, some twelve hours until the next injection.

The door rattled and he quickly lay back down on the bed as Madam Tran entered with the breakfast tray. When she saw him she frowned. "You going to be good this morning? Otherwise no food, okay? You wait until I feed you."

"Yes," Paul said slowly. He had no idea what he sounded like under the drug so he decided it was best to speak as little as possible.

After she fed him, Helmut came in and he had to put up with the indignity of being helped to the bathroom. For the first time he saw in Helmut's face how much the man hated this duty. Why had Otto made him do it? Why not some flunkie? The only answer was Karl. This was the way he wanted it. Helmut and Madam Tran and Otto were the only people who knew that Karl had a twin brother. They were the only people Karl trusted with the information.

But the answer raised more questions than it answered. Why the secrecy? Why had Karl kidnapped him? Where was Karl now? And *who* was George Lish?

Helmut returned him to the bed and left the room. As soon as he was alone Paul got up and checked the door. It was locked. Moving upright after crawling on his hands and knees for so long was, literally, a heady experience. That he could stand firmly and move about on two legs seemed miraculous, but moving around the room quickly told him how weak he still was. After only a few minutes of activity he found himself trembling with fatigue, the strength in his muscles exhausted. He would need to wait until his body had recovered more fully before attempting an escape. Trying to control his impatience, Paul spent the day resting and drinking large amounts of water to speed the drugs out of his system. The hours seemed endless but he celebrated each time he walked to the bathroom and back without falling.

When lunch came he suppressed the urge to rush for the door. Not yet. He did take the opportunity to note the lock on the outside of the door: a metal bar, simple, effective—and without a key.

Madam Tran left. He knew the next time she came back it would be with dinner, and the injection. He looked around now for any sort of weapon but couldn't find one. The bedstead was brass but too well

secured for him to separate a rod from the frame. The wicker nightstand offered little; besides, its destruction might alert whoever came
through the door. Surprise would have to be his weapon; he would
make his break when the next person came through the door. Paul
hoped it would be Madam Tran.

But four hours later, when the door opened, it was Helmut who
came in. Paul pretended to be asleep.

"All right, come on." Helmut shook him roughly. "You want to
piss or not?"

Paul allowed Helmut to help him up. The man, he noted, was
dressed in a tuxedo and smelled like a flower garden, which
explained why he had come in early. He was planning a night on the
town and didn't want to do his chores at midnight.

Paul waited until Helmut had him almost on his feet, then abruptly
stood up, catching the man's arm behind his back and twisting it
around. Helmut grunted in surprise.

"You go first," Paul said quietly, then shoved up on the arm and
pushed forward at the same time, forcing Helmut to lurch ahead.
Moving faster and faster, his free arm flailing as he tried to get his
feet under him, Helmut saw the wall and let out a cry. Remembering
the indignity of the needle, Paul didn't let up. Bent forward at the
waist, Helmut slammed headfirst into the wall and collapsed. As Paul
stepped back, trembling from the exertion, there was a crash behind
him. He turned to see Madame Tran in the doorway, the tray at her
feet.

Paul started toward her but the woman was quicker than Helmut.
She bolted back into the hallway and tried to slam the door. Paul just
managed to thrust his arm into the opening and the door rebounded
off his forearm, numbing his hand. Madam Tran shouted for help.
Keeping her weight against the door, she grabbed Paul's index finger
and bent it back. The pain acted as a catalyst and infused his weakened muscles with new strength. He shoved forward and burst
through the door into the hall.

The force of his effort threw Madam Tran against the wall, and
she quickly pulled a butterfly knife from the folds of her Bao Dai.
With a quick flick of the wrist half of the thin handle pivoted in a
circle and rejoined its mate, back-to-back now, exposing a long,
shiny blade. She jabbed at his face, but it was more a feint than an
attack and her eyes looked beyond Paul to the safety of the corridor
beyond. She wanted out.

Paul was able to dodge the thrust, then deliberately stepped aside, offering the woman an apparent escape route. As her eyes shifted to the hallway beyond him, he kicked out at her hand and sent the knife flying. She tried to rush past but he grabbed her and for a moment the two of them grappled. Madam Tran was strong and wiry, and as he struggled to hold her Paul couldn't believe his own weakness. She tried to knee him in the groin and would have succeeded except that the long folds of the Bao Dai left her off balance. Paul swung her around and somehow managed to push her back into the room with enough force so that she fell to the floor. Before she could get up he slammed the door and slid the bolt home.

He paused for a moment to catch his breath. To his left, a short dark hallway led to an ancient, cast-iron door that was slightly ajar. He approached it warily. Behind him he could hear Madam Tran beating on the door and yelling. Fortunately the walls were thick enough to muffle the sound.

The iron door opened to a continuation of the same hallway, now carpeted and more brightly lit. Music and conversation drifted down a flight of stairs at the bottom of which were two doors, one labeled *Damen* and the other *Herren*. He was in the basement of the Vanilla Rose.

As Paul climbed the stairs, the air around his legs suddenly reminded him that he was still wearing a damn hospital gown. If Madam Tran hadn't showed up when she did he at least could have traded clothes with Helmut. Well, it was too late now . . .

His senses had been deprived for so long that entering the main room of the Vanilla Rose was like stepping into another world. The gaudy extravagance of the decor and the girls in their colored lingerie dazzled him. Sounds were too vibrant and loud, smells rich and pungent. People turned to stare as he crossed the room and some of the men hooted and laughed. "Tell her to give you back your clothes," one of them shouted happily.

Paul gave him a look that shut him up, for the moment anyway. He would have liked to find Otto Wenzler and happily wring his neck, but his muscles were already trembling and the blood was pounding in his head. Obviously his body was still recovering from the effects of the drug and what he'd been through these past few minutes.

Outside, it was just dusk, and the smell of fresh air was like a glorious discovery. Dressed as he was, like an escapee from a hospital, people gave him wide berth and he had to ask five times before someone finally gave him directions to the police station. As he walked there he planned what he would do . . . First, swear out a complaint against Otto Wenzler, then back to the hotel for a bath and a shave and a night's sleep. Would the police loan him money for a taxi? Maybe Ray Tregerdemain could help. In the morning he'd call Bernie and tell him why he'd disappeared. He'd also call Hugh Roark and tell him about Karl. All bets were off now. Karl had betrayed him.

Or had he? Karl could have killed him but he'd put him on ice instead. Paul also remembered what Karl had said about the CIA . . . that they would kill him if they found out or even seriously suspected he was responsible for their agents' deaths. Would they execute Karl if he turned him in? And if they did, could he live with the knowledge that he had caused his brother's death. Could he look his mother in the eye afterward? And wouldn't she find out? After all these years of guilt over abandoning Karl . . . Perhaps he could set up a meeting with Roark, feel him out about a deal—Karl's life in exchange for revealing his identity . . .

He was at the police station now, a stone building that looked like an armory. The lobby had high ceilings with corridors leading off in either direction and worn benches along one wall. The sound of a police radio echoed from a distant room. Behind a broad counter sat a policewoman in a sexless uniform of indeterminate green. She straightened up as Paul entered and hunched her shoulders forward when she saw what he was, and wasn't, wearing.

"It's all right," Paul told her, "I'm not crazy. Someone kidnapped me and I just got away. His name is Otto Wenzler and I want him arrested—"

"And who are you?"

"My name's Paul Stafford. I'm an American citizen. Wenzler's guilty of assault, battery, kidnapping—"

The mention of his name clearly interested her.

"You are Paul Stafford?

"That's right, you probably have a missing-persons report—"

Standing now, she brought a whistle to her lips and blew a loud, shrill sound. Paul assumed she was calling a squad to go after Otto Wenzler, but when the police came streaming out of the back room she pointed at him.

"Paul Stafford. He's the one—*Offizier* Dietrich."

Before Paul could explain, before he could even think, they had him up against the wall with his hands behind his back. He caught snatches of conversation . . .

"Who is he?"

"Stafford, remember?"

"He walked right in?"

"Look what he's wearing."

"Where'd he come from?"

"The one who ran down Dietrich."

"*He's* the one?"

It wasn't until they handcuffed him that Paul finally realized what was happening. And it wasn't until the next day that he actually believed it.

With George Lish's death the final stone in the foundation of the Redeye plot had been laid. Before Karl could dispose of the body, however, he had to apply Lish's fingerprints to pieces of incriminating evidence. In his earlier assassinations Karl never had had to deal with the bodies of his victims. Now it was necessary and he found the task distasteful.

He wrapped Lish's body in a plastic sheet and took it to the bathroom, where he placed it in the bathtub with the head next to the drain. After turning on the shower he cut the carotid arteries with a straight razor. When the blood had drained he carried Lish's corpse back to the stable and placed it on a worktable.

He steeled himself for what came next. In order to implicate the man he needed fingerprints. Karl locked the forearms in a vise and used a hacksaw to cut off each hand at the wrist. He forced himself to work as a butcher worked, treating the body as an inanimate object.

When it was done he put on his surgeon's gloves and, cupping the severed hands in his own, applied Lish's fingerprints to areas of the Winnebago that Lish hadn't touched: windows, cupboard, toilet, both sides of the skylight, the convex mirror, even the spare tire.

He did the same thing to the Redeye, pressing the lifeless fingers to all parts of the launching tube, to the batteries, the case, and the connectors. He paid particular attention to the circular battery receptacle, inside of which he placed the print of an index finger. He planned to do a poor job of wiping the missile clean, as if Lish had tried to conceal his identity, but this print would survive no matter how many others he obliterated.

Karl waited until nightfall, then buried the corpse in an out-of-the-way, heavily wooded part of the property. He knew that bodies were often discovered in what newspapers termed "a shallow grave," but these were usually last-minute expediencies resorted to by killers in a state of emotional turmoil. The graves were little more than depressions covered by dirt and pine needles. But a body four feet deep would never be found. And if the forest floor was left intact, the grave itself would not attract attention.

Karl prepared carefully. Before digging he took a shovel and lifted the topsoil in squares that he set to one aside. Then he put down a plastic sheet and stacked the dirt on it as he dug the grave. Occasionally an axe was necessary to cut through a root but most of the time he worked with a pick and shovel. The work made him hot and the mosquitos made him irritable. By the time he finished it was after midnight.

He placed the body in the grave and filled it in, layered the surface slightly to compensate for the inevitable settling, then replaced the squares of topsoil and watered them. Finally he carried away the excess dirt and sprinkled it lightly over other areas of the property. When he got back to the house it was two in the morning. His arms and back ached and he was hot, tired and dirty.

In the shower Karl stood with head bowed beneath the hot spray of water. His plans were completed. He knew the approach paths to Runways 01 and 19 at Andrews Air Force Base. He had chosen his launch sites, two for each runway, one primary and one alternate. He had the Sony-CIKOP-34F radio with which he could monitor up to three frequencies at once, including the Soviet select air-to-air frequency. And he had George Lish's signature on the Winnebago rental agreement and his fingerprints all over the motor home and the missile. He should have been pleased and optimistic; instead he was uneasy, restless.

Karl analyzed his feelings. It was not the revulsion over the disposal of Lish's body, and it was not the episode with Rita Gaylord. These were matters of necessity and he accepted them as such. It was something else . . .

It was, he realized, and with some surprise, his role in the sabotaging of the Mutual Defense Treaty. As a German, Karl knew all too well how easily a country could be led to its own destruction while confident of victory. It had, after all, happened to Germany in 1939, and by 1945 Karl and his whole generation had begun to pay the price. He rarely troubled himself with political matters, but now, as so-called Summit Monday approached and the newspapers and magazines filled with details of the Mutual Defense Treaty, it was difficult to ignore the seriousness of what he was about to do. He tried to shut out the pro-treaty talk, but it was there all around him. He had to remind himself that Uncle Alex was still the finest man he'd over known. And above it all, that he *owed* Uncle Alex—owed him his life.

It was Friday morning and the General Secretary would not arrive until Monday. Karl was still restless. Wandering through the house, the notion of visiting Paul's house came back, and unlike his brief second thoughts about his mission, it would not go away. Even as he tried to talk himself out of it—it was a risk, after all—the idea took firm hold and he began making plans. He would make sure that Joanna wasn't home, enter secretly and stay for only an hour. If anything looked too dangerous, or felt out of place, he'd forget the whole thing.

As a precaution he called the Gallerie L'Enfant to make sure that Joanna was working. A woman answered. Adopting a nasal, tenor voice, Karl asked for Joanna Stafford.

"She's not in today," the woman told him. "Can I help you?"

"Actually, a friend in Chicago suggested that I ask her advice on some paintings. Do you know when she'll be back?"

"Friday and Saturday are her days off, but she'll be in on Sunday. Shall I give her a message?"

"My name's Dan Julian, but she doesn't know me. I'll stop in Sunday. Thank you."

Karl hung up before the woman could ask the name of his friend in Chicago. As he fingered Paul's house key, he briefly considered going over now . . . He could watch the house and wait for Joanna to leave on an errand. No, too dangerous. Even if she left the house there was no way of knowing how long she would be gone.

Curbing his impatience, Karl took the Kawasaki, drove to Chesapeake Bay and spent the day at the beach. Sunday morning would be soon enough to see how his brother lived his private life.

CHAPTER

22

NEWS OF PAUL'S ARREST SPREAD LIKE A GATHERING wave. The precinct captain in Neukoln called the chief of police in Schoneberg who contacted the American mission in Templehof who communicated the news to the CIA's West Berlin section who relayed it to headquarters in Langley, Virginia. Hugh Roark heard about it as he returned from lunch. What surprised him most was the report that Paul had walked into the police station and given himself up. Indeed, Paul's escape from the hotel had forced him to concede that his ability to analyze people and predict their behavior had failed him. The false passports, the escape and the stolen limousine all served to confirm Maurice's early evaluations, a fact the younger man hadn't let him forget . . .

"You like the guy and you want to believe him. I've got no feelings one way or the other so I see right through him."

"I had the impression you didn't like him."

"I don't like him thinking he can make a fool out of me. Otherwise I'm neutral."

Neutral or not, Maurice's prediction had been that Paul would

224

show up in Moscow, and Hugh needled him about that on the flight
to Berlin. "Probably a ploy, huh?"

Maurice, seated next to him working on a crossword puzzle in the
Pan Am Clipper magazine, looked up.

"What's that?"

"Giving himself up like that. Trying to get our trust, you think?"

"He's not innocent, I know that much."

"Tricky, though. Walking into a police station wearing a night-
shirt. Very damn tricky."

Maurice gave him a black look and went back to his puzzle. It was
the Memorial Day weekend and he had canceled his holiday plans to
go with Hugh after the news of Paul's arrest.

Hugh turned to the window. The Atlantic Ocean was obscured by
clouds, but Hugh remembered the first time he'd flown this route in
an Army C-47. It had been wartime then, the big one, World War II.
But after V-Day came Korea and then Vietnam and all the while the
cold war and the arms race and revolutions all over the place. And
now, something new, the Mutual Defense Treaty with its technology
to end all technologies.

Well, maybe so. He remembered a science fiction story in which a
benevolent radiation belt enveloped the earth and neutralized all electrical current. That was all it affected, just electricity. The result was
no radio or television, no automobiles, planes, space shuttles, computers, *and* no guided missiles. Just the steam engine, the gaslight
and the horse and buggy. The nineteenth century preserved forever.

Wasn't that more or less what the Mutual Defense Treaty promised? A more enlightened, less restrictive version of the same scenario? American and Russain technologies in orbit, ready and waiting
to pounce on any missiles launched in attack? But neither Star Wars
nor the Nevsky technology would change human nature. It was the
human factor that most interested Hugh Roark, not new technologies.
And right now, that interest was concentrated on solving the riddle of
Paul Stafford.

Larry Kincaid met them at the Tegel Airport. Kincaid, with the
Berlin section, had a receding hairline, spoke in a soft voice and
wore a Pierre Cardin suit and aviator's sunglasses. Hugh and
Maurice had met him on their earlier visit and he looked happier then
than he looked today.

"We can't keep the lid on this thing much longer," Kincaid told

them as they had left the terminal. "The police want to bring charges
and the press is already nosing around. By tomorrow morning, the
word's going to be out."

"Where is Stafford now?"

"In a holding cell at police headquarters in Schoneberg."

"Schoneberg?"

"It's the best we could do."

"Can't we get him in a safe house?"

"It's a civilian offense; the Germans want custody. If you knew
the trouble we've caused already . . . the police don't like being told
what to do by the Lord Mayor's office, the Lord Mayor hates being
usurped by USCAB and USCAB is on our ass for making them play
the heavy."

Hugh nodded. He was aware of the delicate relationship that
existed between the local Berlin authorities and the United States
Commandant, Berlin, known as USCAB. USCAB in person was a
two-star general who was officially the ultimate legal authority in
West Berlin. Over the years various protocols and accords specified
the authority and jurisdiction of the police but in the end every German organization was subservient to USCAB.

An *Offizier* at Schoneberg led the three CIA men to an interrogation room with a table and four chairs and a bottled-water dispenser.
A circular fluorescent light in the ceiling buzzed softly. The room
had the bright, antiseptic feel of an operating room.

Maurice looked the room over. "Are we wired?"

Kincaid said, "A wall mike patched to a truck in the parking lot.
Is Stafford the one who took out some of our guys?"

Hugh gave him a sharp look.

"Where'd you hear that?"

"You give and you get, you know how it goes."

Maurice and Hugh said nothing. Kincaid frowned. "Come on,
Roark. I'm giving you backup. How do I bill the time?"

"You want the number?"

"I've got the number, I want the words. Is he the one?"

"He's a direct link," Hugh said. "How and why we still don't
know."

Maurice tightened his lips and Hugh knew what he was thinking
. . . Kincaid had no need to know. But Hugh remembered from his
own experience the resentment of local-station personnel toward the
covert action or special investigations boys who came in from Wash-

ington and ran cowboy operations without coordinating them locally. And Kincaid was right—they needed his help on this one. Give a little, get a little.

Paul was brought in, dressed in a gray prison uniform. He looked pale, drawn. When he saw them he seemed surprised.

"You guys?"

"Hello, Stafford."

"I asked for the American Ambassador."

"You got us," Maurice said.

"You going to get me out of here?"

Hugh said, "I want you to meet Larry Kincaid. He's with our Berlin section."

"I don't care if he's with the Berlin Circus as long as he can get me out of here."

"Take it easy."

"You take it easy. I've been kidnapped and drugged and arrested as soon as I escaped. I want out of here *now*."

"We don't have that kind of authority—"

"Bullshit."

Kincaid said, "He's right. You're being held by the West Berlin police, which means we have no jurisdiction over you."

"Don't give me that. This is an occupied city and the final authority is an American army general. You going to pick up the phone or not?"

He knows the political landscape, Hugh thought. If nothing else, Stafford's time in Washington had been good training in bullshit detection.

"Let's talk first," Hugh began.

"Let's get out of here first."

Hugh shook his head. "Can't do it, Paul. You know that."

Hugh's tone brought home to Paul the futility of insisting on his freedom until these men were convinced of his innocence . . . During the past twenty-four hours in jail he had pieced together the story of what happened at the InterContinental . . . that Karl had returned impersonating him, had been discovered with the false documents and had hurt a police officer in making his escape.

Hugh motioned to a chair. "Why don't you sit down and tell us everything that happened."

"How's this? George Lish is dead."

Paul expected some sort of reaction to the name but he was disappointed.

"Who?"

"George Lish. He's dead and I know who did it."

The men looked puzzled.

"Who's George Lish?" Hugh asked.

"Probably one of your boys. Don't you know?"

They stared at him, waiting.

"Or working for you. One of your assets."

Hugh turned to Maurice. "Know the name?"

"No."

He turned to Kincaid, who spread his hands and shook his head.

"Well, he's dead," Paul insisted.

"How do you know?"

"Two days ago I had another dream. Like the ones before, only this time his name was George Lish, a baby-faced guy, and I killed him with an ice pick. But it's no dream. I was receiving thoughts, direct impressions from the killer." Faced with the reality, there was no room for maneuvering, bargaining about Karl and keeping his identity secret for his mother's sake. For his *survival* he had to convince them of Karl's existence. "His name is Karl Alexander. My twin brother . . ."

"Twin brother?"

"That's what it's been all along," Paul said, pressing forward despite the expression of disbelief on the faces of the CIA men.

"That's why the dreams were so real. I've got a twin brother, and somehow I identify with him when he kills. Intense emotional excitement will—"

The cynical smile on Maurice's face made the anger and frustration of the past weeks boil over, and he moved toward the CIA man with clenched fists.

"I don't *need* this," Paul shouted. "You get out of here—"

"Keep your damn hands—" Maurice began.

Paul tried to grab him, Maurice pushed him off and for a moment they grappled before Hugh moved in and separated them.

"That's enough—"

"Get him out of here."

". . . no position to threaten anybody."

"I said *enough*."

Maurice moved back, smoothing his coat. Paul pointed to him and said, "He waits in the parking lot."

"Mr. Singer is part of the investigation—"

"Mr. Singer's got shit for brains."

Maurice colored. "Only shit for brains would believe some story about a twin brother."

"Talk to my mother, she'll tell you."

"We already did," Hugh said.

The anger left him. "You did?"

"Neither she nor your wife said anything about a twin brother."

"Joanna? You talked to her?"

"We talk to everybody," Maurice told him.

Hugh shot him a cautionary look and added, "We were trying to find you."

"Is Jo home? I want to call her—"

"Let's stay with this, first."

"I want to call my wife."

"So you can tell her what to say?"

"Will you get this asshole *out* of here?"

Hugh sighed and turned to his partner. "Maybe it's best you wait outside."

"You *believe* this crap about twins?"

"I don't know what to believe until I have a chance to hear his story. Neither do you."

"Excuse me," Kincaid said, "I don't want to appear stupid or anything, but what is it we're talking about here, dreams or murders?"

"I'll fill you in later," Hugh said. "Right now I want to hear more about Mr. Stafford's twin brother."

"Karl," Paul said. "His name is Karl Alexander, born Karl Weiss. You can find *anmeld* records up to February of 'forty-six that will list both of us."

"What records?"

Paul told them about the police registration procedures, but when he mentioned that *anmeld* records were in Pankow, Maurice gave a snort of disbelief. Hugh glanced at him and Maurice said, "Pankow's in the East."

"I know that," Hugh said testily, "I was here after the war." And then before Maurice could respond he turned to Kincaid. "Can we get a check on those records?"

Kincaid slid a hand inside his coat and produced a leather-bound note pad.

"There are ways," he said, and began making notes as Hugh returned his attention to Paul.

"All right, let's go back to the starting gate. What happened after you left Washington?"

Paul took a deep breath and began the story. He told them what he'd found out from his mother and why she had never admitted having Karl. When he got to the part about Ray Tregerdemain and the prostitute hitting him in front of the casino, he sensed a change in his listeners. Kincaid looked up from his note pad and Hugh exchanged a knowing look with Maurice.

"What's wrong," Paul said.

"You say Ray Tregerdemain was with you?"

"That's right. He heard the girl's story. He can vouch for me."

"No, he can't," said Maurice. "He was killed about ten days ago."

"Killed?" Paul repeated dumbly.

"Reported as an apparent accident," Kincaid said. "At the zoo. He fell into the polar bear cage and either drowned or was mauled to death, the coroner couldn't determine which happened first."

Paul was stunned. Ray killed, in a zoo. The one man who could back up his story.

Hugh was asking a question. He forced himself to concentrate.

"When was the last time you saw Tregerdemain?"

"Saturday night," Paul said slowly. "The first day I got here. He went into the casino and I went to the Vanilla Rose. I was going to call him the next day—I *did* call him, but he wasn't home. I left a message and that's the last . . ."

He let the words trail off. The implications of Ray's death were all too obvious: Karl had found out about Ray and killed him. But how? How could Karl know? Had he told him? He thought back, trying to remember if he'd said anything about Ray to his new-found brother. They had talked about so many things, he couldn't recall mentioning Ray but he might have. And if he had, then *he* was responsible for Ray's death. The thought brought a sick feeling to his stomach.

"When did he die?" Paul asked. "What day?"

Kincaid answered immediately. "Monday night."

"About twelve hours after you escaped from the hotel," Maurice added pointedly.

Hugh held up a hand. "Easy."

"Pretty convenient accident—"

"I was not involved," Paul snapped. "I was drugged. For God's sake, I was a prisoner until the other day."

"Why don't you tell us what happened?" Hugh said quietly.

Paul got a drink of water from the dispenser and went on with his story, describing his visit to the Vanilla Rose and his meeting with Otto Wenzler. When he told them about the false passports, Hugh went to his briefcase, brought out the passports and opened them to the photos.

"You're saying this isn't you?"

"That's Karl."

Maurice and Kincaid crowded close, comparing the photos to Paul.

"The hair is different . . ."

"Just combed different."

"The lighting's kind of flat."

They kept glancing up at him and back to the photo. Paul felt the way he had when Annie Helms hypnotized him, like a freak of nature, a laboratory specimen.

"Can we finish this," he said. "I want out of here."

"All right," Hugh said, "you came back to the hotel and there was a message waiting. The message told you to go to a certain place the next day—"

"The Spree Bowl at noon."

"And your brother was waiting for you?"

"No, he phoned about ten minutes after I got there. He gave me instructions . . ."

As Paul told them about the meeting with Karl, Kincaid noted down the details: type of car, Karl's name, the Eichwalde Combat School, Treptow Park. As for Hugh, he was particularly interested in the name of the man who raised Karl.

"He wouldn't tell me," Paul said. "But I assume his name was Alexander."

"Alexander," Hugh repeated. "Was he Russian?"

"He didn't say, but I got the impression he was well connected, whoever he was."

"Where did Karl go to school?"

"He didn't say."

"You didn't ask?"

"No, I didn't ask. There were a thousand other things to talk about, we couldn't cover everything in one afternoon."

"But he's an instructor at the Eichwalde Combat School?"

"Yes."

"And he's married and has three children?"

"Yes. Wife's name is Magda. Children are Bridget, Katrina and Wilhelm." His journalist's conditioning to remember names helped.

Hugh turned to Kincaid. "Would you have a dossier?"

"Eichwalde?" He shrugged. "If we don't, military intelligence might."

"See what you can dig up."

Kincaid made a wry face. "It's Saturday."

"I know, but I'd like to confirm or deny the brother before the news breaks."

Kincaid folded his notebook. "All I can do is make the request."

"It's a white priority," Hugh said.

"Coded?"

Hugh nodded and Kincaid smiled ruefully. "A little more than a request, then. Be right back."

After Kincaid left Paul said he wanted to make some phone calls.

Hugh shook his head. "Let's finish here first—"

"Look, Roark. I just dropped off the face of the earth for two weeks and I want to let some people know what happened."

"They think you've gone underground to work on a story."

"Who does?" .

"Your wife, your editor, your mother . . ."

"You told them I was working on a story?"

"You did. At least we thought it was you until . . ."

Maurice said, "It still might be him."

"What?" Paul demanded.

Hugh told him what Bernie Stern had told them: that Paul had called to say that he'd gone underground on an important story. The editor wouldn't give them any details. Maybe he should have, but Paul hadn't expected this, that Karl would impersonate him, appropriate his name and use his identity for his own purposes. Whatever the hell they were . . .

He began asking questions: What had Karl said to Bernie? How long ago? Had his brother called anyone else? Had he called Joanna? Or his mother?

"Not when we last spoke to them," Hugh said.

"When was that?"

"We did a routine call-back, what was it . . ."

"Three days ago, I think," Maurice said.

"Where's a phone? I want to find out."

"We don't have a secure phone," Hugh said.

"I don't care if it's secure or not as long as I can hear them and they can hear me."

"Well, I'm afraid we do care. Can you limit what you say to these people?"

"Meaning what?"

"Meaning no mention of Mr. Singer or myself or of the Agency or of the murders."

"I just want to find out if anyone else has heard from Karl."

"And I'll have to monitor the conversation."

"How about a urine test?"

They called the *Offizier,* who pretended not to understand Hugh's basic German. Paul interrupted and demanded a phone in brisk *Berlinerisch.* The *Offizier* stiffened and marched off to make the arrangements. A few minutes later he led them to what looked like an accounting office. There were neatly stacked ledgers behind glass-fronted shelves and two computer screens on two spotlessly clean desks.

The *Offizier* took his position just inside the door. Paul asked Maurice to wait outside.

Maurice glanced at Hugh, who said, "Why don't you check and make sure that George Lish isn't one of ours?"

"The *alleged* George Lish," Maurice grumbled as he left the room. After he was gone Paul motioned for the *Offizier* to shut the door, but nothing happened until Hugh nodded approval, at which point the man did as asked. Paul made the call collect. Hugh picked up a phone on the adjoining desk and listened.

Saturday was Joanna's day off but only the answering machine was at home. Paul's message was brief: "Jo, it's me. I'm in Berlin and I've got a lot to tell you. There's no number here so I'll call you later." He paused, then, "I miss you."

He waited in silence for seven seconds in the faint hope that she was listening and would pick up the phone. Then he heard the tape click off.

Maybe Joanna had switched schedules and was working. He called the gallery and got Denise, who told him what he already knew, that this was Joanna's day off.

"I don't expect her until tomorrow," Denise said in her deliberate aristocratic lilt.

Paul's next call was to his mother. She was happy and relieved to hear from him but worried about the reports of the hit-and-run incident in Berlin. She told him that "certain men" had been calling and asking questions about him.

"Are you in trouble? If you need any money . . ."

Evidently Karl hadn't called her. Paul considered warning her but decided against it. If Karl meant to get in touch with her, he would have done it by now. He hung up and dialed again while the *Offizier* complained to Hugh, who pretended not to understand German.

This one was to Bernie Stern, who was his usual sarcastic self when he came on the line.

"Damned good of you to contact us. Especially since the CIA knows about your arms-deal story and if you checked in more often you'd know they're hot to trot to find you."

"They already found me. I've got one of them right here."

Hugh gave him a warning look.

"Right where? Where are you?"

"I'm in Berlin. In jail. Now listen, Bernie, whoever phoned you last time wasn't me. Okay? We haven't talked since the day you sidetracked the Rockland-Birdwell story. That day in your office, remember? The man on the phone was my brother."

"You don't have a brother."

"Yes, I do. A twin brother. His name is Karl Alexander and he kidnapped me over here and he's been impersonating me in the States—"

"Oh, sure . . . what the hell are you trying to pull? No, let me guess. There's no story. You've been in bed for two weeks or sucking the sun in Acapulco. There's no CIA connection, no arms sales, no sources, no leads. Am I not perilously close to the truth?"

"Bernie, shut up and listen."

"Better be good, *real* good."

"How about a KGB assassin—"

Hugh waved at him but Paul plunged on without a pause.

"—how about a kidnapping and six—count them—six unsolved murders? How about someone trying to frame me? How does all that sound?"

"Like you're on drugs."

"No drugs, Bernie. This is mainline reality."

Bernie's voice took on a different tone as he considered the possibilities. "A KGB assassin you can actually identify?"

Hugh was looking at him. "Call him a three-letter assassin, Bernie. The phone's not secure."

"So who is this guy?"

Paul gave him an abbreviated, laundered version of what had happened and in return received the details of Karl's phone call. His brother's story about secret arms deals was obviously meant as an excuse for Paul's absence, but the reason for Karl's presence at the Military Ocean Terminal in Bayonne was a mystery. By the time they finished, the *Offizier* was making impatient noises and glancing at his watch.

Bernie had one last question. "Hey, if I believe you, how do I know this is you and not Karl?"

"Who else would tell you to go fuck yourself?"

"At least that makes sense . . . when are you coming back?"

"As soon as the triple-letter gentlemen spring me. I'll call you if and when I get in."

The *Offizier* escorted them back to the interrogation room, where they found Maurice and Kincaid bent over the table paging through an open file. When they looked up there was excitement in Kincaid's eyes but Maurice seemed in shock.

Hugh said, "What's the word?"

"Bonanza," Kincaid said. "We just got a file." And with a near-flourish he brought out an eight-by-ten black-and-white graduation photograph. College students stood on bleachers in front of a wall festooned with ribbons and a bas-relief portrait of Lenin. The students were separated by sex, men in lumpy suits on the outside and women in the center wearing floral-patterned dresses that looked as if they'd been cut from Depression-era window curtains. Paul didn't need the typewritten identification tag to recognize Karl. His brother stood third from the left in the back row, his head lowered slightly, looking warily at the camera.

"There are three other photos," Kincaid said. "None very good. Stasis men don't like to have their pictures taken."

"Stasis?"

"Yes, it seems your brother was a member of East Germany's KGB counterpart. Nominally they're independent but they dance to whatever tune Moscow plays."

"And that's the magic KGB connection," Hugh said. "Which also proves that your dreams are . . ."

"Are real," Maurice finished in a stunned monotone.

The two of them looked at Paul with a mixture of fear and fascination usually reserved for circus freaks.

"I told you *that* a month ago," Paul said.

"You can really do that?" Maurice said. "I mean, read people's minds?"

"I had dreams," Paul said irritably. "It's not mind reading. Come on, you talked to Dr. Helms."

"I have dreams too, but not like that. Not where I can see what's going on in other people's heads."

"You don't have a twin brother."

Now Kincaid was confused. "Excuse me, but did I miss something here?"

The explanations began again, and Paul had to remind himself that these men were only now coming to terms with a phenomenon that he had been forced to acknowledge weeks ago. Hugh recovered more quickly than Maurice, who remained shaken and suspicious, not so much of Paul but of a world that had suddenly changed the rules and made possible something formerly impossible. Kincaid treated it first as a joke, then became apprehensive.

It took half an hour before Paul could return the conversation to the subject of his freedom. He wanted to get out of prison immediately but the CIA men told him that they didn't have the authority to release him. "We'll get you out," Hugh reassured him. "Just be a little patient—"

"You be patient. After you've been drugged and kidnapped and thrown in jail and haven't done a damn thing."

"The Berlin police still think you ran down one of their officers."

"So show them the picture. Prove that it was Karl. Get me the hell out of here."

"We'll get you out. Even if we have to call Washington and have them pull the right strings. Don't worry."

But Paul did worry. And with good reason. While the CIA men were busy pulling strings, he spent another rotten night in jail.

CHAPTER
23

THAT NIGHT, PAUL DREAMED OF RAY TREGERDEMAIN.
They were standing on opposite sides of a swimming pool and Paul
was reaching out, trying to hand Ray fifty marks. They were separated by twenty or thirty feet but still they leaned toward one
another, hands outstretched, until Paul slipped and fell into the pool.

In a dizzying shift of perspective he became an observer, standing
behind Ray, and the man in the water was Karl. Karl yelled for help,
and Ray, thinking it was Paul who was in trouble, jumped in to save
him.

No, Paul yelled, but no sound came from his lips. He could only
watch as Ray swam to Karl, who had gone limp and floated face-
down, shoulders half-submerged. When Ray got to him, he slipped
his arm beneath Karl's shoulders and began swimming back toward
shore. Paul watched as they came toward him, Ray struggling
through the water, breathing in quick gasps with Karl's head, face
upturned and unconscious, resting on his shoulder.

As he approached, a terrible transformation took place. Karl's eyes
opened and a smile spread across his face. The smile didn't stop but

kept going, distending the features, pulling back the cheeks and elongating the mouth and nose until it became the snout of a huge polar bear with glittering black eyes and blood-red lips.

Watch out, Paul screamed silently.

In the water Ray became aware of the transformation. He turned, saw the bear and with a cry of terror released his hold and pushed free. Trying to escape, he swam frantically toward Paul. The bear rolled slowly, nosed under the water and became a shifting pattern of refracted white, moving beneath the surface, beneath the swimming man. Paul extended his hand to help and Ray reached up, but before their hands touched, huge white paws grasped Ray from below and pulled him under.

Paul's hand, still extended, now held fifty marks, the money he'd first offered Ray. Suddenly he knew that the only way to save Ray was to throw the money into the pool. The two forms were visible beneath the waves, rolling one on top of the other, white hair and pale flesh alternating beneath the roiling surface.

Paul threw the money into the water, shouting, *Take it, take it.* Instantly the bear disappeared; in the still water he watched Ray swimming upward, swimming toward him, hands clawing the water, bubbles escaping from his mouth, eyes wide, only now it was no longer Ray, it was—

In a flash of white Ray disappeared and the polar bear rose from the water with Jason's lifeless body clenched in its mouth . . .

Paul woke up and fell off the cot as he flung his arms up. He was drenched in sweat. The image of his son's body seemed to fade slowly, and it took a few minutes before he realized where he was. A guard appeared, blinking under the amber lights outside the cell.

"Was ist?"

Paul picked himself up and waved the man away. Alone, he sat shivering on the bunk, wrapped in a pale green blanket. The image of Jason, blue-skinned in death, was the one he remembered from the mortuary where he'd insisted on seeing his son's body, not embalmed or powdered but immediately, right away, the only way he could believe it. Paul had pushed that moment from his mind. He hadn't thought of it again until tonight, until the dream, where it was all mixed up with Ray Tregerdemain's terrible death.

You let him drown . . . The words came with a shock of recognition, they were the same ones he'd used with Joanna. *You let him drown,* he'd told Jo on the night that she'd come to talk about having another child. And now he had let Ray Tregerdemain drown—

But not in the same way, he silently protested. He couldn't have known that Karl would kill Ray. And yet he hadn't told Ray that they were dealing with a killer. He hadn't mentioned the dreams, hadn't protected Ray by letting him know the true situation. He'd made a mistake in judgment and Ray had paid the price. Just like Joanna. Jo . . . Not until now did he realize the full measure of her desolation. Not only from Jason's death, but from his turning away, his implicit condemnation. How many times had she come to him for comfort and in how many subtle ways had he let her know that no comfort was possible from him? When she blamed herself, he was silent. When she was silent, his correct but distant attitude accused her. All these months he had been punishing her for making their lives needlessly painful, something neither of them needed or deserved. If he had gone that weekend to Charlottesville . . . if he had told Ray Tregerdemain about Karl . . .

Suddenly he felt he *had* to talk to Joanna. He stood up, crossed to the door of the cell and called for the guard. When the man appeared Paul demanded a phone call. The guard, a young fellow with tiny eyes and bushy eyebrows, shook his head. "I have no authority for that; you go back to sleep." He hitched up his pants and returned to his office.

But Paul could't sleep. He spent the rest of the night pacing, his thoughts alternating among Joanna and Jason and Ray Tregerdemain. He hoped the CIA people would be there early and make good on their promise to spring him, but breakfast came and they still hadn't arrived. It wasn't until almost nine that he was led to a processing room where Hugh, Maurice and Kincaid waited.

"It's about time you got here," Paul said.

"It's the weekend," Hugh reminded him. "We had to call Washington and get people out of bed—"

"Yeah, life's tough in the big city. Let's go."

Kincaid said, "We have to wait for the man from the consulate."

"Who?"

"His name is Walsh, he's the only one who can officially receive you into custody."

"And he's got your temporary passport," Hugh added. "So we can get you back to the States."

"I want to make a phone call."

Hugh looked up with a frown, and seeing his expression Paul

added, "Same rules as yesterday."

"Can't it wait?"

"It can; I can't. I've been up since four this morning. Let's go. Let's get something done."

Hugh sighed and turned to the others. "Let us know when Walsh arrives."

They returned to the same office they'd gone to the day before. Paul took one desk and Hugh another. It was after midnight in Washington, early on a Sunday morning. Joanna sounded sleepy when she picked up the phone.

"Hello?"

"Jo? It's Paul."

"Paul?"

"Sorry to call so late. Did you get my message the other day?"

"Umm. Are you still in Berlin?"

"I'm leaving as soon as I can. Listen, there's something I want to know. Forget how strange it sounds but when was the last time we spoke?"

"You know when."

"Please . . . have I called you since you left me the note?"

"It doesn't matter, Paul, I've got my own apartment. I'm moving out . . . We need some time apart. I do, anyway. I can't take the way we've been living so . . . I found a place near DuPont Circle."

"With someone?"

"No, Paul. Alone."

"I see . . . well, whatever you feel comfortable with," he said lamely. "We'll work it out . . ."

"I'm not making any hard and fast decisions," she said. "But I have to stop feeling rotten about myself, and I can't do that the way we've been. I'm not blaming you and I'm not blaming myself—I *can't* blame myself—but you do. I know you do, Paul, and maybe you've got a right to but I can't handle it. Can you understand that?"

"Sure . . ."

"I'm sorry, I didn't mean to tell you like this, but I spent a week alone, wishing I was dead and thinking about everything and . . ."

He could tell from her voice that she was close to tears.

"It's all right, Jo."

Her breath caught and then, in a flat voice, she said, "I wish it was."

He wanted to be with her, to hold her, to feel her arms around him, to tell her what he felt and finally understood, or at least was beginning to understand. He wanted to tell her that he was sorry; but with Hugh pretending not to listen and the German policeman at the door all he said was, "Whatever's right, that's what we'll do. We can talk when I get back, okay? You're going to be there?"

"When are you coming back?"

"Tonight or tomorrow, it depends."

"You don't have to come back on my account," she said stiffly. Then, aware of the hint of hostility in the response, she added more gently, "Sorry."

"Jo, listen, there's something you should know. This is going to be a lot to take at once, but I've got no choice . . . A couple of weeks ago I found out I've got a twin brother. His name is Karl Alexander and he lives here in Berlin. That's why I came over here."

"But you never—"

"I know. I mean, I didn't know. Mom thought he died right after the war so she kept it secret. But you know those nightmares I have?"

"Where you think you kill someone?"

"Right. Well, it seems that those weren't nightmares after all. Just before you left a couple of people from the"—Hugh glanced up—"a certain organization convinced me that those nightmares really happened. I didn't believe it, Jo, but it's true. The obituaries of those same people—their names, anyway—are in newspapers. You can look them up, see for yourself."

"*What* are you saying?"

"Karl works for a foreign government, he's an assassin and he's in the United States. At least he was ten days ago. He even called Bernie and impersonated me—"

"That wasn't you?"

"I've been in Berlin since the day after you left."

So much had happened, Paul realized. The last time they had talked was the night that she'd told him about Luis de Cuevo—the same day that the CIA men had come to him, the day he'd discovered that the death-dreams were real. And he'd never told her. He'd withdrawn from her, as if she were unworthy of knowing what was happening in his life. Talking to her now, it was as if they were strangers again—or getting acquainted again. There was so much about each other that they no longer knew.

At first, like the rest, she was incredulous. Then, as the details of the situation became real, so did the implications of what he was saying. "That's why you asked when we last talked? You thought he might call *me*?"

"I don't know what he might do. All I know is that he's very dangerous and he's impersonating me."

"You're scaring me now, Paul. This isn't funny."

"I know. Listen, do you think you could find someplace to stay for a few days? Maybe ask Denise or go to your parents."

"Does he really look exactly like you?"

"I've got somebody here who could tell you."

Hugh looked up in surprise as Paul offered him the phone, then waved him away.

"Somebody who's helping me find Karl. Until we do . . ."

"Well, I do have this new apartment."

"Good." He thought of suggesting she get the Smith & Wesson revolver that he kept in a file cabinet but decided against it. After all, Karl's appearance in New York had been almost two weeks ago and whatever his business was it had nothing to do with Joanna. If anything, he would want to avoid her and anyone else who might recognize him as an imposter.

"I'm probably overreacting," Paul said, trying to reassure both of them, "but better safe than . . ."

Kincaid stepped into the room and announced that the consular representative had arrived. Paul took down the address of the new apartment and told Jo he'd leave word at the gallery when he was coming back.

Just before they hung up he managed to say what she hadn't heard from him in a very long time. "I love you, Jo."

There was a moment's hesitation. Then, "You're a funny man," she said seriously.

After she hung up Joanna sat cross-legged on the bed. What Paul had said about Karl Alexander worried her as much as his sudden warmth confused her. Two weeks ago his reaction to her affair with Luis de Cuevo—his total, and depressing, lack of anger or jealousy, his cold, unemotional lovemaking had, she thought, told her how little she meant to him. Her brief betrayal had seemed to prove what she most feared, that there was nothing left to betray. And yet, a few moments ago he had told her that he loved her with such conviction that it was impossible to doubt he meant it.

The familiar creak of a tree branch rubbing against the roof startled her. She slipped on a robe and went downstairs and checked each of the doors to make sure they were locked. The empty house felt threatening now . . . She imagined this new-found brother Karl outside somewhere in the yard, watching. She shut the blinds, pulled the curtains and turned on the radio. Her emotions in a turmoil, she made coffee and sat at the kitchen table seriously wondering for the first time since she'd returned from Maine if she was doing the right thing . . .

Joanna had died in Maine—that's how she'd thought of it. She had gone to her family's summer cabin for escape, oblivion, release from a dead heart, a dead marriage. The cabin sat at the tip of a narrow peninsula thrust into Penobscot Bay, a single-story rambling structure with a high peaked roof and screened-in porch on tall bluffs overlooking a rocky shoreline and tumultuous ocean. A local handyman usually opened the cabin but Joanna had not contacted him. When she arrived the windows were shuttered, the screens on the porch boarded up and the electricity off. She opened the cottage herself, hoping that the physical labor would somehow relieve the pain. She released the shutters and latched them open and removed the protective sheets of plywood from the porch screens, getting splinters in her palms. She figured out how to turn on the water and electricity, then cleaned the house, sweeping up the dead bugs, washing the refrigerator, airing the bedding.

These routines soothed her some and she managed to sleep pretty well the first night. When she woke up, though, the memory of what had happened with Paul was too much for her. She pulled out the old trunks and began going through them, looking at memorabilia from her childhood, searching for the little girl who'd gotten lost somewhere along the way. But one trunk wasn't hers—it was Jason's. It held his summer toys—the Tick-Tock book, He-Man, Loomis the stuffed dog with its stitched ear. She'd forgotten about them. In Washington they had given Jason's things to Goodwill and turned his bedroom back into a guest room. Seeing his toys at the cabin brought back too-painful memories: she remembered every toy and how it had come to Jason, the exact occasion. She even remembered the design on the wrapping paper she'd used on some of the Christmas gifts.

The tears came and offered a sort of relief, but one that left her exhausted. She drove to Camden, where nobody knew her, and bought a few cans of Campbell's Hearty Dinners and a case of scotch. Drinking steadily, she courted alcoholic oblivion for days. At some deeper level she realized that she was asking from herself what she felt she'd failed to get from Paul—*attention*. Did she care? Did she care about herself, about anything at all?

The photographs on the mantel above the fireplace showed each of the four generations as children, each one seated on an oddly shaped rock they called Breadloaf: her grandmother, her father, Joanna, and Jason. Each child had been between two and four when the photo was taken. They were a family tradition, and they pierced her heart. Jason's smile, trusting and confident, accused her. Paul's eyes accused her. Her own heart accused her.

She forced the scotch down until she got sick, lay down on the floor and slept for twelve hours.

When she woke up it was an overcast day, raw and windy and cold and she decided to end it, end herself. The decision filled her with a strange exhilaration. She dumped the contents of her father's trunk onto the floor and found his .22 revolver. The gun was unloaded but with it there were two boxes of bullets, one full and one with just a few shells. Selecting the cleanest bullets from the unopened box, she loaded three of the six chambers, every other one. Modified Russian roulette. She would let the fates decide if she was fit to live or not. She no longer could.

The mechanics of what she was about to do gave her momentary pause. If she died in the cabin, who would find her? And after how long? The idea of leaving a mess for someone was distasteful, so she put on a yellow slicker and went outside, where she stood on the bluff overlooking the sea. Forty feet below, the waves crashed against jagged rocks surrounded by angry foam. The tide was just past full, which was good. If she fell, her body would be washed out to sea.

Cold rain and fear made her teeth chatter. She brought the gun from beneath the folds of her slicker. Did bullets fire if they were wet? She didn't know, but she resolved to do this quickly. Holding the gun firmly, she rotated the cylinder, two, three, four times. There was a fifty-fifty chance of a loaded cartridge. Or an empty cylinder.

As she raised the gun and put the barrel in her mouth . . . she began to cry. It was silly, hysterical crying. She felt stupid standing there with the cold metal barrel between her lips so she switched positions and put the barrel to her temple but the tears continued, warm against her rain-soaked cheeks. She could see herself standing there, leaning over the cliff, so melodramatic, so absurd. And she at least knew she didn't want to die.

She moved the gun away from her head, pointed the barrel down at the angry waves and then, about to pull the trigger, she changed her mind. Her hand went around the barrel of the gun, and she threw it as far out as she could into the sea.

"Not my fault," she called after it. "It's not my fault, goddamn it."

Shaking from more than cold, she returned to the cabin and gathered Jason's toys and summer clothing. Each armful she took to the bluff and threw the articles into the sea, one by one. She worked in feverish haste but her mind was clear and she knew what she was doing. After Jason's things came the scotch. She grabbed all the bottles, empty as well as full ones, and threw them into the sea as well.

Back in the cabin, she was shivering so violently that she had difficulty lighting a fire, fingers so numb she could hardly hold the match. Finally the newspaper caught and after a few moments the warmth began to spread across the room. She stripped out of her wet clothes, toweled dry and pulled the blankets off the bed. Wrapping them around her, she sat on the floor close to the fire, staring into the flames. Gradually the trembling stopped.

That night she slept on the floor, curled up with cushions like an animal in its lair. When she woke up eighteen hours later she was no longer the same person, no longer the little girl on Breadloaf rock with fairytale dreams, no longer the young woman in the Ethiopia scrapbook who stood facing the camera with a self-confident smile while somber-eyed Africans looked on. And no longer the bride whose marriage was to be a real-life adventure played out against an exotic, fast-track world of journalism. When she woke up Joanna was a woman who hadn't been able to save her child, who was estranged from her husband, and whose feeling of special dispensation hadn't made her immune from life's natural disasters, after all.

She returned to Washington, considerably saddened but more secure in this new knowledge of herself. She could, she felt, go on from here even if she had to go on alone. She was unsure of how Paul would react to her decision to find an apartment but certain that it was the right thing to do. His two-week absence only reinforced how he felt—or didn't feel—about her . . .

Now, as Joanna sat at the kitchen table cradling her cup of coffee, she seriously wondered if she'd been hasty. On the phone Paul had seemed so genuinely warm and caring, so different from the way she remembered. *I love you*, he had said. For the first time since . . . she couldn't remember. Before the accident, probably. Ironic if after everything she'd done to try and please him that her decision to leave had done what no amount of being stoic and guilty could do—

A noise outside the kitchen window startled her and she jumped, spilling hot coffee on her fingers. She put down the cup and shook her hand to cool it. The sound was the branch of a tree rubbing on the outside wall, a familiar sound now made ominous by Paul's warning. She wished she knew more about this brother of his. Was he some kind of madman? A nut? The vision of someone sneaking around outside sent her upstairs to Paul's study to get the gun from a locked filing cabinet.

Crazy, she thought as she climbed into bed and put the gun in the drawer of the night table. There was a hollow clink as the metal touched glass. Joanna reached beneath a silk scarf and found a pint of Chivas Regal, half full, or half empty . . She recalled putting the bottle there during some distant past life, but the memory was dim, more like remembering something she'd been told by someone else.

She slept restlessly, woke up at dawn and then, comforted by the new daylight, slept soundly for three more hours. When she got up she called the owner of the new apartment and made arrangements to move in that day. Then she called Denise at the gallery and begged off work.

At ten o'clock, she left to get some packing boxes. She paid no attention to the silver-and-burgundy Lincoln Continental parked at the end of the block or to the man inside who averted his face as she passed and then watched her in the rearview mirror until she disappeared around the corner.

CHAPTER
24

AFTER WATCHING JOANNA LEAVE THE HOUSE, KARL drove to a pay phone and called to make sure no one else was there. When he heard the answering machine he hung up. What he was about to do was dangerous, he knew. His background, his training, his instincts all warned against this, but he was powerfully drawn to his brother's existence, as though it were part of his own . . . He had this compulsion to see how Paul lived, how *he* might have lived had their positions been reversed and he had been the one to get sick and Paul been left with Tante Inge. A tiny microbe had changed the course of their lives; he wanted to compare the result. He needed to know. He *deserved* to know.

He did not park on the same street as the house. He left the Lincoln a block away, behind Paul's house. There would be less likelihood of someone connecting him with the car, and if he had to leave quickly he could slip out the back door and cross a neighbor's yard. He had decided against a disguise. A stranger entering the house might cause suspicion, but what could be more natural than Paul Stafford entering his own house? At most he might have to exchange a cursory greeting and he felt confident he could do this. He'd fooled the CIA men.

It was warm and damp as he made his way toward Paul's house. A gang of children played at one end of the street and a man with his back to him was weeding his lawn just two houses away. Karl casually opened the low wrought-iron gate and walked up to the house. He got to the front door without being noticed. The first key didn't work—a back-door key or maybe the key to Paul's office—but the second one slid easily into the lock. Once inside he paused to listen, to smell the air, to let the feel of the place sink in.

The house seemed smaller than it looked from the outside, but by East German standards it was still palatial. There were rooms to either side and a flight of stairs directly in front. As he walked the ground floor it struck him that the house was not so much decorated as arranged. Chairs, tables, lamps, artwork—each piece seemed chosen for itself rather than to fit with a design, yet the effect seemed harmonious.

In the kitchen he reviewed his escape route. There were three doors: one to the cellar, one to the back yard and a third to the garage. Inside the garage he found an Audi. Paul's car, he knew. He had the key on the same ring as the others. The Audi was white, the same as his Mercedes, but it was not a Mercedes, which gave Karl a small satisfaction . . . He had begun to envy his brother's life and it pleased him that his own car was superior.

Upstairs there was a large bathroom and four other rooms: a master bedroom, guest room, office and an artist's studio that looked as if it were in the process of becoming a storage room. He went first to the bedroom. The bed was loosely made, an empty cup with coffee residue sat on a night table. Beside it was a pint of scotch, Chivas Regal, half full. He licked his finger, rubbed it in the bottom of the cup and tasted it. There was no hint of liquor. Did the woman drink in bed? To help her sleep? To drown her sorrows?

A classified section from a newspaper lay on the floor beside a yellow pad, both sandwiched between the bed and the night table. The newspaper had apartment listings, some of which were circled in red; on the yellow pad were brief descriptions and phone numbers. Karl smiled. The impression he'd gotten from Paul was correct; his wife, Joanna, was leaving. She drank herself to sleep. His brother's life was not so ideal as it seemed.

He replaced the newspaper and pad, opened the drawer to the night table and found a gun. Loaded, and on her side of the bed, the side with the scotch bottle on the night table. Which meant what? That Joanna was afraid of prowlers while Paul was away? Or could it be Paul she was afraid of?

Karl was intrigued. Paul's description of Joanna had not hinted at this. Scotch and coffee in bed, a search for a new place to live and a loaded gun close at hand. Karl tried to recall what Paul had told him . . . Joanna had been involved in famine relief when they met—a humanitarian cause—but now she worked in an art gallery in a world of egoism and cultural snobbery. More contradiction. Which meant . . . a woman who didn't know herself? And looking to find out? The sort of self-questioning that was all over the magazines these days . . .

There was a photograph on the dresser that showed Paul and Joanna on a sightseeing boat on the Seine. They stood at the rail with the Notre Dame in the background. Karl picked up the photograph and stared at Joanna. She was smaller than Magda, with jet-black hair and blue eyes the color of the distant sky. Her smile seemed eager, looking ahead. To what dreams? He couldn't, of course, know. But he did know such people could often be duped by offering them their own dreams.

Satisfied that he had discovered an important clue to Joanna's personality, Karl continued his inspection, going through the dresser drawers, noting that Joanna was more casual with her clothing than Paul and that her lingerie was more delicate and stylish than Magda's. From the closet he took a brown tweed man's jacket and tried it on. The fit was perfect. He found a black silk dress and held it up, imagining Joanna inside it, imagining the two of them together, just as in the photograph. If he wanted to he could slip into his brother's life as easily as he put on his jacket—

The doorbell rang and the illusion shattered.

Quietly Karl replaced the dress and closed the closet door. He crossed the hallway to the office, which overlooked the front yard. Positioning himself to one side of the window, he peered out. Whoever was at the door was beneath him, obscured from view, but there was a power lawnmower on the front walk that hadn't been there when he arrived. Now a boy stepped into view, about twelve years old, wearing threadbare jeans with holes in the knees and an oversize baseball jersey. As Karl watched, the boy bent over the lawnmower, adjusted the throttle, pulled the starting cord and the engine roared into life, destroying the quiet of a Sunday morning.

Karl frowned. With the boy out there he couldn't leave unnoticed through the front door. Still, he had been fortunate . . . it could have been a cleaning lady or someone with keys to the house. Besides, it wouldn't take the boy long to mow the lawn, ten or fifteen minutes. He should be gone by the time he was ready to leave.

Karl turned his attention to the study, the room to give him the clearest picture of his brother's life. On the walls were plaques and certificates, framed news stories and photographs of Paul on assignment all over the world, from the jungles of the Philippines to the Antarctic, where he stood in a fur-lined parka with another man, both of them surrounded by penguins.

A desk of oiled teak held a Zenith personal computer, a Rolodex and a stack of bills that must have come while Paul was gone. Someone, probably Joanna, had written Paul's name and beneath it a list of names and telephone numbers of people who had called and left messages on the machine. It was difficult for Karl to believe that anyone knew that many people or that his brother was comfortable being *known* by that many people. When Karl was a child his greatest desire was to be invisible. He could remember hearing Tante Inge—Frau Heusner, he corrected himself—returning home at night. He would shut his eyes, hoping that this would make him invisible, hoping that if he couldn't see her, she couldn't see him.

Going through the desk drawers Karl found a box of blank checks and was struck by an odd idea. But the more he thought about it the more it appealed to him. He took out the wallet he had taken from Paul and studied his brother's signature on his driver's license. The handwriting was remarkably similar to his own. He practiced Paul's signature on a blank piece of paper, and when he had it right he opened the bills on the desk and began making out checks: electricity, gas, Visa, American Express, Woodward & Lothrop—he smiled as he thought of Paul's confusion when he discovered the bills had been paid. Paul might guess who was responsible but could never prove it. And who would care? What law had been broken? What harm had been done . . .?

Karl was so involved in what he was doing that he didn't notice that the variable whine of the lawnmower had sunk to a steady idle, and when the front door opened it took him completely by surprise.

The sound of voices reached him, a woman and a boy.

"Just stack them there, that's all right."

"What about that branch? I can cut it down easy."

"I think we better leave it for the professionals, Danny."

"I can do it easy. My dad's got a chain saw, a Black and Decker."

"Then you ask your dad and see what he says."

"Okay."

During the interchange Karl moved swiftly and quietly. No time now to wonder why Joanna had returned early or if she had gone to work at all. He had to leave this house without being discovered. If he could make it to one of the rooms at the rear of the house he could slip out a window, drop to the ground and leave through the back yard.

He returned the checkbook and the bills to the drawer, moved into the hallway just as the front door shut. Too late. Footsteps on the stairs accompanied by the hollow bump-bump of a cardboard box. If he crossed the landing, Joanna would see him. He slipped back into the office and stood behind the door, from where he had a view of the hall into the bedroom.

Joanna appeared then, carrying one cardboard box and dragging another. She took them both into the bedroom and stood for a moment catching her breath. She wore khaki shorts and a red sweater with sleeves rolled to the elbows. As Karl watched she began packing her clothes, from time to time disappearing into the closet.

He considered the options. The stairway began between the two back rooms and was surrounded by a railing. To escape he would have to make his way around the railing and go halfway down the stairs before he was out of sight of someone in the bedroom. Joanna's forays into the closet wouldn't give him sufficient time, he would have to wait until she went downstairs. And then another possibility as the sound of the lawnmower chugged to a stop. The boy had apparently finished the front yard. Karl waited for the doorbell to ring. When nothing happened he made his way to the window. At one point wood creaked beneath his feet and he froze. The sound of Joanna packing continued without interruption. He reached the window and looked out. The boy had disappeared—he would try to get out the front way.

The window was one of the old, double-sash variety with a movable lower pane. As he unlatched it the sound of metal grating on metal made him wince, but the sounds from the bedroom at least reassured him that Joanna was still busy packing. Placing the heel of his palm against the frame, Karl pushed. Nothing happened. Why couldn't brother Paul live in a modern home with aluminum frame windows? Wasn't this America, all shiny bright and new? And then he heard Joanna coming across the landing toward him. He had just enough time to step back against the wall—and then she was in the room. And he had no place to hide.

Without glancing his way, Joanna crossed directly to the desk, opened a drawer and took out a roll of tape. Her back was to him, but if she gave the room so much as a cursory glance she couldn't help but see him. He fought the urge to crouch, to shrink, to flatten himself against the bookcase behind him. He remained still, barely breathing, willing himself to be invisible just as he once had as a child.

Joanna took the tape and left without glancing his way.

As soon as she was gone a tremor ran through his body and the adrenaline made him dizzy. When he heard Joanna in the bedroom, he quietly returned to his position behind the door and looked out.

He saw her kneeling on the floor, taping the box. Outside the house, in the back yard now, the lawnmower buzzed into life. Good. The noise would cover any sound he might make trying to get the damn window open. He took a step toward the window, then realized that the lawnmower would also cover the sound of Joanna's return if she decided to put the tape back in the drawer. No, he thought, stepping back, better to wait and see what she did next.

He watched through the narrow opening. After taping the box Joanna pushed it into the hallway. He expected her to start packing the next box but instead she went to a linen closet and tried to get something from the top shelf. When she couldn't reach she stepped precariously up on the bottom shelf and managed to grab a small nylon bag, but in pulling it down, a number of boxes tumbled out, raining down on her head.

"Shit," she said, jumping back.

She rubbed her eye, evidently trying to clear it of something. Shaking her head and blinking, she went into the bathroom. All right, this was his chance. When he heard the water running, he moved swiftly onto the landing. All he needed was a moment to get downstairs, then exit by the front door.

As he passed the partially open door of the bathroom he could see Joanna bending over the sink.

Don't look up, he thought. Otherwise . . .

The floor creaked, but the sound of the running water masked his footsteps. And then he was beyond the doorway, out of sight. It took him an extra moment to step around the box she had left at the top of the stairs—as he did the phone rang.

He took two quick steps downstairs and then the water stopped and he froze. He wanted to make a run for the door but remembered how badly the stairs creaked. Any abrupt movement would get her attention. The bathroom was closer to the office, so she could answer the phone there. If he kept still she wouldn't see him, unless she came back to the bedroom.

Which is what she did.

She was toweling one side of her face and was about to enter the bedroom when she lowered the towel and saw him. He had turned around to face upward so that from her perspective it would look as if he had just arrived and was coming upstairs. When she caught sight of him, she jumped, then seemed to relax.

"Paul! My God, you—"

She doesn't know, he realized. *She doesn't know . . .*

"I didn't mean to scare you," he said as calmly as he could. *Play it out*, nothing else to do except—

"With all the racket I didn't hear—"

And then her expression changed and her eyes widened and he thought, she knows. And not only that he wasn't Paul. Her expression shifted again as confusion seemed replaced by fear. She knew who he was; *she knew he was Karl.*

The phone was still ringing as they faced each other on the stairway, neither wanting to admit what he knew to the other. Awkwardly, the game of deception went on.

"I can't stay," Karl said, knowing as he did that this probably wasn't going to work. "I just came to get some notes . . ."

Joanna fought to get control of herself. She gestured weakly toward the office. "Go ahead."

"Aren't you going to get the phone?"

"You can get it."

She backed up to give him room, pressing her shoulders against the wall. Karl came upstairs slowly, and as he did there was a click and the recorded message began: "This is Paul and Joanna Stafford. We're not available right now but if you leave your name and number we'll get right back to you."

Karl was barely aware of the tape. His eyes were on Joanna's, and although he kept his expression pleasant, he was thinking: How could she know? How could she know who he was? Unless Paul had lied to him and had told her before he left. Or had she talked to his mother and his mother had told about him? Or—or just possibly Paul had escaped and she'd spoken to him.

And that would account for the fear in her eyes.

He stopped at the top of the stairs. As the message concluded, a beep announced the caller . . .

"This is Shiela Burney for Joanna Stafford. You can pick up the key from our office anytime after noon today, which is Sunday. Thank you."

At the sound of the voice Joanna said numbly, "It's for me."

She moved to enter the bedroom but he put up his arm, blocking the way.

"Why are you afraid?"

"Paul . . ." the word was strained.

"No." He smiled. "You know, don't you?"

"The phone . . ."

She tried to duck under his arm but he thrust his leg forward, blocking the bedroom door. She stepped back, staring at him.

"Let the machine get it."

"Okay." She smiled but Karl caught the quick hard glint of decision in her eyes and a moment later she was running across the landing to the office. He went after her and got to her just as she put her hand on the phone. He slammed his hand over hers before she could lift the receiver.

"How did you find out?" he said quietly.

The answering machine clicked off.

"Find out what?" Her voice was a whisper.

But Karl was looking at the answering machine . . . He hadn't played back the tape. Now he reached over and flicked the playback switch, and as he did Joanna ran out the door, slamming it behind her. Karl, assuming she was headed downstairs, followed quickly, ready to leap the railing and intercept her on the stairway. Instead she rushed into the bedroom and slammed the door, and he knew immediately what she was after.

Following her into the room, he saw Joanna was digging in the night table for the gun. In two quick strides he reached her as she turned, gun in hand. Cocked, too, he noted with some surprise. As he grabbed the revolver he made certain that his thumb was between the hammer and the cylinder, and the hammer snapped painfully against his thumbnail. She really would have shot him, he realized.

Joanna was strong, fear pumping her adrenaline as they careened around the room. The night table overturned and the coffee cup and scotch and a lamp went crashing to the floor. She let go of the gun and broke away and ran to the window, where he caught her from behind. She slammed an elbow at his chest as he lifted her, and as he swung her around her foot struck the window and the glass shattered, letting in the angry whine of the lawnmower.

He pushed her to the bed, held the gun to her head. "Stop now. Don't make me kill you."

She froze. Outside, the sound of the lawnmower chugged to a halt.

"Mrs. Stafford?" the boy called. "What happened?"

Joanna's eyes shifted from the gun to the window, and Karl understood what she was thinking. "If you say something you will both die."

She hesitated.

"Look at me," Karl demanded. "I will kill you first and him second. He will not get out of that yard."

Her resistance collapsed. She bit her lip and nodded.

The boy called again, "Mrs. Stafford? Are you okay?"

Karl stepped away from the bed but kept the gun trained on her. He motioned to the window. "Tell him it was an accident. Tell him you're fine. Get rid of him. Go ahead, do it."

Keeping her eyes on him, she stood up. Broken glass crunched underfoot as she made her way to the window. Karl stepped close to the wall so that he could watch her face without being seen. Joanna gave him a glance, then, applying a smile, peered out.

Danny was looking up at her, squinting against the sun and bright sky.

"What happened?"

She took a deep breath. "I stumbled when I was moving the boxes, Danny. It's okay. Are you done yet?"

"Did you cut yourself?"

"No I . . . I hit the window with a box. The yard looks real good, Danny."

"Yeah, I'm almost through. You want me to put the glass in the trash can?"

"That will be fine."

As Karl motioned her back to the bed, the damage already done, the full extent to which the Redeye mission had been compromised, began to sink in. It was not so much what Joanna knew about him that worried him but how she knew . . .

As for Joanna, now that she was over the initial shock, she began to collect and even reassert herself.

"What do you want here?"

"Allow me to ask the questions. Who told you about me?"

She looked at the gun. "What are you going to do?"

"I am going to try and save your life, just as I saved your husband's life. But I won't be able to if you refuse to cooperate. Once more, how do you know about me?"

"You didn't save his life, you made him a prisoner, you—"

Karl's hardened expression stopped her. He felt a burst of anger toward Otto. Not only had he paid five thousand dollars, he had provided the Haloparimine, a powerful Stasis-developed sedative sufficient to keep Paul disoriented and weak as a kitten for months. How was it possible that his brother could escape? Goddamn you, Otto . . .

"When did you talk to him?" he said to her.

Joanna glanced at the gun, then back up at his face, studying him. "You're Paul's brother. Would you really kill me?"

"If I have to."

She stared a moment longer, then folded her arms and just sat there, as though daring him to do his worst. She decided cooperating would buy her nothing, only increase *his* options. Of course she had not had Paul's dreams.

Karl knew he could get the information out of her. He could grab her by the neck and stick the gun in her mouth, terrorize her into talking. But as a professional he knew that terror carried its own risks, that it could release hidden forces and produce unexpected results. Joanna might well become hysterical, alert the boy in the yard, or she might become so crazy he would be forced to shoot her. It would be less risky at the safe house on the Toons Creek property. Whether she talked or not, he could not leave her here.

He moved to the dresser, opened the drawer and pulled out a pair of socks and a handful of pantyhose. Joanna began to object, and then a new look came over her face as she realized that he knew exactly which drawer they were in. At his approach, she drew back. He motioned with the gun.

"Face down on the bed."

"Wait. If you leave now—"

Karl smiled. "If I leave you will be a good lady and not say a word? Please . . ." He realized it was dangerous to take her, but far more dangerous to leave her. The easiest way was to kill her, but until he knew how much of a threat his brother had become, Joanna would better serve as a hostage.

In the back yard the lawnmower came noisily to life. The boy must have finished picking up the glass. No longer needing to worry about noise, Karl slipped the gun into his pocket, took hold of Joanna by the shoulders and pushed her face down onto the bed, muffling her scream. Sitting astride her back, he wadded a sock into a ball and stuffed it into her mouth, then used a pair of pantyhose to gag her. He tied her hands and feet and bound her in a fetal position by looping a pair of pantyhose around her neck and running it between her knees to her ankles. When he was finished he wrapped her in a blanket and carried her downstairs to the garage. He put her on the floor, opened the trunk of the Audi and after spreading the blanket inside lifted her into the trunk. He closed it and returned to the kitchen—

A knock at the back door . . . the boy, Danny, stood there, peering in. Karl stepped back but it was too late. Danny had already seen him. Nothing to do now but play out the charade. He stepped back into the kitchen and went to the door where Danny waited.

"Hi, Mr. Stafford. I didn't know you were home."

"I came in last night. I was asleep."

"I'm all done, I even cleaned up the glass—"

"Good." Karl forced himself to survey the yard. "It looks very good."

The boy stood there, and Karl finally realized he was waiting to be paid. How much? Perhaps he could phrase it ambiguously and Danny would tell him.

Karl said, "Have you change for a ten?"

"Not with me but at home I do. I can—"

"That's all right. Just apply the balance to next time."

He handed over a ten-dollar bill and closed the door. As he turned away, Danny's voice reached him.

"Wait, Mr. Stafford."

What *now*?

Danny stood holding the bill, staring up at him with a worried expression.

"This is only a ten, Mr. Stafford . . ."

"*Only* a ten?"

"I did both lawns."

Damn, how much did these spoiled American kids get for mowing a lawn? He added another ten and Danny finally seemed satisfied.

"I told Mrs. Stafford that I could cut that branch up there. Only five bucks. You want me to do it?"

"No, thanks," he said, and shut the door before Danny could come up with some new bright idea.

Carefully he retraced his steps, wiping away his fingerprints as he went. In the bedroom he righted the table and replaced the lamp and other items that had fallen to the floor. When he got to the study he discovered that the answering machine was still on playback. He returned the tape to the beginning and listened, but the only message was the woman who had just called. If he wanted any more information about Paul, he would have to get it from Joanna.

He returned to the garage and opened the trunk. Joanna had obviously been struggling to free herself; her face was red with effort, she was breathing heavily and her neck was raw from the twisted pantyhose.

"We are leaving now," he told her. "Please do not struggle. You will only wear yourself out and there is not much air coming in. It is a forty-minute drive, then I can let you out."

He closed the trunk and got into the car. The driver's seat, rearview and sideview mirrors were all positioned perfectly. Paul's car. He found a radio-controlled device in the glove compartment that opened the garage door. As he turned onto the street he saw Danny, half a block away and coming toward him.

As soon as Danny saw the car, he waved and called out something. Karl's nerves, already stretched thin, could stand no more. Rather than stop and find out what he wanted, Karl simply smiled, waved and kept driving. As he passed he caught a glimpse of a five-dollar bill in Danny's hand. So it was fifteen dollars to do both lawns. The boy was honest, wanting to give him back his five-dollar overpayment. Honest, and a potential danger.

When the Audi didn't stop, Danny continued on to the Stafford house and rang the bell. He intended to give the money to Mrs. Stafford but she didn't answer. He knew she was home because her car was still at the curb and he hadn't seen her with Mr. Stafford. Maybe she was on the phone and couldn't come to the door. Or maybe she was taking a bath. Or maybe—a sudden, secret thought—maybe she was having her period. She might feel sick or something.

Embarrassed, Danny walked quickly back to the sidewalk, whistling loudly to show that it really wasn't all that important, the errand that had brought him to the door. He'd come back tomorrow to return the money. By then Mrs. Stafford should be feeling better.

CHAPTER

25

ON THE FLIGHT BACK TO WASHINGTON THE THREE
men sat side-by-side, Hugh in the middle, Paul next to the window
and Maurice on the aisle. They were in the No Smoking section at
Paul's insistence, which meant that periodically Maurice had to leave
his seat and go to the rear of the aircraft to smoke a cigarette. He
wasn't pleased. It seemed to him as if they had been released in
Paul's custody instead of the other way around. While at the airport
he had taken Hugh aside and suggested that he was treating Stafford
too much like part of the team and not enough like an asset, and a
dubious one at that.

Hugh tended to shrug off Maurice's concerns. He was now pretty
well convinced that Paul was as much a victim as any of the people
murdered, and he had made a decision to treat him as part of the
team, sensing that it was the most effective way to get Paul's confidence and thereby his cooperation.

"But you're not controlling him," Maurice complained. "He's
controlling us—"

"He's sharp, he's got ideas."

"But he's not one of us."

Neither am I, Hugh wanted to say. He hadn't felt like one of "us" since the Tehran fiasco. Maybe that was why he liked Paul Stafford. A natural outsider, Stafford felt no need to be an insider. He'd been impatient that morning with the consular official, a bald man with a double chin named Walsh, who made it obvious what an imposition it was giving up his Sunday morning to come down there and get an American out of jail . . .

"It's real tough for him without that second cup of coffee," Paul whispered loudly enough for Walsh to hear.

With the deputy police chief of Berlin in attendance, Walsh mumbled a short statement about who was cooperating with whom in the matter of Paul Stafford, transfer of custody, jurisdiction of designated agencies, guarantee of appearance within seven days of notification . . . Once formalities were over, Walsh signed his name half a dozen times and disappeared. A police officer with sad eyes and a receding chin then gave Paul a silver plastic bag decorated with a rampant bear, the symbol of Berlin. Inside was the hospital gown he had been wearing on his arrival.

"You can use the restroom," the officer told him. "To change clothes."

"Shove it," Paul told him.

He started toward the door but the officer called loudly after him. "Excuse me, sir, but if you are not returning the uniform issued on your arrival then you must pay for it."

Paul looked down. "Pay for this? You're kidding?"

"Eighty-five marks, sir. Regulations."

"Here," Hugh said, and handed Paul a hundred marks.

Kincaid had gone to get the car, and while they waited for him outside the police station Paul stood with his eyes closed, face tilted toward the sun. A fresh, gusty wind swirled paper debris along the street and pushed patchy shadows of clouds up the face of nearby buildings. Watching him, Hugh could almost imagine the heightened sensation of sun and wind on skin that had been shut from light and fresh air.

"What did you guys find out about Lish?" Paul asked without opening his eyes.

"He's not one of ours," Maurice said. "Not unless he's too recent to be on computer."

"What about the army?"

"Their records show two Lishes, one overseas, the other stationed at Camp Pendleton in California. Neither one's a George and there's nobody at the Military Ocean Terminal by that name. The closest match is a civilian employee named *Litz*—L-I-T-Z. Maybe it looked the same in your dream."

Paul opened his eyes and turned away from the sun.

"It doesn't *look* any way; it's just something I know."

"We're running a check on Mr. Litz," Hugh said. "Just to make sure."

"Why don't you run a check on cargos while you're at it?" Paul said. "I'd like to know what kind of material goes through there."

"You think he was after cargo?"

"He was after something."

It was a good idea, Hugh decided. He turned to Maurice. "Have you called for transport from Dulles?"

"I'll call from the airport. *If* we get there in time."

"When you do, talk to Audrey, have him get a cargo list from the army. Whatever was there the day of Karl's visit."

"And what's come through since then," Paul added.

"Right," Hugh agreed. "The whole works . . ."

And that was the way the day had gone, with Paul acting as another member of the team, Hugh backing him up and Maurice trying unsuccessfully to maintain the boundaries between them. Now, as they headed over the North Atlantic at thirty-six thousand feet, Maurice went to the rear of the aircraft for a smoke and Hugh dropped his tray table and pulled out a notebook and a pencil.

"Let's review what we know," he said to Paul. "Karl Alexander, an agent for the Stasis. Officially a combat instructor, primary assignment is assassination. You find him and blow his cover and what does he do? He doesn't kill you, even though you gave him every chance in the world. Instead he makes you a prisoner. Now we know he's not squeamish about killing so either you're a very small threat—which I doubt—or he didn't want to kill his own brother. What's your guess?"

"I guess he felt a connection . . . with me, my life . . ."

"You want to be more specific?"

"That depends," Paul said. "Let's assume I cooperate and help you find him. What happens then?"

"Well, if you're right about this man Lish and he was killed in America, we could put Karl Alexander on trial for murder."

"Or you could put a bullet through his head."

"Ah," Hugh said. "*You* feel a connection too. You think we're going to kill your brother—"

Paul looked straight ahead. "Are you?"

Before he answered, Hugh glanced back to make sure that Maurice was still in the rear of the plane, then in a more confidential tone said, "I won't tell you that we would never consider killing Karl Alexander, but that's not my job. My job is to identify him and locate him. After that I've got an option to try and grab him. I don't have the authority to execute him." He didn't add that killing was something he had little stomach for. As distinct, for example, from Maurice . . . "But I want to catch him and I want you to help me do it."

"And if you can't catch him?"

"Then Maurice takes over," Hugh said quietly.

Paul had expected something like this. He glanced toward the rear of the aircraft, where Maurice stood with his back against an emergency exit, the cigarette next to his face, eyes trained on a flight attendant preparing a food-service cart. Paul too easily could imagine Maurice being capable of guiltless murder. All in the line of duty. Now he understood why these two CIA men had been paired. By himself Maurice was too cold and off-putting to win trust or elicit information from anyone. But he'd have no problem getting a gun to a man's head and pulling the trigger.

Hugh said that he'd picked the No Smoking section because he knew Maurice couldn't last without a cigarette and they'd have a chance to talk privately. "I want to bring Karl, your brother, in alive. So does Doctor Helms. If you're willing to help us—"

"You talked to her? To Annie?"

"Last night. She's pretty excited. Wanted to get you under hypnosis as soon as we landed but I told her to leave you alone until tomorrow. Anyway, if you'll cooperate I'm hoping the three of us can bypass the fourth of us and save your brother's life . . ."

Paul looked at him. "Why you? I know that Annie's got her sights set on being another Madame Curie, but why should you be so interested in bringing him in alive?"

Hugh hesitated, then: "Okay, I'll go all the way with you. This is my last field assignment. I'd like to see it through to the end. Besides, I'll admit this whole mental telepathy thing intrigues the hell out of me and I want to see you do those tricks—you know, guess how many bananas your brother's holding behind his back.''

Paul made a wry face.

"I'm serious, though," Hugh said. "Your brother's a slippery fish, but one hell of a catch. I'd like to take him alive. What do you say?"

Paul's instincts about people had usually been good, and his antennae were telling him to trust Hugh Roark. But even if he were wrong, did he really have any good alternatives? All his non-cooperation would get him would be one more very hostile CIA agent . . . So he proceeded to tell Roark what he knew of Karl's background, his upbringing under Tante Inge and his resentment that Paul had escaped to America.

"He was very curious about my life," Paul said. "He kept staring at me and asking questions. At one point I had this weird feeling that he was looking at me to see who he was supposed to be. It may sound crazy but I think he thinks I stole his life. He kept talking about what would have happened if our positions had been reversed. I think because I was the one who had to go to the hospital he blames me for what happened."

"That's like blaming the stove for burning the stew."

Maurice's return interrupted them, and Paul turned his attention to the New York *Times*. In a box on the bottom of page one was a story about the heart attack the President's father had suffered on Friday. The President was returning this evening from visiting him. It was the first that Paul had heard of it, and reading the account made him realize how out of touch he had become in just a few weeks.

The words began to blur and he found himself getting sleepy. The tension of the past few days caught up with him and the rush of air past the fuselage dulled his senses. Ignoring the two CIA men now, he tucked a pillow against the window and dozed . . .

He dreamed about Joanna. She was locked in a room and he had the key, but no matter how hard he tried, the door wouldn't open. He became frantic, convinced she was in serious danger. In the odd logic of dreams he knew that he had the right key. Still, the door wouldn't open. Finally he realized he was pulling on a door that opened inward. Pushing forward now, the entire door fell away, hinges and all, but instead of Joanna there was only empty space. Instead of a room, there was sky and clouds and he was staring up at a huge jet airplane plummeting toward him, out of control, one wing tilted toward the ground, its fuselage on fire—

He woke with a start. In the dim light it took him a moment to realize where he was. The cabin was bathed in eerie shadow. The in-flight movie was in progress and most of the windows had been curtained. Roark turned toward him, sliding the earphones to his neck as he did.

"You all right?"

Paul nodded absently, reached up and pushed the call button.

"You had another dream?"

"Not the same kind, not a death-dream."

He explained briefly, while Maurice dozed, and as he did the dream lost some of its frightening impact. It was a more normal dream, the kind where current situations and worries get jumbled around in a surreal blend of fact and fancy. He'd been thinking about Joanna and he was in an airplane . . . the two elements had combined in a normal dream, one of his own dreams, not a reflection of something happening with Karl.

Hugh agreed. "A lot of things can cause dreams. Stress, worry, tension. My wife dreams whenever I'm away and it's no wonder. Half the time I can't tell her where I am, what I'm doing or when I'll be back."

The flight attendant appeared, and Paul asked if the aircraft had an in-flight phone. It did, but they were beyond the range of its use. Paul glanced at his watch. Almost lunchtime in Washington.

Beside him, Hugh had opened his wallet and removed a business card that he held out so Paul could see it. "Ever been to this place?"

The card showed a photograph of an imposing stone structure over looking a lake. Tennis courts and part of a golf course were visible, and the impression was one of a medieval castle surrounded by a country club. The caption at the bottom read: "Marquand Manor House." It was like calling the Taj Mahal a cozy cottage, Paul thought.

"It's on Lake Champlain," Hugh told him. "A gorgeous view, especially rooms that end in '14'—214, 314, 414 and on up. My wife and I go there every year and spend three days together. The manager, Dave Pellston, is a friend of ours. That's his name on the back."

Hugh flicked the card over so that Paul could read the name. Paul nodded politely and settled back in his seat. The dream had left its residual feeling of dread that he couldn't entirely shake. Gradually his attention shifted back to what Hugh was saying . . .

"No one's ever done a study of Company divorce rates," Hugh went on. "But I suspect it's way above average, at least for case officers. That's why Helen and I started doing yearly honeymoons. A chance to renew the marriage and all that. We even had a rule up there, we'd only tell the truth to each other."

The headphones were still draped over his neck and Paul could hear the movie soundtrack, thin and reedy, like midgets talking.

"We have our routines. Breakfast in bed, room service, eggs Benedict with champagne to start the day. Nice tradition. You might want to try it, maybe. You and your wife . . ."

Paul gave him a sharp look, remembering how Hugh had been a party to his conversation with Joanna.

"Just a suggestion," Hugh said quietly.

For the first time Paul was becoming aware of Hugh as a human being rather than a CIA agent. He noticed the tiny broken blood vessels clustered at each nostril, saw the shift in skin texture that marked Hugh's vanished hairline, and recognized the deep cynicism reflected in his pale brown eyes.

Paul took the business card and slipped it into his pocket.

"How the hell," he said, "did a man like you get involved with the CIA?"

"It was the best job in the world at one time."

"Yeah, during World War II."

"And after."

"And then?"

Hugh looked at him to check if he were really interested, then proceeded to tell him. They were three hours from Washington. The time passed quickly.

Trussed up as she was in the trunk, Joanna tried to control her fear and make sense out of what was happening. The gag bit the corners of her mouth and she was stiff from lying with her knees drawn up to her chest and her cheek pressed against the lumpy blanket. The warm air was thick and stale. Her immobility, the darkness and claustrophobia were worse than having a gun pointed at her. Afraid that she might suffocate if she struggled, she lay still, and tried hard to think . . .

Why had he done this? She searched her memory for everything that Paul had told her about his brother. He had said that Karl was a killer for a foreign government. But didn't that mean he killed only on assignment? He had no reason to hurt her. But she remembered the look in his eyes when he had threatened to kill Danny and the way he had handled her as soon as the loud noise of the lawnmower drowned out any other sounds.

She saw again the way that he'd gone unhesitatingly to her underwear drawer. He knew which one it was. The implications were obvious—he'd been in the bedroom before. Was it today or had he been there earlier? He had Paul's keys so he could have come anytime, even while she was there, maybe while she was sleeping. The image of Karl entering at night and standing in the room while she slept made her sick. She thought back over the past few weeks, trying to remember if any of her panties or bras were missing. Nothing special came to mind.

She knew when they got to the freeway because the car picked up speed and they were no longer stopping for traffic lights. Immediately she had tried to keep track of how long they traveled in each direction and which way they turned, but it soon became confusing. Now, as they left the city, Joanna became aware of a lump in the floor of the trunk pressing against her hip. She tried to shift her weight but every time she moved, her bonds pulled tighter.

Suddenly, without warning, the Audi braked and lurched to the left. Joanna was thrown forward against the metal cross-braces of the rear of the back seat. The squeal of an approaching vehicle's brakes built and an air horn sounded directly behind them, so close that the trunk resonated with the sound. Joanna braced herself for the rear-end collision that she knew was coming. Instead, the car swerved back to the right and accelerated again, leaving behind the sound of the angry truck horn.

Her heart pounded, her forehead hurt where it had struck the forward wall. Two weeks ago she had wanted to end her life but found the will to carry on. Now, it seemed, she was going to die in a stupid traffic accident, crushed in the trunk of her own car. Either that or Karl would kill her and dump her body on the side of the road or in some empty field.

Her head still pressed against the rear seats; she shifted position, and as she did something pinched the little finger of her left hand. A moment later her fingers identified the object as a bottle cap, left over from some picnic or a vacation that she and Paul had taken together during some distant, safer time. She clutched it like the hand of an old friend.

They turned off the main road, and the further they went, the more certain she became that he was going to kill her. The muffled wail of a passing train hinted that they were near an Amtrak route but Joanna was too upset to speculate on their location. If only she had a knife or a piece of glass or a—

The bottle cap. She could feel the sharp edges between her fingers. It might be enough to cut through the pantyhose if she could just manage to get it in the right position. She twisted it in her fingers and began pushing at the bonds. She had only limited movement of the fingers of her right hand and couldn't tell if the cap was doing any good.

Then the car slowed and stopped and Karl got out. Joanna struggled to slip the bottle cap into her back pocket before he opened the trunk. The cap was like a charm now. As long as she had it with her she would be safe. She was still trying to reach her pocket when Karl returned to the car, drove forward and stopped again.

She heard him get out once more just as she managed to slip the cap into her pocket. Outside the car she heard a dull metal clang. A moment later, they were driving again, this time slowly. Moments later, the car stopped for the last time and Karl turned off the engine. She would know now if he meant to kill her.

The sound of the key sliding into the lock was magnified by the confined space. She tensed. The trunk opened and she squinted against the light. Karl stood above her, a knife in one hand. She drew a sharp breath and stiffened as he leaned toward her.

"Don't be afraid," he said, "I intend to untie you."

His voice sounded friendly. The knife slid behind her neck and she flinched. There was a sharp tug and the gag came free. Thrusting her tongue forward, Joanna pushed the stocking, wet with saliva, from her mouth. Her lips were raw and her jaw was stiff; she worked her mouth a moment. One by one Karl cut the remaining bonds and then helped her out of the trunk.

"I'm sorry you had to travel that way," he said. "But there was no time to explain and I could not take a chance on your making an upset."

He sounded so pleasant, so much like Paul talking . . .

They stood before a large, isolated farmhouse that sat on the crest of a shallow hill surrounded by forest. To one side was a stable and beyond it a corral overgrown with weeds. No other homes were visible and no sound of human habitation interrupted the cicada's intem-

perate buzz or the mockingbird's occasional call. She took a deep
breath. The warm air was cool against her damp skin. It was country
air, familiar from her childhood, and it struck her with a sweetness
and richness that made her dizzy. She allowed a sense of new hope.
Maybe Karl meant no harm after all—

And then she saw the gun. Karl had drawn it from his jacket
pocket and stepped back.

"Wait . . ." Joanna gasped.

He smiled, an engaging smile, just like Paul's.

"Don't worry." The barrel of the gun swept upward until it
pointed at the sky. Karl pulled the trigger, and a sharp *crack* echoed
into the hills.

Still speaking pleasantly he said, "Now you know that we are
alone and I know that the gun works. No one will help you if you try
to run away."

He slipped the gun back into the jacket and motioned toward the
house with a nod of his head, another familiar Paul gesture.

"Please," he said. "You should be my guest rather than my prisoner."

Inside, he led her to the kitchen, a cheery room decorated in a
country style with yellow-trim bay windows and blue-checked curtains. The blue-checked pattern was duplicated in the tablecloth.
There was a deep double sink, a laminated wood counter and a cast-
iron stove with a row of copper-bottomed pans hanging suspended
above it.

"Would you like something to drink? I have root beer, ginger
ale."

"Water is fine."

"Perhaps wine?"

"Just water."

He got two glasses from the cupboard and filled them at the sink,
turning his back to her. She stole a glance at the back door, wondering if it was locked, trying to estimate if she could possibly outrun
him in a dash to the wooded area at the bottom of the hill.

"Please don't try to run," Karl said without turning.

She stared at him in amazement. He brought the water to the table,
smiling at her confusion.

"Your reflection is very clear in the kettle," he said, indicating
the shiny chrome kettle beside the sink.

Again it was like seeing a part of Paul's personality, imperfectly, as if refracted through flawed glass. Paul, too, was incredibly alert and aware of the world around him, but whereas Paul showed his interest openly, Karl kept his awareness hidden, like the gun concealed in his jacket pocket.

Karl was watching her with interest. "I really did not mean for you to see me this morning. If I had known you were not going to work I would never have come."

"Why did you come?"

"To the house?"

Joanna nodded. The question had brought an imperceptible change in Karl's expression, a slight hardening of the pleasant smile that she recognized as one of Paul's defenses against a question he was uncomfortable answering.

"I suppose," he said slowly, "that it was a matter of curiosity. I was curious to know how my life would have turned out if Paul had been the stronger one of us and I the weaker."

"The stronger? What do you mean?"

"Didn't he tell you?"

Joanna shook her head. "There wasn't time."

"Then you haven't seen him."

"No, I—"

He was watching her intently, waiting for an answer. When she stopped in mid-sentence he smiled.

"You talked to him on the telephone," Karl concluded. "Which means he is still in Berlin."

His evident self-satisfaction made her angry. "He's in jail," she said, "because of *you*."

"In jail?"

"For running down a policeman."

"Of course," he said. "They would blame him . . ."

"For something *you* did."

"Poetic justice, I believe you might call it. Paul lied to me. He told me that he had come to Berlin alone. He said that the Central Intelligence Agency did not know of my existence, but when I went to the hotel, there were CIA agents, who tried to capture me."

"You've got an answer for everything, just like him."

Karl's eyebrows went up in surprise. Then he smiled, genuinely this time. "You think we are similar? Beyond the physical appearances? Let me ask you: Would you have known it was me on the stairs if you had not talked to Paul first?"

"Of course."

"How? How would you have known?"

He leaned forward, watching her eagerly.

"Paul isn't ugly," she said.

"Ugly? What do you mean?"

"He would never have done something like you did to me, on the bed and putting me in the trunk."

Karl shrugged that off. "But on the stairs, or sitting down like this, across the table from one another, would you have known?"

She regarded him closely. Who *was* this man and what was he after?

"Maybe not for the first few minutes," she said slowly. "But after a while . . ."

"Then what?"

"Paul can be gentle," she said.

He stared at her with an expression that seemed to Joanna a mixture of astonishment and bitterness.

"The world is not a gentle place," he said stiffly. "If you knew that you wouldn't be here, Paul wouldn't be where he is. Gentleness? You find it only when protected by strength and courage. You are lucky, people like you who live under the protection of others, but when that protection is taken away, then you learn."

He stopped abruptly, stood up. "I had no breakfast," he announced. "There is ham and cheese and hard-boiled eggs. Would you like some?"

"No thank you," Joanna said.

She was still thinking about his outburst. One thing was certain: he was eager for her reaction to him and how she thought he compared to Paul.

Joanna said, "Why did you bring me here?"

"So you wouldn't tell the authorities. My presence in Washington is a secret."

"Why?"

"If I told you, your life would be in danger."

"From you?"

"Perhaps."

He began slicing the cheese. She decided to challenge him.

"Paul said you were an assassin for a foreign government. Is that true?"

He paused, turned and his gray eyes regarded her silently.

"Occasionally—rarely—killing is one of my duties."

"Like now—?"

"No," he said with an amused smile, "that's why I brought you here."

But she recognized the smile from Paul's face. It covered a lie. And now she was convinced that unless she got away from this place she would die here.

Surprisingly, the knowledge had a cold, calming effect. She was no longer as frightened as she'd been lying in the trunk of the car. He had revealed something of himself—not enough yet, nothing she knew how to use, but he was no longer as unknown an entity as before. And she felt she had one advantage: she could read his expression better than he could read hers. Living with Paul had schooled her in the subtle art of discerning the truth behind the protective half-truths and reflex deceits that grew like ivy over the invisible walls of their marriage. I know you better than you know me, she thought as she watched Karl, now cutting cheese at the counter. She also knew which of her own responses were effective in dealing with Paul and which were not. She wondered if Karl had any of the same vulnerabilities. If he did . . .

She got up and came toward him. "Here, let me help with that."

He turned, knife in hand, and stared at her. Slowly a smile worked its way across his features. He held the knife toward her. "Would you like to cut the ham?"

Joanna hesitated, then realizing that he expected her to take it, she shook her head.

"I'll tell you what," she said casually. "Why don't I make some coffee? Have you got some?"

"In there." He pointed to a cupboard.

Joanna felt his eyes on her as she crossed the room. All right, she thought. Now it begins. Cat and mouse. Mouse and cat. Her survival would depend on which was which.

CHAPTER

26

THE CIA HAD SENT A CAR TO MEET THEM AT DULLES
International. The driver handed Hugh a briefcase with an inset combination lock.

"Audrey says this is up to the minute," he said. "You don't have
to come in until tomorrow."

"That's damn nice of him," Maurice said. "He must have been
promoted since we were gone."

Hugh offered Paul a ride, then waited until they were inside the
car before opening the briefcase, which contained computerized cargo
manifests from the Bayonne terminal. The three, including Paul now,
studied the information, passing the sheets back and forth. Most of
the cargo that had been shipped during the previous ten days was
household goods for officers going overseas. There was also a consignment of web belts and leggings and a variety of food stores going
to the navy: gallon cans of spaghetti, five-pound cartons of cereal,
tins of powdered eggs . . .

"Look at this stuff," Maurice said in disgust. "Powdered milk,
powdered eggs, ice cream powder . . ."

"What about this?" Paul said, pointing to two cargos listed as "Contents Classified."

"What about it?"

"Can we find out what they are?"

"We?" said Maurice.

"You find out, somebody find out."

Hugh nodded. "We'll put in a request on Monday."

"Why not today?"

"It's not priority and this is Sunday," Hugh reminded him. "Any extra manpower is likely working security for the Mutual Defense summit."

Mention of the summit reminded Paul of how long he had been away. The drugs had confused his sense of time, made him feel now like Rip Van Winkle. The summit, still weeks away when he left for Berlin, would begin tomorrow. He hadn't even known that the President's father was in the hospital until he picked up the newspaper on the plane.

As they approached Highway 124 Paul was about to tell the driver to turn right when Maurice leaned forward and gave him directions to Paul's house.

Paul smiled grimly. "I see you know all the best ways to get to my house."

"We know where you live," Maurice said.

"And no doubt how much I've got in the bank."

"Officially, no."

Paul had to restrain himself from making some reference to Maurice's less than savory activities. After what Hugh had told him it was hard to be civil to the man but he didn't want to betray Hugh's confiding in him.

When they arrived at the house the garage door was open and Joanna's red Alfa was sitting at the curb. Paul's first thought was that the Alfa's starter was acting up again. Then he remembered that Jo was moving and probably needed the bigger car to transport her things.

Before Paul got out of the car, Hugh gave him his home phone number. "In case anything comes up," he said.

Considering what Hugh had confided about himself, Paul suspected the man was talking as much about coming to terms with Joanna as he was about finding Karl.

The lawn had been newly mowed, he noticed, as he walked up to the house. It was Sunday; Danny McVey had been here. The familiar neighborhood routines were still being observed. There were times when a neighbor's preoccupation with a manicured lawn or waxed BMW irritated him, but today he found it comforting. It was good to be home.

He reached behind the porch light for the spare key. It wasn't there. He checked the ground beneath the light. Had Jo forgotten to leave it? The anxiety he'd felt on the plane began to trickle back. Then he realized: that's why Jo had left the garage door open, so that she could go in through the kitchen. Maybe she hadn't been able to find the key.

He entered the house from the garage, half expecting to find a note on the kitchen table. Nothing. He called Joanna's name. No answer, but he hadn't expected one. The house was empty.

In the front hall the empty boxes brought home for the first time the reality of Joanna's leaving. He continued upstairs. There was a box in the hall, this one full, and another in the bedroom, empty but with one side crushed, as if someone had stepped on it. Then he saw the broken window and walked slowly toward it. From the shards of glass left in the frame he guessed that the window had been broken from the inside. What the hell . . . ?

Moving close to look into the yard below, glass crunched beneath his foot. He knelt down and found two chunks of glass next to the wall, but when he looked outside there was no debris in the yard. He turned from the window. The bedspread was mussed, and so was the Chinese rug. Lingerie dangled over the side of an open dresser drawer.

Moving quickly now, he checked the other rooms. The red light was flashing on the answering machine. There were two messages, one from a real estate agent who wanted to coordinate schedules so that Jo could pick up the key to the new apartment, the other from Denise asking Jo to call. Paul called the real estate woman first and confirmed what he already feared: Joanna had never kept her appointment. Then he called the gallery, where an irate Denise complained that Joanna had asked for the morning off and then hadn't shown up at all.

"I just hope it's an emergency," she said, "because I had to cancel my plans this afternoon."

"Yeah," Paul said, "maybe she's been in car wreck or something."

"I didn't mean *that* kind of emergency," Denise said archly.

He hung up and called Danny's house. His mother, Cassie McVey, answered. Paul asked to speak with Danny.

"Did he screw up the lawn?" Cassie wanted to know.

"The lawn's fine, Cass. I just want to ask Danny a couple of questions."

"No problem, but listen, I told him to bring you your change. I don't want him spending money he hasn't earned—not until he has a credit card, anyway, you know what I mean?"

"What change?"

"For the lawn. You gave him twenty, right? Well, he's not a Savings and Loan—that's what I told him. I said, if you're not paying interest you're not borrowing money."

"*I* gave him twenty? Is that what he said?"

"Well didn't you?"

"Cassie, just put him on, will you? There's some confusion over here. I'll straighten it out."

"If he's lying again—"

"Will you just get him?"

The pause on the other end of the line told him she was hurt by his abrupt tone.

"Please," he added in a conciliatory tone.

She answered with careful precision. "If you'll be patient for one moment."

Paul could hear her in the other room talking over the sound of a televised football game. A normal Sunday afternoon in the suburbs, only nothing was normal anymore. Not since he found out about Karl . . .

Danny came on the line. "I got your five dollars, Mr. Stafford. I was going to bring it over on the next commercial—"

"Danny, listen carefully. I've got a couple of questions for you. They may make no sense to you, it may seem like I should know the answers but I want you to answer anyway, okay?"

"Sure."

"You mowed the lawn this morning, didn't you?"

"Sure."

"How long ago?"

"How long?"

"What time did you mow the lawn?"

"I didn't have my watch on. I guess about ten-thirty."

"Who was here?"

"Come on, Mr. Stafford. You know."

"I was here, wasn't I?"

"Sure. You paid me and everything."

Paul's grip on the phone tightened. "Okay, now listen. Pretend like I've got amnesia, I can't remember a thing. Was Mrs. Stafford here?"

"Sure."

"The window in the bedroom is broken. Did you see what happened?"

"Well, it was like all of a sudden the glass came down right in front of me. If I'd have been a little closer it might have sliced my ear off. And Mrs. Stafford said she hit it with something. Not her hand, a box I think."

"She told you that?"

"Sure. I asked if she was cut and she said no."

"Listen, Danny, and this is important. Was anyone else here when the window broke?"

"Besides you and Mrs. Stafford, I didn't see anybody . . . What's going on, Mr. Stafford?"

Paul hung up, then dialed the police. A switchboard operator passed him off to Detective Perlmutter, a man who asked questions with a thick southern accent.

"How old is your wife, sir?"

"She's twenty-nine."

"Any mental or physical impairments?"

"No."

"Why do you believe she's missing?"

"I told you, there's a broken window in the bedroom. There's also signs of a struggle. The bed is all mussed up, the side of a box is smashed and the rug's all bunched up."

"Any sign of physical injury?"

"Like what?"

"Bloodstains, hair or tissue, anything of that nature."

"No, *nothing of that nature*." Watch it, he told himself. You need him . . .

"All right, sir. We'll send an officer over to take your report."

As soon as he was off the phone he had second thoughts. Could he be sure Joanna was with Karl? What if she'd gone to find someone to replace the pane of glass? Or taken a box of clothes to her new apartment? Could she have gone with Karl of her own volition? No, he couldn't believe she would do that. Not after what he'd told her about Karl . . . There was no use pretending. Karl had kidnapped Joanna. But it made no sense unless . . . unless Karl had found out about his escape. He could have talked to Otto or read the story in the newspaper and decided to go after Joanna, take her hostage.

Again, why?

And more important, what did he intend to do with her?

He dialed Hugh Roark's home number and talked to his wife. Roark hadn't gotten home yet.

"Just tell him that Karl surfaced. Ask him to call me at home."

Needing to do *something*, Paul went over the house again, looking for any clues, hoping he wouldn't find any of Detective Perlmutter's kind of evidence. Vague unease had hardened into a ball in his stomach. The more he thought about it, the more he was sure Jo was in serious danger. If only he knew why Karl had come here, why in hell he'd gone to Bayonne and what he was doing in Washington.

He needed answers. Well, this was his town, his territory, and he was supposed to know how to get answers. Let the CIA work bureaucrat's hours, he would track down this George Lish and find out what was in the Bayonne shipments and he would do it now, today, not waiting until Monday.

He got out the *Herald* phone directory and looked up the home numbers of researchers. Kathy Craven was his first choice but she wasn't home. Next he tried Pam Markowitz, who was home and willing to work on Sunday for double-time.

"Good," Paul said. "Are the computers up?"

"They were when I left."

"Here's what I want you to do. Access National Phone Service Directory and find me every damned George Lish in America. Then call and find out which one's dead."

"Which one's what?"

"Dead. I got a tip that a man named George Lish was killed three days ago. I want you to find out the who what where when why. I want a quick and dirty bio."

"Are you serious?"

"Someone's life may depend on it. Can you get down to the office right away? I'll meet you there as soon as I can. If you find anything first call me at home."

When he hung up, Paul felt a little better . . . at least he was moving, and it made him feel more in control.

The next call was more difficult. Vic Daniloff was a friend from army days. They had flown together in Vietnam, and Vic had then gone career army and transferred to intelligence. Now he was a lieutenant colonel stationed at the Pentagon. Paul had used Vic for confirmation of primary-source information but had never sourced him directly. It was an article of faith between them that he would never trade on their friendship by asking Vic for primary information. Now there was no other way.

"Hello, captain," Vic greeted him cheerily. "What's all this I heard about you in a hit-and-run in Berlin?"

"Wasn't me."

"That's good to know. I tried calling but nobody was home—"

"Vic, listen, something real serious has come up and I need your help. If there was any other way I wouldn't come to you but Joanna's in the middle of it. I think she's in trouble."

"What happened?"

"Someone's holding her as a hostage—I'm sure of it but I can't prove it, not until I get more information. That's where you come in."

"Keep going."

"Two cargos were sent from the Military Ocean Terminal in Bayonne, their contents classified. I've got the lading numbers, shipment dates, all that. What I don't have is what's in them. That's what I need from you."

Vic said slowly, "You want me to access classified information."

"I wouldn't ask if there was any other way."

Vic was silent for a moment, and when he spoke there was an edge in his voice. "I knew you'd do it someday. Come to me for some story that—"

"It's not a story, Vic. It's *Joanna*. Her life's in danger, for Christ sake."

"How in danger?"

"You want the short version or the long version?"

It was an old routine: the short version was *trust me*, the long version was *please trust me*.

"Blind faith, huh?"

"It was enough at LZ Bird," Paul said, reminding Vic of the first time they'd flown together. Vic had just arrived and he'd been assigned area-familiarization as Paul's co-pilot. They'd gone into

Landing Zone Bird at night and Paul had taught Vic how to hold position by tucking in close enough to see the instrument lights on the ship ahead. It was dirty pool, Paul knew, reminding him of Vietnam. Vic knew it too.

"Don't give me that," he said.

"I saved your ass a couple of times."

"I saved yours, too."

"We were a good team, Vic."

"It's not a team, now, Paul. It's not just the two of us in a cockpit. I've got a career, I've got a wife. I've got Linda and the kids and a house with a mortgage. We're not yahoo flyboys now. Passing classified information isn't like faking a terrain familiarization on a beer run to Khe Sahn. Don't come at me with something like this."

"No choice, Vic."

There was a long silence and Paul let it sit there, big and empty enough to fill with memories of LZ Bird.

"Paul . . ." The voice was tight and controlled. "You make a career of bucking the system. I made a career supporting it. I can't live outside the system."

"I'm not asking you to."

"If it gets out—"

"I've never blown a source, Vic."

He sighed. "All *right*, I can't promise anything but I'll see what I can do."

"That's all I'm asking."

"You be at the office tomorrow?"

"Not tomorrow. Today."

"I have to go to the office for this. I don't have a secure line here . . ."

"I'm sorry."

"We almost went to Cape May this weekend," Vic said. "Never mind . . . what are the goddam cargo numbers?"

Paul gave them to him and Vic repeated them back, then said, "Are you at the *Herald*?"

"No, but I'll be there soon. Leave a message with the operator if I'm gone."

In the background Paul could hear the television: the football game.

"And Vic?" he added, "It needs to be ASAP."

"I *got* the message."

* * *

A few minutes after Paul hung up, the police arrived. There were two of them, one a stocky black man with drooping melancholy eyes, the other a white man with a jaw that thrust forward like the prow of a ship. The black man was in charge. Before he spoke, he glanced at a thick note pad he carried in one hand, checking Paul's name.

"Mr. Stafford? You phoned a missing-person report?"

"My wife. She was here this morning with a man who's been impersonating me. I can prove that. Now she's gone and there's evidence of a struggle."

The two officers exchanged a look and Paul knew it was going to be difficult.

The first officer said, "Where was the forced entry?"

"What forced entry?"

Again he consulted his notebook. "Broken window. Signs of forced entry."

"Upstairs," Paul said. "But I didn't say it was a forced entry."

"Are these your boxes, sir?"

"My wife's."

"Is she going somewhere?"

"She just got an apartment in D.C."

The officers said nothing but Paul could sense their growing skepticism. By the time he'd shown them the window and explained about Joanna, their notebooks were back in their pockets. The window looked like an accident, nothing was stolen, Joanna had keys to the Audi, Paul had admitted that they hadn't been getting along . . .

"That's not the point, damn it. The point is that someone was here in this house with her this morning and she would have never left with him of her own free will. I *know* that. I spoke with her last night and warned her about him."

"About who?"

"A man named Karl Alexander. My twin brother."

It sounded foolish so he added, "He's a murderer," which sounded even more foolish.

"A murderer," the black officer repeated somberly. "Well, sir, that sounds like a job for homicide."

His partner with the bony face clenched his teeth to keep from smiling.

It was useless, Paul realized. The more he said, the more far-fetched it sounded. Given time he could get witnesses. Given time, he could prove that Danny saw a man who was impersonating him at the same moment that he was on Flight 491 inbound from Germany. Given time he could prove he had a twin brother and maybe even prove that Karl was a suspected killer. But by then it would be next week and God knew where Karl would be or what might have happened to Joanna . . .

The officers began an explanation about freedom of movement for adult Virginia citizens with no history of senility or mental illness. Paul cut them short and ushered them out of the house. Out on the sidewalk some of the neighbors had gathered, curious about the police car. Paul assured them that nothing was wrong and chatted long enough to satisfy himself that none of them had seen Karl earlier or had seen the Audi leave. He went back inside and stood staring at the empty boxes in the hallway, all addressed to the local Safeway store. Danny had said that Jo had arrived with them just this morning. And then what? Karl surprised her? Forced his way inside?

No, of course not. He had my keys.

Anger surged through him. What the hell was Karl doing? He'd taken his wallet, his car, the keys to his house, and now the son of a bitch had taken his wife. He'd impersonated him in Bayonne and even carried off a conversation with Bernie. His brother was taking over his life, stealing his identity like some sort of leech, sucking his existence away bit by bit.

The more he thought about it, the angrier he got. Yes, in the beginning he'd tried to understand Karl, even tried to sympathize with him, with the horror of his childhood, the arbitrary, rotten bad luck he'd had. But no more. This was far more ominous than simply kidnapping him and keeping him prisoner. In some perverse way Karl was beginning to take over and live Paul's life. Including his wife.

He felt he had only a limited amount of time to find Karl and stop him. It was as if Karl was stealing elements of his life until some critical mass would be exceeded and Karl would actually *become* him.

"No you *don't* . . ."

Two could play this game. He had always been more sensitive to what Karl was doing than the other way around. Well, now he would use that sensitivity to stop him. He returned to the office and called Annie Helms. The business card she had given him had disappeared with his wallet, but her number, in Jo's handwriting, was on the list of phone messages. He sat down heavily, pulled out the bottom drawer and rested his foot on it as he listened to the phone ring.

Be home, be home . . .

A moment later a low voice answered. "Annie Helms."

"Hello, it's Paul Stafford. I need to—"

He stopped in mid-sentence, his attention caught by the sight of a check inside the drawer. Not just one check but a lot of them, *his* checks, made out and already signed.

"Paul," Annie said eagerly. "I'm glad you called. I talked to Hugh, he told me what happened. The link is your brother, right? A twin brother named Karl Alexander?"

Paul barely heard her. He leaned down, picked up the stack of checks and bills and put them on the desk The first one was made out to American Express in the amount of his two tickets, from Washington to Miami and Miami through Frankfurt to Berlin. The handwriting looked like his, the signature looked like his, but he had never seen the bill, never made out the check. The check bore today's date.

Annie was calling his name. "Paul? Are you okay?"

Paul stood up slowly, teeth clenched, feeling dizzy.

"God*damn* you," he gritted. "Goddamn you."

"What? What is it?"

"It's him. He even made out my checks. He's paying my bills—"

"Who? Karl?"

"Yes. He took my checkbook—I've got them right here—American Express, the gas, the electricity—he signed *my* name. He's trying to—"

An edge of renewed excitement was evident in Annie's voice "Karl signed *your* name to *your* cheeks?"

"God damn it, I want him. I want into his mind. How soon can you get here?"

"To your house?"

"Wait, you're in Silver Spring. Let's meet at the *Herald*. You're going to hypnotize me. How long will it take you to get downtown?"

There was an imperceptible pause, then she said, "Give me twenty minutes."

"I'm on my way."

"Wait," she said quickly. "What happened?"

"He's got Joanna. He's . . . he's trying to steal my life. Trying, hell. He's doing it. I'll see you down there."

"Bring the checks."

He hung up, and when he unlocked the file cabinet to get his gun, it didn't surprise him that the gun was gone. The son of a bitch had his wife, his wallet, his car, his clothes and now his gun

CHAPTER

27

IT WAS A CAT-AND-MOUSE GAME, AND BOTH OF THEM
knew it. Each wanted something from the other, but neither was altogether sure what the other knew.

Karl was certain that Joanna was trying to lull him into a false
sense of security, but each time he thought he could predict her
response she surprised him. He had even given her opportunities to
escape—apparent opportunities, anyway—turning his back, placing the
knife within her reach, leaving the room one time—but she made no
move. Mostly she acted almost friendly, engaging, which he suspected was a ruse, although it intrigued him. As did her answers to
his questions about Paul. The more he learned, the more he continued to feel drawn into his brother's life . . .

As for Joanna, she made a decision to try to act as natural as possible. The effort was exhausting, and the eerie physical similarity to
Paul was more disconcerting than she'd expected. As he leaned
toward her across the table, he seemed to go in and out of focus, the
edges blurring between him and Paul so that sometimes she all but
lost the sense of Karl as a stranger. There was always that physical

presence, the uncanny likeness to Paul. It was almost easier to believe that some alien intelligence had invaded and taken over Paul's body . . .

Karl's hunger to know all about Paul not surprisingly spilled over into a persistent curiosity about Joanna and he began questioning her about her life. He seemed particularly pleased to hear she was an only child.

"Did you feel special with the attention of two parents, or were you lonely without brothers and sisters?"

The question stumped her because she had only her own experience, there was nothing to compare it to. He was also intrigued by her knowing how to fly, wanted to know why she decided to become a pilot. That one was easier.

"My father had a plane," she told him. "When I was little I would sit on his lap and he let me handle the controls. Later I took lessons and got my pilot's license."

"Then you come from a wealthy family."

"Not wealthy. There was land they sold when I was six. Most of their money came from that."

"Do you think it helped draw you together, you and Paul, this interest in flying?"

"I don't think so." She felt herself getting edgy, nervous as he moved into personal areas.

"He said he wanted to fly with you to Ethiopia and you refused."

Joanna tried to conceal her surprise. One of her problems trying to carry off this exchange with Karl was that she had no idea what Paul had told him. More than once he had referred to things she assumed he had learned from Paul.

"Taking Paul would have meant less space for food," she said. Besides, the *Herald* was paying his way over.

"Still, I think Paul was attracted by a woman who could share his interest in flying."

"Did he say that?"

"He did not, but I know that I would be attracted by someone who shared my interests."

"What are your interests?"

He smiled. "That is what I am finding out."

He turned the conversation back to Paul and his life. He wanted to know how Paul got along with his parents, why he had decided to be a journalist, how long he had known Joanna before they decided to get married, where they had gone on their honeymoon, why she was moving away now. Like Paul, she thought, he seemed almost obsessive about details. Joanna forced herself to satisfy him, alternately piquing his interest and satisfying his curiosity as she played for time and looked for a real opportunity to escape. It was as if Karl was on the trail of something and she was leading him, but she had no idea where she was going or what, ultimately, he wanted or intended.

When they moved to the living room Karl offered her the couch but she sat in an overstuffed chair. Without the table between them, her bare legs made her self-conscious. She wished she wasn't wearing shorts. To mask her unease, she tried again to turn the conversation around.

"What about you? Are you married?"

"Of course. I have a wife and three children but with none of them have I ever had a conversation such as the one that you and I are having now."

Joanna hadn't thought of it as a conversation so much as an interview, and an extended one at that.

Karl pulled a rocking chair close and settled into it. "Tell me, what was the first thing you noticed about Paul? That first time you saw each other, where was it? The parking lot of the store with the odd name?"

"A Safeway store."

"Safeway, yes. When you saw him there, what first attracted you to him?"

She felt like Scheherazade, spinning stories to save her own life. She had better make them as interesting as she could.

"The contrast between his smile and his eyes. I liked his eyes, disliked his smile."

"Go on. Give me an example."

"Well, he was watching me argue with the store manager and his eyes seemed warm and curious but he had a smile with the downturned lip that seemed cynical. Eyes and smile tended to fight each other. I couldn't figure out which one was the real Paul . . . What about you? What was the first thing you noticed about your wife?"

"I liked her looks," he said flatly. "But with Paul, at what point did you decide that you were in love with him? How did you know?"

God, this was the same dogged pursuit of a subject that was so characteristic of Paul when he was interviewing someone. Ask ten questions, answer one, ask ten more . . .

"I think I fell in love the first time we talked," she said. "He asked what I was doing and when I told him he listened with such close attention that I felt like what I was telling him was the most important information in the world. He listened to me like he really cared what I thought. Not many men do that . . ."

"I care what you think."

"Why?" She tried to sound casual, not at all sure she wanted to hear his answer.

"Because if *I* had been the weaker one and Paul the stronger, then his life with you would have been mine."

She stared at him. So that was the reason for all his questions? To find out what some alternative life might have been like?

Karl misunderstood her expression. "He didn't tell you that part, did he? How my life was sacrificed for his? I am sure he avoided that part."

"What?"

His words were still echoing in her mind: *"His life with you would have been mine."*

"Did he tell you how he came by his charmed life?"

"What charmed life?"

"The famous journalist with awards and plaques all over the walls. Did he tell you why it happened to him and not to me?"

"He earned the awards," Joanna said, trying to hold back her irritation. "I wouldn't call it a charmed life."

"That depends on your point of view. Paul was not the strong one. He was sick. He would have died, but my mother took him to an American hospital and left me with an old woman who used me in ways which would disgust you. Paul's good life is built on my suffering. The strong carry the weak. I saved him twice: once when we were children and again only two weeks ago. I could have killed him two weeks ago but I saved him. Now I pay the price. Just as I did before."

She was stunned. With this outburst she realized how she'd misunderstood what he was after. She had tried to humanize, to make herself and the life she shared with Paul attractive. She'd given a picture of their relationship to win his sympathy. The strategy had backfired. To Karl, every cherished moment was more damning evidence of the life that Paul had stolen. In trying to build a case for Paul and herself, she'd built a case against them.

"Why do you look at me like that?" Karl demanded.

"What?"

"You look at me as if I am some sort of monster."

Think. Pretend to see things from his perspective. *Do* something . . . "I'm sorry, of course I know you're not a monster—"

"How do you know that?"

Now he was toying with her, and she was the mouse in the cat-and-mouse game. His tone was light, he smiled, but behind the words she sensed that the answer was important to him. She struggled to appease him.

"I don't believe anyone is inherently evil—"

"What do you believe?"

"I . . . believe in people—their basic goodness."

Wrong answer. Karl's lips formed a condescending smile. "You don't really believe that."

"Yes, yes, I do. Really."

"What about me? Do you believe in my basic goodness?"

"Yes, I do, but I think you try to defeat it—"

His smile hardened. Quickly she saw her mistake. Sympathize, don't criticize.

"I don't say I'm right . . ."

"No, no, do not back down. That is what Paul finds attractive in you, your strength, that you stand by your principles. I find it attractive, also. So go ahead. Analyze me. Tell me why you think I defeat my . . . basic goodness." No smile this time.

"I don't . . . know you well enough."

"Sure, you do. I'm Paul, only stronger."

Oh my God, she thought. He really believes that.

What to do? She couldn't continue this but she didn't dare stop. She had to have some relief from his terribly intense scrutiny. She needed to let her face reflect her true feelings, if only just for a moment.

"All right," she said, "I'll try . . . but first you've got to let me go to the bathroom."

For a moment she thought he might object, then he relaxed, leaned back in the rocker and waved toward the hallway. "Use the one on this floor, beneath the stairway."

She got to her feet, hoping he didn't notice how unsteady she was. But she felt his eyes on her as she crossed the room, and when she turned into the hallway she caught a glimpse of him looking at her legs. After years of living with Paul, Joanna recognized and understood that look . . .

As soon as the door was shut, the fear she'd hidden until now sickened her. The coffee burned her stomach. She gripped the wash basin until her fingers ached. Nausea came over her, and she had just enough presence of mind to turn on the water so that Karl wouldn't hear as she gave in to it.

She flushed the toilet, rinsed her mouth and forced herself to breathe deeply. No more, she had to get away. There was a narrow window in the bathroom. She pushed the curtains aside and inspected it. It was a new aluminum window, small, but if she opened both panes, large enough. One hundred feet away were the woods.

Her fingers had moved to the latch before she noticed Karl standing at the living room window, staring into the distance. The configuration of the house gave him a good view of the exterior bathroom wall. She pulled back, hoping he hadn't seen her, fighting down the panic that came from knowing she was trapped. Karl wasn't stupid. He knew about the window. He wasn't going to let her go anywhere.

She fought to stay calm. Instinct ordered her to act, to get away, to run into the woods until she could run no more. Or to the Audi. She remembered the spare key that Paul kept tucked under the radiator just in case he ever lost his keys in the field or on assignment. The key was in a metal container the size of a matchbox with two thin magnets on one side. Jo recalled that they had once used the spare key when Paul inadvertently locked his keys inside the car. That was two years ago. Now she imagined the key tucked away inside its magnetic container, waiting for her to retrieve it . . . If only she could break free long enough to find it . . . But to do that, somehow she would have to put Karl out of commission . . .

But how? She had never even hit anyone in her life. How much force did it take to knock a man unconscious? And would she be able to do it if she had the opportunity? Karl had said he meant to let her go. But his words said one thing, his tone, expression, body language said something else. He never meant for her to leave here alive . . .

She had been in the bathroom long enough. Don't arouse his suspicions now, not after working so hard to offset them, refusing opportunities to run away, acting warm and friendly. And he had responded, whether he knew it or not. There was no mistaking the desire in the look he'd given her as she left him.

His life with you would have been mine.

No wonder Karl was attracted to her . . . all day long he'd been living *Paul's* life. What if she offered him a chance to live Paul's life for real? What if she . . . if she went to bed with him?

The thought made her cringe. She could never do it.

But would she have to? What if she made him think she was willing, then surprise him . . . Maybe a few preliminaries. Could she do that? She would have to. And she would have to choose the right place, somewhere with something hard that she could use as a weapon.

If she failed it would be worse than ever. If she hurt him but didn't get away . . . But she couldn't wait any longer. She had to try.

She checked herself in the mirror, took a deep breath, opened the door and stepped into the hallway. Because he was still at the window, Karl wasn't immediately visible.

"Karl?" She used his name for the first time. "Can I take you up on that glass of wine?"

As he came toward her, he looked surprised, and pleased.

Good, Joanna thought. Be surprised.

"I'll join you," he said.

She followed him to the kitchen, dipping one shoulder in a way that she knew Paul always found attractive. Now all she needed was a weapon.

CHAPTER
28

ON HIS WAY TO THE *HERALD* PAUL WAS FORCED TO detour around Seventeenth Street, which was barricaded and guarded by district police in preparation for the Soviet leader's arrival the next morning. The Russian embassy, a five-story brownstone, sat in the middle of the block, its wrought-iron gate temporarily removed to accommodate the armored Soviet limousine that would meet the General Secretary at Andrews Air Force Base. On the roof a security man stood watching the street below.

Normally Paul enjoyed the sense of excitement that permeated Washington during the visits of a foreign leader, but today, intent on his private business, the detour annoyed him. When a confused motorist stopped in the middle of the intersection to ask directions of a policeman, he honked his horn angrily. The policeman gave him a sour look. When he arrived at the *Herald*, Annie Helms hadn't showed up yet. Paul told the receptionist that he would be in research and went to see if Pam had discovered anything. He found her seated at the computer terminal, the remains of a Big Mac lying in its plastic container between her keyboard and the telephone. She sat with one leg tucked under her and, as if to proclaim that this was her day off, wore bluejeans and a checked cotton shirt with rolled-up sleeves. Her eyes brightened when she saw Paul.

"It's a good thing you didn't ask for *Jones*," she said. "I'd be here until Christmas."

"What about Lish?"

She showed him a list of names.

"Eighty-seven Lishes in the United States, almost a third of them up in the Seattle area. They must have come on the same boat— salmon fishermen or airplane designers."

"How many *Georges*?"

"Five Georges, two accounted for by phone—Savannah and Detroit." She lowered her voice suggestively. "Savannah George sounds very nice. I think I'll call him back and see if he ever comes up to Washington."

"What about dead George?"

"Three possibilities: Seattle George, whose roommate says he *thinks* George is on a hunting trip but they work different shifts and he hasn't seen him for a while. That's one. Then there's Nashville George, where nobody answers. Finally we've got Houston George, who left on a business trip and never came back. He runs a boarding kennel and his dogs were starving."

"Sounds good."

"Not for the animals. Dogs and cats mostly and one poor parrot. The SPCA people were there when I called. When Houston George didn't come back there was nobody to feed the animals so somebody called the SPCA."

"Where'd he go? What kind of business trip?"

"They didn't know. They were just there to figure out what to do with God's little dears—that's what this lady called them, '*God's little dears*.' "

"What about the police? Have any bodies been found?"

"Who knows? I haven't had time to call."

Paul reached for the phone. "What's Houston's area code?"

"Seven one three."

Pam stood up and stretched while Paul made the call. The police had no reports of George Lish, dead or missing. As soon as he hung up, the phone rang. It was the receptionist with news that Annie Helms had arrived. Before he left he gave Pam new instructions.

"Check with the police in Nashville and Seattle. If none of those

Lishes are missing or dead, get me background on Houston George. I want to know marital state, employer, if he's connected with government agencies or defense contractors, if they're in debt—you know the routine."

"Oh, sure," Pam said. "I'll just give them your name, they'll tell me everything I want to know."

"Pretend you're a prospective employer, pretend you're TRW, pretend you're Publisher's Clearinghouse and you want to give Lish a million dollars, whatever you want. Use your imagination."

On his way upstairs Paul met Dicky Lazarus, the photographer who had been in his office the day the CIA men first showed up. Dicky, wearing two Nikons, did a double-take when he saw Paul.

"Hey," he said. "What are you doing here?"

"I work in the building, remember?"

"This morning somebody said you were in jail in Berlin."

"Must have been my twin brother," Paul said. "Where are you going?"

Dicky wrinkled his nose in disgust. "The President is landing at Andrews. The usual grip-and-grin stuff. Hey, what about the cop? You really run him over?"

They reached the entrance to the building where Annie Helms was waiting.

"Tell you tomorrow," Paul said.

Annie greeted him with a firm handshake and a thousand questions. Ever since Hugh Roark called her from Berlin and told her about Karl Alexander, she'd been berating herself for not coming on her own to the truth. Twins. It seemed so obvious. In college she had done a research project on the twin studies carried out at the University of Minnesota. She remembered the remarkable incidence of shared personality traits and the symbiotic emotional responses that characterized twin groups, and she was irritated that she hadn't immediately investigated the possibility with Paul.

As he escorted her upstairs now, Paul told her what he had found at the house and filled her in on the details of his miserable time in Berlin. The experience had left him the worse for wear, Annie decided. He was pale and drawn, his hair messy, clothes wrinkled and he needed a shave. Tension and worry were evident in the set of his mouth and the narrowed eyes, and his voice was flat with controlled anger when he told her about Joanna's kidnapping.

"He's still impersonating me," Paul finished grimly, "and he's got Joanna."

"But you don't know that for sure."

"I know it. I can't prove it but I *know* it, just like I know a man named George Lish is dead but I can't prove that, either."

"What reason would he have to kidnap her?"

The buzz and staccato chatter of printers swelled as they entered the city room. Annie was surprised at the number of people who were working on a Sunday. A young man called to Paul as they passed. He nodded acknowledgment but continued talking to Annie.

"I don't know, that's why I want you to hypnotize me. I need some kind of clue—where he is, what he's up to, something. We know he's in the area so it should be easier this time."

"Not necessarily," she said. "Mental energy hasn't been scientifically quantified, but the available evidence indicates that physical proximity isn't as critical as the intensity of the emoting experience and the harmony of the receptor."

"Emoting?"

"Forget the jargon. Emotional, will do."

"Whatever, all I know is that I want a look into his mind. I want Joanna."

They reached Paul's office, which was smaller than Annie expected, just enough room for two chairs, a desk and file cabinet. On one wall was a large bulletin board with announcements pinned to it. There was a wire-mesh basket on the desk with pink message slips. Beside it a photograph taken on a merry-go-round showing Paul and a young woman standing beside a child who sat astride a carved unicorn.

"No couch," Paul said, "but the floor's okay."

Annie glanced down. It wasn't ideal but the environment was familiar to Paul and that might help him to relax.

Paul said, "Loosen my belt and all that crap?"

"Whatever makes you comfortable."

Paul kicked off his shoes and lay down.

"I don't guarantee this will work," Annie cautioned him.

"Why not? It worked before."

"Not exactly. We were doing something different. We were searching your memory, and the incidents we discovered all fit the same pattern—your brother was in a state of high emotional excitement and you were asleep."

"Let's just do it, okay?"

Annie looked around the room. "We need something you can concentrate on."

"I'll concentrate on Karl."

But she meant something concrete to focus his attention. There was a Luxor lamp attached to the desk. She swiveled it and extended the arm so that the head was positioned above Paul. Then she seated herself on the floor beside him.

"All right, Paul. I want you to relax. Let your mind clear of thoughts, of worries and fears. Concentrate your attention on the light bulb, listen only to my voice, and relax, relax . . ."

She led him through the relaxation procedure, calling attention to each part of his body, working her way from the extremities inward, through his torso to his face.

"Your eyes are becoming heavy now," she said in a low lilting monotone. "You are growing sleepy, your eyes are so heavy you can't keep them open . . ."

Paul closed his eyes, but it wasn't working. He wasn't becoming drowsy. His mind was racing just as it did when he was working against a deadline. It was like a searchlight, picking facts out of the darkness. He couldn't dim the light or diffuse the focus and facts kept reappearing as clues in different combinations.

"Your arms are growing heavy, the weight is spreading from your shoulders down to your fingertips, a weight like lead, so heavy now that you cannot move your arms. Your right arm is thick and heavy and you cannot move it no matter how hard you try. You can't lift your arm because it is so heavy. Your arm, your whole body is like lead. No matter how hard you try you can't raise your arm. You can try it now, Paul. Try to raise your arm and feel how heavy it is, feel how immobile your arm has become . . ."

Paul lifted his arm and opened his eyes. "It's not working."

"You're fighting the suggestion."

"I'm *trying*."

Annie shook her head. "I can see it in your body. When your hand relaxes there's a frown on your face; when your face relaxes your shoulders are tense; when your shoulders relax your hands are tense. You're not letting it happen. You're thinking too much."

Paul sat up. "I can't help it. I keep trying to put the pieces together. George Lish, the Bayonne terminal, Joanna—they're all connected somehow."

"Stop thinking. Empty your mind."

"I'm trying."

"No you're not, you're not concentrating."

"All right, do it again."

Paul lay down and closed his eyes. This time Annie thought she did manage to induce a light trance. She told Paul to imagine he was watching a signal coming from Karl, a beam of light emanating from Karl's eyes, like a slide projector beaming an image onto a screen inside his mind.

"The image that you see is what Karl sees. You're looking through his eyes now, you're looking through Karl's eyes and you see what he sees. On your own mental screen you can see what Karl sees. Tell me what it is, Paul. Tell me what you see on your mental screen."

Annie could see the movement of his eyes beneath the closed eyelids.

"Let your mind remain blank, a blank screen, and let the image from your brother's eyes play on that screen. Whatever Karl is looking at, right now, that's what you're seeing. Light and shadow, form and color, it's all becoming clear. Karl's world is becoming clear before you. You see what he sees, the two of you are one, the two of you see the same things now. Tell me what's on the screen, Paul. What image do you see?"

He frowned.

"Don't force the image," she said. "Just relax now. Relax and let it appear naturally . . ."

Paul could feel himself fighting her suggestion. There were times when Annie's voice soothed him into something resembling a trance, but all the time he was aware of his mind resisting. He didn't want to relax, he didn't want to give up control. He wanted inside his brother's mind and yet he didn't.

It was no good. He opened his eyes. Annie's face, just a few feet away, was backlit by the curtained windows facing the city room.

"It's not working," he said, and stood up.

Annie was still sitting on the floor, watching him. "We could use drugs—"

"No, no drugs."

"You want to find her, don't you?"

"Not dead."

The words slipped out and surprised them both. A look of new comprehension came to Annie's eyes. She got to her feet. "That's it.

That's why you won't go into a trance. You're afraid you'll experience her death. That's why you can't relax.''

As soon as she said it Paul knew she was right.

"That's it, isn't it?" Annie persisted.

Paul nodded. "It's like I've got control over her life. I feel like if I go to sleep or into a trance he'll kill her. As if my conscious will is some sort of a shield. It's crazy but that's how it feels."

"Maybe not so crazy."

Paul gave her a sharp look. Annie's eyes were alive with excitement. "Maybe you *are* keeping her alive," she said. "Maybe your desire for your wife's safety—the importance she has for you as a human being—maybe those feelings are apparent to Karl. Not consciously, but manifested as a feeling.''

"Then I *shouldn't* go into a trance."

"It's all speculation," she said in a voice of wonder. "But what if it's true? What if you are keeping her alive?"

Paul was frustrated. To save Joanna he had to find Karl, to find Karl he had to establish a mental link with his brother, but to do that required hypnosis that could endanger Joanna. It was a full circle with no solution.

He picked up the phone and dailed 4478. There was only one way left, the hard way, the plodding step-by-step way, the accumulation of facts until a pattern began to form.

"Research. It's me."

"Pam, what have you got?"

"Not much on Nashville and Seattle Lishes but Houston Lish sounds like a real nut case."

"What do you mean?"

"Come on down, I'll show you."

"Over the phone, Pam. What have you got?"

"Okay, okay. Mr. Houston Lish turns out to be a member of the Rank—you know, the looney tunes who killed that radio guy in Texas?"

"They sent a bomb through the mail, right?"

"And anonymous death threats to the judge who sentenced them. If you're doing a story on these bozos you better start opening your mail with tongs."

"What about Lish?"

"He was one of the founders of the Rank back in the seventies. He wasn't charged in the bombing but at the trial he was forcibly removed from the courtroom twice for demonstrating."

Paul made notes. After hanging up he told Annie what Pam had come up with.

"He left Thursday morning," Paul concluded. "And I dreamed his death Thursday night. With the time difference, that would be Thursday afternoon in Houston."

"You think Karl killed him in Houston?"

"I don't know. Pam's trying to find out where Lish was going. But if he *was* killed in Houston, we've got Karl in three locations: two weeks ago in Bayonne, three days ago in Texas, and this morning at my house. New York, Houston and Washington. There's got to be a connection."

"Never mind the connection," Annie said. "Let's just concentrate on where he is now. We've got to find him and investigate the mental link that exists between you. That's what's important."

Paul's face clouded and Annie added quickly, "And to find your wife, Paul. I know that comes first."

Paul doubted that it did, at least not to Annie. Before he could respond, the phone rang. It was Vic. The first thing he wanted to know was if Joanna was still missing.

"The situation hasn't changed," Paul answered.

"Then I've got your information," Vic said. "But I don't like what I see."

"What?"

"DE 3186 SF is shipment, ten each, Communications/Data Link Jammer type AN slash MLQ dash T six."

"A data-link jammer? What's that?"

"Security system for radio transmissions. And your second shipment—"

"Wait a minute," Paul grabbed a pen and sheet of paper. "Give me the numbers again. Alpha Mike—"

"Alpha *November* slash Mike Lima Quebec dash Tango six."

"Okay. What's next?"

"QL 4416 HS is two hundred and fifty-six each Redeye tactical weapons, type XM41E2."

As soon as he heard the word *Redeye* the image of a doorway open to the clouds blossomed in his mind.

"Redeye," he repeated.

"X-ray Mike four one Echo two, you get that?"

Paul scribbled quickly. "Yeah, okay."

"Just remember, my ass is hanging in the wind on this one. Don't expose me to Charlie, huh?"

"I won't. Thanks, Vic."

As he put down the phone Annie was watching him closely. "What?"

"A Redeye missile," Paul said slowly. "And a dream I had. On the plane. It came back to me just now."

"What dream?"

Paul explained about the dream and how he remembered it when Vic mentioned the Redeye missile: the room with Joanna locked inside and the door that opened onto the sky with a jet—

He paused, his thoughts churning.

Annie said, "That sounds like a normal dream, not a link with Karl."

Paul wasn't listening. With the news of the Redeye shipment the facts had begun to shift, forming a dim pattern that was gradually emerging like a ship from the fog.

"Wait a minute, wait a minute," he said. He began pacing nervously. "Forget about Lish for a moment and focus on the Redeye. Maybe that's why he was at Bayonne, not for a victim but for a weapon. What if he went to Bayonne to steal a Redeye?"

"And just what is a Redeye?"

"A heat-seeking missile used to shoot down jets. But if that's why he's here, to shoot down a jet . . ."

Thoughts tumbled one after the other, each one modifying the one before, shifting the context, changing the import of his perceptions. *Had* Karl come to America to steal a Redeye and shoot down an aircraft? If so, why? Why not use a bomb? Why not sabotage an aircraft in a way that would look accidental? There was no reason to use a Redeye unless—

Unless the aircraft were impossible to approach in any other way. No . . . unless the *victim* were impossible to approach in any way. A man so well guarded—

Paul stopped. There was only one answer.

"Christ! The President . . ."

"What?"

He turned to Annie. "His target isn't Lish, it's the President of the United States. That's why he needs a Redeye!"

Annie just stared at him. Paul grabbed her by the elbows.

"The *dream*," he said, voice cracking. "The jet falling. It wasn't my dream, it was Karl's. He's planning on shooting down Air Force One.''

Paul released her and turned for the phone, taking Hugh Roark's number from his shirt pocket.

"Wait a minute," Annie said. "That's a big leap—"

"It fits, it all fits . . ."

"But was a missile stolen?"

"Yes."

"Is that what the man told you?"

"No."

"Then how do you—"

Paul was already dialing. Annie stepped over and put her hand on the receiver.

"Paul, will you wait? Wait just a minute."

"I'm calling Hugh. The President's in danger—"

"You don't know that."

"I *do* know it. I can't prove it but I know it. I'm sure Karl somehow got a Redeye and he's going to use it to shoot down the President's plane. Anybody else he'd kill another way, one-on-one, like all the others. But the President—how do you kill one of the best-guarded men in the world? You don't. You kill the plane he's on."

Paul turned back to the phone but Annie grabbed his elbow.

"Paul, *why*? You said Karl works for the Russians. Why would the Russians assassinate the President when their leader is coming tomorrow to sign the treaty?"

Paul stared at her. He felt like he'd just walked into a brick wall. He was certain he was right but he saw with equal certainty that what Annie said was true. Why would the Soviets want to shoot down the President now?

"I don't know . . . maybe to stop the treaty, to make a tougher one with a new President . . ."

"You see?" Annie said gently. "You're reaching, jumping to conclusions. I know you had a dream about a jet falling, but that's not unusual. You were on a plane. Considering everything you've been through, it would have been strange if you *hadn't* had dreams. And when you think about this missile, how could one man steal something that big? He'd need help."

"No, no," Paul shook his head. Annie's reading list obviously didn't include *Jane's Weapons Systems*. "It's a shoulder-launched missile. It's portable. You can pick it up with one hand."

"Still, it wasn't reported stolen, was it?"

"I don't know."

The look in her eyes was one of professional understanding, and concern. Paul pulled away.

Annie said quietly, "Why don't you sit down, Paul? Take it easy—"

"Don't patronize me, Annie."

"I'm not."

"You damn well are."

"All right, but before you make any decisions, at least think things through."

Paul looked at his watch. "The President lands in less than an hour. I think there's a good chance that Karl's out there with a Redeye missile waiting to shoot him down. And I know he's got Joanna. What would you suggest? Are you willing to take the responsibility for the President's death? Or for Joanna's?"

Annie's self-assurance began to waver. "What about George Lish?"

Paul had forgotten about Lish. For a moment the scenario he'd built threatened to collapse. Then he remembered something about one of the CIA victims.

"Jim Wilson," he said. "Remember how he was found? In the trunk of his car with his throat slit and a note that was supposed to be from some anti-American Turkish group. Only the note was fake, remember? To throw suspicion on someone else."

"What are you saying? That George Lish—"

"Could be a scapegoat," Paul finished. "Maybe he never was the intended victim."

For the first time the awful implications of what Paul was saying became clear. This time Annie didn't protest when he dialed Hugh Roark. The CIA man had gotten Paul's earlier message and had been calling the house for half an hour.

"I'm not at the house," Paul said. "I'm at the *Herald.* Annie's with me."

"What's she doing there?"

Paul quickly told him what had happened since they'd parted. He made it as brief as possible but even so it was hard for Hugh to keep up. He kept saying, "Whoaa, whoaa," and asking Paul to repeat or explain something. When Paul told him he thought Karl meant to shoot down the President, he stopped Hugh cold.

"Are you serious? You really think he's got a Redeye?"

"Hugh, I do. I can't prove it and Annie thinks I'm crazy—"

"I didn't say that," Annie called out.

"But your source," Hugh said. "Can't he tell you if one was stolen?"

"Not now. The President lands in forty-five minutes. You want to take the chance?"

"No. You stay there, I'll get right back to you."

"I won't be here. I'll be where *he'll* be. Where the President's plane is scheduled to land. Andrews Air Force Base."

"No, you can't do any good out there—"

"If I find him I find Jo."

"The Secret Service will want to talk to you. You better stay put."

"No way."

"Paul—"

"I'm going after Jo, you take care of the rest."

"Wait. Let me talk to Annie."

Paul held out the phone. "He wants to talk to you."

While she talked with Hugh, Paul went outside to another phone He dialed the National Weather Service and listened to a tape-recorded forecast and review of current conditions. Only one statistic interested him: the wind direction. He had covered his share of presidential arrivals over the years and was familiar with the runways at Andrews. When he heard that the wind was from the south he knew that Runway 19 would be in use. If Karl positioned himself on the approach path he would be north of the airport.

He put down the phone, called to Annie and started toward the elevator. By his calculation they had less than an hour to find Joanna, and save the President's life.

CHAPTER

29

BEFORE HE KILLED HER KARL WANTED HIS BROTHER'S
wife. He wanted to possess her in every way, including spiritually.
That Joanna had to die was a decision he had made on the way to the
Toons Creek house. His failure to kill Paul had already endangered
his own life and now threatened the security of the mission. He
would not make the same mistake again.

And yet as the afternoon wore on his feelings underwent a subtle
change. In the beginning he had been interested in talking to Joanna
for the insight she could provide to Paul. By the time they moved
from the kitchen to the living room his interest and attention had
shifted increasingly to Joanna. They were involved in a battle of wits,
he and Joanna. Or were they? Her responses seemed endlessly variable; one moment she was earnest and sincere, a moment later, whim-
sical and ironic, a moment after that, apprehensive and fearful. Every
comment that indicated she misunderstood everything that was going
on was balanced by one of such unerring accuracy that he almost
imagined that Joanna could read his mind. Her moods were mercu-
rial; attempting to capture her thoughts was like trying to grab a fish

from a running river.

It was in the living room that her physical presence took on a sex
ual dimension—the way she sat, her trim legs tucked beneath her,
head thrust forward, the well-defined lips half-parted, sometimes flat,
sometimes curling inward, changing form and redefining themselves
with every shift of emotion. He was aware of the way the sweater
hung on her shoulders and the swell of her thigh where it disappeared
into dark recesses beyond the thick cuff of the shorts. His gaze slid
over her long hands and restless fingers that kept adjusting the
sleeves of the sweater. There was a wedding ring, a gold band inset
with tiny diamonds, the same as Paul had. Suddenly he wished he'd
taken Paul's ring along with his passport.

Standing at the living room window while she was in the bathroom, he began to fantasize sex with her. He imagined her standing
close to him, her desire matching his, her eyes glistening. He would
place his hands on her hips, then slowly follow the contours of her
body upward, his hands sliding beneath the sweater, feeling the curve
of her waist, the faint ripple of ribs disappearing beneath the soft
swell of her breasts. She would return his embrace, leaning into him
stretching her arms around his neck, her face turned to his, their
mouths joined, teeth sliding against one another, the soft warmth of
her cheek against his face.

Lost in the fantasy he paid no attention to the tiny alarm bells
sounding deep inside and it wasn't until she came out and called in
an obviously seductive voice, "Karl, can I take you up on that glass
of wine," that the spell was broken and he knew . .

She was going to try to seduce him.

And he also realized with a shock how far he had been drawn into
the fantasy that he and Paul were somehow the same person, that
Joanna was his wife as much as Paul's, that her attraction to Paul
would somehow translate into a corresponding attraction to him. It
was an illusion of his own making, he realized, but she had recognized and encouraged it. She had offered the most seductive fantasy
of all: that for the first time in his life he had met someone who
understood him. And he had fallen for it

Until she overplayed her hand.

"You want wine?" he called, quickly recovering.

Joanna came into view, one shoulder lowered suggestively.

"Please."

No, Karl thought, you're going too far. The voice, the shoulder, too much.

"I'll join you," he said.

He stepped quickly past her so that she wouldn't see the satisfaction in his eyes. Or the admiration? What was it Paul had said? That Joanna was the most emotionally astute woman he'd ever known. Now Karl knew what he meant. Joanna had ferreted out weakness where he thought none existed. She had discovered his long-buried need to be understood, perhaps even accepted?

Now that he clearly saw what she was doing, he was amazed that she had brought him this far. A moment ago he had been fantasizing making love to her. Now, he again envisioned the two of them together, but this time she was the aggressor, kissing him, undressing him, running her lips across his body, encouraging him . . . with her long, delicate fingers, exciting him and then what? Would she try to grab the gun? Smash a knee into testicles? How far would she go?

He went to the cupboard, got out two wineglasses and placed them on the table. Joanna stood at the table, watching.

"It's funny being here with you like this," she said. "I keep thinking you're Paul."

In spite of himself, Karl again felt he was taking over part of his brother's life, but this time he also recognized and understood the reaction. Careful to maintain a light tone, he said, "Except that Paul is nicer and more gentle?"

"Maybe, but of course I haven't been with you in the best of circumstances . . ."

This time there was no body movement to go with the words, her tone was less obviously suggestive. Had she realized she was coming on too strong, Karl wondered? Had she read him that well and made an adjustment in her performance?

"Maybe we can compensate for that," he said.

Karl opened the refrigerator and took out a chilled bottle of white wine. He had already decided what he would do with her. First, encourage her to drink. If she was playing a role as he believed she was, she would need the courage the alcohol would provide. He remembered the bottle of scotch on the table beside the bed and guessed that she often turned to liquor in times of stress. He hoped so, because it would give more credence to her death. It would look like she broke her neck when she missed a turn and the car tumbled into the Patuxent River. And if she had a significant amount of alcohol in her system, so much the better. In the meantime it would be amusing to watch as she tried to seduce him and discover just how far she would go. He would not be easy to get into a state of sexual abandon—Joanna would have to work very, very hard.

"I hope you like white wine," he said as he placed the bottle on the table beside the two glasses.

When Joanna saw the label she smiled. "I don't believe this."

"What?"

"Did Paul tell you he liked Orvietto Classico?"

"Does he?"

"It's one of his favorites, didn't he tell you?"

Karl shook his head, watching her closely. She seemed to be sincere now.

"Well," she said lightly, "maybe you two have the same tastes in life."

"It seems we do."

He turned to get a corkscrew. Joanna might start the seduction but he was going to finish it. He wanted to see her face when he was deep inside her. He wanted to—

He had just gotten the corkscrew from the drawer when something—a movement reflected in the distant kettle or a rustle of quick-moving fabric or a slight grunt of physical effort—something alerted him. He turned, crouching, just in time to see the raised arm descending, the wine bottle a green blur . . .

As he raised his arm to block the blow he caught a glimpse of her face, the expression now so different from a moment ago. Her teeth were clenched, eyes bright with fear and hate. He was looking at the real Joanna at last—Joanna, the enemy.

His arm partially blocked her at the wrist but the momentum sent the bottle crashing against his temple. A sheet of white sparks jumped before his eyes. As he grabbed for her, his knees buckled, and he collapsed to the floor.

Something moved, something tugged at his coat. He blinked, saw her crouching over him, her arm extended as she tried to get at the gun in his pocket. When she saw his eyes open she moved quickly away, but he managed to grab at her and caught her ankle. She tore free and ran out of the room, leaving him gripping her shoe.

He stumbled to his feet and started after her. In the hall a wave of dizziness made him career off the wall and knock a Winslow Homer reproduction to the floor. He paid no attention. By the time he reached the front door he had the gun out.

She was twenty feet away, running past the stable, heading for the woods.

"Stop, right there," Karl ordered.

She changed direction, veering to the stable. He fired a quick shot as she reached the door. She was thirty feet away. He went into a marksman's crouch but there were still ferris-wheel spots dancing in his eyes. As she threw open the door he squeezed off another shot and saw the wood fly above and to the left.

Then she was gone.

All right, he thought as he stood up. Now she was trapped. The only door to the stable was at his end. He walked deliberately forward. His head throbbed but when he touched his temple he felt no bleeding. He breathed deeply and his eyes cleared. She had managed a lucky blow. She would never have a chance at another.

As soon as he and Annie arrived at Andrews Air Force Base Paul realized what an impossible task he'd set for himself. Less then fifteen miles from Washington, the base was situated in an area where housing developments, shopping centers and industrial parks alternated with small farms, rolling fields and thick forests, any one of which offered too many opportunities for concealment. At least he had had the foresight to bring along a map of Prince Georges County, and though this helped narrow the area of the search there were still too many places beneath the approach path to Runway 19 where Karl could be.

They had made the drive in record time, weaving in and out of traffic, with Paul alternately thinking out loud as he tried to re-create his brother's reasoning and cursing at cars that got in his way. Most of the time Annie sat gripping her seat. She disliked sports cars, and the Alfa Romeo's seatbelts didn't even have shoulder straps.

Paul pulled into the parking lot of a 7-11 store and grabbed the map from Annie's lap. Across the street a tall fence marked the boundary to the air force base. The main gate was visible with uniformed, white-gloved military police waving vehicles through.

"You think it's crazy, don't you?" he said as he pored over the map.

"I don't know," she said. "If you think that he's out here . . ."

Paul frowned in concentration, lifted his head and stared outside.

"No," Paul said slowly, "it's more than him. Jo's in danger, and this son of a bitch has got a Redeye missile. I'm sure of that . . ."

Except the words that had come with increasing conviction now lost some of it. "I don't know if he's *here*. I'm not . . . responding to it, to this . . ."

"You mean the base?"

"Everything. I've got this feeling, this urgency the President's in terrible danger—" He stopped, frowned. "Or Jo. It could be her, not him. Except what the hell would Karl be doing with a Redeye unless it's the President's who?" He put his hands to his temples and pressed inward, shook his head and slammed a fist against the steering wheel.

"Hold it, Paul. Just try to let your mind relax," Annie said quietly.

"I can't, can't relax. *Something's* going to happen, and it's got to do with Joanna and the Redeye and Air Force One . . ."

The Winnebago gave Joanna a moment of hope. It blocked her view of the rear of the stable and it wasn't until she ran around it that she realized there was no back door.

It had been a foolish choice, ducking into the stable, but the gunshots had unnerved her. Their sharp reports echoed in her ears and her hand tingled from the way the door jumped when the bullet struck it. The stable had seemed her only chance. Now, the folly of that decision became too apparent. In addition to the Winnebago there was a worktable surrounded by shelves and cupboards and three propane tanks standing against one wall, and that was all. There was no place to hide except the Winnebago, and what was that but another box inside a box?

Needing to do something, she opened the door to the Winnebago. And had an idea. Instantly she dropped to the ground and wriggled beneath the motor home. The earth was uneven and smelled of damp dirt; she could feel the undercarriage pressing against her back. With her face turned to one side she could see the base of the stable walls between the underside of the Winnebago and the floor. The narrow band of light that streamed in from the open doorway dimmed when Karl entered.

She froze.

Karl was only visible from the knees down. At any moment she expected he would stop, his knees would bend, and his head would come into view as he looked beneath the Winnebago and found her. But he walked down the right side of the Winnebago, toward the door that she'd left open.

He thinks I'm inside it, she thought.

As he passed her, she began to work her way toward the rear of the motor home, where it was closest to the outside door. Her hair caught in something and she almost cried out. She reached around and tried to free it. No use. Karl mounted the step to the Winnebago and his shoes disappeared from view. She had to move—*now*. She shoved forward, heard and felt the clump of hair rip from her scalp, and crouching low, ducked out the door and around the front of the house to where the Audi was parked.

When she turned around she half-expected to see Karl coming at her. Not yet. The sun was low, long shadows bathed the yard. Tranquility at odds with the reality.

Moving quickly, she located the magnetic keyholder beneath the front bumper. Her fingers fumbled to open it, and when she did the key flipped to the ground. She dropped the holder, recovered the key and got into the car. By habit she slammed the door and instantly regretted it. Karl was sure to have finished looking in the Winnebago and was probably outside by now.

The seat was too far back but she couldn't take time to adjust it. Perched on the edge, she jammed the key into the ignition and started the car. If he hadn't heard her before, he had now. She let out the clutch and the car lurched forward, and died. She hadn't released the parking brake.

She wrenched it free and started the car again. This time when she let out the clutch the Audi shot forward and she found herself holding onto the steering wheel to keep from being thrown back too far to reach the pedals. A glance in the rearview mirror still showed no sign of Karl as she rounded the curve and the farmhouse was lost in the trees.

She let out a deep breath, pushed the button and rolled up the windows. The skylight was open too, but before she could close it a wrought-iron fence came into view. For a moment she was tempted to smash through it, but crashing the fence might puncture a tire or smash the radiator or shove a fender into the wheel. A glance behind showed her that the road was empty. She pulled to a quick stop, left the motor running, got out and pushed open the gate. Back in the car, she realized how naked she felt outside it.

The road behind was still empty so she took a moment to lock the door and adjust the seat. When she reached to close the skylight a flash of movement caught her eye, not from the empty road but from the woods off to the right.

He was coming toward her, open coat flapping, palms chopping the air.

She threw the car into gear and headed out of the gate, tires spitting dirt, rear end fishtailing as she turned onto the road. The Audi straightened and Karl slammed shoulder-first into the right side of the car. He clutched the door handle, half-running, half-dragged alongside as he tried to get in. But the doors were locked and she had rolled up the windows.

But there was the open skylight.

As the car surged forward he lost his footing and grabbed the sunroof just in time. His legs banged against the car but he held on. When Joanna looked over, Karl's face was pressed against the window, his features flattened and distorted as he struggled to maintain his hold.

She wrenched the wheel back and forth trying to shake him loose. But he had both hands on the sunroof now, and as she swerved toward him he used the motion of the car to help him climb aboard. A moment ago it seemed impossible he could hold on. Now he lay across the roof, his legs visible in the rear window, his fingers curled around the inner lip of the sunroof.

She accelerated and at the same time reached over and activated the switch to close the sunroof. A pickup truck appeared, coming straight at her, horn blaring. Gripping the wheel hard with both hands she swerved back to her side of the road. She slowed down then, thinking that maybe, somehow the people in the truck would help, but it went right past, peppering the side of the Audi with grit. All she got was a glimpse of the driver's face scowling at her.

He thinks we're fooling around, she thought.

Karl's arm plunged through the five-inch gap in the sunroof and grabbed at her face. She ducked away but the hand kept clawing at her. Fingers raked her cheek, then gripped her forehead and went toward her eyes.

She slammed on the brakes, the car skidded wildly. There was a thump, Karl plunged into view, disappeared over the hood. The car was skidding sideways in a slow spin. She fought to regain control and had almost succeeded when the Audi slammed rear-end into a telephone pole.

The impact was solid but not wrenching, like falling over backward in a chair. The engine died and in the new silence the wail of an approaching train sounded. To the left, in the direction that she'd been heading, the road climbed to meet the railroad tracks, and beyond the tracks was a busy highway. Behind her, through a drifting cloud of dust, she saw Karl get to his feet and start toward her.

She started the car and tried to drive ahead. The Audi rocked forward, and stopped, rear tires spinning. The engine roared but the rear wheels only dug in deeper. She began rocking the car, putting it into reverse, then forward, reverse and forward, rocking it back and forth. With each cycle the trunk rose higher. Karl was close now, she could even see the expression in his eyes. Not wild, not crazed. Weirdly calm, professional. Now the car had bounded back onto the road. Joanna swung the wheel to the left and fishtailed away.

Karl was less than five feet from the rear bumper when the Audi began to pull away. She watched in the rearview mirror as he made one last effort to catch up, then slowed and collapsed to the roadside—no, not collapsed. He had gone into a crouch with one elbow braced on his knee, the gun held out with both hands. She hunched down and yanked the steering wheel back and forth to throw off his aim. Any moment she expected to hear the shot, and she wondered if he hit her in the head would she die before she heard the bullet?

He did not fire. Instead he stood up, pocketed the gun, and began coming after her. It was so crazy it scared her more than the gun. He couldn't hope to catch her, then why—?

And then she heard the diesel's wail and saw the train approaching the crossing. A long train that would cut her off from the safety of the highway. It was over. Unless—

She shifted to fourth and put her foot to the floor. If she stopped, he would kill her. If she died at least it would be trying to get away, not passively trapped like some animal. She leaned forward, pushing the steering wheel, urging the car onward, afraid to shift her gaze from the opening between the two railroad crossing signs, afraid to see the train bearing down on her.

The scream of the diesel's horn was constant now and joined by another sound, the shriek of metal as the train's wheels locked in a final attempt to stop. The road lifted as it met the railroad bed, and she felt her stomach drop as the Audi vaulted into the air. She was aware of a black thundering mass and a single sweeping headlight off to her left and a world of noise. The tracks flashed beneath, and a moment later the car was buffeted by a shock of rushing air. The train's horn shifted in tone as the Audi slammed down on the other side of the tracks, and the train swept past and behind it, a blur of quick-changing colors in the rearview mirror.

Before she could recover from the shock Joanna saw the Stop sign fifty feet ahead, and beyond it the busy highway. She was going over seventy miles an hour

She slammed on the brakes, knowing as she did that it was useless. All she could do was try not to hit anyone, and with that thought she deliberately steered off the road and into an embankment. The right fender struck, the Audi vaulted into the air and turned slowly on its side. When it hit the pavement, it flipped over again and again and again.

CHAPTER

30

LE SORBET RESTAURANT WAS HALF A BLOCK FROM the Secret Service field office on G Street. It was here that Agent Eliot Ingerman, assistant director of the Secret Service Protective Division, received news of the Redeye threat to Air Force One. For six weeks he had been working twelve-hour days coordinating security arrangements between the various intelligence agencies in preparation for the Russian General Secretary's visit. He had gotten only five hours' sleep the night before and had been stuck in his office all day. At five-thirty he slipped away and walked to Le Sorbet, where he ordered a seafood croissant and a cup of coffee. The beeper went off before the food arrived. Now, as he stood at the pay phone and listened to the incredible possibility that a Redeye missile had been stolen and would be deployed against Air Force One, he couldn't help feeling that the threat would never have materialized if he had stayed in his office and sent a secretary out for food.

"What's the quality of the intelligence?" he asked grumpily.

"Single source but no confirmation. The officer running him rates him solid but admits it's more gut-level than long-term experience."

"Who's the officer?"

"Hugh Roark. He's one of the old guard, working a special assignment through Security. He seems solid."

The man on the other end of the line was Tommy Lecrazny, CIA liaison officer. Also on the line was Ingerman's assistant, Barbara Ziegler, who had received the incoming call and patched the CIA man through.

The smell of food made Ingerman's stomach growl. He glanced toward his table where a waitress held up his seafood croissant. Ingerman smiled and nodded to her and continued questioning Lecrazny.

"Who's the primary?"

"Paul Stafford, reporter over at the *Herald*."

Ingerman's senses sharpened. Paul Stafford wasn't the most well-loved reporter in Washington—especially by some of the defense contractors and their politician pals—but no one doubted his credibility. Or the accuracy of his sources.

"The tip came through Stafford's source?"

"Not exactly. It's Stafford's brother."

"The tip came through his brother?"

"No, the brother's the assassin."

"*Stafford's* brother?"

"That's how I get it."

"And Stafford called him in?"

"Yep."

"Well, fuck a duck," Ingerman said softly.

All his Secret Service training emphasized avoiding emergencies; advance planning was the order of every day. The President and his family never went anywhere that had not been prepared beforehand. Emergencies were anticipated so that they were no longer emergencies but contingencies. There was a contingency plan for everything, including the substitution of Dulles Airport for Andrews Air Force Base. The question now was whether to activate the Dulles option. It was a matter of individual judgment and the chance of making an error was magnified by both lack of information and the necessity for a quick decision.

Ingerman glanced at his watch. The President was scheduled to land in twenty-eight minutes.

"Okay, I'm on my way back. Leave a number with Barbara and stay close to the phone."

"I told you this one was out of left field."

"Barbara?"

"I'm here."

"Okay, listen. Call the Bayonne terminal and confirm the integrity of the Redeye shipment. Then double-check the PTA for stolen or missing Redeyes or any other kind of ground-to-air missiles."

He was referring to the Potential Threat Analysis, a report prepared by the Office of Protective Intelligence, which listed all individuals, organizations or activities that might become a threat. Stolen Redeye missiles definitely fell into the PTA's jurisdiction.

"Next thing," Ingerman went on, "locate Paul Stafford and have him stand by. Then alert Kenny—he's doing the arrival at Andrews—give him a sitrep and tell him we'll get back. And get a current ETA for the landing. After that find me Colonel Coswell or Bud Hollingsworth—somebody who knows the capabilities of a Redeye and how much threat it poses to Air Force One. Hollingsworth's number is on a zip card. I'm at Le Sorbet and I'm leaving now."

After hanging up Ingerman detoured past his table, grabbed the croissant and left a five-dollar bill. Outside, he walked briskly down the street, wolfing his food as he went.

Joanna's decision to outrun the train took Karl by surprise. When her car did not slow down but shot across the tracks he expected it would be crushed like an aluminum can. Instead, it disappeared from view, leaving him staring in disbelief, unable to believe that Joanna had gotten away. Yet there he was, standing in the middle of the road, dirty and bruised, trying to catch his breath, while she was no doubt on her way to the police. How she had started the car he still couldn't figure out . . . the keys to the Audi were in his pocket.

As the shriek of the train's brakes and wail of its horn subsided his anger and self-recrimination boiled up. Part of his arsenal was to recognize and exploit the weaknesses of his victims, and he was an expert at it. Yet in this case he had been betrayed by *his* weaknesses . . . especially the illusion of living his brother's life that had taken such hold of his imagination. Joanna had recognized it and used it. She had played to it, built and encouraged it for her own purposes. He had known that her seduction was false; why then hadn't he also realized that she would make her move before it even began?

Because he had so badly wanted the seduction to happen.

He threw the gun to the ground. Everything was in jeopardy now.

She would go to the police and she would tell them about the Toons Creek property and the Winnebago. The police would come looking for him; they might even discover Lish's body. When he thought of the trouble he'd gone to kidnapping his brother, stealing the Redeye, placing Lish's fingerprints everywhere. And what of Ikhnovsky? The old man had said that his life was in Karl's hands. Had he traded his mentor's life for his brother's?

Karl was still sorting through his angry thoughts when the train passed and he saw several cars stopped on the highway beyond the crossing. For a moment he thought that Joanna had flagged down motorists to come and get him. Then someone lit a purple flare and went running to put it on the road, and Karl suddenly realized: Joanna had not escaped, after all. She had missed the train but hit something else, apparently another car on the highway.

Rage evaporated, relief flooded in. He began jogging toward the accident. He ran easily now. With this reprieve his thoughts regained their equilibrium and he was able to begin planning his next move. Joanna would, he hoped, be dead, and if so his only problem would be getting back to the safe house.

He slowed to a walk as he reached the crest of the railroad tracks. One lane was blocked and someone had taken on the task of directing traffic. His eyes read the story in the long shallow furrows that angled off the road and up an embankment, where they disappeared. The splintered stump of a Stop sign stood at a forty-five-degree angle; beyond it the highway was covered with broken glass and bruised with patches of white paint and silver metal.

She had obviously lost control, gone up the embankment and cartwheeled into the street where she had struck another car, a Ford Escort, he noted. The left front panel of the Ford was staved in, its metal ripped, the engine cocked to one side, its steaming radiator dangling like a broken tooth. Two men were leading a hysterical woman from the Ford. Nearby another man was lying on the ground, alive but clutching his arm.

A larger crowd had gathered around the Audi, which had come to rest in an upright position but was in much worse shape than the Ford. Its wheels were bent almost parallel to the road, all the glass was broken and the openings, which had been windows, were barely recognizable. The roof, buckled and twisted, hugged the car like a metal blanket, and all the corners and sides were mashed inward, as if a giant had used the car for a piece of clay. It seemed unlikely that anyone could have lived through the crash.

As he approached, two men and a young woman eased Joanna's body through the gaping windshield. A fourth man wearing shorts stood to one side giving nervous advice . . . "That's got it. Here she comes, here she comes." . . . Someone called out, "Is she alive?" No one answered but the comments continued as more people gathered around. "Okay, gently now." . . . "Shouldn't we get her away from the car?" . . . "You don't want to move her; if she's got broken ribs you could puncture a lung." . . . "But the car, I smell gas." . . . "No cigarettes."

The man in shorts turned and began yelling importantly, "Nobody smoke, there's gasoline here. No smoking."

Karl moved forward. Joanna was lying on the side of the road, her face cut, blood streaming from her head. She was deathly white and Karl couldn't tell if she were breathing. One arm lay twisted at an impossible angle, the jagged tip of glistening white bone poking out of her sweater. A woman came running with a blanket. Karl took one end and helped cover her with it.

"Is she alive?" he asked.

"Just barely," the man on the ground beside her said. "Has anybody got a bandage? Something to stop the bleeding?"

A young man pulled off a tee-shirt with a picture of Bruce Springsteen on it. Karl placed his index and middle fingers on Joanna's neck and felt for a pulse. It was there, but faint. The man who had gotten the tee-shirt began using it to staunch the flow of blood. He looked up at Karl and shook his head.

"I don't think she's going to make it."

Karl nodded and moved back, letting others fill the role of Good Samaritan. Joanna was a threat. She had made herself a threat. She had to die. This was good. This way it looked like a simple accident without his having to arrange it.

He left the scene and began walking back to the house. When he heard a distant siren he thought what a shame that they had come so quickly. He hoped the man with the tee-shirt was right. That Joanna was almost dead. It would be best if she died on the way to the hospital.

Air Force One was over Wheeling, West Virginia, when the call came through. The President was in the First Family's lounge, sitting near his wife, who ignored what he was saying. She had good reason: the President was speaking in Russian. He sat with his feet up, eyes closed, wearing tiny earphones and a boom mike, listening to a tape of Russian phrases he intended to use during the meeting with the Russian leader. His father's heart attack, mild as it was, had left him with a heightened sense of mortality that gave added significance to the Mutual Defense Treaty. If he could leave this a more peaceful and secure world than the one he'd been born into he would count his life, and his tenure in office, well spent.

Someone knocked at the door. The President, who liked to travel in casual attire, assumed that it was his valet with a fresh shirt, his coat and tie. Instead he found Lee Knudson, his chief of staff, waiting for him.

"Eliot Ingerman's got something for you."

Lee did not say that it was important but he didn't need to. The layout aboard Air Force One was such that the President's compartment and First Family's quarters were in the forward section of the plane, followed by compartments for the White House staff, Secret Service detail and press pool. By tradition, occupants of one section were free to visit those behind them but did not move forward without an invitation. Unless it was something very important.

The two men went to the President's compartment, a hybrid modern office and communications center. From a single telephone the President could link through the National Command Authority to every communications system, civil and military, closed, ciphered, encrypted or open, in the Western world. In this case the man on the other end of the line was Eliot Ingerman. The President didn't know Ingerman well but what he did know encouraged him to trust his judgment, which was why he was surprised that the Secret Service man thought it necessary to brief him on a situation that seemed far-fetched at best.

After explaining the situation Ingerman said, "Colonel Coswell tells me the aircraft has a defense screen that would knock out a Redeye but I've got a detail on the way to Dulles just in case we want to make a preemptive defense."

"What are you saying, Eliot?"

"I'm saying, sir, that if you'd like to order the Dulles option, we can move on it right away."

No, the President thought, that is exactly what I would not like to do. There were four members of the White House press pool aboard the aircraft, not to mention the reporters and photographers at

Andrews; any deviation to Dulles would be all over the papers and networks within hours. He could imagine the lead story: "THREAT TO AIR FORCE ONE FORCES LANDING AT DULLES." He could imagine the effect this would have on the Russians, particularly the KGB contingent in charge of the General Secretary's safety.

"You wouldn't ask my opinion if you could confirm a definite threat, would you?"

"No, Mr. President."

"Are you prepared to execute the Dulles plan based on what you know now?"

"Without independent confirmation of reporter Paul Stafford's story, and based on what I'm told about our air defense capabilities, my judgment says no."

"You've been doing this longer than I have," the President said. "We'll go with your judgment.

"Yes, sir." Ingerman didn't sound happy.

The President smiled. "You were hoping I'd make it easy for you?"

"Damn right, sir."

"All right, Eliot. Thanks for the briefing. You'll let me know where all this started."

The President hung up and exchanged a speculative look with Lee Knudson.

The chief of staff said, "Son of a bitch probably taped the conversation to cover his ass in case we go down in flames."

The President shrugged. "It goes on all the time. We just don't hear about it."

"You mean venality, subservience, evasion of responsibility?"

The President smiled again. Lee's exaggerated sarcasm offended some people but the President enjoyed it.

"The threats. They get handled. We never know—"

"We'll know this time if they don't get handled."

The President's smile faded. He turned to look out the window. Some thirty thousand feet below, the country crept silently westward as they began the descent into Washington.

Two Air Force helicopters began circling lazily over the approach area as Paul and Annie checked the spot that seemed best situated for an attack: an industrial park located in a wooded area just beyond the base. There were a couple of older wood homes that once might have been farmhouses but most of the buildings were of concrete construction, one, two or three stories high: a printing company, an auto body shop, a design studio, a self-storage facility and half-a-dozen anonymous warehouses.

Paul was sure that Karl wouldn't be wandering, carrying the Redeye like a fishing pole, but he described the missile to Annie so she knew the size and shape of what they were looking for. They drove slowly up and down dead-end roads and saw dozens of places that Karl might be, but no sign of him or of Joanna. At one point they stopped at the self-storage facility and asked about anyone who looked like Paul, realizing as they did how peculiar the question must sound. A young man with a Jamaican accent said he couldn't help them but let them go up to the roof.

Paul shook his head as he surveyed the surrounding area. "He could be on that roof or that roof or still inside a building waiting for the plane to come in sight. Or he could be out there in the woods."

"We'll know in a minute," Annie said.

Paul followed her gaze and saw a Boeing 707, low in the sky, turning toward them. He checked his watch. It wasn't yet six o'clock.

"Not him," he said. "That's the backup plane. Air Force One will be about ten minutes behind."

Annie gave him a look of renewed appreciation. Paul decided not to tell her that he had worked the White House beat for six months.

They went back to the car and decided to check the roads that passed beneath the approach path: Interstate 95, Highway 337, the Marlboro Pike and Suitland Parkway. It was a rolling terrain, and the roads were usually bordered by woods. They passed a car parked at the side of the road with its hood open and stopped to inspect it. Paul peered in the window and walked around the car. Annie followed. Every time a truck passed, the air buffeted them and the suction tugged at Annie's skirt.

Paul ran a speculative eye over the back of the car. "The trunk would probably be big enough to carry the missile," he said. "And who knows if anything's really wrong with the engine?"

"But where would he go?"

Paul turned and looked at the trees some ten feet away. He began walking toward them. Annie caught up to him and suggested they spread out. The woods weren't particularly thick but they would cover more area by separating. And they didn't have much time.

She seemed caught up in the search as much as he was, and for the first time Paul considered what might happen if she came on Karl, toting a Redeye missile and with the 38-caliber Smith & Wesson.

"I know you don't want to hear this," he said. "But did it ever occur to you that he might kill you if you try to stop him?"

"I won't try to stop him. I just want to find him."

Before he could figure out what she meant by that he saw over her shoulder, ·in the distance, the President's plane, Air Force One. It was only a silhouette as it turned slowly onto final approach but Paul recognized it. His face hardened then, and Annie turned to look over her shoulder.

"That's him?"

Paul didn't answer. He was already charging through the woods, shouting Karl's name. Anything to disrupt him, flush him from his hiding place. Annie took a divergent path and followed some thirty feet off to his right. She added her voice to his, which Paul thought was just as well. The more people Karl thought were after him, the more likely he was to bolt.

The earth sloped upward, then began a gentle descent. There was a flash of color just ahead, through a clump of trees, and a moment later Paul found himself in the open, standing on the shoulder of another road, not the freeway this time but the Allentown Road, which bordered the base.

The flash of color was a sweeping red light from a Highway Patrol car parked in the center of the road. Two officers stood beside the car, chatting. On the road, in the distance, Paul could see another police car blocking the road. This car was turning away traffic.

One of the patrolmen spotted him and his smile died. "The road's closed, sir."

The man's partner turned around just as Annie came out of the woods.

"Karl?" she called out, then stopped short. She saw the police and she saw Paul and she looked confused. The police looked suspicious.

"Can we help you folks?"

Before Paul could answer Annie recovered and gave a quick innocent explanation.

"Someone had trouble on the freeway," she said brightly.

"There's a car with nobody around. We thought maybe they'd come this way."

The older patrolman had heavy jowls, but he was evidently a man of the old school; he tipped his hat and said, "If they did they're not here now, ma'am. This road's closed until the President lands."

"Then maybe somebody gave them a ride," Annie said. "Thank you anyway."

She took Paul's arm and led him back the way they'd come. The whine of the approaching jet made them both look up. Trees pointed like tall fingers at the hazy blue sky beyond. The noise swelled, and Air Force One slid overhead. Now they could see the blue-and-white markings and the Presidential seal. Annie took a quick breath and involuntarily tightened her grip on Paul's arm.

The sight of the plane triggered something in Paul, a dislocation of memory, the sense that something was wrong. It had to do with the shape of the aircraft, with the engines, lunging forward from their pylons beneath the sweptback wings. It was wrong . . .

The plane disappeared from view.

"That's not the one . . ." Paul said.

Annie turned to him, realized she was holding his arm and released it. Paul was still staring into the trees.

"That's not the plane."

"It's another backup?"

He turned to her. "*No*, it's not the one I saw. You know, in my dream. Or whatever you call it. I remember *clearly*, one wing was broken and it was heading straight for me. But there were no engines. No engines on the wing. They were in back, attached to the fuselage. Rear-mounted engines, just below the tail."

"You mean like a 727?"

Paul shook his head. "*Four* engines, two on each side, mounted in—"

It hit him like a physical blow. He knew the aircraft type now: paired engines, two on each side, mounted in tandem. And the sweptback tail topped by a horizontal stabilizer, just like a 727 except it wasn't a 727, it was a Russian jet, an Ilyushin 62. It was Aeroflot . . .

"My God."

Annie stepped back. *"What?"*

Paul's face was a mask of wonder, and disbelief.

"It's not the President. It's the Russian. Karl's going after—"

"Who?"

"That's why he's here. *He's going to kill the Russian General Sec-*

retary. ''

Annie could only stare at him. She heard what he was saying but it made no sense. For the first time she questioned her own judgment and wondered if Paul was indeed crazy. She felt like Alice running after the White Rabbit. Every time she turned around a pumpkin had become an orange, or a mushroom a birthday cake.

"He's going to kill the Russian," Paul announced. "I'm *sure* of it."

He started back to the car. Annie ran to catch up.

"But you said—I thought Karl was working for the Russians."

"He is."

"Then why—?"

Paul opened the door to the car and turned to her. "I don't know. But I saw four engines mounted in twin pairs and that spells Aeroflot and that means the leader of the Soviet Union. Let's call your boss."

"Wait." Annie put a hand on his arm. "Paul, stop and think a minute. If he's working for the Russians he's not going to shoot down their leader. And if he's not working for the Russians . . ."

Her reasoning ran into a dead-end. Paul looked at her closely. "What are you saying? That he's working for you guys? For the CIA?"

"No, no," she said quickly, and then, with less assurance, "at least I don't think so."

For a moment they both considered the possibility that Karl was somehow working for the CIA. Paul felt his mind stretch to the breaking point as he tried to juggle the facts into a new interpretation. If Karl was actually working for the CIA, then who were the original victims? KGB agents? And why would Hugh and Maurice need Paul's help in tracking him down? Or were they supposed to be KGB agents too?

No. He'd confirmed Hugh and Maurice's credentials. They were CIA. That was a fact. And he had dreamed the murders; that was another fact. And he had good reason to trust Hugh Roark; that was a fact too.

"No," he said firmly, "it doesn't work any other way. I don't know why he's after his own boss, but I know he is . . . Come on."

He slid into the car and Annie followed him.

"Don't tell anyone but Hugh," Annie warned. "If the Russians hear about it, even if it's not true, they may try to kill him."

He looked at her. "Just as long as they don't kill Joanna."

"He's your own brother," she said.

Paul didn't answer. Annie watched him for a moment, then turned to the window. When she spoke again her tone was almost reflective. Peculiar, he thought, at a time like this.

"You don't realize how rare it is, this link you have with Karl. Maybe in its special form it's unique. The two of you are very valuable people."

Paul shook his head.

"It's true, damn it. I know it sounds extreme, but your lives are one of a kind, worth more than—"

"Than my wife's, than the President's?"

She didn't answer him, but as he looked at her he realized that was exactly what she thought.

CHAPTER

31

BECAUSE OF HIS PREMATURELY GRAY HAIR, AS WELL as a certain knack for navigating the treacherous political waters of governmental bureaucracy, his colleagues had given Eliot Ingerman the nickname "Gray Fox." Ingerman played to this image by projecting an urbane, authoritative exterior that was sometimes at odds with the turmoil he felt during those rare times he had to put his judgment on the line. This was one of those times.

He had returned to his office on G Street and with Barbara's help had talked to a dozen people in as many minutes. He hadn't been able to get in touch with Paul Stafford, for which he blamed the CIA. After all, Stafford was their source. But he had talked to Hugh Roark and everything that the CIA man told him served to confirm his assessment that the Redeye threat was empty. Stafford's brother, a twin it turned out, was a man Stafford had never met or even known about until a few weeks ago. The brother, Karl Alexander, was supposed to be working for the KGB through an East German organization called the Stasis.

"He's a trained killer," Hugh Roark had told him. "And very

effective.''

Maybe so and maybe not, Ingerman thought. The CIA wasn't infallible. It put too much emphasis on collecting intelligence and not enough on analyzing it. Stafford was a case in point: what kind of Byzantine plot would have a Russian hitman going after the President now, on the eve of the Mutual Defense Treaty? Hugh Roark had no answer for that one.

No, the whole thing seemed more likely to have sprung full-blown from this Paul Stafford's imagination. The report from the Bayonne Military Terminal was negative: there were no reports of any security breaches or missing cargo. And Colonel Coswell assured him that Air Force One was infra-red protected.

"We've got a Hot Brick system," Coswell explained. "That puts out a variable-frequency waveform that'll confuse the hell out of a heat-seeking missile like the Redeye. Which, of course, is not to say that I'd like to have one fired in my direction.''

Or the President's direction, Ingerman thought. Despite the reassurances, the Gray Fox had taken two precautions: he had warned the President about the threat and he had arranged to videotape the landing. If anything *did* happen he wanted a filmed record for both clues and evidence.

Now, as he watched the video monitor, he felt a familiar burning sensation in his stomach. It was going to be a rough week for his ulcer. The scene on the monitor showed the arrival area at Andrews, where a small group of people waited to meet the President. The camera operator, one of their own men, was on the roof of the terminal. He didn't have a tripod and the picture was jerky.

"Tell him to hold still," Ingerman called to Barbara, his assistant. "Give us a steady picture.''

Barbara sat at an adjoining desk with a telephone to her ear. She was a plain, middle-aged woman who was as efficient as she looked.

The camera operator's voice reached them through the monitor. "Okay, here he comes.''

The image abruptly shifted and settled on the far end of the runway, where Air Force One was visible descending from a hazy sky. Ingerman waved Barbara over and they both held their breath as the plane slowly, imperceptibly approached the runway. As it was about to touch down a phone rang, making them both jump. Barbara returned to her desk to take the incoming call.

The plane touched down and Ingerman's stomach growled in relief.

The damn CIA boys had spooked him.

The camera operator said, "Is that it?"

"Stay on it," Ingerman instructed. Just in case. Always, just in case.

He opened his desk drawer, took out a pill for his stomach and walked into the hallway for a drink of water. When he came back to the office the air force was rolling out the steps to Air Force One.

Ingerman said, "The cooler in the drinking fountain is on the blink again, better call someone."

Barbara looked up from the phone, her face ashen.

"What?" he demanded.

"That was Bayonne," she said slowly. "A security team just inspected the warehouse. They found a ventilator, up on the roof, where somebody broke in. It looks like it happened during the last month."

Ingerman felt icy fingers on his backbone. He turned to the television monitor, where the President stood at the top of the ramp, waving to friends and reporters.

You lucky son of a bitch, he thought. And then he thought it again, this time for the President.

Karl alternately walked and jogged back to the Toons Creek house. He was in good spirits. He had meant to devise a traffic accident to kill Joanna and now it had happened with the added benefit of eye-witnesses. His only concern, of course, was that she might not have died. He had no idea whether she recognized the Redeye packing case in the back of the Winnebago but he didn't intend to take any chances. As soon as he got home he took out the phone book and began calling hospitals. Joanna had been taken to Glenway Memorial Hospital in Upper Marlboro. A nurse in the emergency room told him that she was in surgery.

"How badly hurt is she?"

"I don't know, Mr. Stafford. You'll have to talk to the doctor when he comes out of the operating room."

"Was she conscious when she was admitted?"

"No, sir. She was brought in comatose and in shock."

"But she's expected to survive, is that right?"

"You'll have to talk to the doctor about that, Mr. Stafford."

"All right, I'll come right down."

After hanging up Karl considered the situation. If Joanna survived she would come out of surgery under sedation. Judging from what he'd seen of her injuries they would probably put her in intensive care, where she would be hooked up to a lot of machines and monitors. She would be getting an intravenous solution and would probably be on a respirator. The nurses would be watching, so he had to be careful. He could do nothing physical.

The obvious choice was a drug. A whiff of hydrogen cyanide would induce a heart attack, but there was no way to administer it if she was on a respirator. Besides, he had no hydrogen cyanide, only Haloparimine, the same sedative he'd given Otto to use on his brother.

Karl smiled as the idea took hold. He went to the bathroom and found his toilet kit, a compartmentalized soft leather bag he had purchased in Turkey. He took out a small round bottle with a syringe top. The label indicated that this was medicine for use with an ear infection. In fact, it was highly concentrated Haloparimine. One syringe would induce a sleep so heavy that a man's bedroom could be searched with a crowbar and he wouldn't wake up. Two syringes could induce a coma; the entire contents would kill a person.

All he needed to do was dump the Haloparimine into the IV solution. The first symptoms of the drug, shallowness of breathing, would be masked by the respirator. By the time Joanna's blood pressure began dropping, he would be gone and the drug would have progressed too far to be reversed.

Feeling more confident than he had since Joanna had surprised him that morning, Karl changed clothes and began packing the Winnebago. He wore gloves so as not to leave any of his own fingerprints next to George Lish's. The house itself didn't matter—there was no way he could get rid of all of "Ron Tednick's" fingerprints even if he wanted to. But it wouldn't be necessary. Joanna was the only one who could link him to the Toons Creek house and she was not going to survive.

It was a small and select group of men who gathered in the Briefing Room of the Secret Service field office on G street. Eliot Ingerman had called the meeting after talking to Stafford on the phone and deciding that the man was sane. Unfortunately, Stafford sounded more credible than he looked. When he showed up for the meeting Ingerman was dismayed to find him hollow-eyed and pale and obviously on edge. It didn't help that most of his assertions couldn't be checked, based as they were on dreams and premonitions and hypnosis and what seemed psychological mumbo-jumbo.

The woman, Annie Helms, made a more substantial impression, although her theory about brain waves and genetic compatibility was equally out of left field as far as he was concerned. Ingerman had talked to them both on the phone and decided that if he had to make a decision based on such elusive evidence, he wasn't going to do it alone. It was at that point that he called a meeting of the Summit Security Unit.

The six men who sat around the oval table represented various intelligence and security agencies: the Secret Service, FBI, CIA, Defense Intelligence Agency and the State Department's INR—the Bureau of Intelligence and Research. In addition, Ingerman had asked Colonel Buzz Coswell, an expert in airborne defense systems, to attend. Hugh Roark and Annie Helms were there with Paul Stafford. Conspicuously absent were the KGB security-specialists who had flown in from Moscow weeks ago. Ingerman thought it best to wait until the American contingent had a chance to evaluate Stafford's story before opening themselves up to Russian alarm or criticism. Or ridicule.

Ingerman took off his jacket, unbuttoned his cuffs and rolled them neatly twice to emphasize the importance of the meeting. As soon as the last man arrived, he stood up.

"Gentlemen, thank you for coming on such short notice. Obviously I wouldn't have called this meeting unless the circumstances were extraordinary and they are that. Many of you will recognize the man on my right by name, if not on sight: this is Paul Stafford, from the Washington *Herald*. Next to him are two members of the Central Intelligence Agency, Hugh Roark and Dr. Anne Helms, both of whom are closely associated with the events that have led up to this meeting. In a nutshell, Mr. Stafford has information that leads him to believe that a man—in fact, his own brother—has stolen a Redeye missile and intends to use it to shoot down the Soviet General Secretary tomorrow morning."

There had been some complaints about calling a meeting during the dinner hour but this little bombshell effectively stilled them.

D. L. McNally from the State Department finally made himself heard above the others.

"Wait a minute, Eliot. Where are Vronsky and Dekanozov? Why aren't they here?"

"I think you'll understand the reason when you've heard Mr. Stafford's story."

"Just so you understand, the protocol guarantees the KGB security section a voice in any decisions concerning the General Secretary's safety."

Ingerman was annoyed. He knew as well as McNally what the protocol provisions were.

"That's all well and good," he said, "but according to Mr. Stafford it's the *Russians* who are behind the plot."

There was a moment of stunned silence that Ingerman allowed to linger in the air a bit longer than necessary before he turned to Paul. "All right, Mr. Stafford, the floor is yours."

Paul stood up and looked around the table. "Three weeks ago," he began, "I wouldn't have believed a word of what I'm about to tell you." And then, briefly as he could, he told them about the death-dreams, about Roark and Singer coming to him and about the discovery of his brother. He told them how he had tracked down Karl and how his brother kidnapped and then impersonated him, first at the hotel, then at the Bayonne terminal and finally at his own home. He described the dream of George Lish's death and the most recent dream of a doorway opening to the sky where an Ilyushin 62 was falling in flames.

The reaction of his listeners was mixed. Some of the men masked their reactions with impassive faces while others were openly incredulous. One man sipped his coffee and toyed with the cup while another slumped back in his chair with folded arms and lowered head. At one point Doug Weems, the FBI man, interrupted with a question that Ingerman delayed with the suggestion that they wait until Paul was finished.

"I know that George Lish is dead," Paul said. "I know that Karl Alexander has a Redeye missile, I know that he kidnapped my wife Joanna and I know that he's going to try to shoot down the General Secretary's plane tomorrow morning."

"Is that it?" Doug Weems asked. "That's the extent of your evidence?"

"That's it. I can't prove it but—"

"Then I'd like to know what the hell we're doing here?"

"Wait a minute," Tommy Lecrazny began.

"No, I mean it," Weems said. "We've got a file full of crackpot death-threats six feet deep. That doesn't mean we—"

His words were drowned in a flurry of delayed reactions as several began talking at once. Paul exchanged a glance with Annie Helms, who rolled her eyes as if to say, What did you expect?

Ingerman let the uproar continue for a few moments and then moved to regain order. "All right, all right, let's take things one step at a time. Doug, your point is that there's not sufficient evidence to merit taking any action, is that what you're saying?"

His initial outburst over, the FBI man became more cautious. "Take action how? By investigating, sure. But let's not run off half-cocked. We've got a list of everybody who's made death threats on the Russian and none of them involve anything like a Redeye missile. That takes a conspiracy and conspiracies don't happen overnight and they don't happen without involving a lot of people and a lot of people don't make conspiracies without leaving a trail. I can tell you right now there's nothing in Bureau files and we know there's nothing on the PTA. So, sure, investigate, but why all this? Why an emergency meeting? The only hard evidence is that a warehouse up in Bayonne was broken into."

"Warehouse E," the DIA man reminded him. "That's a security warehouse and that's where the Redeyes were shipped from."

"Shipped intact, isn't that right?"

Ingerman nodded. "Padlocked and sealed before arrival at Bayonne, both intact when they arrived, both intact when the container was loaded."

McNally pulled out a pipe and began a dredging operation in a pouch of tobacco. "Have we checked with the shipment consignee in Costa Rica?"

"The shipment hasn't arrived yet. The *Coralis* is still at sea. We're trying to get authorization to break the container and do a cargo check."

Weems said, "Back to square one. The only hard evidence is a busted ventilator in a security warehouse."

"And six dead CIA assets," Hugh said.

"That's an altogether different case—"

"Not if the same man is responsible."

"Excuse me," McNally said. "But the more important issue here is motivation. According to what I've heard, this Karl Alexander works for the KGB, isn't that right?"

"No," Hugh said. "He works for the East German Stasis."

"I know, but he takes orders from the KGB, correct?"

Hugh nodded. "Assassinations would have to be approved by Moscow."

"So fundamentally we're saying the same thing: he works for the KGB and my question is, what I'd like to know, how does that square with shooting down the Russian leader?" McNally sat back with a satisfied expression.

"I've got a reason," Paul said. "Karl told me the finest man he'd ever known was a Russian. When I pressed him, he wouldn't tell me who it was, but according to his file, Karl was the protégé of a Russian KGB man named Alexander Ikhnovsky."

"What file was this?"

Hugh said, "Our station in Berlin."

McNally raised an eyebrow. "And you passed it around?"

"I passed it to Mr. Stafford."

"Who has a clearance, I assume?"

"Let's get back to the point," Ingerman told him. "What about Ikhnovsky?"

"He worked his way up to Deputy Director of the KGB," Hugh went on. "One of the old guard who was pushed aside when this new guy and his reformists took power. It's possible a group of reactionaries, hardliners, wants to get rid of him."

"And blame it," Paul added, "on George Lish and the Rank."

". . . There's always a wolf waiting to grab the baby," McNally said. "That's nothing new in Russian politics . . ."

Weems looked around the table. "I think we've lost track of the real point, which is that everything we're talking about is based on this man's dreams."

He nodded toward Paul, who again had the feeling he was an animal in a zoo. Before he could respond Annie spoke for the first time.

"They're not dreams, not in the conventional sense of the word. They're intense impressions that Paul—Mr. Stafford—picks up sporadically and without volition from experiences his brother is having."

"That's reassuring," Weems said. "For a moment there I thought we might have to make a decision based on dreams. Now we can make it on mind reading."

"Or on missing your dinner," Paul added.

Weems shot him a surprised look and Ingerman quickly intervened.

"I think Dr. Helms should give us her view of the psychological aspects of the situation. Mr. Stafford, perhaps you wouldn't mind waiting in my office? I'll have Barbara take care of you. Gentlemen, if you'll excuse us for a moment.''

Paul followed the Secret Service man into the next room. It was after normal working hours but there were still a number of people on duty. The low sound of radio communications and zip of laser printers reminded Paul of the *Herald*. There was the same feel of round-the-clock activity.

"I trust you don't mind being out here," Ingerman said. "but you understand the type of controversy that your story generates.''

"Yeah, I'm a human mini-series.''

Actually now that he'd told his story there wasn't much that Paul could do except try to find Joanna before tomorrow morning. Somehow the two lives were intertwined, he thought . . . such as, if the Russian leader survived, Joanna wouldn't. And vice versa.

Ingerman's assistant, Barbara, took him in hand. She was a matronly woman with soft features and the beginning of a double chin, but she spoke with quick precision and her eyes reflected an intelligence to match. She showed Paul to the couch in Ingerman's office and offered to get him a soft drink or coffee.

"Coffee, please,'' Paul said. "And I'd like to use the phone.''

"You go right ahead. Punch the green button, that'll get you an outside line.''

He called home, half-hoping that Joanna had called, half-fearful that if Karl was holding her hostage, there might be a message threatening her life. Instead the answering machine played back a message from the police:

"Mr. Strafford, this is Officer Cruikshank of the Maryland Highway Patrol . . . There has been a traffic accident involving Mrs. Joanna Stafford. She's been taken to Glenway Memorial Hospital. That's in Upper Marlboro and if you need to get in touch with us, here's a number—''

Paul slammed the phone down and dialed the information operator for the number of the hospital. A traffic accident? Where? How? And what about Karl? Was he in it? Above all, was Joanna all right?

When he got through to the admissions desk Paul explained who he was and the operator put him on hold while she paged the doctor. Paul found himself clenching and unclenching his hand. If Karl had hurt Joanna . . .

Barbara returned with his coffee and put it on the desk. She saw from his face that he was upset and gave him a questioning look.

Paul turned away, ignoring her, and she went back to her desk.

"Mr. Stafford, this is Dr. Halby."

"I want to know about my wife. How is she? Is she all right?"

"Your wife should be fine," Halby told him. "A CAT scan showed no skull fracture or cranial bleeding. She did suffer a ruptured spleen that required immediate surgery, but the operation went well and she's recovering now in ICU."

Paul slumped down. "But she'll be all right, you say?"

"Barring any further complications, she'll recover fully."

"What happened, doctor? Do you know?"

"Your wife was in an automobile accident, a fairly serious one by the extent of her injuries."

"Was she alone?"

"As far as I know. You'd have to talk to the police."

"Were there any other injuries?"

"Aside from the concussion and the spleen she has an exterior fracture of the left arm and two fractured ribs, lacerations of the scalp and lip and some minor cuts and bruises. The internal bleeding was the biggest danger but I believe we've stopped that now."

"So she'll be okay?"

"As I say, barring any further complications. We'll know more when she regains consciousness."

"Was she conscious when she came in?"

"I don't believe she was."

"Then she didn't say anything? About the accident?"

"You have to understand, your wife was in a state of shock when she arrived."

"I want to see her."

"You can do that, but only for a few minutes. She's in intensive care."

"You just take care of her. I'll be right there."

"One more thing, Mr. Stafford. Are you the same Paul Stafford who writes for the *Herald?*"

"Yes."

"Well, that article on malpractice suits was right on the money. I wish I could make it required reading for all my patients."

"Talk to you when I get there," Paul said.

Before he left he wrote a brief note explaining to Annie where he'd gone and left it with Barbara. As long as Joanna was safe, the experts could concentrate on the Russian.

CHAPTER

32

AIR FORCE TECHNICAL SERGEANT MARINA ADIEVA should have been nervous but she felt nothing. She was not a woman who harbored doubts. Outside the window of the Electronic Maintenance Facility she could see Aeroflot 86540, code named *Plamenny*, flame. This was the aircraft which would take the General Secretary from Moscow to Washington, D.C. Marina's crew had just completed an on-board inspection of the electronic systems. Now they sat crowded around an ancient black-and-white television watching a soccer game.

Marina surveyed the brightly-lit room with its steel gray work benches and complicated test equipment. There was a tool kit someone had left on the bench nearest the door. Bobokov. He was the most careless and slipshod member of her team. Marina casually drifted over to the table and, when no one was looking, picked a thin screwdriver from its slot and slipped it into her pocket. Then she called out sharply.

"Bobokov, is this your tool kit?"

Bobokov turned with a confused smile.

"I say, is this yours?"

"I was in a hurry—"

"And where is your number four?"

"What?"

Marina picked up the kit and carried it to him. The other technicians either turned to watch or hunched closer to the television.

"Your number-four screwdriver," Marina said. "Where is it?"

Bobokov took the kit and frowned. He lifted some of the other screwdrivers from their slots.

"I'm sure it was here . . ."

"You didn't leave it in the Wildfire system did you?"

Bobokov paled. It was a cardinal rule that when performing maintenance on a delicate piece of electronic equipment all parts taken out for testing were to be replaced and nothing foreign left behind. An air crew's life depended on such attention to detail, as did the careers of electronic technicians such as Bobokov.

"No, no," he protested, "I know I had it when I left the aircraft. It must be here in the shop."

"I hope so, because I intend to check the aircraft."

Marina left the shop and crossed the tarmac to Aeroflot *Plamenny.* A yellow fuel truck crouched low under one wing as ground crewmen finished making their preparations. The guard, an air force corporal in knee-high boots, paid no attention to Marina as she boarded the aircraft. She was wearing her identification badge and he had seen her before.

Inside the plane Marina made her way to the cockpit. Behind the pilot and co-pilot seats there were two work stations, one for the flight engineer, the other for the ADO, the air defense officer. The ADO's desk faced a bewildering array of switches, lights, digital readouts, display panels, gridded screens and radar scopes. They were all as familiar to Marina as the pattern on her bedspread.

She turned her attention to the Wildfire IRCM system, a defense against infra-red, or heat-seeking, missiles. The system was actually two separate components: DeTect and DeCoy. DeTect consisted of infra-red sensors able to pinpoint any high-temperature heat source moving toward the aircraft at over sixty knots. It would alert the ADO to a potential threat and tell him range, bearing and speed. It was a passive system used for identification and tracking but unable to defend the aircraft.

DeCoy was the active system. It used a heated ceramic element whose radiant energy was mechanically modulated to confuse an incoming missile about the aircraft's whereabouts. Attempting to follow the apparent wild gyrations of its target, the missile would make ever-larger corrections until it exceeded its maneuverability limits and went out of control. DeCoy was Aeroflot *Plamenny's* protection, and it was this component that Marina meant to disengage.

But cleverly. The control panel, the arming switch, indicator lights, frequency selectors, test indicators—all these things must look and respond normally. The ADO would mistakenly think that they were protected, while DeTect would accurately register what was happening . . . Oh yes, they would see it coming, all the way in. And realize too late that they were naked.

Marina sat down and went to work. She had designed and built a circuit board that would disengage DeCoy's ceramic element without alerting the ADO. All she had to do was remove the cover plate, snip five wires and reroute them through the new board. She had practiced the procedure at the test bench; it would take three minutes and twenty seconds.

Unlike Karl's Uncle Alex and his coterie, it was not politics that motivated Marina. It was strictly personal. Marina was in love with Colonel Feliks Grigorenko. She had been in love with him ever since she graduated from the air force's advanced electronic school and began her duties as one of the maintenance team for Aeroflot *Plamenny*. At the time of their meeting, another Soviet leader was in power and Grigorenko, then a captain, was his pilot. Marina was twenty-two and had never been in love; Grigorenko, in his late forties, was unhappily married and had been in love many times.

Marina was not a beautiful woman, although a hint of Mongol blood gave her features an unusual look that stopped short of being exotic. She was uneasy with people and had few interests, but those she had she pursued with an intensity and singlemindedness that sometimes intimidated her peers. She seemed more interested in micro-chips and circuit boards than in socializing, which made it all the more surprising when she fell so much in love with Grigorenko, a casually vain and slightly overweight man to whom flying came as naturally as seduction.

The affair blossomed quickly and might have run its natural course, ending in disillusionment for Marina, had not the then General Secretary died. When the new one replaced him, he also replaced the pilot of Aeroflot *Plamenny*. Grigorenko was sent to an air base on the Kamchatka Peninsula, where he distinguished himself as the interceptor pilot who incorrectly identified Korean Air Lines Flight 007 as a U.S. Navy RC-135 reconnaissance aircraft.

Grigorenko's error was never officially acknowledged. In fact, to prove that no mistake had been made, he was promoted to colonel. But he was taken off flight duty and within the Soviet air force his name became synonymous with the English expression "blind as a bat." When he eventually returned to Moscow, it didn't take long for him to gravitate toward Alexander Ikhnovsky and the others plotting to overthrow the current regime.

In the meantime Marina remained steadfast. Without planning or explanation or understanding, she had taken Grigorenko into her heart as she had not done with any man before him nor would do with anyone after him. It was a commitment that could not have been more absolute had it been memorialized with wedding vows and a public ceremony. After his departure she threw herself into her work and devoted herself to the letters she wrote him each day but could not send. She had no close friends; the depth of her pain and the extent of her bitterness on his behalf remained hidden.

It took Marina three months to work up the courage to make contact with Grigorenko after he returned to Moscow. Under the domed ceiling of the Marxistskaya subway station, the former lovers met for the first time in years, and under the peeling ceiling of Marina's apartment they became lovers again. The next morning, with Marina lying exhausted on top of him, Grigorenko asked if she would risk her life for him. Without hesitation she answered yes . . .

A faint vibration shook the aircraft as someone mounted the outside steps. For the first time she felt a twinge of alarm, but she stayed calm and began screwing the cover plate back in place. As long as it wasn't the ADO, no one would know what she was doing. As she finished she heard someone step into the compartment behind her.

"Something wrong?"

Marina finished tightening the last screw and turned around. A burly KGB man in civilian clothes was staring at her. He frowned when he saw her coveralls and her badge.

"We were given an all-clear on electronics. Why are you here?"

Marina stared back impassively and held up the screwdriver.

"One of my men left this aboard. I didn't want it rolling around loose."

The KGB man grunted and turned his attention to the cockpit. "Has the captain been here?"

"I haven't seen him."

When she left, Marina paused at the top of the stairs and ran her hand over the fuselage of Aeroflot *Plamenny*. After so many years, the aircraft was like an old friend. For that brief and only moment, she felt sad.

Annie's presentation didn't last long. No sooner had she begun a discussion of mental affinity in twins than Barbara Ziegler slipped into the room and whispered in Ingerman's ear. When her audience turned its attention to the newcomer, Annie paused.

Ingerman stood up. "Excuse me, Dr. Helms, I'll be right back. Please continue."

Annie waited until he was out of the room and then picked up where she had left off.

"Tests at the University of Minnesota have shown a high correlation of image-affinity grouping in active-passive mental states," she said. "It's similar to the way that iron filings align themselves along the magnetic lines of force when they come into proximity with a magnet. In the case of twins, the passive mental state picks up images from the active mental state."

It was not the most receptive audience she had ever faced. These were practical men whose job it was to defend against concrete realities like bullets and bombs. Annie found herself speaking more and more rapidly in an effort to convince them. Just as she felt she had gotten their attention, Ingerman returned. All eyes turned toward him and Annie paused again.

"Sorry," Ingerman said, "I keep interrupting you. We just got word that Paul Stafford's wife is in the hospital. I spoke to the police who tell me that she was involved in a car accident this evening. She ran a Stop sign at high speed and lost control of the car. Right now she's in serious condition at Glenway Memorial Hospital."

"Where's that?" someone asked.

"Upper Marlboro. It's out near Andrews."

"Near Andrews? What was she doing out there?"

"The police had no idea."

"Where's Paul?" Annie asked.

"He's on his way to the hospital."

McNally took the pipe from between his teeth. "Was Mrs. Stafford alone or was she with this Karl Alexander?''

"She was alone.''

Weems nodded. "So much for Stafford's kidnapping theory.''

"We don't know that for sure.''

"We don't know *anything* for sure. Why call a meeting without much information, that's what I'd like to know.''

"Because,'' Ingerman replied with more patience than he felt, "I wanted everyone to be apprised of the situation and I wanted everyone to meet Paul Stafford since his credibility is a key consideration here—''

"Which at the moment,'' Weems put in, "is not so high.''

Frank Delgado, an overweight man from the Defense Intelligence Agency, was squirming. "Could we abbreviate this, please? If we're here to consider a threat, then let's consider a threat. I don't know about the rest of you but I don't have time for speculating on science fiction—no offense Dr. Helms—but let's keep to what we know.''

"He's right,'' Tommy Lecrazny said. "Let's assume the worst case: there's a Redeye missile out there with somebody who intends to use it. It doesn't matter whose brother he is or how he got a missile or whether he killed or kidnapped anyone. All that matters is, how real a threat is a Redeye missile and what do we do about it?''

"What do you mean, how real a threat? If he can shoot down the General Secretary's plane . . .''

"Can he? My understanding is that the Redeye is pretty much outmoded. I mean, we've got counter-measures for something as primitive as a Redeye missile, don't we, colonel?''

Colonel Coswell, hands folded on the table in front of him, nodded. "That's affirmative.''

"So, I assume the Russians have some kind of counter-measures, too.''

"I'm sure they do,'' Coswell replied. "Something comparable to our Hot Brick system. The DIA would have more on Soviet air defense systems.''

"We do,'' Delgado agreed. "But we don't know just what kind of a package they've got on this aircraft.''

"There's a good way to find out,'' Ingerman said. "Let's ask them.''

Karl parked the Winnebago in the hospital parking lot. Clouds had crept over the night sky, and from deep within their recesses distant lighting glowed. There was a close, muggy feeling in the air that presaged a change in the weather. Before he went into the hospital Karl walked around the building, familiarizing himself with the layout and the grounds in case a quick escape became necessary. In addition to the main entrance there was a side door, an emergency room entrance and a loading dock on a lower level.

The hospital was a new one with glass doors that opened automatically at Karl's approach. Cool air enveloped him as he entered the reception area. To the left was a lounge made up of slab couches grouped around a planter with abstract graphics decorating the walls. The reception desk was directly ahead, manned by a nurse wearing a green nametag. Karl told her he was Paul Stafford and that his wife had been brought to the hospital after a car accident.

The nurse, a thin black woman whose nametag said "Raylene," typed a few quick entries into her computer and looked up.

"Your wife is recovering from surgery, Mr. Stafford. She's in intensive care. Just sign in and I'll give you a pass and you can go on up."

She handed him a pen and Karl signed Paul's name in the ledger. It didn't even feel odd any more, signing his brother's name.

Raylene also handed him a pink card encased in plastic with the word "VISITOR" on both sides.

"That's on the third floor, Mr. Stafford. You just take one of the elevators down the hall on the right."

"Thank you."

Karl walked down the hallway but rather than stopping at the elevator he continued until he found two double-doors leading to a stairway. He went downstairs and made sure the doors were unlocked. Through the thick windows he could see a long, brightly lit hallway with lab technicians and maintenance people going about their business. The loading dock was at this level. If he needed to, he could escape through the basement.

When he got to the third floor he had to stop at a desk outside the intensive care unit. After showing his pass and explaining who he was, he went through a set of double-doors and entered a hushed environment in which the rhythmic beeps and tones of monitoring instruments seemed loud. The physical layout of the ICU was like the spokes of a wheel, with glass-walled rooms extending outward from the nurses station at the hub. From the ceiling, banks of display screens stared down, each telling its own story of some particular portion of the anatomy.

There were three nurses in the room, one behind a circular desk, the other two standing outside it. They were talking quietly when Karl entered; at his approach a hawk-faced woman with a brittle smile came toward him. Her nametag identified her as "Margaret."

"Mr. Stafford?"

Karl nodded, momentarily taken aback that they knew his name. Seeing his confusion, Margaret said by way of explanation, "They told us you were on your way. Your wife is right over here."

There was only one other patient in the ICU, an old man whose emaciated body raised barely a ripple in the sheets covering him. Joanna was in the adjoining room. She lay pale and still, connected by tubes to equipment on wheeled carts that surrounded the bed. One small tube went into her nose, another made its way between her loosely parted lips and the third, to which Karl paid particular attention, disappeared beneath a white bandage on her arm.

"I know it looks frightening," the nurse was saying. "But she's actually doing very well."

Karl turned and stared down at her.

"Then she won't die?"

"I should say not," Margaret said, apparently offended by the suggestion. "Barring any complications, your wife should recover quite nicely."

After cautioning him that he could stay only a few minutes, she returned to the nursing station. Karl approached the bed. Joanna's head was bandaged and one side of her mouth was swollen and bruised. Her upper lip was drawn slightly where stitches had been taken.

As he stared down at her, Karl noticed the silken strands of black hair that crept from beneath the bandages. Her eyes, shielded behind delicate, translucent eyelids, were still. About to place his fingers against her cheek he caught himself. If he touched her, he might change his mind.

That was the danger in pretending to be Paul; it was making him susceptible to some of Paul's emotions, which had been so alien to him. What was it Joanna had said? Paul was gentle? Well, Paul could afford to be gentle. Everything in life had been handed to him, tied and wrapped like a Christmas gift. He, Karl, could afford no such luxury.

He withdrew his hand and glanced up at the nurses. They were visible through the open door and side window, talking softly, not paying much attention to him but still aware of what was going on. They were sure to notice if he brought out a knife and tried to cut the IV bag. Then he noticed the pale green curtain hanging against the wall that could be drawn around the bed to provide some privacy.

He went back to the nursing station. "Excuse me, Margaret. I would like to pray for my wife. Would it be all right to draw the curtains, just for a few moments?"

She hesitated.

"Please?" Karl added in a low voice.

"All right then, but just a few moments, Mr. Stafford."

Margaret went to the room and drew the curtains around the bed. "You mustn't touch her."

"I understand. And thank you."

After one last glance at her patient, Margaret left him alone.

The curtain did not completely mask the bed, but it obscured the area in which the clear plastic IV bag dangled from a metal pole. Karl moved close to it, careful not to trip over anything. While the respirator cycled softly in the background, he took out a Swiss army knife, opened the small blade and quickly made an incision along the seam at the top of the IV bag. He then exchanged the knife for the bottle of Haloparimine.

For a moment he hesitated. For a few hours her opinion had mattered to him. But, he reminded himself, it had all been false on her part. Just play-acting to escape. Do it. He squeezed the bag to open the incision and poured the Haloparimine into the bag, creating a faint pattern where the two liquids met. He then gently shook the bag and the disturbance cleared.

Karl stared at Joanna one last time. It would be a painless death. At least he could give her that.

Arkadi Vronsky disliked Washington, D.C. He disliked America and all Western nations in general, not on political grounds but because they made his job so incredibly difficult. Vronsky was the director of security for the General Secretary, a job that was difficult enough in the Soviet Union and almost impossible in America, a society that seemed always to be on the brink of anarchy. Whenever he and his team suggested even the most modest security precaution they were told they couldn't do it without infringing on somebody's constitutional rights. The Americans could not even go to the grocery store without insisting on a constitutional right to overspend and indulge themselves. That was why, when Eliot Ingerman told him about the Redeye plot, Vronsky assumed it to be the work of an American. He was shocked to learn that the suspect, Karl Alexander, was alleged to be a member of East Germany's Stasis.

"That's a very serious allegation," Vronsky said. "The GDR is our ally. To accuse it of planning an attack on the General Secretary's life is as irresponsible as it is absurd."

"I didn't say the GDR planned the attack," Ingerman told him.

"Who, then?"

"We think it's possible that someone in your own government is behind the plot."

Vronsky stared at Ingerman and wondered what kind of a game this man was playing? He found something suspect in Ingerman's expensive and impeccably tailored suits and his well-groomed mane of gray hair. The man was too conscious of himself and the impression he made; Vronsky would have liked a glimpse below the surface of Ingerman's gleaming facade, particularly at this moment. Was he serious in suggesting a Soviet-directed plot against the General Secretary?

"Mr. Ingerman," Vronsky said, "if ever there is a Soviet plot to destroy a Soviet leader, I guarantee that you will be the last to know."

"Could be. But our information is that Karl Alexander is the protégé of an ex-deputy director of the KGB, a man named Alexander Ikhnovsky."

Vronsky was familiar with the name; he'd even met Ikhnovsky years ago. But the man was retired now and too far removed from the political arena to effect any changes in the government. There were other men, old-line, reactionary members of the Politboro and some army leaders who were much more vociferous in their condemnation of the current leader's policies and who constituted real threats. The KGB was aware of these men.

"What do you suggest we do, Mr. Ingerman? Arrest Alexander Ikhnovsky? And on what charge? Can you give me any proof of this conspiracy?"

"It's not up to me to prove conspiracies. I'm only interested in getting your General Secretary in and out of Washington in one piece. We've got a missile shipment we're going to check, and when we do we'll know if there's a Redeye missing or not. In the meantime maybe you can find out if Karl Alexander is in Berlin.''

"You mean you don't know if he's in Washington?''

"We have a single-source report. I'm looking for supporting evidence, one way or the other. Also, I'd like to know how well protected your aircraft are from something like the Redeye?''

"As well as your own aircraft are protected, I'm sure.''

"You might want to find out.''

After the American left, the first thing that Vronsky did was to contact Air Marshal Lyalin, who actually laughed at the mention of a Redeye missile.

"The Redeye is from the horse-and-buggy era,'' Lyalin boomed through the phone. "It has no IFF, no narrow-band frequency selection, not much range and is a follow-only weapon. It's been replaced three times over. I thought the Americans had given them all away.''

"That's what they're doing, only now they have one less to give away than before.''

"They lost one, did they?''

Lyalin seemed to think this a fine joke. There was something about the air marshal's relentless good humor that grated on Vronsky's nerves. At least Lyalin was able to reassure him that Aeroflot *Plamenny* was protected from a Redeye missile by something called the Wildfire system.

"A blind man chasing a greased pig,'' Lyalin said. "That's the Redeye chasing Aeroflot *Plamenny.* The missile will more quickly end up in someone's living room than in the General Secretary's lap.''

"Still, you might want to pass along the information to Moscow,'' Vronsky suggested drily.

"I shall, I certainly shall. But Wildfire will be operating whether the Americans have lost a Redeye or not. That is standard procedure.''

The air force had its standard procedures and Vronsky had his. He went to the radio room and encoded a priority request for a copy of Karl Alexander's Stasis file and confirmation of current whereabouts. He could already tell that this would be a long night.

CHAPTER
33

PAUL FELT THE FIRST DROP OF RAIN AS HE CROSSED the hospital parking lot. From beyond the horizon came the rumble of distant thunder. As he approached the building, an illuminated sign bordered in green caught his eye: "Glenway Memorial Hospital." A feeling of recognition tugged at the edge of his consciousness. Had he been here before? As the sliding glass doors opened automatically at his approach the feeling intensified, along with a vague foreboding.

Paul went straight to the reception desk and announced himself. "I'm here to see my wife. Joanna Stafford. She's in ICU."

The nurse, Raylene, ran an eye over him, and a slow smile spread across her features.

"How'd you do that?" she asked.

"Do what?"

"Change clothes so fast? How'd you do that?"

It took Paul a moment before the full impact of her words struck him.

"*Joanna*. Where is she?"

"Wait a minute now, you got to sign in again."

"It's not *me*, I didn't—"

He saw the ledger on the desk and grabbed it. His own signature stared back at him. Karl had been here. He shoved the ledger aside and turned on the nurse. "Where's intensive care?"

"Calm down, Mr. Stafford. You just—"

Paul reached across the counter and grabbed her by the shoulders. "Where *is* she, damn it? What floor?"

Raylene tried to pull away, eyes wide. From across the room a uniformed guard approached.

"Just a minute, sir."

Paul turned and headed down the hallway. The guard, a man about sixty, tried to stop him but Paul shoved him aside and ran down the hall. The guard yelled and a couple of attendants turned to look. Paul jumped for an elevator and slipped inside just as the doors closed. A nurse's aide stood behind a patient in a wheelchair.

"ICU," Paul said. "Which floor?"

The aide, scared by his manner and look, seemed tongue-tied.

Paul looked around. Above the doors was a building directory: "Intensive Care" was on the third floor. He jabbed the button and a moment later the elevator bumped to a stop. A maintenance man was mopping a narrow strip of linoleum between two portable signs that read "Caution: Wet Floor." At the end of the hallway there was a desk, and behind it were double-doors leading to the ICU.

A male nurse looked up at his approach but Paul walked right past him. The man called after him, "Excuse me, sir . . ."

Three nurses at a circular desk looked up in mild surprise at his approach.

"Joanna Stafford? Where is she?"

The oldest nurse frowned. "Now, Mr. Stafford, I told you—"

The male nurse had followed him in. "Excuse me, sir. You can't just barge in here."

Paul turned to the windowed rooms as the oldest nurse, Margaret, came toward him. And it was then he spotted Joanna lying with her eyes closed, head swathed in bandages, tubes running into her nose and mouth, another into her arm. Paul rushed to her bedside. She looked so pale and . . . lifeless that he was sure Karl had already killed her. Then her chest moved and he realized she was still breathing, she was alive. Or was it the respirator breathing for her? What could he tell with her hooked up to all these damn machines?

Margaret came in after him and took his arm. "Mr. Stafford, you have to leave here, now. I told you that before."

Paul wrenched free and picked up Joanna's hand. He felt for a pulse.

"Mr. Stafford, please . . ."

Paul turned on her. "He's trying to kill her. The man who was here a few minutes ago, it wasn't me. He's trying to kill her . . ."

Margaret stared at him. Joanna's heartbeat came to his fingertips, faint. But instead of relief he felt a growing dread. Something was wrong. Karl had come here for a reason . . .

"All right, Mr. Stafford," Margaret said gently. "Why don't you come out here and sit down—"

"Check her. Find out what's wrong."

His fingers were still on Joanna's wrist, feeling her heartbeat, but feeling, too, something lurking just beyond the boundaries of his consciousness. An image began to form of a narrow opening—

"She'll be all right if you just come outside . . ."

Margaret placed a hand on his arm and gently but firmly tried to pull him away.

"Don't." Paul yanked his arm free. The male nurse stepped forward, his palms upraised.

"Take it easy, Mr. Stafford. You don't want to hurt your wife, do you?"

The image faded, leaving only a residue of unease. What the hell had Karl done? What?

"Something's wrong with her," Paul insisted. "I don't know what, but the man who was here before, he did something. Check her vital signs, her blood, everything."

Margaret and the male nurse exchanged a glance. Another nurse was watching from the doorway. Obviously none believed him.

"Was I wearing these clothes?" Paul demanded. "I wasn't, right?"

For the first time a faint look of uncertainty crossed Margaret's face.

"You see what I'm saying? I know it sounds crazy but I think he might have poisoned her or injected her with something or—"

He noticed the IV bag and now an image exploded in his brain: the narrow opening, an incision in plastic, something . . . poison . . . draining into the bag, into Jo's veins—

The male nurse was motioning to two uniformed guards who had just arrived.

Margaret said soothingly, "She's really all right, Mr. Stafford. The machines tell us that."

"No she's *not*." He moved to the IV monitor and yanked the tube free. An alarm bell went off as the tube snaked across the floor and glucose gushed from the bag. He pulled out the tubes and wires attached to the other machines. The room came alive with beeping and alarm bells and blinking lights.

The guards grabbed him and hustled him out of the room as nurses converged on Joanna.

"Do a blood test," Paul yelled. "See if there's poison."

"Just come along now," one of the guards said.

They had him by the arms, one on both sides with an aide behind him.

"My wife . . . tell them to check the IV—"

"Sir, you're upset, but you're also disrupting this hospital."

As they wrestled Paul to the other side of the room, Dr. Halby arrived. He was younger than Paul imagined, a short, wiry man with bushy black eyebrows and lips too well-formed for his features. He went immediately into Joanna's room.

"Someone's trying to kill her," Paul called to him. "Check her blood and change the IV."

At least there was a flurry of activity in Joanna's room. At least they were paying attention to her condition now.

"I'm *okay*," Paul told the guards, pulling his arms free. After a few minutes, Dr. Halby came out.

"Is she all right?" Paul demanded. "Did you check her?"

"You're Paul Stafford?"

"Did you do a blood test?"

"Wait a minute. Let me try to understand something. You're the Paul Stafford I talked to on the phone? The one who wrote those articles on medical malpractice?"

"Yes, what about my wife? Is she all right?"

"No thanks to you, I'm afraid."

"Did you check her blood and change the IV?"

"The IV was contaminated so we changed it. There's no need to check her blood. Now suppose you tell me—"

"Doctor, I believe someone's trying to kill my wife," Paul interrupted. "A man impersonating me was just here. You can ask the nurses. He was wearing different clothes. He's my twin brother and he has a history of using drugs to incapacitate and kill people."

He could tell Halby didn't believe him.

"I *know* how it sounds," Paul said quickly. "But I can prove what I say. Call the CIA and ask for a man named Hugh Roark. He'll confirm what I'm telling you."

The wrong thing to say. Halby's skepticism turned to incredulity at the mention of the CIA. Paul felt his frustration mount.

"Will you just for God's sake check her blood? If she was poisoned, how could you find out? Where would it show? Just *check*."

Halby rubbed the bridge of his nose. "Mr. Stafford, will you take a moment and consider what you're saying. Just think what you're—"

"I know goddam good and well what I'm saying."

"You're distraught, which is only natural under the circumstances—"

"And what if she dies? Is that only natural under the circumstances?"

"If you'll allow me to, I'll prescribe something—"

Margaret came out of the ICU holding the empty IV bag.

"Excuse me, doctor, you might want to look at this." She showed Halby the bag. "Either the seam broke or else, maybe . . ."

She let the words trail off. Halby inspected the bag while Margaret eyed Paul.

"That's it," Paul said. "You left him alone with her, didn't you? The first man who was here?"

Margaret gave him a look and said nothing until Halby glanced up. "Was someone alone with her?"

"*He* was. He asked to close the curtains to pray," she said, still staring at Paul. "I didn't see any harm in it."

"Not your fault," Halby snapped, but his face was flushed with anger. "I want an immediate blood test and prepare an emergency transfusion. I want the contents of this bag analyzed."

Margaret returned to Joanna's room and Halby turned to Paul. "If you're right, either I owe you an apology or you owe the police an explanation."

"Just save Joanna, okay?"

Halby was already in motion. The guards took Paul to the security office to fill out a report. He was still there when Annie Helms arrived.

The problem with the KGB's centralized bureaucracy was that all messages were routed through Moscow. In Vronsky's case, his priority request for confirmation of Karl Alexander's whereabouts brought a quick response from the Berlin Karlshorst section: Karl Alexander was on temporary duty with the KGB training facility at Yaroslavl. Because the night signals clerk in Moscow received the response as he was going off duty, his replacement enciphered the message and transmitted it to Washington. In the process he misunderstood the origination code so that when Vronsky received it, he thought the information came from Yaroslavl rather than Berlin. By midnight, he was on the phone to Eliot Ingerman with the good news: Karl Alexander was six thousand miles away.

It was the second piece of good news for Ingerman. The American and Soviet air defense specialists had already conferred and the consensus was that a Redeye missile wasn't sophisticated enough to pose a threat to the Soviet air defense screen.

"They won't go into details," Coswell told him, "But from what they say and what we already know, it's probably something like our Hot Brick system."

Ingerman didn't pretend to understand Hot Brick systems but he was willing to accept Coswell's assurances. His job was to protect the Russian leader once he was on the ground; it was up to the air force to get him there. Still, he wished they had been able to discover whether or not a Redeye was missing. But the *Coralis*, with the containers lashed to her deck, was battling a tropical storm in the Caribbean. It would be at least forty-eight hours before a physical inventory could be made.

And then there was Paul Stafford, whose credibility had just reached zero. If Karl Alexander was in Yaroslavl, then it must have been Stafford who visited his wife both times in the hospital. He recalled what Hugh Roark had told him about Stafford's marital problems and his wife leaving him. Had Stafford tried to drug his own wife? And then lost his nerve and gone back and saved her? Or had he planned it that way from the beginning? To save his wife and effect a reconciliation as the heroic husband?

A chilling possibility occurred to him: what if Stafford was one of those multiple personalities? The Dr. Jekyll and Mr. Hyde type, in which neither personality was aware of the other's existence? He had read articles about such people and even studied case histories during a course on criminal psychology. It made more sense than dreams and mental telepathy.

Besides, what reason did anyone else have for killing Joanna Stafford?

When the test results showed a lethal amount of sedative in Joanna's IV solution, Annie's testimony and her CIA credentials helped convince both Dr. Halby and the police of Paul's story. After the reports were filed, Paul insisted on returning to the third floor. He could not stay in the ICU, but Dr. Halby arranged for him to wait in the lounge at one end of the hallway. It didn't matter to Paul as long as he could monitor who had access to Joanna. He had apparently arrived just before much of the sedative had a chance to enter Joanna's system. Now that she was safe he wasn't going to trust fortuitous timing again. He was going to stay there until Joanna regained consciousness, which Halby anticipated might not be until morning. Annie opted to stay with him.

"You should go home," he told her.

"I'll stick around."

"Why?"

"Well, to be truthful, I want to find your brother."

"You think he's coming *back* here?"

"No. But if you fall asleep tonight I'd like to be here in case you have any dreams."

"I'm not going to sleep," Paul said. "Not until I know that Joanna is all right."

They were sitting on the couch. Paul leaned forward, put his elbows on his knees and rested his chin on his palms. Annie sat with him in silence. Later, she said, "They don't think he can shoot down the General Secretary with a Redeye."

"Who doesn't think so?"

"They were talking about it after you left. There's some kind of a defensive screen. The Redeye can't get through it."

Paul nodded absently, his mind on Joanna. Annie became silent, aware that he was not in the mood to talk. Twice she went to the cafeteria and brought back coffee. Around two in the morning she began to doze off, each time sliding sideways against Paul. He moved to a chair and let her curl up on the couch. Later one of the nurses covered her with a blanket.

Paul's eyes remained transfixed on the entrance to intensive care, and there were times when his mind went blank and he was looking at nothing. Dr. Halby stopped twice to check on Joanna and to reassure him. Just before dawn the fatigue caught up with him and Paul found himself falling asleep, only to wake up with a start when his hand dropped from the arm of the chair or when his head fell forward. He had not had a good night's sleep in three days.

Annie woke up at six-thirty. Unable to persuade Paul to come to the cafeteria for breakfast, she went alone and brought back coffee, a pint of blueberry yogurt and a Danish. At eight-fifteen Joanna regained consciousness, but Paul had to wait until Dr. Halby checked her and the nurses removed her from the respirator before he could go in. When Joanna saw him her first reaction was fear. Her eyes widened and she let out a hoarse cry.

Dr. Halby put a hand on Paul's arm. "Wait."

"Jo," Paul said. "It's me. Paul . . ."

"Paul?"

"Yes, *yes*."

He came toward her but she drew away.

"Hand," she said, pointing.

Paul held out his right hand but she ignored it and reached weakly for his left. Only after she turned his fingers and saw the wedding band did she begin to relax and her eyes filled with tears. Paul knelt by the bed and pressed her hand.

"You're all right, you're all right, darling . . ."

"He was here," she whispered to him, still hoarse.

"I know."

"Tied me up, I had to get away."

"Joanna, Joanna . . ."

"Tore my hair."

She raised her hand to her head and when her fingers met the bandages she seemed surprised. "That bad?"

"You were in a car wreck, Jo."

"A car wreck? No, I remember my hair . . ."

"Your hair's okay."

"I tore it. One of those motor homes. I crawled underneath it to get away . . ."

She remembered escaping from Karl but she remembered nothing about the accident. When Paul told her about it she frowned. "I hurt the car?" It struck such a note of incongruity that he had to smile. Jo looked confused for a moment, then smiled too when she realized. The stitches at her lip made her wince.

"Ow."

"Don't smile."

"Don't make me laugh."

She pointed to a pitcher of water. Paul poured her a glassful and watched her sip it, favoring the injured lip. When she was done he put the glass back on the nightstand. He took hold of her hand. "Do you know how much I love you?"

"Tell me."

He leaned close and told her, realizing it was long overdue.

The General Secretary asked to be awakened when Aeroflot *Plamenny* passed over the North American continent. The steward brought dark Turkish coffee, and the Russian leader tucked a lump of sugar behind his lower lip and sat sipping as he stared out the window. Dawn's hard-edged light reflected the plane's white underbelly but had not reached the land below, emerging gray and shapeless from the night.

His wife entered the stateroom then and sat down across from her husband.

"You got some sleep?"

"Enough. What about you?"

"Enough," but the enigmatic smile told him a different story.

She was worried about the trip, he knew that. She had an unerring instinct when it came to sensing the mood of her country. When he graduated from Moscow State University it was she who told him to let their peers go to the high posts in Moscow. He should return to Stavropol and local politics. It had been the most astute move of his career.

She had been correct, too, about the speed with which he carried out his reforms. When he assumed the Soviet leadership she had urged caution. But he had pushed ahead, perhaps too quickly. The high expectations had led to disillusionment and, in the last few months, to feelings of unrest. Which was what worried her.

"The mood is wrong," she had said last week. "Remember the atmosphere just before Brezhnev replaced Khrushchev?"

"I am not Khrushchev," he reminded her. "And this is not 1963."

"You could get sick, postpone the summit."

It was wishful thinking. There was no way to postpone the summit. The Mutual Defense Treaty was the key to furthering the shift from a military economy to a peacetime market economy. The Mutual Defense Treaty, he had said in a speech to the Politburo, was mankind's last great attempt to save itself "from the endless cycle of wars whose battles echoed down the corridors of time." The Mutual Defense Treaty was his legacy to the nation that had given him birth and nourished him and raised him to the highest office in the land.

There was a quotation that he had heard his grandparents use, a biblical reference that stuck in his mind. The words came back to him now: "When I was a child, I spoke as a child and I understood as a child and I thought as a child: but when I became a man, I put away childish things." That was how he felt about the Mutual Defense Treaty. It was time now to put away childish things.

The first rays of the sun touched the land below, setting white fire to mists that ran like veins among the rolling forests. An escort of United States Air Force jets had replaced their own MiG fighters during the night. They were in U.S. hands now.

She reached across the table and took his hand.

"It will be good," she said, wishing she really believed it.

He nodded. It would have to be good. There was no other way.

Karl awoke refreshed after a good night's sleep. It was clear and cool, a good omen. He went to a truck stop called Dixie's Diner, ordered a breakfast of sausage and eggs, and enjoyed his last moments as an anonymous American. The commuter flights left hourly from Washington National to New York, where he would catch a four o'clock flight to Brussels. After that, a connection through Rome to Berlin. By tomorrow at this time he would be home.

The thought brought him no particular joy. His career in the Stasis was over. By now Paul was sure to have talked to the American embassy officials and probably the CIA. Karl had no illusions about his brother. Having been betrayed, Paul would make good his threat to tell the CIA who was responsible for the deaths of their agents. The CIA would send someone, maybe a team, two or three men. His death would appear accidental but to anyone inside the intelligence community the message would be clear: judgment and execution.

Karl could see his future as if looking through a crystal ball. He would take Magda and the children and move to Russia, where Uncle Alex would insure that he was given an adviser's role at some KGB or army training school. In the aftermath of the General Secretary's death, he would be an unsung hero of the new faction, but only as long as Uncle Alex was alive would he be safe. After that he would be a liability to the plotters—the one man who could disprove their legitimacy.

No, Karl thought, from now on, he would be a man on the run. He would have to plan an alternative life while Uncle Alex was still able to protect him. He would need to put away money in a Swiss bank account, he would need false identity papers, and when the time came, a credible death. Otto could help him; he could make amends for letting Paul escape.

Karl paid the bill and left the change stacked neatly in a cone on the table. When he returned home he would have no American money to serve as a tell-tale clue indicating where he had been. He left the restaurant, drove to a shopping center and positioned the Winnebago at the eastern edge of the lot facing the direction from which Aeroflot *Plamenny* would make its approach. The winds were light and from the south, which meant that Runway 19 was in use. The Ilyushin would make its approach from the north and land on a heading of 190 degrees, almost due south.

Karl unloaded the Kawasaki motorcycle, started it and let the engine run a few moments. His escape route would take him out the back of the shopping center and through a playground that opened onto Marlboro Pike Road. It was thirty-five minutes to National Airport.

After letting the engine warm up Karl parked the motorcycle where he would need it for his getaway. Back inside the Winnebago he removed the Redeye from its case, installed the cylindrical battery and checked the voltage. The missile was ready. Finally, Karl brought out the CIKOP-34F radio in its Sony housing. The radio had multi-channel reception, which allowed him to access three channels at once. He tuned in Andrews Air Force Base approach, tower and ground control frequencies. It was eight-thirty. The General Secretary had one more hour to live.

CHAPTER
34

ELIOT INGERMAN ARRIVED AT THE SECURITY COMMAND post at Andrews Air Force Base at seven-thirty. The command post was a small room on top of the terminal that had a good view of the runway and arrivals area. Ingerman could see the Russian leader's special limousine, flown over from Moscow, along with a rank of government cars. Reporters and cameramen were setting up near a roped-off area, and at the periphery were the ubiquitous television vans with their dish antennae pointed at some distant relay station. Everything looked normal for such an event, calm and under control.

And then Paul Stafford called from Glenway Hospital. His wife had regained consciousness and corroborated what Paul had told them before: Karl Alexander was in Washington and had kidnapped Joanna.

Ingerman remained deliberately calm.

"That's very interesting, Mr. Stafford," he said. "Particularly since we confirmed last night that Karl Alexander is at a training camp in the Soviet Union."

"Confirmed? How? Did anybody see him?"

358

"I assume someone talked to him—"

"Not unless it was a local call. He's here and I'm betting he has a Redeye and is going to use it on the Russian—"

"I'm also informed that a Redeye missile has no chance of success against the Soviet air-defense screen."

"According to who? The same guy who talked to my brother last night?"

Stafford's certainty worried Ingerman more than he wanted to admit.

"Your wife," he said. "Is it possible to talk to her?"

There was a pause. "Are you saying you don't believe me?"

"I'm not saying anything beyond the obvious and that is that Karl Alexander can't be two places at once. It would help if I could talk to your wife."

"Then you better talk to the doctor."

The doctor refused to let Ingerman talk to Joanna Stafford directly but agreed to relay one question and one answer. Ingerman wanted to know if Joanna was positive that her husband's twin brother was in Washington. The answer was a definite yes. Ingerman asked to talk to Paul again.

"He's gone," the doctor said,

"Gone where?" Ingerman demanded.

"I have no idea. Mr. Stafford is not my patient, his wife is. If you'll excuse me . . ."

It was Ingerman's worst nightmare come to life: two pieces of absolutely critical and absolutely contradictory evidence. He had a half hour to decide whether to switch to the Dulles option, with all the attendant publicity that would involve. Of course, an attempt on the Russian leader's life, no matter how easily defeated, would mean worse publicity.He cursed softly and Colonel Coswell looked over.

"That was Stafford?"

Ingerman explained the situation but Coswell seemed unconcerned. "The Russkies say the Redeye is non-deliverable. You should hear the old air marshal—he acts like he'd welcome an attack just to show what Soviet counter-measures can do."

Ingerman's stomach was churning. He had no intention of letting the Russians prove they could fend off an attack that the U.S. wasn't able to prevent.

"We've got no choice," he said. "We're going to have to go to Dulles and I'm going to have to explain it to the President."

He moved to the phone.

"You serious?" Coswell asked.

"What else can we do? Flip a coin to see if Karl Alexander is in Russia or out there on Interstate 495? I'd rather deal with the Dulles repercussions than chance an attack. Unless I'm overruled."

Coswell turned a weather eye to the runway as Ingerman picked up the phone and asked the Comlink operator to connect him to the White House.

"You know," Coswell said, "this runway is almost ten thousand feet long and the winds are less than seven knots. That's not too much of a tailwind component for an Ilyushin 62."

Ingerman frowned and told the operator to hold the line. "What are you suggesting?"

"If there *is* anybody out there with a missile, they're going to be positioned for aircraft landing on Runway 19. Seems to me the simplest solution would be to switch directions. Have them land on Runway 01."

Ingerman looked out the window.

"Where's that?"

"Right there. It's the same piece of concrete but each end has its own runway designation."

"You mean switch the direction they'll land?"

"Right."

Ingerman replaced the phone.

"We can do that?"

"It's not recommended. You land with the wind behind you and it takes longer to come to a stop and wears out the brakes. But we've got ninety-seven-hundred feet of concrete here and with winds less than seven knots an Ilyushin shouldn't have much problem. If there's some guy out there in the bushes, we leave him with his thumb up his ass watching the wrong side of the sky."

The more he thought about it, the more Ingerman liked the idea. It seemed simple and foolproof. And it avoided any negative political repercussions.

"Okay," Ingerman said, "let's see if we can clear it with the Russians."

The plan was simple but not, as Ingerman imagined, foolproof. The emergency vehicles at Andrews, the crash trucks, were routinely positioned one-third of the way from the approach-end of the runway.

When the runway designation was changed, the crash trucks were notified of the change over the ground control frequency, one of several channels that Karl was monitoring. He was adjusting the mirror at the rim of the sunroof when the call came through:

"Attention all ground vehicles, Andrews active runway is now changed to Runway Zero One. Repeat: Active runway designation is now Zero One. Confirm by station."

When Karl realized what they were saying, he sat down at the dinette table and turned down the volume on the other two channels. One by one, each unit acknowledged the change.

"Crash 3, positioning Zero One."

"Crash 4, on the way to Zero One."

"Crash 5, uh, I don't know what the winds are like for you guys but from where I sit, they're still from the south."

"Winds are two one zero at five," the ground controller confirmed. "Be advised that Summit One will be landing downwind."

An unidentified low voice growled, "Ain't that just like a Russian."

Karl jumped up. It was almost nine o'clock. He had barely half an hour to change his position to the launch site south of Andrews, a housing development called Linwood Acres. He shoved the motorcycle back inside the Winnebago, covered the Redeye with a blanket and took off.

Why? The question dogged him as he manuevered the cumbersome motor home down streets that suddenly seemed clogged with traffic and stop lights. Why had they changed runways? Airplanes always landed into the wind. Always. It didn't make any sense for them to change the procedure, not unless they knew.

The thought that the mission might be blown was too much to accept. But if it were, something must have gone wrong in Moscow. It hadn't come from him. The only loose end he'd left was his brother, and even if Paul escaped the jail in Berlin, he knew nothing of the Redeye mission.

A less ominous possibility occurred. Perhaps the Americans were doing this as a precaution—a last-minute change in plans to avoid just such an attempt as this, however unlikely . . . As he approached his destination Karl became mired in a traffic jam. With time critical, he was suddenly bumper-to-bumper on a country road that led to a small suburban neighborhood tucked into the woods.

Then he saw what was causing the delay. Up ahead a number of cars were turning into the Piscataway Golf Course. A sign at the entrance announced: "Memorial Day Tournament." It was the damned holiday. He made a mental note to take the opposite direction when he left.

After he passed the golf course the road became clear. Oddly enough, it was clear in both directions; he would have expected an equal number of cars coming the opposite way. A moment later he saw why. A police car was blocking the road.

Karl felt in his jacket pocket for the Smith & Wesson. He had two shots left and there were two officers standing at the car. As he stopped, one of the policemen stepped over to the Winnebago.

"Are you a resident, sir?"

"What's going on?"

"Only residents of Millsford and Linwood Acres beyond this point. I've got to see a driver's license or some proof of address to let you through."

Karl thought quickly, remembering a street name from his earlier reconnaissance.

"I'm visiting the Wilsons on Arrowhead Drive."

"Well, you'll have to call and get them to come meet you. Or have a cup of coffee somewhere and we'll be out of here around nine-thirty."

"What's it all about?"

"Who knows? They just want the road closed. But if you want my guess, it's the Russians. They got their head honcho coming in to Andrews today."

Karl turned the Winnebago around, trying to remain cool, trying to consider his options. The land at this end of the Air Force Base was rural and wooded. Could he park the motor home and hike through the hills? He doubted that there was enough time. Then he remembered the Kawasaki. It was made for off-road use. He'd be conspicuous as hell with the Redeye over his shoulder, but if he stayed clear of roads and houses and kept to the woods, he might make it. Unless he was spotted by the helicopters, which were now flying patterns over the approach area.

And then the Piscataway Golf Course appeared and gave him a better solution. He remembered from studying maps of the area how a triangular wedge of the course extended next to the approach path. Without a second thought he turned in, parked and ran to the clubhouse. Five minutes later he was back at the Winnebago with a golf cart and a set of clubs.

He dumped the clubs unceremoniously to the floor, got out a knife and sliced the leather dividers at the mouth of the golf bag. The longest part of the Redeye, the barrel, fitted easily down the bag, but the handgrip and eyepiece were too bulky and the overall length too great to completely hide the unit. He slipped off his jacket and draped it around the remaining portion of the missile. It might not look exactly like golf clubs but at least it didn't look like a Redeye missile. Particularly not to the helicopters overhead.

He put the golf bag into the back of the cart and headed to the eighth hole, just another sportsman out for a little exercise with the oddest set of clubs on the fairways.

Paul and Annie drove to Andrews for the second time in twenty-four hours. Paul was determined to prove that Karl Alexander was real. His brother was too much of a threat to go free—to Joanna and himself as well as to the target of his assassination. Who knew when Karl might impersonate him again or for what purpose? The only way was to stop him.

Annie sat beside him, leaning forward in her seat. "You know," she said, "in a way I hope they don't believe you. I think I can get to Karl, make him come over to our side—"

"I already tried that."

"You threatened to expose him. You didn't offer him a new life."

"Is that what you're going to do?"

"I want to get him amnesty if he'll come over."

"What about me? Maybe I'll go over to the Russians."

She looked up quickly, realized he was being sarcastic.

"You still don't understand the significance of the gift you've got."

"It's not a gift, believe me."

They arrived at the Chevron Station, where they had arranged to meet Hugh Roark. The CIA man was leaning against a Ford Taurus dressed in slacks and a lightweight beige sportcoat over an open-necked shirt. By contrast, Paul hadn't shaved, slept or changed clothes in over two days. Annie didn't look too much better. Her eyes were less hollow than his but her dress was badly wrinkled and the leather boots seemed to sag around her calves.

Hugh spread a map on the top of the car and showed them the

areas he thought they should check. He seemed to be the only one except for Annie who believed that Karl Alexander existed. At one point he glanced at the Alfa and asked if it had a radio. Paul shook his head.

"The mobile phone was in the Audi."

"Then I'll take the highways here—337, 4, I-95, Westphalia and the Suitland, as well as this industrial park. You cover these two neighborhoods and this shopping center."

Hugh wanted to know if Joanna had specifically meant a Winnebago or was she speaking of motor homes in general? Paul wasn't sure so they decided to check all motor homes.

As they left, Annie called to Hugh, "If you find him, remember our deal."

Hugh barely nodded and took off in his Taurus.

"What deal was that?" Paul asked.

"Hugh agreed he'd try to take Karl alive."

"Too bad you didn't ask Karl if he'd take Hugh alive."

Annie opened her mouth to respond, then thought better of it. They spent ten minutes checking a shopping center and found three motor homes, none of which showed any sign of Karl or a Redeye missile. They then drove the streets of a local neighborhood. At one point they spotted an actual Winnebago parked on the street, but the curtains were drawn making it difficult to see inside. A man came to the door of the adjoining house and called to ask what they wanted. It turned out to be his Winnebago and, no, he hadn't seen any other motor homes in the neighborhood that morning.

They ended up at the same 7-11 where they had stopped the day before. It was nine-fifteen. Looking at the map, Paul wondered about the areas they had checked, the ones left for Hugh. Annie was scanning the sky.

"Where will the plane appear?"

"That direction." Paul pointed. "He'll come right across there. Look through the fence and you can see the runway."

The fence was on the other side of the road. Beyond it, in the distance, a row of air force jets was visible in front of a huge hangar. Low in the sky two helicopters were circling over the approach path the same way they had when Air Force One landed.

The approach path.

Paul turned back to look in the direction he had pointed out to Annie. The sky was empty.

"I'll be damned," he said.

"What?"

"He *did* believe me. Son of a bitch, he believed me, after all."

"What are you talking about?"

"Look out there, beyond the base. What's in the sky?"

"Just a helicopter. It's not a plane."

"Two helicopters. They always fly security over the approach path. Remember yesterday?" Paul turned to the car. "Come on."

"But this is the—" she stopped as the import of his words became clear. She slid in beside him. "They changed runways?"

"You got it. They're going for a downwind landing."

The tires squealed as Paul accelerated out of the parking lot. Annie grabbed for the dashboard. "If they did switch runways," She yelled. "What makes you think Karl knows?"

"If he doesn't, Hugh's got him all to himself."

Annie struggled to keep the wind from whipping the map off her lap as she gave Paul directions and tried to pinpoint the area beneath the approach path. It took ten minutes to reach the other side of Andrews. When they passed the golf course, Annie called out, "We're close now."

And then they were at the roadblock. When the officer saw Paul, he did a double-take, then looked the car up and down and slowly smiled.

"Well, sir," he said, "it's a lot smaller but it still ain't going to get through."

A rush of questions revealed that Karl had been turned back in a Winnebago not more than ten minutes earier.

"There's a motor home at the golf course," Annie said. "I saw a couple of them."

In fact there were four motor homes, two of them Winnebagos. They started looking through windows, and in the second Winnebago they found a motorcycle and pile of golf clubs on the floor.

They went to the clubhouse, an open, airy building of varnished white pine, where the pro shop was busy selling golf balls, sun visors and bags of tees. The tournament didn't start until noon but the place was already full of both serious golfers and families out for a picnic.

Paul pushed his way to the rental desk. "Have you seen a man who looks like me?"

The kid behind the counter wore a green blazer with the club insignia. He grinned at Paul and said. "Well, it was either you or your twin brother.''

"My brother," Paul said. "Did he rent a cart?''

"Just a little while ago.''

"What color?''

"White, like all of them.''

"Which way did he go?''

"Couldn't tell you.''

"I need a cart.''

"Excuse me," said a man wearing checked pants. "But I was here first.''

"This is urgent—''

"Sure, but get in line.''

"Look, this is a matter of life and death—''

Annie jumped in then. "His brother is on medication. He took the wrong bottle this morning. He's got digitalin instead of insulin and if he uses it he'll have a seizure.''

"Oh, well, sure, miss.''

The man stepped aside, and a few minutes later Paul and Annie were navigating the fairways as fast as the cart would go. They took a shortcut between the fourth and eighth holes directly to the eastern border of the course. As they arrived, a couple who had just teed off was leaving. Nearby was an empty cart.

"Did you see who left this?'' Paul called.

"I think it's broken," the lady answered. "It was here when we came.''

They were at the eastern boundary, the beginning of the area beneath the approach path to Runway 01. The gently rolling hills beyond the rough were lightly wooded and offered Karl plenty of opportunity for concealment.

Paul checked his watch. It was 9:30. As they entered the woods Annie suggested they split up. "We'll double the chance of finding him.''

Paul shook his head. "Too dangerous. He's got my gun, remember?''

"I've got this.'' Annie pulled a Deutonics automatic from her purse. Paul looked at her in surprise.

"You know how to use it?''

She gave him a scathing look and said, "Just yell if you see him.'

They split up and began the search.

* * *

The golf bag, with its shoulder straps and heavy construction made a good carrying case for the Redeye. Karl's first objective was to find a vantage point from which the missile would have a clear view of the aircraft. The ideal position was a water tower directly beneath the approach path. It rose from a hill and commanded a view of both the golf course and Andrews, but with the helicopters patrolling the area Karl decided it was too risky to station himself there. The tower was painted a red-and-white checkered pattern and drew attention to itself.

He finally found a clearing near the crest of a neighboring hill, a location that allowed him to remain sheltered by the woods until the last moment. With the missile lying against the golf bag, he used earphones to monitor the approaching target. The Soviets were running slightly behind schedule; it wasn't until 9:30 that the Ilyushin made contact with the control tower.

Karl stepped clear of the trees and took a position with his back to the incoming aircraft. The Redeye rested on his right shoulder, pointing high, waiting for the Ilyushin to enter his field of view. Because he wasn't on the crest of a hill the airport was hidden from view, but by using the water tower as a reference point Karl knew he was positioned directly beneath the approach path.

Through the earphones he heard the Soviet pilot report his position in heavily accented English.

"Summit One is now entering downwind for landing Runway Zero One."

"Roger Summit One, winds two two zero at six, altimeter three zero one four."

Karl flicked off the safety with his right thumb and bent his head to the eyepiece. There was a faint whine as the Redeye's gyroscope came up to speed.

From his left, a woman's voice said, "Karl Alexander."

He froze, then raised his head from the eyepiece and turned to find a woman with unkempt blonde hair pointing a gun at him.

"Don't be afraid," she said. "I'm not going to hurt you. I need your help and you need mine."

"Who are you?"

"My name is Anne Helms. I'm a research scientist with the Central Intelligence Agency and I know all about you and Paul."

"Paul!"

"Listen to me. It's over. What you're doing now is useless. If you

kill him another leader will take his place, maybe liberal, maybe conservative, it doesn't matter. In the end you'll accomplish nothing.
Only your own death because they know—the CIA, the Russians,
everyone. You're blown, Karl. It's all over, but I can help. I can
offer you a new life . . ."

She moved toward him slowly, speaking quietly but intensely, the
gun always pointed at his chest. He gauged the time it would take
him to lower his right hand and get the Smith & Wesson from his
pocket. Too long.

In the earphone he heard the Soviet pilot report turning the base
leg. The woman was still talking . . .

"Karl, listen to me. I can offer you asylum. Come over to our
side and nobody will hurt you. You can do something bigger and better than anything you've ever thought of. What you and your brother
share is a priceless gift, a mental identity of such accuracy—"

"How do you know this?"

"I know about the dreams. I know you share an affinity so rare
that it could be years before another case comes along, if ever. You
and Paul are worth more than any political leader, do you understand
that? You have a gift and I can save it. I want both of you to join
my research program, you and Paul—"

"Did Paul send you?"

"He's here, he's with me."

So Joanna had lied. Paul was free, or had escaped. Over the earphones he heard the Soviet pilot, "Summit One is turning final."

"Roger Summit One. Cleared to land Runway Zero One."

The woman was still talking, faster now. "I'm *trying* to save your
life, Karl. I'm not going to shoot you. If you go ahead with your
plan I can't protect you. If you stop, I can save you."

Karl's eyes were on the gun in her hand, judging the threat, judging the distance. If only he wasn't weighed down with the damn missile, if his hands were free . . .

"Karl, please, you've *got* to trust me. Here."

And so saying, she tossed the gun aside.

Karl realized then: the wild hair, the wrinkled clothes, the strange
expression—the woman was crazy. He reached into his pocket and
took out the Smith & Wesson.

"I'm not here to stop you," Annie said, extending her hands.
"I'm offering you a new life."

The sound of the approaching jet reached them. It was time. Karl raised the gun and shot her once, dead-center, in the forehead.

Paul heard the shot from the other side of the hill. He called Annie's name and began running. The low whine of the approaching jet grew in volume as he got to the crest of the hill and paused. Karl must be close, but where?

Through the woods, twenty feet down the slope, the trees cleared. Karl would need an open space to fire the missile. Paul ran toward the opening, jumping over fallen branches and stumbling over half-buried logs. A shadow washed over the land as the Ilyushin thundered overhead and Paul burst into the clearing. Karl stood not ten feet away, the Redeye resting on his shoulder, his head tilted to the eyepiece. At his feet lay the still form of Annie Helms, her blonde hair matted and stained with blood . . .

Karl hadn't heard his brother's arrival. When the Ilyushin swept into view, he positioned the aircraft in the ranging ring while his left thumb uncaged the gyro and engaged the guidance system. A high-pitched acquisition signal announced that the infra-red sensor had locked onto the jet's exhaust. Raising the launcher slightly to place the Ilyushin in the target dish, Karl pulled the trigger . . .

As Paul rushed headlong toward him, Karl's every movement seemed magnified. He saw the tension in the arms, saw Karl's final adjustment of the launcher, saw the finger tighten on the trigger . . . he threw himself forward in a flying tackle that caught Karl from behind. The two men crashed to the ground, and as they did the missile vaulted from its launch tube with a muffled *whomp*.

Paul's impact deflected the muzzle of the launcher and altered the heading of the emerging missile. The booster charge sent the Redeye twenty feet into the air, where it seemed to hang for a moment before the main engine ignited. The steering fins snapped open, but the infra-red sensor had lost its target. The Redeye surged blindly forward at treetop level as its gyroscope attempted to recover the original heading. For a moment it veered wildly, then the sensor picked up the target, now at the very periphery of the missile's ability to correct course. With the Ilyushin's four closely positioned jet engines a bright bullseye, the Redeye began its swift upward trajectory.

In Aeroflot *Plamenny* a flashing red light and intermittent warning tone brought the air defense officer bolt upright in his seat. The

Wildfire DeTect system had picked up a high-temperature heat source. The ADO hated these alerts. The DeTect system was so sensitive that even such innocent objects as fireworks and flares often created false alarms. But they were in the United States now and the possibility of a missile . . .

A quick glance at the blue panel-light reassured him that the DeCoy system was engaged. Unaware of Marina's sabotage, the officer turned his attention to the DeTect display screen and noted that the relative bearing of the heat source was 176 degrees, almost directly behind then.

"Hot flash," he called out.

"Identification?" from the co-pilot. But the ADO could not tell him. The heat source had vanished.

Paul's interference, crashing into Karl, had given the Redeye an erroneous trajectory that betrayed it. No sooner had the sensor picked up the Ilyushin's engines than the descending jet disappeared behind the water tower. The missile was sensitive only to heat; it had no radar to warn of intervening obstacles. Its exhaust trail described a quick corkscrew as it searched blindly for its target, and then slammed into the water tower. There was an explosion, followed by a cascade of water that sparkled like a Niagara Falls bursting from mid-air. The tumbling cataract momentarily drowned the sound of the disappearing jet. When it was over, the tower stood jagged and gaping, with water dripping slowly down its legs.

The two brothers were still on the ground. Now, as they turned toward one another, Karl was the first to speak.

"*You* . . ."

He reached for the Smith & Wesson but the gun lay on the ground between them and Paul was already moving toward it. By the time Karl lunged forward, Paul had the revolver in his hand. Karl froze. Paul got slowly to his feet and Karl followed. Keeping the gun trained on his brother, Paul moved to Annie's crumpled body and confirmed what he already knew.

"Go ahead," Karl said calmly. "Shoot me."

Paul's hands trembled as he tried to control his anger.

"Do it, Paul. Kill me like I killed her, like I killed your wife, like I could have killed you when I had the chance. Go ahead. Kill me, damn you."

Part of Paul badly wanted to pull the trigger, but another made

him hesitate . . to shoot any man in cold blood . . and here a man
in his own image . . .

Karl sensed the hesitation

"You can't do it, can you? And do you know why? Because in
killing me, you would become like me."

"I'm not like you—"

"Oh, I think you are. Deep down, Paul, we are the same. Brothers. You will kill . . ." He began walking toward him.

"Don't Karl—"

"You think I'll make it easy for you? No, we've come full circle
now. You are the killer and I am the victim."

"You're no victim."

"I will not be a prisoner, you see? So you will make the final
choice after all."

Paul understood what Karl was doing—forcing on him the burden
of execution . . . and betting that he would not accept it. Karl continued to advance, eyes fixed on him. Paul stepped back.

"No closer."

Karl extended his hand.

"Use the gun or give it to me."

Paul pulled back the hammer with a click.

"Put your hands on your head, Karl. *Your* choice, not mine."

A moment of doubt. Karl stared at the gun. An eyebrow twitched.
"Then become me."

He grabbed for the gun, and Paul had no choice.

He pulled the trigger . . .

EPILOGUE

IT TOOK WEEKS FOR JOANNA TO RECOVER FULLY FROM the accident. During that time Paul was tender and attentive, almost as if he were making up for his earlier coldness. When she was well enough he took a two-week vacation and they went to the cabin in Maine. It was a time of renewal and of healing for both of them. There were no more recriminations about either Jason's death or her affair with Luis de Cuevo.

Three weeks after their return to Washington, Joanna missed her period. She lay in bed that night, watching Paul get undressed, wondering if she should tell him now or wait until the doctor confirmed what she suspected—that she was pregnant. Paul stood at the dresser, shirtless, staring into the mirror. Joanna felt she knew what he was thinking. He was haunted by his brother's death, she knew, unable to free himself of the notion that Karl's blood was on his hands. There were times since they had been reunited when he became distant and distracted, even in the middle of a conversation, and on occasion the half-glimpsed image of himself reflected in a store window or mirror would startle him. When he came to bed, Joanna decided, she would tell him about the possible pregnancy. Maybe it would take his mind off the past, focus his thoughts on the future.

"Hey," she called. "You're doing it again."

He turned and gave her a quick smile.

"Sorry."

"Come on, come to bed."

He came to the bed, sat down and took her hands in his.

"I keep thinking about him—"

"I know."

"He could have run. I don't think I could have shot him in the back. If he wasn't threatening me I doubt if I could have done it. But he came at me—"

"He didn't think you'd pull the trigger."

Paul shook his head. "I think he knew. I think he did it to prove we were the same in *every* way. Both killers—"

"You're not a killer, don't even think that."

"I think he was trying to turn me into him."

"*That's* creepy."

"If it had happened the other way—if he had grown up in this country, with mother and father, and a normal family life—would he have been me and would I have turned out to be him? Was it all a trick of fate, an accident of upbringing?"

Joanna shook her head. "No, no, no," she said softly but firmly.

"You're sure?"

"I'm positive. There was something missing in Karl, and it can't just be blamed on an accident or geography. If he had grown up in America he might not have been a killer but he'd never have been you. I forget the psychological term for it, but I don't think he was ever capable of feeling real love or even sympathy for anyone else. Loyalty, duty, yes. But—"

"But if I'd been brought up the way he was—"

"You would have been you, regardless. If anything I bet you'd have gone the opposite way, to compensate. Maybe you'd have become a doctor or priest . . . ."

Paul ran his eye over her body, outlined in relief beneath the sheets.

"Not a priest, I hope."

Joanna put her arms around his neck and put her forehead against his.

"No matter how or where or what, you'd still be you—the man I want. Now."

He pulled her close and kissed her. Their need for each other surged into quick passion. Of late there had been an extra intensity to their lovemaking. She was grateful for it, and wondered if it was because they'd come so close to death that this most elemental affirmation of life had taken on a new and powerful dimension.

Paul moved to kiss her breasts but Joanna restrained him, still embarrassed by the angry red scar that disfigured her body.

"Turn out the lights," she whispered.

Paul got up and crossed the room. He stepped out of his pants and reached for the light on the dresser. A neat stack of coins caught his attention: quarters on the bottom, then nickels, pennies and dimes. With a frown, he pushed the stack over, then turned off the light and crossed the darkened room to Joanna.